Michelle Douglas has be since 2007, and believes sl██████████ She lives in a leafy suburb of Newcastle, on Australia's east coast, with her own romantic hero, a house full of dust and books and an eclectic collection of sixties and seventies vinyl. She loves to hear from readers and can be contacted via her website: michelle-douglas.com

After writing more than one hundred books for Mills & Boon, **Stella Bagwell** still finds it exciting to create new stories and bring her characters to life. She loves all things Western and has been married to her own real cowboy for forty-four years. Living on the south Texas coast, she also enjoys being outdoors and helping her husband care for the horses, cats and dog that call their small ranch home. The couple has one son, who teaches high school mathematics and is also an athletic director. Stella loves hearing from readers. They can contact her at stellabagwell@gmail.com

SECRET BILLIONAIRE ON HER DOORSTEP

MICHELLE DOUGLAS

HIS FOREVER TEXAS ROSE

STELLA BAGWELL

MILLS & BOON

First Published in Great Britain 2021
by Mills & Boon, an imprint of HarperCollins*Publishers* Ltd,
1 London Bridge Street, London, SE1 9GF

www.harpercollins.co.uk

HarperCollins*Publishers*
1st Floor, Watermarque Building,
Ringsend Road, Dublin 4, Ireland

Secret Billionaire on Her Doorstep © 2021 Michelle Douglas
His Forever Texas Rose © 2021 Stella Bagwell

ISBN: 978-0-263-29923-6

0221

MIX
Paper from
responsible sources
FSC™ C007454

This book is produced from independently certified FSC™ paper to ensure responsible forest management.

For more information visit: www.harpercollins.co.uk/green

Printed and bound in Spain
by CPI, Barcelona

SECRET BILLIONAIRE ON HER DOORSTEP

MICHELLE DOUGLAS

For sweet little Mikayla. Welcome to the family.

CHAPTER ONE

OWEN PERRY GLANCED at the clock on the wall of the lawyer's office and then at the lawyer.

Mr Dunkley cleared his throat and adjusted his tie before shuffling the papers on his desk. 'Ms Nicholls only arrived in New York yesterday. It's a long flight from Sydney. She's probably jet-lagged and still finding her feet.'

Owen ground back his impatience. He had no idea why Mr Dunkley was determined to make allowances for Callie Nicholls. He knew as well as Owen did how many letters Frances had sent to Australia. And they both knew exactly how many letters she'd received back in return.

None.

Not one.

With a deep breath Owen forced his jaw to relax and glanced at the envelope on top of the folder in front of him—his godmother's final message to him. He'd brought it along as a reminder, to help him keep his resentment in check and to honour Frances's memory. Frances wouldn't want him telling Callie Nicholls exactly what he thought of her. She wouldn't want him to feel resentful or bitter on her behalf. She'd want him to be professional...and kind.

Unbidden, grief smothered his heart like a pillow pressed to his face, making it hard to breathe. His name, written in Frances's familiar looping handwriting—in fountain pen rather than ballpoint, because she'd had a thing for fountain pens and coloured inks—made him ache.

He wished he could sit in her living room just one last time to argue politics over a game of chess. That, of course, could never happen, and that letter addressed to him had been written in black ink, rather than a whimsical aqua or tangerine, as if to signify the formality of its contents. As if to symbolise death.

Stop being maudlin.

She'd give him a stinging set-down if she could see him now and be privy to his thoughts. But she couldn't and she wasn't. All that was left was her letter.

Darling Owen, you owe me nothing…

He owed her everything! Which was why he'd do what she'd asked rather than give Callie Nicholls a piece of his mind. He'd help this rotten woman however he could, keep an eye on her for as long as she was in New York—which he hoped to God wasn't going to be too long—and he'd be *neighbourly.* Just as Frances had requested.

He might have more enthusiasm for a root canal treatment, but he'd do it anyway. *For Frances.*

The intercom on Mr Dunkley's desk buzzed. 'Ms Nicholls for her ten o'clock appointment.'

Owen's gaze flicked to the clock. Ten twenty-five.

'Send her in,' the lawyer responded.

The door opened and a young woman burst into the room in a flurry of coat-shaking and swift gestures, and for a moment Owen had an impression of colour and sunshine and spring breezes.

'I'm so sorry I'm late!' She unwound a startlingly pink scarf from around her throat. 'New York is insane!'

The lawyer immediately leapt to his feet. Owen did the same, doing all he could to squash the defiance rising through him.

'Does it ever get quiet here?'

He couldn't help himself. 'You're late because of the noise?'

Blue eyes swung to him, a keen intelligence brightening them to the colour of a cobalt glass marble he'd once treasured as a kid.

The corners of a mobile mouth twitched. 'My hotel is right next door to a fire station, and either there are a lot of fires in New York or there's something wrong with their alarm. But, even given my disrupted sleep, I was awake nice and early—bright-eyed and bushy-tailed.'

Bright-eyed? *Tick.* Bushy-tailed…? He refused to let his gaze drop.

'The taxi driver I thought I'd been *so* lucky to hail dropped me three blocks away, swearing black and blue that your offices, Mr Dunkley, were just "right there"—he even pointed to a door—and then charged me twenty dollars for the privilege…which seemed a lot.' She rolled her eyes and set her raspberry-coloured coat on the back of a chair. For the briefest moment her lips tightened. 'I have a feeling I was just taken for a ride—*literally.*'

'Where are you staying?' he asked.

She named a nearby hotel—budget and far from fancy. Not the kind of hotel Owen would want his sister staying at.

'It would've been quicker to walk.'

Her brows rose at his tone and his shoulders knotted. He'd promised to be helpful. Sniping at her wasn't helpful.

Pulling in a breath, he did what he could to temper his tone. 'Your hotel doesn't have the best of reputations. Other arrangements will have to be made for you.'

Those blue eyes narrowed. 'We haven't been introduced.' A small pointed chin lifted—a very determined chin—and a hand was thrust towards him. 'Callie Nicholls.'

He clasped it. 'Owen Perry.' He released it again immediately, his hand burning.

'The executor of my grandmother's will?'

'That's right.' His hands clenched. Why hadn't she written Frances just one letter? Had it really been too much to ask?

'Well, Mr Perry, let me assure you that I'm perfectly capable of making my own arrangements in regard to my accommodation. And whatever else I choose to do while I'm in New York.'

He'd just bet she was.

'So, please, don't trouble yourself on my account.'

She was welcome to stay in a dumpster for all he cared. Still…

'Your grandmother would want you to be comfortable *and* safe for the duration of your stay.'

'That can be solved easily enough,' Mr Dunkley inserted hastily. 'Ms Nicholls, please have a seat.'

They all sat.

'I think it would be prudent for Ms Nicholls to stay in her grandmother's apartment,' said the lawyer.

'No!' Owen's denial was instant, automatic and involuntary.

Both Mr Dunkley and Callie Nicholls stared at him. The non-existent collar of his woollen sweater tightened about his throat. It was just… He couldn't imagine anyone else living upstairs. Didn't *want* to imagine it.

Callie glanced at the lawyer, who swallowed and leaned towards Owen a fraction. 'Why on earth not?'

If Callie moved in he'd no longer be able to go upstairs and sit in the half-dark to breathe in Frances's familiar scent and just…remember her.

'Well…?' Callie prompted now, not unkindly, but with a perplexed furrow ruffling the skin between her eyes.

Damn it all to hell! This woman didn't deserve to profit from Frances in death when she'd refused to come near her in life. He closed his eyes and bit back the howl that pressed against his throat.

This is what Frances wants.

That was what he needed to focus on. Not on how Callie had done Frances wrong.

'The apartment hasn't been touched in over eight weeks. It'll need a thorough airing and cleaning before anyone can move in, and—'

'All taken care of,' Mr Dunkley said with forced cheer. 'I took the liberty of hiring cleaners yesterday. The apartment is ready—' he shrugged '—for whatever Ms Nicholls wishes to do with it.'

Owen ruthlessly pushed all sentimentality away. He couldn't afford it at the moment. 'How *forward-thinking* of you, Mr Dunkley.'

The salient fact was that as soon as Frances's granddaughter signed the paperwork a significant portion of her grandmother's estate would pass to her—including the apartment block her grandmother had lived in. It was a modest complex by New York standards—only eight apartments in total—but it was located in the heart of Greenwich Village, one of the most exclusive neighbourhoods in New York, and worth millions of dollars.

As soon as she put it on the market, he planned to buy it. They got down to business.

'Your letter informs me that I have inherited a small legacy from my grandmother, Mr Dunkley, which I'll confess was unexpected.'

Owen only just managed to contain a snort.

'But it's terribly exciting. What can you tell me about Frances?'

'She was born Frances Victoria Allbright and grew up in Maine. At the age of nineteen she married Thomas Nicholls, an up-and-coming stockbroker. Thomas tragically drowned over forty years ago, leaving Frances and your mother reasonably well off. Frances, however, never one to rest on her laurels, began playing the stock market. Thomas had apparently taught her everything he knew, and she did rather well for herself.'

As the lawyer spoke Callie moved closer and closer to the edge of her seat, her face glued to Mr Dunkley's.

Avaricious. That was the word that stuck in Owen's mind. It made him sick to the stomach. Frances had deserved so much better.

'She remarried when she was forty-six, but it only lasted four years before ending in an acrimonious divorce.'

'Who did she marry?'

'Richard Bateman…' Mr Dunkley paused, as if waiting for more questions, but when they didn't come he continued. 'A year or so after the divorce she moved from her apartment on the Upper East Side to Greenwich Village, which is where she lived for the last twenty years.'

Which was how Owen had met her. His mother had been Frances's cleaning woman.

Callie leaned forward again. 'Mr Dunkley, these are all interesting facts, but you say you've been my grandmother's lawyer for over thirty years?'

Mr Dunkley removed his glasses. 'What is it you want to know?'

'I want to know what my grandmother was like. What sort of person was she? Did she have a quick temper? Was she fond of cats? Did she have any hobbies? Who were her friends?'

'Your grandmother could be brusque to the point of rudeness, but underneath she had a kind heart,' Owen found himself saying. 'She was fond of neither cats nor small children. She could play a mean game of chess, and she continued to follow the stock market until the day she died. She didn't have many friends—probably because she was insanely private—but those she did have she cherished. She was a philanthropist; she gave generously to a range of charities. And she spent every Christmas alone.'

Callie turned to him, eyes wide and lips parted, as if hungry for his every word. Things inside him tightened.

Things he didn't want to tighten. Or clench. Or burn. She looked the epitome of wholesome small-town goodness—the quintessential girl next door—with her shiny chestnut hair, her wide smile and glowing skin. She looked like the kind of woman who hid nothing—what you saw was what you got.

In other words: trouble.

Owen knew better than to accept anyone at face value. Fiona had taught him that lesson in the most ruthless way possible. He'd base his opinion of Callie on her actions, *not* what she looked like. And, based on her actions so far, she was only out for what she could get.

It took all his strength not to drop his head to his hands. Frances deserved so much better…

The longer Callie stared at the enigmatic and utterly perplexing Owen Perry, the more the breath jammed in her throat. Instinct told her he was the key to everything. This man had *known* her grandmother. If anyone could tell her everything she needed to know, it would be him.

Which was going to be interesting, because every instinct she had told her he didn't like her. How odd… He didn't even know her! Still, in her experience men didn't need an excuse to act either illogically or belligerently, and there was no way on God's green earth she was kowtowing to another privileged male, securely entrenched in his sense of entitlement, so help her God.

She'd find out everything she needed to without his help. She knew how to follow a trail of breadcrumbs to put the past back together. It was what she did. She was a trained historian, for heaven's sake. She didn't need Owen Perry.

'Anything else?' he asked.

While polite, she couldn't help feeling his words were a taunt she didn't understand.

'I'm just envious, that's all. Until recently, I didn't know Frances existed.'

He'd known her grandmother. He sounded fond of her.

'But you knew her—you liked her, I think. What was your relationship to Frances?'

'She was my godmother.'

Godmother? Owen was Frances's *godson*? Her heart, her spine and everything inside her softened. What she'd taken as aversion was grief.

'Oh, Owen, I'm so sorry for your loss. You must miss her a great deal.'

He didn't answer, just glanced away.

Mr Dunkley cleared his throat. 'Let's move on to the legacy, shall we?'

She immediately straightened and turned back to the lawyer, gripping her hands in her lap.

Please, please, please let Frances have left her a letter, explaining why she'd never contacted her. Please, please, please let her have left her a family tree she could finally start to trace.

'Your grandmother was a wealthy woman...'

Automatically she nodded, waiting for the lawyer to present her with the yearned-for letter.

'Your grandmother owned the apartment block she lived in, and she's left that to you—along with a trust fund she started for you when you were born.'

Her pulse quickened. *When she was born?* Had she met her grandmother as a baby?

Both men stared at her expectantly as she shuffled to the very edge of her seat. 'And...?'

The knuckles on Owen's hands turned white. 'You want more?'

'*Yes!*' Her heart hammered so hard she could barely breathe. 'Didn't she leave me a letter, explaining why she never contacted me? Why would she leave me anything when she never tried to pursue any kind of relationship with me? Why start a trust fund for me?'

None of it made any sense.

Owen leapt to his feet and started pacing. As if… She frowned. As if he were furious and needed an outlet. His actions made no sense either.

The man's grieving, she told herself.

'Your grandmother didn't leave you a letter,' the lawyer said.

Her heart shrank. No letter? Then—

'But she has left you a comfortable nest egg. The trust fund totals five million dollars.'

As if money made up for not knowing her grandmother, her family. As if— Whoa!

'What?'

'In all, the value of the apartment block and the trust fund totals more than twenty million dollars.'

She gaped at him. It took a moment before she could find her voice. 'You *cannot* be serious? In your letter you told me I'd inherited her apartment—not an entire apartment block. *Twenty million dollars?* That's not a comfortable nest egg. It's…outrageous!'

'Agreed.' Owen's mouth tightened and he flung himself back in his seat. 'It *is* a lot of money, Ms Nicholls.'

'Callie,' she corrected automatically.

Her grandmother had left her ridiculously wealthy. But *why*? None of it made any sense. She wanted to drop her head to her hands. Instead she pushed her shoulders back. A letter would've made things easier, but she wasn't giving up. She'd uncover the mystery of her family's past if it was the last thing she did.

But apparently she'd do it as a wealthy woman.

Only if you keep the money.

The thought filtered into her brain and stuck there.

Did her mother know about all this wealth? She *had*

to know. And yet she'd scorned it throughout the financially difficult years of Callie's childhood. She'd chosen to work hard and struggle alone on her small wage rather than rely on her family's wealth and support. She continued to shun it still.

There had to be a reason for that. A *good* reason.

Her mother had always said rich people made up their own rules—subscribed to a different moral code than the rest of the world, thought they were above everyone else and untouchable. And she hadn't meant it in a flattering way.

It appeared she'd been speaking from experience.

If that was the case then maybe Callie shouldn't accept the legacy? She didn't want to profit from a family that had victimised her mother.

She clenched her hands so hard her fingers started to ache. Dragging air into cramped lungs, she focussed on her one definite course of action and the reason she'd come to New York in the first place—to piece together her family tree. That would help to keep all the emotions at bay— the panic, the hope, the fear. Once she'd traced her forebears she'd be able to put together a step-by-step account of how she'd done so. She was hoping that would earn her a prestigious research position with the TV series *Mystery Family Trees*.

That was all she needed to concentrate on for the moment.

She'd think about the money later.

Besides, once she'd found out the truth she'd know what to do with the money, right?

If she kept it… She swallowed. If she kept it she'd never have to work again. It was like being handed a winning lottery ticket. But she couldn't imagine not working. Not working was wrong on way too many levels.

She'd loved her previous job. For good or ill, it had defined her. A familiar anger fired through her. She pictured the look on Dominic's face when he found out she'd won the TV job—the knowledge that in having her fired from her university position he'd pushed her to win the job he most wanted… Oh, there would be something so Karma-perfect about that.

Her heart slowed and satisfaction warmed her veins. Her success would chafe him from the top of his too-tight shirt collars to the soles of his feet. How sweet that would be.

'Spending the money already, Ms Nicholls?'

The words were said lightly enough, and from someone else they might even have been teasing, humorous. But there was an edge to them…an edge to Owen Perry. Still, people grieved in different ways. She had to make allowances for that.

'Not yet, Mr Perry. Believe it or not, my mind was far more pleasantly engaged.'

'On?'

She couldn't stop her smile from widening. 'Revenge,' she purred.

And it would serve Dominic right for every self-serving second of his mean-spirited treachery.

Common wisdom said revenge was a dish best served cold, but she wasn't so sure. She was still furious with Dominic, not to mention the head of the history department at her university back home, and revenge fantasies were her greatest source of satisfaction at the moment.

She'd never considered herself particularly hot-headed or grudge-bearing before, but now she knew differently. Now she knew she'd simply never had a reason to be hot-headed. And apparently, given the right set of circumstances, she could hold a grudge like a champion.

'How…delightful.'

Owen Perry's drawl snapped her back. *Concentrate.* She had a family tree to unravel and she needed a trail to follow.

'Mr Dunkley, may I have a copy of the will?'

'Why?'

Owen Perry leaned towards her as he spoke, and for the first time she noticed the innate sensuality in the disturbingly firm set of his mouth. It made things inside her flutter and twitch. With his square jaw and grey eyes, Owen Perry was a disturbingly attractive man.

'Curiosity, I suppose.' And because she was searching for breadcrumbs. But she didn't say that out loud. 'Is there any reason why I shouldn't see the will?'

He sat back with a shake of his head. 'Of course not.'

She did her best to ignore him after that. She had a sneaking suspicion jet-lag was catching up with her. Maybe that was why she'd become so aware of him. Jet-lag could be making her misinterpret the vibe he gave off. After all, the man had no reason whatsoever to dislike her, did he?

It wasn't easy to ignore him. Owen wasn't a diminutive man—he had broad shoulders and a long, lean frame that put him at just over six feet. And he was hard too—muscled, as if he worked out. And all that bristling masculinity vibrated with an intriguing intensity beside her.

She moistened her lips. 'Were there other bequests?'

Other bequests meant there'd be other people she could talk to about Frances—and even if they couldn't tell her about the falling-out that had obviously occurred between Frances and Callie's mother, at least they'd be able to paint a picture of Frances for her.

'There were no other bequests—except to your mother.'

Her heart sank.

The lawyer adjusted his glasses. 'Your grandmother left the rest of her money, along with the family estate in upstate New York, to your mother, Donna Susan Nicholls.'

There was a *family estate*? She straightened. That wasn't just a breadcrumb. That was an entire loaf of bread!

* * *

Callie Nicholls's face lit up at the mention of the family estate and a gargantuan weight slammed down on Owen's shoulders. It took all his strength not to bow under its force. He didn't even have the energy to swear. Clearly twenty million dollars wasn't enough for Frances's granddaughter—she wanted the family estate too. He was glad his godmother wasn't here to witness such a travesty.

'What happens if my mother refuses the bequest?' asked Callie.

It was a circumstance Frances had foreseen. She'd placed a twelve-month timeframe on her daughter's acceptance of her inheritance, with instructions to her lawyer to ignore any letters from Donna refusing the bequest during that time.

Mr Dunkley relayed that information, and then removed his glasses. 'If after that time your mother still refuses her inheritance, it will go to a cats' home.'

Callie turned to Owen. 'You said she didn't like cats.'

It made no sense to him either. He squared his shoulders. 'Nevertheless, I can assure you that the likelihood of winning, if you were to contest the will and seek to have your mother's share of the estate settled on you instead, is extremely unlikely.'

She waved his words away and he had a disturbing impression that she'd barely been listening to him.

'Mr Dunkley, how much money are we talking, here?'

'Five to six times what your grandmother left you. So, somewhere in the region of one hundred to one hundred and twenty million dollars.'

She sagged. 'That's an obscene amount of money... How could I not know my grandmother was one of the richest women in New York?'

'She wasn't. Not by any means,' said the ever-pedantic

Mr Dunkley. 'The richest woman in New York is worth a hundred times that.'

Owen didn't blame Callie for the look she sent the older man. He watched with a detached but fascinated interest as she straightened, wondering what game she planned to play now.

'Mr Dunkley, do you know what it was my mother and grandmother fell out about?'

Owen's eyebrows rose. Was she hoping to heal that breach and inherit that 'obscene amount of money' in turn when her mother died?

Mr Dunkley pursed his lips into a prim line. 'Your grandmother never took me into her confidence.'

She turned to Owen and raised an eyebrow, and for a disconcerting moment he wondered if he'd misjudged her. All he could see in her face was bafflement. There wasn't an ounce of guile, and no—

Don't be an idiot. It was simply part of an act. The same kind of charade Fiona had played.

'What about you, Mr Perry? Do you have any idea?'

Owen shook his head. He had no idea what had happened between Frances and her family.

Mr Dunkley shuffled some papers. 'Let's get this paperwork done, shall we?'

It took a ridiculously short amount of time to dispose of a fifth of Frances's estate. A few signatures, Callie's bank account details, and the key to Frances's apartment promised in the next day or two. A fifth of Frances's life—gone, just like that.

A fist reached into Owen's chest and squeezed hard. It should be more difficult. It should take longer. Callie Nicholls should be forced to jump through hoops and prove her worth. There should be…

There should be more than this clinical practicality!

Callie Nicholls should be damn well *grateful* to her

grandmother. And she should've given Frances the time of day when her grandmother had been alive. She could've answered at least one measly letter. Was it too much to ask in exchange for twenty million dollars?

They left the lawyer's office together. As they took the elevator to the ground floor his conscience chafed him. Damn it all to hell! He was supposed to be fulfilling his promise to Frances.

When they reached the foyer he pulled his business card from his pocket and handed it to her. She raised a dubious eyebrow, and for some reason that set his teeth on edge.

'My card,' he said. 'If you need anything while you're in New York, I hope you'll contact me. I'll help in whatever way I can.'

Very slowly, she reached out and plucked it from his fingers, careful not to touch him. 'That's surprisingly kind of you.'

He deserved that.

Her lips pursed and her eyes suddenly narrowed. 'You say you were my grandmother's godson?'

He lifted what he knew was a crushingly supercilious eyebrow, but he couldn't help it. 'Would you like to see my baptism certificate?'

Just for a moment humour made her eyes sparkle. 'You've no idea how tempted I am to say yes to that.'

When her lips curved up like that, they looked suddenly and irresistibly kissable. Her humour, and the direction of his thoughts, took him entirely by surprise. He had to bite back a smile—totally inappropriate. He had no intention of falling for this woman's charm. A charm no doubt honed and practised to take in gullible fools like him.

She slipped his card into her handbag. 'If you're Frances's godson,' she said slowly, 'and the only bequests she left in her will were for my mother and me...'

He frowned. Where was she going with this?

'Do I need to make you some kind of monetary reparation? If you were expecting something and didn't receive it…' She shrugged. 'That would explain it.'

He clenched his hands so hard he started to shake. Was money all this woman could think about?

'Explain what?' he managed to ask in a credibly even tone. He, for one, *would* do Frances proud.

'The distinct impression I get that you don't like me.'

He dragged in a breath. Evidently he'd have to work harder if he truly wanted to do Frances proud. 'I'm sorry if that's the impression I've given you. It's been a…difficult day.'

Her face softened.

'And, no, you do *not* need to make me any financial recompense. I would refuse it if it were offered. So please save yourself the bother and me the offence. Frances gave me everything I needed while she was alive.'

He didn't need any handouts from the likes of Callie Nicholls! Frances had saved both him and his mother. She'd given him a top-notch education that he'd forever be grateful for. But more than that she'd given him her love and support. Nothing could replace that. *Nothing.*

Her lips thinned and her eyes narrowed. 'I see. Well… It was a…*pleasure* to meet you, Mr Perry.'

Her inflection told him she meant the exact opposite.

Without another word she turned and stalked out onto the busy downtown street, head held high and with a sway to her hips that, despite his fiercest efforts, had male appreciation heating his blood.

The moment she was out of sight he threw himself down onto one of the foyer's strategically placed sofas, raking both hands back through his hair. That could've gone better…

His phone rang, jolting him back into the present. It was the new intern he'd recently taken on. Christopher used a wheelchair, and worked remotely from his home in Ohio. Owen talked him through a coding issue, channelling some much-needed patience.

No sooner had he ended the call, however, than his phone rang again. He didn't recognise the number, and hesitated to answer it, but eventually he pressed it to his ear and barked a curt, 'Hello?'

'I'm sorry to trouble you, Mr Perry, especially so soon after having met with you, but you did tell me to call if I should need any assistance…'

Callie Nicholls!

Darling Owen, help her in whatever fashion she needs.

'And I meant it. How can I help?'

'My hotel room has been burgled. Naturally, I'd prefer not to stay here now. I've just spoken to Mr Dunkley and he said you have a key to Frances's apartment. I mean, he has one too, but it's currently still with the cleaning company he hired. And while he's expecting them to drop it off this afternoon…'

Her words petered out, as if she'd run out of energy, and a sudden wave of compassion threaded through him.

He deliberately hardened his heart. Concern was reasonable, but instinct warned him against anything more benevolent or generous.

'I'll be right there.'

CHAPTER TWO

CALLIE LEAPT OUT of the armchair in her hotel's misleadingly respectable foyer, unable to sit still for another moment. As much as she hated to admit it, Owen Perry had been right. This hotel was a disaster. Beyond its shabby-grand foyer, with its chintz armchairs and ostentatious chandelier, the rooms were poky and plain. And, while Callie had never considered herself a stickler, they weren't scrupulously clean either.

She could make do with poky quarters and a bit of dust—she'd once lived in student digs, for heaven's sake—but the appalling lack of security was scandalous. She should've done more research before booking…read some reviews, made some comparisons.

She huffed out a laugh. *Yeah, right.* She'd been knocked so far sideways on receiving the registered letter notifying her of her grandmother's death that it was extraordinary she'd managed to arrange flights and accommodation in the first place.

Her pulse skittered. She had a *grandmother*.

Correction—she'd *had* a grandmother.

She folded her arms tight. And now she'd not only lost her grandmother, but every darn thing she'd brought with her to New York bar the clothes on her back and the handbag slung over her shoulder. Said handbag didn't contain all that much either, as she'd heard all the usual horror stories about tourists having their bags snatched, yada-yada-yada, so she'd deliberately left most of her money and valuables in the safe in her room, thinking they'd be…well, *safe*!

Apparently she'd been wrong about that as well.

'Callie?'

A warm and ridiculously comforting voice had her swinging around. *Owen.* While her sixth sense still told her he didn't like her, the sympathy in his face and the concern alive in his eyes had her fighting the urge to throw herself into his rather capable-looking arms to sob her heart out and let him fix everything.

She rolled her shoulders. That was just the jet-lag talking. She wasn't a sobber. And she never abdicated responsibility. Not any more.

Her initial instinct had warned her to stay on her guard around Owen, and she meant to listen to it. The man had obviously fleeced Frances out of as much money as he could while the poor woman had been alive. He couldn't be trusted.

Her fingernails made half-moons in her palms. 'That was quick. You've obviously mastered the flagging a cab thing better than me.' Things inside her pulled tight. 'So... would you like to gloat?'

His brows drew together and her words seemed suddenly small-minded and petty.

'Gloat?' he repeated.

'You told me this hotel wasn't up to scratch. And you've been proved right.'

His lips thinned as he glanced around the foyer—almost as if he was trying to pinpoint her robbers, though they'd be long gone.

'I'd have rather been proved wrong.' His gaze returned to hers with a sudden and startling sharpness. 'You took offence when I suggested you should change hotels. Why?'

'Because it wasn't a suggestion—it was an instruction. It sounded patronising, and it implied that I couldn't look after myself.'

He was silent for a moment, his lips pursed, as if he was replaying their earlier conversation in his mind. Eventually he nodded. 'You're right. It did. I apologise. I didn't mean it to.'

Okay. Um…wow…

'I'm glad you called. I'm the most logical person to help you as I'm the one who has a spare key to your grandmother's apartment.' He nodded, more to himself than her. 'So, yes, I'm the logical person to escort you there.'

He'd used the word *logical* twice. Right…they were going to be *logical*, then.

She made a 'logical' decision not to ask why he was the keeper of the key—she wasn't sure she wanted to know. She just wanted to get away from this hotel. It was starting to give her the heebie-jeebies.

'The thieves took everything?' he asked.

'Right down to my toothbrush.'

'Was anything of value taken?' He raised his hands. 'And, before you take offence, I'm not implying that your clothes or suitcases aren't valuable.'

'But they can be easily replaced,' she agreed. 'As can my toiletries. Can you believe they didn't leave me a single lipstick? They even took my shampoo.' The sheer thoroughness of the robbery astounded her. 'The room was picked clean. I didn't want to carry too much cash, or keep all my cards on me—or my passport—so I put them in the room safe.'

'And, let me guess, the safe is gone?'

'Bingo. I've cancelled the cards and contacted the embassy.' She glared across at the reception desk. 'I asked the hotel if there was some way they could give me some cash against my card. I mean, they have my credit card details and they have charged me for my stay, but that's too hard, apparently, and God forbid they should actually put themselves out to help a guest.'

'They *charged* you?'

That had irked her too. 'Technically, I did stay the night.'

'Excuse me for a moment.'

He strode across to the reception desk without waiting for her reply. She watched, wondering if he'd have any more luck than she'd had. Words were exchanged and, while she couldn't make them out, the tone Owen used had her biting back a smile. The manager was summoned and before she'd realised what had happened she was being offered an apology and her bill was being refunded—in cash—along with a series of vouchers to an array of New York tourist attractions thrust into her hands.

'How did you manage that?'

He didn't answer, just ushered her out of the hotel. 'Let's get you settled at your grandmother's.'

Ten minutes later she found herself standing in the small entrance foyer of an unprepossessing apartment building. He pointed to the stairs. 'We're heading to the top.'

They trudged up to the fifth floor. 'These stairs must've become difficult for Frances as she got older.' Callie was breathing hard herself. 'How did she manage them?'

'She didn't.'

'There's a lift?'

His lips pressed into a tight line. 'She didn't go out.'

Something he'd said back in the lawyer's office clicked into place. 'She was a recluse?'

'Of sorts.'

That wasn't going to help her breadcrumb trail. She opened her mouth, but instinct warned her that questioning him further would be fruitless, so she snapped it shut again.

Unlocking the door, he ushered her in, but didn't follow. His grey eyes had darkened and she sensed a storm building in their depths.

'You're not coming in?' she asked.

Dear God, did she have to sound so *needy*? She wasn't some distressed damsel.

Chin up. Shoulders back.

'How thoughtless of me. You must be busy…probably need to get back to work. I'm sorry to—'

'There's nowhere I need to be. I'm not working today.'

Uh-huh… Right, then…

She gestured behind her at the apartment. 'Then would you like to come in?'

He let out a long breath, coloured with something she couldn't put her finger on. What she did know was that it wasn't enthusiasm.

'Fine.' He marched in. 'I'll put the kettle on.'

For a moment she wanted to tell him to forget about it and go home, where he could be a grump on his own time rather than hers. But she bit the words back. The man had come to her aid without a murmur of complaint. He'd prevented a bad situation from getting worse. He didn't deserve her rudeness.

The apartment wasn't cavernous. Callie had figured anyone with as much money as Frances would live in something wildly opulent, but while it was comfortable, the apartment was by no means luxurious. It was also painted a dull brown that certainly didn't show it off to its best advantage.

The front door opened onto a large room with one corner given over to a kitchen and dining area. To the left of that two three-seater sofas stood at right angles to each other on an enormous Persian rug. An entertainment unit with a TV and top-of-the-line stereo system rested against the far wall. Various dressers, side tables and bookcases were scattered around the room. It was unsophisticated, but comfortable, and not what she'd been expecting.

Owen pointed at the two doors that stood either side of the entertainment unit. 'They're the bedrooms.'

She peeked inside the nearest, which had a view over the street. It had evidently been Frances's and she closed the door hastily, feeling like an intruder. The other, exactly the same size, was a guest room. She'd sleep there. It had a balcony, which was a bonus, even if it did only look out onto the backs of other apartment buildings.

'And the bathroom is on the other side of the kitchen wall.'

Just for completeness, she stuck her nose inside there as well. It was clean, and more generous than the bathroom she'd had at the hotel. It even had a bathtub. She made a mental note to grab some bath salts.

When she emerged back into the main living area, Owen handed her a steaming mug. 'It's black, I'm afraid. There's no milk. I'll organise a few staples to be delivered.'

She opened her mouth automatically to refuse, but closed it again. Who knew how long it would be before she had access to her own money again? 'Please keep a record of all that I owe you. I'll settle with you as soon as I can.'

He gestured at the room. 'What do you think?'

The question was freighted with far more meaning than she could decipher. It made her hesitate, but eventually she shrugged. 'It's comfortable. I like it.'

'You hate it.'

'Not true.'

It was just… The apartment might be generous by New York standards, but it was far too small for someone to have remained cooped up there as a recluse.

'Did my grandmother die here?'

He sipped his coffee, those grey eyes cool and reserved once more. 'Would it bother you if she had?'

It wasn't her grandmother's death that bothered her. It was the way she'd chosen to live her life. She sipped her coffee too. It was far stronger than she was used to, but she refused to grimace.

'You just answered a question with a question, so I'm guessing that's a yes.'

She wished she could get a handle on him…read him better. Just a tiny little bit would help.

'I'm not squeamish about staying in a place that somebody has died in.' She sent him an apologetic smile, because the words felt as if they should come with an apology. 'I'd just like to know, that's all.'

'Frances was taken ill here, but she died in hospital.' He paused, as if fighting with himself. 'If you're not squeamish, why ask?'

And there it was—the latent hostility that rose and bristled from him like a wolf's hackles. It had raised its head a couple of times in the lawyer's office, and she knew now that she hadn't imagined it.

She took another sip of her drink, her pulse picking up speed. 'Because I know nothing about my grandmother's last days.' And she needed to find out everything she could about the woman. 'Was she alone?'

She wasn't asking just in the hope of finding a contact who could help her fill in all the blanks in her family tree either. She sincerely hoped Frances hadn't died alone. Nobody should die alone.

'Did she have someone with her at the end?'

'Yes.'

She straightened when she realised who that person had been. 'You?'

'Yes.'

After leaving the lawyer's office, she'd had every intention of having nothing more to do with Owen Perry, but it was beginning to dawn on her that he might be the only person who could tell her all she needed to know.

She refused to let her shoulders sag. Refused to let her sudden exhaustion show. 'Why don't you want me staying here?' The question blurted from her, but she needed to know.

His mouth tightened. 'Do you mind if we take care of a few housekeeping things before I answer that?'

'Housekeeping?'

He lifted his phone and punched in a number. 'Rachel, I need a favour. I've an acquaintance who's just arrived from Australia and, long story short, she finds herself with nothing except the clothes she's standing up in.'

And twenty million dollars she wanted to say, just to annoy him. Though she didn't know why she wanted to annoy him. Except his using the word *acquaintance* had stung. It shouldn't have. It was the truth. But that hadn't stopped it from sounding so damn dismissive.

'That's exactly what I'm hoping.'

There was a pause while he listened to the person on the other end.

'So if I text you her picture you'll be able to gauge her size and have some essentials sent round?'

There was another pause.

'Excellent. Charge it to the company credit card.'

He gave the address of the apartment and then rang off.

'May I?' He held up his phone as if to take her photograph.

She tried not to focus on the way the thin woollen material of his jumper pulled taut across a pair of tantalisingly broad shoulders, or how the charcoal colour brought out the colour of his eyes.

'Why don't I just tell you my sizes?'

'They can be different between countries. Rachel is a wizard. She'll take one look at your picture and know your size.'

She nodded. She did need some basic essentials ASAP, and it was just easier to go with the flow.

He took the photo and then sent it to this unknown Rachel.

She stared at him. And then realised she was staring, so

forced her attention back to her coffee. 'What do you do? For work, I mean.'

His gaze turned sharp. 'Why?'

'Why do you have to be so suspicious?' She set down her mug. 'All I want to know is if your boss is going to be okay with you charging personal items—*female* personal items—to your company credit card. I've caused you enough inconvenience as it is.'

He swung away, stowing his phone in his back pocket. 'I'm a software engineer. I develop programs and apps for mobile devices. There won't be any trouble.'

Lucky him. His employer was evidently far more understanding and fair-minded than hers had been. Still, Owen was a man, and from where she was standing it seemed there were different rules for men.

'Next,' he said, his voice businesslike as he reached for his wallet, 'how much cash do you have on you?'

She wrenched her gaze from his strong thighs. Owen made jeans and a jumper—*sweater* in New York, she corrected herself—look like a work of art.

'Oh, please, put that away! Thank you, Owen, but you've already done enough. I'm very grateful, but I have enough cash to last me a few days.' *If she was frugal.* 'I promise,' she added, when he opened his mouth. 'Especially with the refund you scored for me back at the hotel. And if I find I'm running low I'll call on Mr Dunkley and make him earn the no-doubt outrageous fees he's been charging Frances all these years.'

'A fee he's now charging you.'

'Is there any other "housekeeping" we need to take care of?'

'I don't think so.' His nostrils flared. 'Everything in this apartment now belongs to you. You're free to do with it what you will.'

And he hated that fact. That much was obvious.

'Are you going to answer my question now?'

He turned away, his jaw clenching. 'I didn't want you staying here because—' He raked a hand through his hair, before swinging back. 'Look, it's not personal, okay? *I miss Frances.*'

His intensity took her off guard. 'Okay...'

'And over the last few weeks I've been letting myself in here and sitting down in my usual spot on the sofa to watch *Law and Order*, like I used to do with her when she was alive. It...' He trailed off with an impatient shrug.

Her heart burned, because she could see the grief stamped on his face and, despite all her suspicions, she knew it wasn't feigned. 'It made you miss her less?'

'Not really. It was a small comfort, that's all.'

And now she'd taken that away from him. She should leave...stay somewhere else. 'I guess it's too much to hope that there's a vacant apartment in the building?'

'They're all tenanted.'

Of course they were.

'What?' he demanded, when she continued to stare at him.

'I just don't get you. You obviously cared about Frances and yet you...'

'I *what*?' he bit out.

'Took her for a ride—took advantage of her. Or is all of this resentment and hostility...' she waved a hand at him '...because your meal ticket has run out?'

Owen's head rocked back. What the hell...? *Meal ticket?* He didn't need a meal ticket. He was a *giver* of meal tickets.

But Callie obviously didn't know that. She had no idea who he was—that he was the name and the brains behind Perry Apps. He was more than happy for it to stay that way too. Avarice was this woman's middle name. He didn't need the hassle of yet another gold-digging woman trying to infiltrate his life and his heart. Callie was pretty, but she wasn't *that* pretty.

Are you sure?

He rolled his shoulders, angry with himself. He might have a weakness for her particular brand of fresh-faced wholesomeness, but he was neither a fool nor a masochist.

'You're accusing me of financially profiting from your grandmother, when it's *you* who has inherited twenty million dollars?'

'The fact that I've inherited part of Frances's estate has seriously irked you—'

You bet it had!

'Despite the fact I couldn't possibly have taken advantage of someone I'd never met and had no contact with…'

Sing another song, sunshine.

Her hands clenched, as if she could read the scorn in his heart. 'You *told* me you'd fleeced her.'

What?

'When?'

'When you said, *"Frances gave me everything I needed while she was alive"*!' she shouted at him.

He stilled at the fury in her eyes. He tried telling himself her anger was because she thought he'd stolen what was hers, but instinct told him otherwise.

Instinct? *Ha!* What use were instincts? They'd proved so monumentally fallible where Fiona was concerned that they couldn't be trusted or listened to or taken into account. He'd honestly thought Fiona had loved him for himself. Not his money.

A vice tightened about his chest until he could barely breathe. If she'd succeeded in her plan he'd have been bound for the rest of his life to a ruthless, rapacious woman he couldn't respect. He'd had a narrow escape. And it had been dumb luck, not reasoned deduction, that had revealed

Fiona for the woman she was rather than the woman she'd wanted him to believe her to be.

Instincts had no place in his world view any more, or in his decision-making, or in any course of action he embarked upon. He wasn't making the same mistake twice. The only thing he'd rely on now was evidence and cold hard facts.

And what *were* the facts? From the sparks flying from Callie's eyes and the way her hands had clenched in white-knuckled violence… Callie was furious. *Fact.*

'It seems like you preyed on a lonely old woman, which is a truly despicable thing to do.'

It would be if it were true.

Callie slammed her hands to her hips. She wasn't some tiny, fragile-boned pixie girl—she had curves. Curves that had his groin tightening and a thirst rising through him. She had muscles too, as if she worked out or played sport. She didn't have a large build, but he had a feeling that if she threw a punch there'd be enough force behind it to wind a guy.

And she looked as if she'd like nothing better than to punch *him*. The realisation lightened some of the weight that engulfed him.

Then her shoulders lost some of their tightness. 'And yet you were with her when she died. You didn't let her die alone.' She cocked her head to one side and surveyed him. 'Which I guess makes you a wolf with a conscience.'

He was tempted to let her continue believing the worst. He neither needed nor wanted her good opinion. At that precise moment, though, Frances's face rose in his mind, with that knowing eyebrow raised as if to ask, *Really?* and he found himself huffing out a breath.

'You managed to put the worst possible interpretation on those words, didn't you?'

Her chin lowered a notch. 'What *did* you mean, then?'

He drained the rest of his coffee and then strode across

to the sofa and sat. In Frances's seat. Because he couldn't bear the thought of seeing anyone else in it—especially if that someone was her undutiful granddaughter. She hesitated and then took a seat too, at the other end of the sofa, curled up against its arm in a spot where he couldn't remember anyone ever sitting.

'My mother was Frances's cleaning woman. I was four when Mom starting cleaning for her—not at school yet—so my mother often had to bring me to work with her. The first time I came here, Frances taught me to play checkers.'

Callie smoothed her hands across her skirt and for a moment all he could see were her knees—really pretty knees. He shook himself. Pretty knees? Was he losing the plot?

'I thought you said she didn't like small children?'

'For some reason she made an exception for me.' For which he'd always considered himself blessed. 'My father was an alcoholic, and sometimes violent.'

Callie's gaze speared his and he found himself shrugging.

'He never hit my mother or me, but he punched holes in walls, broke dinner plates, threw things. We knew it was only a matter of time.'

As a little kid, he'd lived in fear of his father. It wasn't something he liked to dwell on.

'Frances helped my mother leave him—gave her cheap accommodation here in this apartment block. She took an interest in us—in me.' Loss hollowed out his stomach. 'She was the grandmother I never had.'

Callie sucked her bottom lip into her mouth. When she released it, it was plump and red from where she'd worried at it…and disturbingly fascinating.

'Where's your father now?' she asked.

'As soon as he realised he couldn't force my mother to come back, he told us we were dead to him. We haven't seen him since.'

'So... Frances, your mother and you were a family of sorts?'

They had been, and he didn't have enough family to be blasé about losing any of their number.

He refused to allow his attention to fix on her lips.

'She paid my college tuition fees. Without the benefit of that education I'd be pulling beers in some bar or lugging bricks around a building site. And, while there's absolutely nothing wrong with either of those things, she gave me the opportunity to find my place in the world. That education opened doors that had been previously shut to me.'

Her brow cleared. '*That's* what you meant when you said she'd given you everything you needed while she was alive?'

Exactly.

'I'm glad.' But she didn't smile. She stared across the room, her brow once again furrowed.

Owen... Frances's voice sounded a warning through his mind.

He ground his teeth together. 'What's wrong? You don't look pleased?'

Her gaze swung back to his. 'You and your mother looked after Frances?'

'We all looked after each other.'

She made a noise of frustration, lifting her hands. 'So why didn't she leave her money—her estate—to the two of you, instead of me and my mother?'

'We didn't want her money!' His throat burned. 'That's not what our relationship was based on.' He leaned towards her. 'But, speaking of despicable...' He was incapable of keeping the edge from his voice.

Their gazes clashed and she raised an eyebrow in exactly the same way Frances used to do, and for a moment he couldn't speak.

'What have I done that's despicable?' she asked. 'Besides being late for this morning's meeting and choosing the wrong hotel?'

Don't raise your voice. Don't yell. Don't roar at her that Frances deserved better.

'You said you wanted revenge on Frances.'

Her jaw dropped. 'I said no such thing!'

She wanted to deny it? He'd been there!

'Just after Mr Dunkley told you about the inheritance.' He dragged in a breath. 'You were smiling, and I asked you if you were already spending the money.'

She stared back, and then her face cleared. 'I wasn't referring to my grandmother when I said I wanted revenge.'

'Who were you referring to?'

'None of your business.'

Bizarrely, he had to fight a smile.

'Until a couple of weeks ago I didn't even know my grandmother existed. Why on earth would I want revenge on her?' She slumped back. 'She's given me all this money. What I don't understand is why she never tried to contact me when she was alive.'

He shot to his feet. 'Can we just cut that pretence? I know the truth.'

She stared at him and rose too. Something had changed in the depths of her eyes—the blue was neither so brilliant now, nor so clear.

'Would you care to explain that? Are you saying Frances *did* try to contact me?'

He'd just told her how close he and Frances had been. Did she honestly think him ignorant of the letters? Hell, he'd posted an awful lot of them himself.

He strode across to the antique dresser on the far wall and pulled open the top drawer, gesturing for Callie to come and take a look. The moment she drew near, the scent of spring flowers filled his senses. He backed up a step. Callie might look pretty, and she might smell pretty, but her heart was as black as pitch.

He kept his face trained on hers as she drew out the letters—hundreds of them—some of them addressed to Callie and others to her mother. She took them back to the sofa and stared at them. With her lower lip caught between her teeth, she sorted through them, checking the dates on the postmarks and collating them into two piles—hers and Donna's.

Eventually she glanced up at him, her eyes suspiciously bright. 'She wrote to me...'

He didn't bother dignifying that with an answer.

Her lips twisted. 'Oh, that's right. You're being a typical discerning male. I suppose it's *logical* to think that because they were returned *I* was the one who returned them.'

He blinked, felt something scratching through his chest. Was it possible he'd read her wrong? She didn't look guilty. Unlike Fiona when he'd caught her out in her lies. Of course that could simply mean she was a better actress than Fiona.

Or it could mean you have this wrong.

Facts. He needed to focus on facts.

She drew a pen and a scrap of paper from her handbag, scrawled something on it and then held it out to him. Forcing his frozen legs to move, he took it. She'd written *Return to Sender*. Then she handed him one of the letters addressed to her.

He studied the handwriting. With a mouth that had gone as dry as the Arizona desert, he reached for one of the letters addressed to Donna. The instruction on both letters was written in the same hand, but it was different from the sample that Callie had written on the scrap of paper.

He lowered himself back down to the sofa. 'Your mother returned all of these?'

He didn't know why he asked the question when the evidence in front of him provided the answer.

'So it would seem.'

'So when you said you weren't aware of your grand-mother's existence…'

'I wasn't lying.'

He rubbed the back of his neck. 'I didn't believe you.'

She shrugged, gesturing at the letters. 'I can see why you came to the conclusion you did.'

They were both quiet for several long moments. Eventually she glanced up. 'You thought *that* of me—' she pointed to the letters '—and yet you still came to my rescue at the hotel today. Why?'

He hesitated, reluctant to tell her the truth, but suspecting he owed it to her. 'I promised Frances I would provide you with every assistance if you should ever come to New York.'

'And, despite how you felt about me, you were determined to carry out her wishes.' She tapped a finger against her lips. 'Which turned out lucky for me.'

'Callie, I'm sorry. I—'

She waved his apology away. 'It doesn't matter.' Her accompanying smile was strained. 'It at least explains why I sensed you didn't like me.'

Her eyes clouded as they travelled back to the letters and Owen's temples throbbed. Her mother had deliberately kept them from her. Why would she do that? There must have been seriously bad blood between the two women. It was beyond him to understand why Donna had refused to patch things up when Frances had proffered an olive branch, though. They were *family*! Family should mean something.

'Did Frances ever speak about my mother and me?'

He shook his head. And he'd never asked. He'd known that Frances had been married twice, and that she had a daughter, but his mother had warned him never to pry into Frances's affairs. They'd been so grateful to her, and neither of them had wanted to cause her pain or discomfort. It had been unspoken, but they'd both known that Frances's family was the one topic that was off-limits.

He'd respected her privacy. Wishing he'd done otherwise now was pointless. She'd never have told him anything anyway, and he'd have only vexed her.

'I guess these now belong to me.' Callie gathered her letters into a pile. 'Which means I'm free to read them.'

He gestured at Donna's letters as Callie collected them up and returned them to the drawer. 'What are you going to do with those?'

'I haven't a clue. I've a feeling my mother should read them.'

'But…?'

She swung round and the light from the windows caught the auburn highlights in her hair. 'My mother isn't an unreasonable woman, Owen. She's…lovely. She's smart and fun and I respect her. We're close.' She moved back to trace a finger across the letters. 'I'm beyond shocked to find she's kept these from me. It goes against everything I know about her.'

He rested his elbows on his knees, searching her face. 'What are you saying?'

'I'm saying she must have a very good reason for not wanting me ever to meet or even know about Frances.'

He stiffened. 'Then she'd be wrong.'

They were both suddenly on their feet, eyes flashing and breathing hard.

'Of course that's what you'd say. You only knew the best of her.'

'In the same way you only know the best of your mother.'

She wheeled away. 'The fact is neither of us knows what happened between them.'

That was true enough. He'd loved Frances, but she'd

been far from perfect. Still, she hadn't been imperfect enough to not be forgiven by her own flesh and blood.

Callie folded her arms. 'I have a feeling I'm not going to like Frances.'

He scowled back. What right did she think she had to judge her grandmother?

'That's right. Keep an open mind. Doesn't the fact that she's left you ridiculously wealthy mean anything?'

'I'm not keeping the inheritance if I don't like her!'

What?

'You signed the paperwork!'

'If I hadn't, what would've happened to the money, huh? Would it have gone to a cats' home?' She shook her head. 'I don't have anything against cats, but I can direct that money into better channels.'

'Like…?'

'Amnesty and the Red Cross…and that charity that distributes mosquito nets—it's a far from sexy one, but it's rated as getting great results.'

'The Against Malaria Foundation?'

'Yes! That one.'

They stared at each other, a little nonplussed. He shook himself. While Callie might've named three of his personal favourite charities, it was not what Frances had wanted her to do with the money.

'You'd really give the money away? The amount Frances has given you is life-changing.'

'Maybe I don't want my life changed.'

Something hard settled in the pit of his stomach. Frances would hate this outcome, and he was going to do everything he could to prevent it. By the time he was through with her, Callie Nicholls was going to acknowledge that her grandmother was a saint. Okay, maybe not a saint, but—

'Do *you* want it?' she asked.

He recoiled. 'No!'

She spread her hands as if that explained it all.

The reasons behind her initially tepid reaction to her inheritance hit him then. He'd thought she'd been hoping for more—for everything. He'd thought she'd been disappointed in the legacy Frances had left her. Instead, she'd been interested in Frances herself.

He dragged in a breath. While he already had his own twenty million dollars—and the rest—would he be able to just walk away from that sum, as Callie was threatening to do?

'The money doesn't have to be life-changing. It doesn't have to mean anything,' Callie said. 'Signing Mr Dunkley's paperwork will simply make accessing information easier. And frankly, Owen, that's all I'm interested in.'

'What kind of information are you after?' he asked.

While he might have been wrong about her returning Frances's letters, that didn't mean Callie Nicholls wasn't still trouble with a capital *T*.

CHAPTER THREE

EVER SINCE CALLIE had entered Frances's apartment, she'd grown more and more aware of Owen. Maybe it was because the apartment was an undeniably feminine space. Not in a pink and frilly way, but there were vases dotted about, waiting for flowers, scented candles lined the windowsills, and a plethora of cushions covered the sofas—more cushions than a man would ever put up with. Furthermore, the bookcase overflowed with novels—most of them romance and women's fiction.

The apartment was a feminine space, and Owen was undeniably masculine.

Or maybe it was the fact that she now understood why he'd been so angry, even though he'd tried to hide it. He'd thought she'd callously shunned a woman he'd cared about deeply. She didn't blame him for feeling the way he had.

What on earth had happened between her mother and Frances?

A chill chased across her scalp. Maybe she should leave the past where it was and not disturb it. Except…

She wanted to know, ached to learn all she could.

Here was a chance to discover where she came from, to find out if she had any other family and fill in all the blanks she'd been hungry to fill as a child. Here was a chance to *finally* get to the bottom of a mystery that had chafed at her for her entire childhood.

For as long as she could recall it had only been her and her mother. But they hadn't been alone in the world, as her mother had always claimed. She'd had a grandmother.

Her hands clenched and unclenched. She couldn't lie to herself. Her mother would have a good reason for keeping it from her. She suspected there'd be a price to pay for sating her curiosity. But also a prize to be won! And she couldn't forget that tracing her family tree would give her the chance to win an amazing job—one that would have Dominic grinding his teeth in envy and frustration.

She thrust out her jaw, resolve setting like concrete in her chest. Getting a new job, getting her life back on track and feeling in control again was her number one priority. She wasn't walking away now.

As for her inheritance and the money—she could make a decision about that at a later date.

She blinked herself back into the present to find herself staring at broad shoulders, lean hips and grey eyes that had turned as bleak as the mist her plane had flown through on its descent into New York.

In spite of what Frances had or hadn't done to Callie's mother, Owen had loved the older woman and he missed her. Her chest burned. She was intruding on that grief and taking away his sole source of comfort. She wanted to get to the bottom of this mystery, but not at the expense of other people.

'You know what, Owen? I really appreciate everything you've done, but I think I should find a nearby B&B. Maybe you'd be kind enough to suggest somewhere suitable and—?'

'What on earth are you talking about?'

She planted her hands on her hips. She stared at his strong thighs and her mouth went dry. *Don't stare.*

'And…uh…maybe you could hold the key for me until I'm ready to go through Frances's things?' His eyes narrowed, and she swallowed. 'Also, while I think of it, maybe there are a couple of Frances's things you'd like for yourself—for sentimental reasons. You should give it some thought and—'

'No, Callie.'

His face had cleared and he shook his head, his tone a strange combination of gentleness and implacability.

She blinked. 'I beg your pardon?'

'I'm not letting you do that.'

She puffed herself up, doing her best to feign offence. 'What do you mean *letting* me? It's *my* decision. The thing is, I'm sure I'll be much happier in a B&B.'

Beneath the soft wool of his jumper, his shoulders flexed. 'I know what you're doing, and I'd rather you didn't. Your grandmother would wish you to stay here. She certainly wouldn't want me coming here to wallow and be morose.'

'But—'

'It's time for me to move on. Now that you're in New York, I won't be coming here again without an invitation.'

'Fine! But you don't have to move on right this minute, you know? You can take your time and—'

He took her hands and squeezed, his smile warming his eyes. Her heart pressed hard against her lungs, making it difficult to catch her breath.

'Callie, I appreciate the thought. I really do. But it's totally unnecessary. This is just a place, and these are just things. I have my memories. That's enough.'

Her shoulders sagged, but some of the guilt lifted. 'If you're sure…?'

'Positive.'

He scanned her face and then nodded, as if satisfied with what he saw, but for a fraction of a moment his gaze lingered and the moment lengthened and slowed. She felt as if she were being tugged towards something unknown… something that promised richness and depth and meaning.

But then he blinked and dropped her hands, stepping back so quickly that instead of drifting along on a warm current she found herself having to plant her legs to keep her balance.

'Is there anything else I can do for you?'

His words emerged clipped and terse, and she automatically shook her head and pulled herself into straight lines.

'No, thank you. I don't need anything else.'

Drifting along on a warm current...? Had they been making eyes at each other? Surely not!

He glanced away, the muscles in his jaw bunching. 'I should take you out to dinner tonight...'

Except he didn't want to. That much was obvious. And she wasn't a damn charity case.

'No, you really shouldn't. Thanks for the thought, but no. It's been a hell of a day and jet-lag is catching up with me. I just want some quiet time to process everything that's happened.'

As she spoke, she moved towards the door, hoping he'd follow and leave. The absolute last thing she needed in her life was another complicated man.

'A quiet night in is exactly what the doctor ordered. I have your card. Why don't I give you a call sometime in the next couple of days and we can catch up over a coffee or something?'

Given his earlier desire to leave, he was now moving with studied reluctance. At the last moment he diverted to the kitchen, held up the apartment key, and set it on the counter.

She nodded her thanks. 'Like I said earlier, I appreciate all your help today.'

'It was nothing.'

They stood there for a moment in agonising awkwardness. What was the correct way to say goodbye to him? Kissing his cheek would be far too familiar, and yet shaking his hand felt too formal and wrong.

Eventually he nodded. 'Take care, Callie. If you need anything, don't hesitate to call.'

'Thanks.' She dug out a smile and offered a dumb little wave. 'See you.'

He turned and set off down the stairs and she closed the door, leaning back against it and blowing out a breath.

Even with their misunderstanding cleared up, she and Owen mixed like oil and water. It might be wise to spend as little time in each other's company as possible.

The sixteen-hour time difference between Sydney and New York didn't make for a restful night's sleep, even given Callie's exhaustion. At three a.m. she woke, ravenous enough for a three-course meal, but forced herself to remain where she was. She didn't fall back to sleep until after six, and then woke groggy and disoriented at nine.

A shower helped her feel halfway human, but before she could sally forth to find herself some breakfast and buy a phone charger a knock sounded on the door.

'Grocery delivery for Callie Nicholls.'

Owen had organised groceries for her? She'd been too beat to head out yesterday and find a store. She'd simply heated up a tin of soup she'd found in the pantry and made do with that.

The deliveryman set several bags on the kitchen bench and left again with a cheery 'Have a nice day.'

She made coffee and toast, and was flicking through the newspaper when a second knock sounded. Another delivery—one she had to sign for. When she opened the package she found a phone charger.

For all his reserve, there was no denying that Owen was taking his duty to assist her seriously. She pulled her phone out and started to call him—and then stopped.

He'd probably be at work by now. She texted him instead.

Thanks for groceries and charger. Dinner on me when new c card arrives.

He replied promptly with a thumbs-up emoji. She waited, but that was it.

'What more do you want?' she murmured, shaking her head and setting her phone on the charger, doing what she could to push thoughts of Owen from her mind.

Last night she'd decided to spend the day at the New York Public Library. She was a researcher, she wanted to find out all she could about her family, and where was the best place to research anything? A library.

She fell in love with the Fifth Avenue building the moment she stepped inside its grand marble foyer. And it was a love that only grew as she climbed the grand staircase to the third floor and the Rose Reading Room—a room the size of a football field, with arched casement windows that flooded the space with light, row upon row of antique wooden desks, and murals on the ceilings she stared at so long her neck started to ache.

She happily lost herself in its depths for several exhilarating hours.

Frances's family—*her* family—had links she could easily trace to sixteenth-century Europe. The family of Thomas—Frances's first husband and Callie's grandfather—was going to take a little more work, but she could already tell it wasn't going to be impossible.

She wasn't in the least interested in Frances's second husband Richard, as he had no blood ties to her, but it was impossible to avoid the headlines and photographs of them in the social pages—especially of their wedding and subsequent divorce. The wedding pictures showed a lavish affair, with the happy couple beaming at the camera. Frances looked absolutely ravishing, and much younger than her forty-six years of age. While Richard Bateman, twelve years her junior, was movie-star-handsome.

Callie fanned herself. *Way to go, Grandma.*

The divorce, though, had been an acrimonious affair.

From all accounts, Richard had been fundamentally incapable of fidelity. Callie winced at the far from flattering photo of Frances snapped only four years later, looking every inch her fifty years.

Maybe falling for jerks ran in the family.

Stop it. Her grandmother's first marriage sounded rock-solid. Everyone was allowed one or two romantic mistakes in their lifetime. Unfortunately, Frances's mistake had cost her several million dollars in the divorce settlement. At least Callie had only lost her job.

She stuck out her jaw. But not for long. Soon she'd have an even bigger, better, shinier job, and Dominic would be gnashing his teeth in envy.

And *that* would be perfect.

Returning to the apartment block mid-afternoon, she pushed open the door and a pint-sized dog, all cute honey-coloured fur, bolted from the foyer inside.

'Oh, no, no, no…little puppy, wait!' She pulled the door open wider, expecting to see the owner hurtling down the stairs after it, but nobody appeared.

'Don't even *think* about escaping,' she told the dog in her sternest teacher voice, not relishing the thought of chasing it all the way across New York.

But no sooner had the dog relieved itself against a nearby railing than it dashed back past her and inside again to race up the stairs. Oh, well. At least it was toilet-trained.

A door on the next landing opened, but the dog didn't pause. Callie called out a greeting as a woman emerged, but she only sent Callie a glare and returned inside, slamming the door behind her.

'Wow, so the locals are friendly, huh?' she muttered, setting off up the stairs. Still, this was a big city, not a country town where everyone said hello to each other.

She pulled up short when she reached the top floor and found the little dog sitting right outside Frances's door.

'Who do you belong to, little guy? Because you sure as heck don't live here?' There'd been no dog basket or water bowls in the apartment. He looked clean and well cared for, though, and he wore a collar. Someone in the complex must own him.

'You're lucky I like dogs,' she told him. 'Come in and have a drink and then we'll see if we can find where you live.'

It was time to introduce herself to the neighbours anyway.

He drank deeply from the bowl of water she set on the floor, and groaned in delight when she scratched his ears and rolled onto his back for a tummy rub.

'You're a little charmer...' she read the tag on his collar '... Barney.' There was no accompanying address or phone number.

She unpacked the few things she'd brought home with her from the library—a book and some printouts—before turning back to her four-legged visitor.

'C'mon, Barney. Let's see if we can find out who you belong to.'

She scooped him up from where he'd settled himself on the sofa. Rather than squirm or struggle, he licked her hand and happily settled in her arms.

'You're *so* good,' she cooed, tucking the key into the pocket of her jeans.

She decided to start on the fourth floor and work her way down. 'Hello,' she started brightly when a man answered the first door, 'I'm just wondering if this little guy belongs to you? I'm staying in the apartment upstairs and—'

'No, it doesn't.' The man glared at her. 'You got something against pets?'

'Of course not. It's just—'

But she found herself talking to the door that had been closed in her face.

'Did I hear Claude say you've got something against pets?' demanded the occupant of the other apartment on this floor.

'No, I—'

'Wanna kick me out 'cos I have a cat?'

She stilled. 'Do you know who I am?'

'We *all* know who you are.' And the woman shut the door in her face too.

She continued down to the next floor. The woman who hadn't returned her greeting earlier didn't even answer the door, though Callie could've sworn she was at home. She turned to find the door of the apartment opposite open, and a man glaring at her.

'Not my dog,' he growled.

'How did you—?'

'Heard you upstairs.'

Were the walls that thin around here?

'You coming down here to tell me you're increasing the rent?'

She moistened dry lips. 'Nope.'

'You expect me to believe that?'

Her spine stiffened. 'Yes.'

'Well, I don't. And don't go disturbing Jilly in Number One. She works nights and needs her rest.'

'Right. Thank you. I—' She rolled her eyes. 'And I'm talking to another door.'

By the time she reached the basement apartment she was feeling ragged. She raised her hand and knocked, not sure if she hoped to find the resident at home or not. A firm tread sounded.

She pushed her shoulders back. No matter how glaring and bad-tempered this person might be, she would not turn tail and run. She lifted her chin, determined to give as good as she got.

The door opened, she hiked up her gaze…and her jaw dropped.

'Owen!'

Callie Nicholls stood on his doorstep, and at the sight of her something low down in Owen's gut sprang to life. He tried to stamp it out, exterminate it. For pity's sake, if he concentrated hard enough he *would* conquer the inconvenient heat flooding his veins. He just had to try harder.

A glance at her face, though, and all that was forgotten. The corners of her mouth drooped, her shoulders were hunched up towards her ears, and tiny lines fanned out from her eyes. She looked dragged down, worn thin…exhausted.

'What's up?'

'You really don't want to know…' The bitter edge to her words made him stiffen. 'But maybe you can answer a few questions for me.'

'Right, hit me with them.' He'd meant the words to sound rallying, encouraging. Instead they'd emerged clipped— like a command—making him wince internally.

Get a new hotel.

Treat your grandmother with respect.

Tell me your questions.

Way to woo a girl, Owen.

Not that he had any interest in wooing this girl. He had no interest in wooing *any* girl. He might find her attractive, but he wasn't making a play for her.

She stuck out a hip and his mouth dried.

'One: why does everyone in this building hate me?'

Ah.

'Two: does this dog belong to you?'

He glanced at the little dog cradled in her arms, but before he could answer she powered on.

'Three: why didn't you tell me you lived in the basement apartment of the block I've inherited? What's the big secret?'

It took all his strength not to fidget.

'And four,' she continued after a short pause, 'are you going to invite me in?'

In answer to her last question he pushed the door open wider and waved her in. 'But before you put the dog down, let me close my office door.'

His office was the first room off the hallway that led to the rest of the apartment, and the door stood wide open. He'd been working when she'd knocked.

Her eyes widened when she glanced past him and caught sight of his computer equipment. 'You have some fancy-schmancy computer gear there, Owen.' She ruffled the dog's ears. 'And we sure as heck don't want you getting in there and causing havoc, Barney.'

'Most of the equipment belongs to my company.'

'The company you work for?'

'Yep.'

He omitted the salient fact that he owned the company. He wasn't ready to trust her. He tried telling himself that who he was and what he did was no concern of hers, but it didn't ring true. Whatever. It had no bearing on their current conversation.

'You can put Barney down now. It should be safe.'

Her lips twitched. 'Fingers crossed—but I refuse to give any guarantees. Barney and I aren't all that well acquainted yet.'

They followed the little dog as he trotted down the hallway and into the open-plan living room.

'Oh!' Callie pulled up short when she saw it. 'I thought it'd be dark and poky down here, but it's…'

'Not?' he finished for her, moving towards the fridge.

'It's amazing.'

It was. Light flooded into the room from the French

doors that led outside to a small private courtyard. The living room walls were painted a warm cream, and the pale furniture reflected back the light, making the room appear airy and spacious. He could afford something much grander these days, but he didn't want grander. Not at the moment.

'Beer?' he said.

'Beer?'

She swung from surveying a picture on his wall, her eyes widening and her lips curving in a way that chased away all the shadows.

Don't focus on the lips.

'Yes, please!'

Her enthusiasm made him grin. 'I forgot. Aussies and beer go hand in hand, don't they? Or is that an outdated cliché?'

'Nope, it's pretty much a national standard. Trying American beer is on my list of must-dos while I'm here.'

'If it's not up to scratch I can point you towards a couple of local liquor stores that probably stock Australian beer.'

She stared at him, and then she smiled, and for a moment the world tilted.

'That's kind of you.' She hiked herself up to sit on one of the stools at his breakfast bar.

He handed her a beer. And then remembered his manners. 'Glass?'

She shook her head, glancing back behind her to see the dog lay sprawled in a patch of sun, completely at ease. 'This little guy has a habit of making himself at home wherever he is. So…?'

She turned back, eyebrows raised. He ordered himself not to stare.

'How about I answer your questions in reverse order?' he said.

She sipped her beer, her eyes not leaving his.

He didn't move to take the stool beside her, but remained

leaning back against the kitchen bench, the breakfast bar between them. Cool, casual, unruffled—those were the things he needed to be.

'First up—yes, I am going to invite you in.'

A current of electricity surged through him when her lips twitched.

'Thank you. I'm honoured.'

'I didn't mention the fact that I live in the same building as Frances because it slipped my mind. And it didn't seem important. I moved back into the block eight months ago, but it's only a temporary measure.'

She set her beer down carefully. 'You didn't tell me you live down here because you don't trust me. That made sense when you thought I'd been mean to someone you loved, but it's still the case now...' She stared at him. 'I suppose that means your natural default position is suspicious?'

He straightened. 'No, it's not. I...'

The denial petered out and he forced himself back into an attitude of casual slouchiness. The little dog trotted over to sit at his feet, staring up at him. He welcomed the change of focus.

'You thirsty, little guy?'

He set a bowl of water down for the dog, but Barney rolled onto his back instead, begging for a tummy rub. With a low laugh, Owen obliged before forcing himself upright again.

'It never used to be my default position,' he made himself say. Before Fiona it hadn't been. But now...

'So I shouldn't take it personally?'

'You shouldn't take it personally,' he agreed.

They stared at each other, neither moving, and in that stillness something changed—stirred and unfurled, charging the air. A fist reached into his chest and gently but inexorably squeezed the breath from his body. Panic fluttered at the edges of his consciousness and he had to wrench his gaze away before he did something stupid. Like walk across and kiss her.

What the hell...?

His heart pounded and Callie's dazed expression, the way her fingers tightened about her beer, the way her jaw tightened, told him she'd recognised what he hadn't been able to disguise—that he found her attractive...that he wanted her.

She took a long pull on her drink, looking everywhere but at him. Had he made her feel uncomfortable? Or—worse—unsafe?

He didn't want her feeling unsafe around him.

'Sometimes you remind me of Frances.' The words dropped into the silence that surrounded them. 'And it catches me off guard.'

It was the truth, but it wasn't what that moment had been about. Still, it would provide him with some kind of excuse, at least. And hopefully help her feel at ease again.

She froze—head tilted back, bottle of beer to her lips. Nothing moved except her eyes as they returned to his. Eventually she lowered the bottle, but she didn't speak.

'It's in the way you raise your eyebrows. Especially when you quirk just one of them.' He huffed out a laugh. 'Exactly like you're doing now.'

She lifted a hand to her eyebrow, as if committing the mannerism to memory.

'You have a rather precise way of moving your hands... And your chin,' he added with a frown, the resemblance only striking him now, 'is the same shape as Frances's.'

'It's the same shape as my mother's too.'

She traced it with her fingers and he tried not to imagine following the action with his own hand, then tilting it so he could lower his mouth over hers and—

He pushed away from the bench. At her questioning glance he gestured across the room. 'The sofa's more comfortable.' He needed to sit.

His sofa was a deep, L-shaped affair, but before he could plant himself in the far corner the little dog had beaten him to it.

'That's a little bold, Barney,' she scolded, scooting across to lift him onto her lap. 'Owen might not want you sitting on his sofa.'

Owen took the seat furthest away, aware now of her fragrance. She smelled like spring flowers. Or maybe that was because his courtyard was filled with a profusion of the spring blooms his mother had planted.

'I don't mind him being on the sofa.'

She glanced around and huffed out a sigh. 'But he's not yours, is he?'

It was more of a statement than a question, and things inside him pulled tight. He was a dog person. What was it about his apartment that gave her the idea he wasn't?

'No dog bed or food bowls or dog toys,' she continued, and his shoulders loosened. 'You wouldn't happen to know who he belongs to, by any chance?'

He shook his head. 'What made you think I would?'

She told him how she and Barney had become acquainted.

'He must be local,' he agreed, curbing the temptation to reach over and fondle the dog's ears. It would bring him too close to Callie. 'He looks well cared for.'

She nodded.

'Right.' He stood. 'Lost dogs are usually found within the first hour of going missing. I suggest we walk the nearby streets to see if anyone is searching for him.'

'Excellent plan!'

They returned to his apartment an hour and a half later, none the wiser and with Barney still trotting obediently on the length of cord Owen had dug out of the bottom of a drawer. They flopped down onto his sofa, nursing bottles of water.

'He can stay with me until I find his owner.' Callie glanced at Barney and then at Owen. 'I get the feeling you're a dog person too?' He nodded, and her eyes lit up. 'You work from home, right?'

'What makes you say that?'

These days he volunteered as little information about himself as possible. He'd been too trusting, too open, with Fiona, and it wasn't a mistake he meant to repeat.

'Your office is huge. So I just thought…' She shrugged. 'I figured it meant you worked from home sometimes.'

'Sometimes I do.'

He refused to meet her eyes. He had to go into the office occasionally. When he had meetings with clients, or his team of programmers, but it was rare. He left the day-to-day running of the company in the capable hands of his office manager. Ninety-five per cent of his work he did in the comfort of his own home.

'Then we can share custody of Barney, if you like. I'm doing some research at the New York Public Library. It'd be great if I could leave him with you for a few hours each day when I do that.'

'Sure, why not?'

Lissy had been on to him for ages to get a dog. Barney would provide the perfect trial run. Maybe he could use Barney as an enticement to get Lissy to come and stay one weekend soon…

He reached across and tugged gently on Barney's ear. 'How'd you feel about that, Barney Boy? We can have some guy time. You can kick back over a bowl of kibble while I slave over a hot computer.'

He eased back, doing his best to ignore the scent of spring and the impulsive restlessness it sent surging through his veins. So, the New York Public Library…? What was she researching?

He watched as Callie rubbed the little dog's neck and

shoulders, and laughed when Barney groaned his delight, kicking his back legs.

'It might be worth putting some posters up around the area to help track down his owner. I could take Barney's picture, make a poster, run a few copies off… What do you think?'

'That's a great idea. Someone has to be fretting about him, and we ought to spread the word. First thing tomorrow I'll ring around the local vets. They might know who he is.'

Her face grew serious again and the silence stretched, making Owen's nape prickle.

'You do know you still haven't answered the first of my earlier questions?'

He scratched a hand over his face.

'Why do all the residents here hate me, Owen?'

'They don't hate you. They're just worried. Worried you're going to evict them or hike up their rents and force them out.'

'I see.'

She folded her arms and Barney leapt off her lap to pad over to the warm patch of sun outside, where he proceeded to stretch out as if on a minibreak at Waikiki Beach.

'Really strategic move, being rude to me, though… Right? That's the perfect plan to have me warming to everyone and feeling sympathetic and benevolent.'

He bit back something rude and succinct. How did he explain the motley crew that made up the residents of this apartment block?

'Joan in Number Six is a victim of domestic violence. Her now ex-husband is in prison for assaulting her. He contravened a restraining order—wasn't supposed to be within a hundred yards of her.'

She flinched.

'Stuart in Number Four turned to drugs and alcohol as a teenager, due to childhood sexual abuse. He's clean now, but it's a constant struggle for him. He works part-time and is on a disability pension. He sees a therapist several times a week.'

She swallowed.

'Ana from Number Three—her parents were illegal immigrants. When her father was extradited back to Ecuador he was murdered. She and her mother, who is nearly crippled with arthritis, are fighting to stay in the country.'

'Okay, okay…' She waved her hands in front of her face. 'I get it. Everyone here has had a tough time.' She pulled in a breath. 'Change—any kind of change—will be frightening for them.'

'They have zero expectation of receiving kindness from strangers, Callie. It's not what they've been taught to anticipate.'

Behind the startling blue of her eyes, he could see her mind turning over.

'Frances took each of them in?'

'Yes.'

'She offered them a safe place and cheap rent, just like she did for your mother?'

His gut twisted. Now came the moment of truth. If Callie really was a gold-digger she'd hike up the rents. She could get ten times what everyone here was paying. She could price them out and force them out.

His back molars ground together. He wouldn't let that happen. If he had to, he'd subsidise the tenants' rents. Not that he had any intention of telling her that. The people here had been through enough for one lifetime. Frances had wanted to give them a safe place to shelter and rebuild their lives. He'd continue that legacy for as long as he could.

'I've no intention of changing things for the foreseeable future, Owen.'

His heart hammered against his ribs. 'What *are* your plans for the foreseeable future?'

CHAPTER FOUR

'WOW, YOU MUST be really good at your job!' Callie couldn't help but be impressed with all the high-end equipment in Owen's home office.

'Or just a tech nerd.' He didn't glance up from manipulating an image of Barney on the screen for the promised poster.

'You said you create apps?' At his nod, she added, 'Would I be familiar with anything you've worked on?'

His gaze remained glued to his screen, but he named a couple of apps that had her eyebrows shooting up towards her hairline.

'Wow! If you worked on those then no wonder you have an office at home like this.'

'What do you mean?' He swung around, his tone clipped.

She blinked. 'I just meant it's clear your company will do whatever it can to keep you happy...so you'll keep working for them.'

With a curt nod he turned back to the computer.

She soldiered on past the awkwardness. 'I guess the beauty of working from home is you can ditch the power suits and work in jeans and a tee.' Although Owen didn't strike her as a power suit kind of guy... 'Or even your PJs, if you want.' Though Owen might be one of those guys who wore nothing at all to bed.

Her cheeks grew suddenly hot and her palms clammy.

His lips twisted. 'I bet you like a guy in a power suit.'

There was an edge to the question that raised her hackles. 'Mmm, you bet... What woman doesn't, right? I mean it's *dreamy*.'

She wondered if she'd overdone it, but he swung back

to his computer with a scowl. 'The commute is *mmm, dreamy* too.'

There was clearly something about her that made him want to snipe at her. And vice versa. Grief on his part, maybe? And the shock of being thrust into this seemingly alternative reality on hers? This ruffling and needling and poking at each other should feel stressful, fraught…nerve-racking. It didn't, though. It felt enlivening…*energising.*

For a moment earlier she'd even thought Owen had wanted to kiss her. It had sent a thrill of something gloriously reckless powering through her veins and—

Don't even go there.

She wasn't getting involved with anyone at the moment. She wasn't in the right frame of mind to start a relationship, so what was the point?

Fun? The word had some of the hardness inside her wanting to soften and thaw, but she refused to let it. That kind of fun would distract her from working on the things that really mattered—work and stability. The distraction might look tempting, but it wasn't worth it. Not in the long run.

She tossed her head and forced herself back to the conversation. 'The downside of working from home, of course, is not having workmates,' she said.

She missed her work colleagues. Not Dominic and the Head of Faculty—she didn't miss them one little bit. But the rest of the staff in the history department had been a fun bunch. They'd welcomed her, advised her, and on occasion challenged her. They'd taught her so much about becoming an efficient researcher and a good teacher. She missed them. She missed her students too. She'd hate to work from home like Owen did.

She glanced down to find cool grey eyes assessing her. He leaned back in his chair, the poster evidently forgotten. 'You miss the people you work with, Callie? I'm guessing you're not a computer nerd. What is it that you do?'

'Did,' she corrected. 'Past tense. I was a junior history lecturer at a university back home.'

'You were fired?'

'Nothing so dramatic. I was *"let go".'* She made air quotes. 'My contract wasn't renewed.'

His eyes gentled. 'Downsizing?'

'The powers that be are always trying to downsize the arts.' Not that she'd really been a victim of downsizing. She'd been a victim of sexism and an old-style boys' club mentality. It wasn't a mistake she'd make again.

She glanced around his office. 'It must be nice to be so good at something and to be valued for it. I envy you.'

'I'm sure you were very good at what you did.'

She'd thought so too. She'd thought she was safe. 'Maybe if I'd been better at it I wouldn't have been *let go*.'

'We both know that workplace politics comprise so much more than a worker's individual worth, Callie.'

'Truer words…' she quipped, refusing to dwell on her sense of injury and the stinging injustice of it all. She'd keep her eyes firmly fixed on the main prize. 'Currently I'm between jobs, but there are prospects on the horizon—' *good prospects* '—and I'm quite sure work colleagues will feature in my future.'

'Good for you.'

'What about you? Don't you miss having work colleagues?' she asked as he turned back to the screen. 'Though I suppose you're an island complete unto himself.'

His lips twitched, and she had the oddest feeling she could stare at those lips all day.

'I might not go into an office on a daily basis, but I'm not a hermit. I have online meetings, brainstorming sessions with other programmers. And outside of work this apartment block is a little community in itself.'

One she was currently excluded from. Being excluded sucked. She needed to do something to change that.

'I also see my family and friends regularly,' he said.

She held up a piece of sporting memorabilia—a pewter man swinging some kind of bat mounted on a shiny walnut base. 'And who do you attend ballgames with?'

'Don't drop that—it's a limited edition. Not cheap.'

She very carefully placed it back on its shelf. 'What sort of ballgame…?'

'Baseball. And the fact you had to ask tells me you know nothing about ballgames.'

'Not a thing.' And, strangely enough, her life didn't feel the poorer for it.

'And sometimes,' he continued, 'when I'm wrestling with the logic of a particularly difficult piece of code, I'll work at a nearby coffee house.'

She clapped her hands beneath her chin. 'Like the one in *Friends*?'

He laughed. 'It looks nothing like the one in *Friends*. It's larger…more beaten up…no sofas.'

'It sounds kinda cool.'

'It is. You'd probably like it. Lots of guys in high-powered suits.'

'Oh, I'm sold! Address, please? I'll make sure to drop by.'

His hand stilled on the keyboard. Above the photo of Barney that was centred on the page he'd written *Found* and beneath that he'd written *Answers to the name of Barn*.

'You want to meet someone while you're here?' he asked.

A temporary fling with a like-minded guy would be the perfect way to drive Dominic from her mind and her heart once and for all—that and the job. Her heart pounded up into her throat. *The job…* She *had* to convince the producers of that show that she was the perfect candidate.

She released her breath and shook her head. 'I can't afford the distraction of a fling at the moment.' She pointed to his screen. 'It's Barney. With an *E-Y*. *B-A-R-N-E-Y*.'

He typed *E-Y*. 'Distraction from what?'

She couldn't work out if he was grilling her or if he was genuinely interested. 'When I told you I didn't know what my plans were, I meant about my inheritance and this building.' Now that she knew he lived here and worked from here, his concern made more sense. 'But I have a job plan I'm working on.'

He spun around on his chair. 'Which is…?'

She gestured to his spare chair, silently asking if she could sit in it.

'Knock yourself out.' He grabbed the pile of files on it and set them on his desk.

'Have you heard of the TV programme *Mystery Family Trees*? It's a British TV series that's proved so popular in the UK they've made an Australian version too.'

His brow creased. 'The show where they trace a celebrity's genealogy?'

'That's the one. Well, they're now in the process of putting a team together to make an American version of the show.'

'Uh-huh…'

'And I'm an historian.' She spread her hands and kinked an eyebrow. 'See where I'm going with this?'

'That mouth of yours is going to get you into trouble one day.'

But one corner of his own mouth lifted as he said it, and then his gaze lowered to her lips and time seemed to stand still. The murmur of a sighing breeze brushed through her, transporting her somewhere warm and sultry, like a tropical beach. Doors firmly shut inside her cracked open a fraction and—

Owen snapped away and swung back to his computer. She blinked, the warmth inside her icing over as the present crashed back.

Keep talking. Don't let the silence stretch. Pretend nothing happened.

Nothing *had* happened. And nothing was *going* to happen.

'So, my plan is to put together a little video of me uncovering my own family tree to send in with my application.'

She was sure she didn't imagine him pushing several inches away on the wheels of his office chair before turning back towards her. The expression in his eyes, though, was alive with interest, and she could almost see him joining the dots.

'So the discovery of your grandmother…?'

'Has opened heretofore unknown doors.'

'And the research you've been doing at the New York Public Library…?'

'Has been to trace my family history. Which, I have to say, has been pretty straightforward. I've been able to go back five generations. I've hunted out locations I can visit to add colour to my personal documentary. And there's the possibility of a skeleton in the closet, with a younger son mysteriously missing in the eighteen-hundreds—"missing" as in I've not been able to find any further records of him yet. I suspect the family shipped him off somewhere to hush up some scandal. I also suspect, given enough time, I can get to the bottom of it.'

He stared at her. 'That's a good plan. Actually…it's inspired. It should land you the job for sure.'

She wrinkled her nose. 'Except my area of expertise is Australian history, rather than personal or family history. But research is research, right? Regardless of the topic, the skill-set is the same.'

'I'd have thought so—especially if you can showcase those skills in action.'

She slumped. 'The thing is…'

He leaned towards her. 'What's the thing?'

'While I might be finding it easy enough to trace my mother's side of the family…'

'Yes?'

The grey of his eyes looked like smoke—all misty and mysterious like a Scottish moor she'd like to explore.

'Callie?'

She snapped back. 'The problem is I've absolutely no idea who my father might be.'

'What, nothing?'

'*Nichts. Nada.* Nothing. My mother refuses to talk about him, and his name isn't on my birth certificate. Something really bad must've gone down.'

'But this is your *father*. Everyone has the right to know who their father is.'

'You think so?'

She was less convinced. It didn't stop her from aching to know where she had come from, though. She hitched up her chin. Besides, there was the job to consider. She was determined to do everything in her power to win it.

'Of course they do. Even if it's just to access a medical history. That stuff can be important.'

'But what if he's violent—a criminal? What if he beat my mother up and raped her? I can't see how me knowing that will help anyone.'

He rubbed a hand over his face.

'And even if he didn't…' things inside her hardened '… I just know he has to be a nasty piece of work. What I do know is she loved him.' The kind of heartbreak her mother had evidently suffered only came from the deepest love…and the deepest betrayal. 'And, as I was born only four months after my mother emigrated to Australia, I'm thinking it's a fairly safe bet that he's American.'

Owen nodded.

'I'm guessing that when she told him she was pregnant he wanted nothing to do with her or a baby.' But of course she had no proof of that.

'Or perhaps she loved him so much she left to protect him from a scandal? Maybe he was someone important?'

'Or already married.' She surveyed him for a moment. 'You said you and Frances liked to watch *Law and Order*. Does that mean you enjoy a good mystery?'

'I must do. I work with computer code. It's a lot like trying to put the pieces of a jigsaw puzzle together.' He raised an eyebrow. 'Does your mother know what you're trying to do?'

'I haven't said as much, but... She knows me. She knows I'll dig. I haven't told her about the job yet, or how I plan to win it.'

He rested his elbows on his knees, his eyes gentling. 'Callie, don't you think if you told her how important this job is to you she'd tell you the truth?'

He smelled like warm cotton and talcum powder, and something homemade baking in the oven.

'You've been watching too many sappy rom-coms,' she teased, to hide the way her pulse had quickened.

Breathing him in felt nourishing in a way the tin of soup she'd heated up for her dinner last night hadn't. She battled a bolt of pure temptation. It would be so easy to lean across and kiss him.

She shot to her feet to pace around his office, in an attempt to distract herself from the shape of a mouth she had a feeling would now figure prominently in her dreams.

'You don't want to distress your mother?' he asked.

'She's just become engaged.' She glanced over her shoulder to smile at him. 'I'm so pleased for her. I've never seen her so happy.' She traced a finger along a square glass case that held a signed ball—a baseball, she supposed. 'You really like these Mets, huh?'

'More than life itself.' He paused. 'And your mother?'

She was going to be facetious and say she was pretty sure her mother wasn't a Mets fan, but she bit it back and returned to her seat instead. 'This is the first time I've seen her truly happy in a romantic relationship.'

Understanding dawned in his eyes. 'And you don't want to mar that by bringing up the past?'

'Correctamundo,' she said, doing her best Fonz impression. 'It's cool. I'll just work it out for myself. In fact I *want* to work it out myself. Only then will I be able to prove my worth and convince the producers of *Mystery Family Trees* to hire me.'

'Except you don't have a single lead.'

'You think? I'd place all my twenty million dollars on a bet that Frances knew what happened. I'm betting that's what they fell out about. And I'm guessing Frances wished she'd given my mother more support and has regretted not doing so ever since. Hence the letters.'

'It's a possibility… But Frances wasn't a prude or a stickler. She wouldn't have cared about her daughter becoming a single mother.' He glanced up. 'What's your plan?'

'To read Frances's letters and see if she makes any mention of it, or see if there's some clue in them. Other than that… She must have an address book somewhere. I could ring her friends…tell them who I am. Maybe they'll agree to meet with me. Someone will know what happened back then. They always do.'

He stared.

She stifled the urge to roll her shoulders. 'What?'

'You're going to all this trouble for a job?'

'It's a good job.' She hitched her chin at his office. 'This looks like a good job too—seems to me you're getting to call a lot of your own shots. What lengths would you go to to keep it?'

He huffed out a laugh, as if acknowledging the hit. 'Okay… The thing is, Frances didn't have many friends. If she did before I knew her, she'd lost touch with them by the time my mother and I moved here.'

A four-year-old kid going through the kind of upheaval Owen had been would've noticed everything. He would've kept watch and noted every person who entered the building, working out who belonged and who didn't. He'd have kept watch for the father who scared him. Her heart burned at all he must've gone through.

'I do know the few people she did keep in touch with, though. And I remember the names of those she occasionally talked about from the good old days.'

He did...?

He leaned back slightly. 'I'll make a deal with you.'

'What kind of deal?'

'I'll do whatever I can to help you find out who your father is...'

Her heart leapt. He was smart. He knew how to put a puzzle together *and* he had inside information. She'd be crazy to refuse his help.

'And in return?'

'If you decide you're going to donate your inheritance to charity...'

'Yes?'

'Will you sell the apartment block to me first, rather than donating the building lock, stock and barrel?'

She stared. 'You can afford to buy it?' Just exactly how good was this job of his?

In the next moment she dismissed the thought. If he had that kind of money he wouldn't be living in a basement apartment—not even one as nice as this.

His eyes had turned opaque. 'There's a co-op I know that would be interested in taking it and its current residents over.'

A charity? It was funny... Yesterday she wouldn't have thought he was the kind of man to concern himself with the down and out. Today she could see how wrong she'd been.

'I'm not asking for a discount—you'd be offered the market value.'

It was a no-brainer. 'You have yourself a deal.'

'Or,' he continued, 'if you decide to keep your inheritance but sell the building—'

'You'll have first dibs.'

'Thank you.'

They shook on it.

'A party!' She leapt to her feet as the inspiration occurred to her. 'That's what I'll do. I'll throw a party for everyone. A block party. And then they'll all like me. Just you wait and see.'

'So what *is* she like?'

Owen glanced at his mother as they passed into Washington Square Park through the western entrance. Sixteen-year-old Lissy trailed along behind, dragging her feet and looking bored in the way that only a teenager could.

'She seems nice enough.' They stopped to watch a game of chess in action. White Knight moved to C4 and he could see at a glance how he could win the game in three moves if he were playing black.

'And all the letters Frances sent?'

They walked on. A squirrel scampered across the grass, all twitchy motion, and he started to feel twitchy too, though he had no idea why. 'It appears she knew nothing about them. It was Donna who intercepted and returned them all.'

'That makes a strange kind of sense.'

It did? He stared at her before swinging around to find Lissy had fallen even further behind and had started talking to some guy who was *way* too old for her. And who was eyeing her up in her short, short skirt like a Rottweiler would a piece of porterhouse.

He slammed to a halt. 'Lissy!'

With an eye-roll, she gave the guy a wave before continuing towards them. 'Spoilsport,' she muttered, drawing up on his other side. And then she rolled her eyes. 'Relax… I know him, okay?'

'How?' he demanded, and winced. He didn't mean to sound so damn censorious, and he could've kicked himself when her face closed up and she didn't bother answering. 'Look, Lissy, I'm sorry. It's just—'

But he was talking to thin air. Lissy had hurried on towards a small group of girls.

His mother shook her head. 'When are you going to learn, Owen?'

The mild reprimand made him feel even smaller. But, *damn*, his little half-sister had turned into a ball of sarcastic prickliness over the last year. The sunny-natured kid who'd once adored him was long gone. She worried the heck out of him. She was boy-mad, and the clothes she wore were designed to attract the attention of every male in a ten-mile radius.

He ground his teeth together. The kind of attention from the kind of guy that had a brother's every protective hackle rising.

They were moving in the direction of the fountain in the middle of the park, with the familiar shape of the Washington Square Arch up ahead on their left, when he saw Callie and Barney seated on the grass with three teenage girls around the same age as Lissy. He halted and stared.

'Owen, if I didn't know you better I'd say you were ogling that young woman.'

He snapped to attention, shook himself. 'That's her. That's Callie Nicholls.'

'It appears she's made some friends.'

When? How? When did she have the time…?

Lissy ambled back, but the barely suppressed excitement in her eyes belied her affected nonchalance. She surreptitiously pointed to one of the girls in Callie's circle. 'That's Angelina Michaels.'

She said it in a reverent tone that clued Owen in that Angelina was *somebody*. He racked his brain. 'Who is she again?' But then he remembered. 'The basketball star at your school?' From memory, she was a year ahead of Lissy.

'She's a goddess. You should see her play. Amazing!'

A smile built through him. Maybe this was his chance to redeem himself a little in her eyes. 'Would you like to meet her?'

She shushed him. 'We can't just go over there!'

'What if I can swing a casual introduction because I know the person she's talking to?'

Lissy stared, a gleam starting up in the depths of her eyes. 'Then I might, *perhaps*, forgive you for being such a bossy bore so far today.'

His jaw dropped. 'Bossy bore?'

'The moment you clapped eyes on my skirt this morning you started being as prissy and snippy as an ancient aunt in one of those Dickens or Austen books I have to read for school.'

'If you had more sense I wouldn't have—'

'I'd like to meet her.'

His mother's voice broke through their bickering, reminding Owen that he was supposed to be the older and wiser sibling. It was just that he worried so much for Lissy—was worried she'd fall in with the wrong crowd, worried that some guy would treat her the way his father had treated his mother. He'd do everything he could to protect her from that.

It was Barney who saw them first, giving a clear, resounding bark—he had a big bark for such a little dog—and straining on his lead towards Owen. Callie glanced around, her lips curving into her trademark smile when she saw him. Jumping to her feet, she shook both his mother and

Lissy's hands when he introduced them, before introducing her own trio of… Acquaintances? Friends?

He glanced at the girls and gestured to the books and laptops. 'What are you all up to?'

'Callie's helping us study for our Math final,' one of the girls said.

He couldn't hide his surprise. 'But Callie's a History major, not Math.'

'They're not mutually exclusive,' she teased. 'I was probably better at Math than I was at History. I just enjoyed History more.' Her face lit up. 'Hey, you might be able to help. Micah is having some trouble with her computer science elective and it's beyond my skill-set.'

Before he knew what he was about, Owen found himself sitting on the grass tutoring Micah while Callie skilfully steered the others into a discussion about basketball when Lissy mentioned her admiration for Angelina's game. Then she smiled at his mother and led her to a nearby bench. 'I was hoping I'd get a chance to meet you and maybe chat a bit about Frances, Mrs O'Sullivan.'

'You must call me Margaret.'

And that was all he heard. But as he took in Lissy's glowing face when Angelina invited her to shoot some hoops with her one afternoon the following week, and heard his mother laugh at something Callie said, he found he didn't mind sitting in the spring sunshine explaining the vagaries of the Math that Micah was struggling with. They were a nice bunch, and he enjoyed the good-natured way they teased each other, and the way they included Lissy in both their discussions and their teasing.

He'd have been happy to sit there for another hour, except Micah gave a start as she glanced at her watch. '*Gah!* I have to go or I'll be late for my shift at Burger Co.'

Angelina groaned. 'I promised Mom I'd babysit tonight. If I don't get home soon it'll be panic stations.'

The three girls said their goodbyes and were soon gone.

'That was awesome,' Lissy breathed as they joined their mother and Callie. 'Angelina is the best point guard our school has had in ten years.'

Callie smiled. 'They're a fun bunch.'

Owen stared at her. 'How did you meet them?'

When the muscles in Callie's jaw tightened, Lissy rolled her eyes and his mother shook her head.

He grimaced. 'Sorry, I didn't mean that to sound so…'

Lissy folded her arms. 'Bossy?'

He resisted the urge to run a finger around the collar of his sweater. 'Like I was giving you the third degree.'

Callie glanced at Lissy. 'You get this a lot?'

'All. The. Time.'

Callie raised an eyebrow at him. 'It's a bit much, isn't it?'

A scowl built through him, but before he could reply his mother spoke. 'We're having dinner with Owen this evening. We'd love it if you could join us, Callie.'

What on earth…?

Callie glanced at him, as if she sensed he might be feeling less than hospitable. He checked himself internally and discovered he wasn't as averse to the idea as he probably should be.

He huffed out a laugh and shook his head. 'We would,' he confirmed.

'Then I'd love to.'

Her smile seemed to make things inside him click into place—which made no sense. *She* made no sense. He frowned. Actually, now that he thought about it, could he retract the dinner invitation?

The women all seemed completely at home with each other, strolling along and chatting, and Lissy was utterly delighted to be handed Barney's lead. He felt oddly left out. Eventually they turned back the way they'd come, and it was only as they drew abreast of the collection of chess tables that the idea hit him.

'Do you play, Callie?' He wanted to trounce her. At just one thing. He knew the impulse was childish, but he couldn't contain it.

'I do.' Blue eyes assessed him. 'And I'm pretty good.'

'So am I.'

She turned to face him fully. 'Are you challenging me to a game?'

He wanted to wipe the floor with her—figuratively speaking—and get a sense of control back. He glanced at his mom and Lissy.

'It's too early to start preparing dinner yet,' his mom said. 'I'm happy to sit here in the park in this lovely sun.'

'Don't do it,' Lissy said to Callie. 'He's really good.'

'So am I, baby doll,' Callie said, affecting a gangster stance and pretending to straighten her non-existent collar.

Lissy giggled and slipped an arm through Callie's, apparently BFFs.

Callie played white. He was black.

And she whooped his butt.

And to his shock he found that he didn't mind at all.

'Where did you learn to play like that?'

'My mum is obsessed with the game. It's a rare occasion that I can beat her.'

Owen's stomach burned. Had Frances taught him to play because the game had reminded her of her daughter?

Callie swung to Lissy, the glossy auburn highlights in her hair gleaming in the sun. 'Did you hear I had all of my things stolen?'

Lissy's mouth dropped open. 'All of your clothes too?' She whimpered at Callie's nod. 'I'd have bawled my eyes out.'

Had Callie wanted to cry? He squirmed as he recalled

what he'd thought about her...how mistaken he'd been. He should've been more sympathetic, kinder...gentler.

'Your brother was great—he had some essentials delivered and took care of everything. I was so grateful.'

She sent him a smile that made him feel like a million dollars.

'But I still need to buy some clothes. Are there any stores around here you can recommend? I've no idea, and—'

'I could go shopping with you!' Lissy's face lit up. 'Tomorrow? It'd be fun.' She grinned at her brother. 'Owen would let me crash for the night. I mean you've been nagging me to stay for, like, for *ever*, right?'

She was volunteering to stay *the whole night*? He did his best not to sound too eager. 'Sure.'

'Is it okay, Mom?'

'Sure, honey—but only if it's okay with Callie. She might have plans.'

'No plans.' Callie nudged Lissy's shoulder. 'I'd love it.'

He wanted to hug her for the grin she sent his little sister.

'And maybe we could all watch a movie after dinner,' Lissy added.

'Sounds like fun,' Callie agreed.

Both of them turned to him and he raised his hands in surrender. 'Any chance I get to choose the movie?'

'None at all,' Lissy said, with a cheerfulness that warmed him all the way through.

'Fine...' he pretended to grumble. But the plan sounded absolutely perfect.

CHAPTER FIVE

SEEING OWEN WITH his family was like viewing him through an entirely new lens. He'd lost that almost unconscious edge he had whenever he was around her. He'd relaxed. *Properly.* And a relaxed Owen was doubly potent.

It sent warning bells clanging through Callie's mind. All she wanted to focus on was finding a new direction in life—starting with the TV job. And then she'd make a decision about her inheritance. And she planned to do all of that footloose and fancy-free, thank you very much. She wasn't letting any man into her life until she was damn certain everything she'd worked so hard for couldn't be pulled out from under her. She wasn't putting her livelihood at the mercy of some guy's whims. She'd learned that lesson the hard way.

And she had an extra reason to worry now too. If word got out that she'd inherited so much money, how could she be certain that any man would want her for herself? How could she be certain he wasn't interested in her money instead?

Even Owen. After all, how much did she really know about him?

She glanced across at him in his soft worn jeans that looked as comfortable as air and his loose long-sleeved tee. A girl could admire a good-looking guy without it meaning anything, though, right?

'Are you sure there's nothing I can do?' she asked.

'Just keep sitting there, looking suitably impressed with my kitchen skills. It's doing wonders for my ego.'

He said it with the same teasing half-grin he used on

Lissy and it made her feel as if she belonged, that she wasn't an unwelcome intruder.

Dangerous. The word whispered through her. Still, the man prepared a salad with an elegance that was *very* easy on the eye…

'You know your way around a kitchen better than I do.'

'I like to cook. It gives me time to think. Figuring out how to make an app work can take a lot of thinking time.'

Margaret ambled over from the sofa, where she'd been flicking through a newspaper, to perch on a stool beside Callie. Lissy and Barney were out in the courtyard. Callie could hear Lissy talking on her phone.

'It's something you do very well,' Margaret said. 'Your apps are inspired.'

'Obviously the company he works for thinks so,' said Callie. 'I saw his office. It's amazing.'

Margaret sent her son a swift glance, but he was busy slicing onions. 'He's too modest,' she said drily.

Callie did her best not to get mesmerised by the sight of those large hands, with their short, slightly squared nails, effortlessly slicing and chopping.

'Coming up with ways to make a lecture or a tutorial engaging and fun can be a bit like that,' she said. 'But doing my thinking time in the kitchen would be a disaster. The food would either be half raw or burned to a crisp.'

His grin hooked up one side of his mouth and her heart started pitter-pattering away as if it had donned tap shoes and was learning a brand-new dance routine. He scattered sliced red pepper over the lettuce and red onion already in the salad bowl before adding cherry tomatoes and sliced cucumber. She blinked when he pulled extra virgin olive oil and a bottle of gourmet vinegar from the pantry.

He made his own dressing?

The fork he whisked with faltered for a moment as he

sent her a sidelong glance, and she suddenly realised she was staring. She had to get over this awareness. It was crazy!

She swung to Margaret. 'What's the thing you remember most about Frances?'

A sigh Callie didn't understand eased out of the older woman. 'I have a lot of memories. But honestly…? It's her sadness I find myself remembering most.'

Owen stopped whisking and stared at his mother as if her words had speared straight through his heart.

She sent Callie a small smile. 'Frances helped me escape an unpleasant situation and I'll be forever grateful to her. I loved her. I just wish I could've done…more.'

She reached out to touch Margaret's arm. 'I'm glad she was able to help you. But from what Owen has told me, you all helped her tremendously too.'

Margaret nodded. 'Owen especially.'

Really? She filed that under her *Things to Pursue Later* list.

'I also remember her political rants,' Margaret added with a laugh. 'She could be scathing when she disagreed with whoever happened to be in power at the time. Hilariously so. She'd have us all in stitches, but nodding in agreement.'

'That sounds like fun.' And it did.

Margaret nibbled a piece of cucumber Owen had pushed her way, as if he was inherently attuned to what she'd like. He glanced at Callie and raised an eyebrow. She pointed to the red pepper, so he cut a nice long slice, speared it on the end of the knife and held it out to her. It made her feel ridiculously cared for.

Margaret gestured towards her son. 'Owen did most of the cooking in our household from the age of twelve onwards.'

Her eyebrows flew upwards. 'Really?'

'Mom worked long hours. Cleaning houses all day is hard work. It seemed the least I could do.'

'He traded me chores—told me he'd cook if I did the dishes.'

'Doing the dishes is my least favourite chore ever. Besides…' he grinned at his mother '…back then Mom had three standard meals that she cooked on rotation.'

Margaret winked at Callie. 'And he wasn't a fan of any of them.'

'And she'd cook them up in these huge batches, so we'd be eating the same thing for days on end. I like variety.'

His shoulders lifted in a careless shrug and Callie tried to not let her mind dwell on other things that involved variety—things she really shouldn't be thinking about.

'So you taught yourself to cook?' she said in a rush, hoping it would hide where her thoughts had gone.

He and Margaret shared a swift glance, a beat of silence passing between them, and Callie found herself nodding.

'Frances taught you how to cook.'

They both turned, as if concerned the revelation might upset her.

'It's okay,' she said, touched that they didn't want to hurt her feelings. 'You can't miss something you never knew you had.'

'Not true.' Owen rinsed the fork before turning back and searching her face.

She thought of the little boy who'd probably been terrified of his father. He'd have missed his parents not having a harmonious marriage. He'd have missed not having a father who couldn't control his temper.

'You can,' she agreed slowly.

She flashed to an image of her ten-year-old self, sitting in her classroom on Grandparents' Day. It was a memory that stuck with her to this very day.

'Do you guys do Grandparents' Day at school? It's where

grandparents spend half a day at school in the classroom with their grandkids. I wasn't the only kid in my class who didn't have grandparents, but the split would've been about eighty-twenty. And on that day I *really* wanted grandparents. And aunts and uncles and cousins and siblings and everything in between.'

She smiled, but a thread of sadness for her younger self remained. She'd yearned for big family picnics and huge Christmas celebrations and spending holidays with people who belonged to her.

'At the end of the day I raced home and told my mother that if she married again and gave me a stepfather, I would adopt his mum and dad as my grandparents.'

Owen leant his hip against the bench. 'What did she say?'

'She asked me what would happen if she fell in love with a man who didn't have parents any more, just like—' She pulled up short, suddenly conscious of how callous that would sound to Owen and Margaret—people who had loved Frances.

'Just like her,' Owen finished. He shook his head. 'It's okay, Callie.'

Actually, it wasn't. But she pasted on a smile anyway. 'I told her she was only allowed to fall in love with a man who had a mum and a dad and six brothers and sisters, all with little kids, so I could have first cousins and second cousins and third cousins twice removed.'

Margaret's eyes twinkled. 'Did she manage to keep a straight face?'

'Not for a moment!' Callie laughed. 'Though I didn't understand at the time why she thought my plan so funny.'

'When I met Jack—Lissy's father—Owen was fourteen at the time, and he took him into the courtyard out there and told him that if he ever raised either his hand or his voice to me he'd drop his cold, dead body in the river.'

Callie clapped both hands over her mouth. 'You didn't!'

His grin had her heart setting off on another tap-dancing routine. 'I obviously had an over-inflated sense of my own power. Jack weighed twice what I did, and he had arms like—' He made a big circle in the air the size of a pumpkin.

She swallowed. 'What did he say?' And where was Jack now?

'He said that if he ever did either of those things he'd help me find the best spot in the river to dump his cold, dead body.'

She pressed her hands to her chest. 'Perfect answer.'

Margaret took the salad to the small dining table as Owen lifted chicken breasts in a fancy salsa from the oven. He sent Callie a wink. 'You'll be pleased to know there has never been cause to find that spot on the river. Jack is at his monthly poker night tonight. He'll be sorry to have missed meeting you. He and Frances became great friends.'

It appeared then that everyone had been on the best of terms with Frances. Everyone, that was, except her mother.

'I've contacted three of Frances's oldest friends.'

Callie had been kneeling on Owen's living room rug, greeting Barney after returning from the library, but she shot to her feet again now. 'Friends?' *Old friends?*

'Childhood friends.'

It was three days since she'd had dinner with Owen and his family. She flew across to the breakfast bar. 'Do you think they'll talk to me? Maybe let me visit them?'

He glanced up from pouring coffee beans into his machine. 'I've organised for us to meet with them at the Russian Tea Rooms for high tea this Friday at two o'clock. It was the only time I could get them together at the same time, and I thought it'd be better to meet as a group. Their memories might spark off each other.' He halted. 'I hope that's okay? I wasn't trying to be high-handed—'

'Of course you weren't.' She reached out to squeeze his arm. 'I'm really grateful.'

Beneath her hand, his forearm burned warm and vibrant, and a bolt of energy transferred itself from him to her, making her breathe deeper and adding colour to all the things in his kitchen, as if her eyes were seeing them in a more vivid light. She suddenly felt more alive than she could remember feeling. *Ever.*

He'd stilled at her touch and he stared down at her hand now. 'We have a deal. And I mean to keep my side of the bargain, Callie.'

She reefed her hand back. That was what this was all about—the bargain they'd struck. He didn't want her short-changing the residents of the apartment block. Nothing more. Which was exactly as it should be. But her heart gave a sick thud all the same.

'I'm still grateful. Thank you.'

He shrugged, his attention on the coffee machine again and thankfully not on her.

'Hopefully they'll be able to provide you with a couple of leads.'

She hoped so too.

'Coffee?' he asked.

'Um…no thanks.' She'd shared one with him yesterday, and the day before too, but she couldn't let herself get too comfortable and cosy with him. Men were off her agenda for the foreseeable future. Her sole focus was to get that TV job and find a new direction for her life.

If you keep your inheritance you can take things easy, take your time, have a holiday…

She shook the thought off. She still intended to work. Sitting around in the lap of luxury might sound appealing at first, but she had to do *something* or she'd go out of her mind with boredom. She had no intention of being a good-for-nothing layabout. She pulled in a breath. Bottom line—

no guys until she was once again gainfully employed and her life felt as if it belonged to her again.

She edged towards the door. 'I might just dump my gear upstairs and then take Barney for a walk.'

She didn't ask him if he wanted to join her. They weren't friends. All she was to him was a duty to discharge.

'C'mon, Barney.'

The little dog scrambled to his feet and scurried across the room to her. The two of them had started towards Owen's front door when Owen called out, 'What do you do at the library, Callie?'

Working at the library sounded romantic—as if she might be sitting in a lofty vaulted room poring over dusty tomes, but the reality was vastly different.

'Basically I just use their computers to access genealogical databases and old newspapers…and print off whatever looks useful.'

'You could do that from here.'

'Except my laptop was taken in the robbery. And as I have access to my emails on my phone, I figured I wouldn't bother replacing it until I got home.'

'I have a spare computer you can use.'

The day she'd been in his office he'd had three computers all fired up and on the go at the same time. She'd figured they were all necessary for whatever it was he did. Besides, the thought of working beside him day after day…

She shook her head. 'I've intruded enough on your time as it is, Owen. You don't need me under your feet. The library is fine.'

He stared, and then his eyes widened and his mouth puckered as if he'd sucked on a lemon. 'I wasn't suggesting you work in my office.'

She folded her arms and raised an eyebrow. *Nice*.

'Sorry, but I'm not good with distractions—noise,

music…other people moving about. It breaks my concentration.'

She unbent a fraction and glanced at Barney.

Owen shook his head. 'Barney is as good as gold. He just lies on his bed—' they'd both bought Barney dog beds for their respective apartments '—and we enjoy each other's company.'

'You're such a good dog,' she cooed, scratching Barney's hindquarters until he groaned his pleasure.

Owen frowned. 'He doesn't chew anything he shouldn't. He doesn't bark when he hears any of the other residents coming or going…'

'And on walks he's always polite to other dogs. He loves choosing random people to make friends with. He's sociable and well adjusted.' She blew out a breath, nodding. 'I know… *Someone* has to be missing him.'

'No word yet?'

'None.' She checked the posters they'd put up in various shop windows and on trees in the park every time she and Barney went for a walk. Just to make sure they were still there and didn't need replacing.

'Okay—back to the subject of the computer. I was going to suggest we set up a spare computer and printer in your apartment. You're welcome to use it for as long as you're in New York.'

She swiped her hands down the sides of her jeans. 'Are you sure you can spare one?'

'You *have* seen my office, right?'

His hands went to his hips and it made him look tall and broad and delectable. Her tongue stuck to the roof of her mouth. She did her best to unglue it. 'If you can spare it, then a computer would be very welcome.'

'Done. Let's do it.'

He strode into his office and she followed in his wake, slightly bemused.

'Can you manage the printer?' He opened a door to a storage cupboard and effortlessly lifted out a printer. 'If not I can make a second trip.'

'Give it here. Of course I can manage. I'll head on up and open the door,' she added as he started to haul out a computer. And cables.

'I'll be right behind you.'

The printer wasn't heavy, but by the time she'd climbed the stairs she was short of breath.

'I need to get fitter, Barney.'

But she knew there was nothing wrong with her fitness levels. It was just that the guy downstairs had a habit of stealing all the oxygen from her lungs, and it always took too long for her to get it back.

Callie's face when they entered the Russian Tea Room was priceless. The red leather banquettes, dark green walls and twenty-four-carat gold ceiling made a striking statement—and that was before you took into account the priceless artworks on the walls.

'It's amazing,' she breathed.

Owen had wanted the three older women to feel spoiled. He's hoped it would make them more amenable to answering Callie's questions.

She swung to him. 'I will, of course, be paying for this.'

'Already taken care of,' he said, and pointed across the room to one of the red leather banquettes against the far wall to distract her. 'Josephine, Betty and Eliza are already here.'

He refused to question too closely why he'd wanted to cover the cost of today's expedition. Heaven only knew Callie now had more than enough money to cover the expense for a hundred such afternoon teas, but...

On Saturday night he'd seen something hungry in her—

something that had made him want to draw her into the warmth and ease of his family circle.

For the greater part of his childhood it had been only him, his mother and Frances. They had constituted the people he could rely on. On Saturday night he'd realised that for *all of Callie's life* it had just been her and her mother. He understood loneliness, and he'd recognised it in her.

It had made him…

He rolled his shoulders, suppressing a frown. It had made him want to pay for today's afternoon tea, that was all.

Thrusting his disturbing thoughts to one side, he set about the task of introducing Callie to Frances's contemporaries and smoothing the waters to encourage conversation. 'Callie never even knew she had a grandmother—Donna never told her—so she's hoping to get to know Frances through the memories of the people who knew her.'

Over cucumber, caviar and salmon sandwiches, and glasses of French champagne, the older women reminisced about the days when they'd all been girls together—from schoolgirls to debutantes and then society wives. Callie had told him she wanted to discover the identity of her father—that it was the main reason she wanted to meet her grandmother's friends—but that consideration seemed to go by the wayside as she hung on to their every word as if each one was pure gold…as if she couldn't get enough of their stories.

'It all changed, though, when Frances married Richard,' said Eliza.

'In what way?'

Callie nibbled a miniature lemon tart as if only mildly interested in that statement…as if it hadn't sent a quiver through her entire body. Owen suspected nobody had noticed but him.

'Did you not like Richard?' she asked.

All three women hesitated. 'It's not that,' Eliza said eventually. 'He was…very good-looking.'

Callie nodded. 'I've seen pictures. He was movie-star-handsome.'

'And charming to go with it,' Betty added. 'Maybe Frannie had been on her own too long—it took her a long time to get over Tom's death—but she completely lost her head over Richard. In her eyes, he could do no wrong.'

Callie laughed lightly, but there was no real humour in it. 'That's a rookie mistake right there, isn't it? No one's perfect.' She glanced up from pushing a crumb around her plate. 'I take it you ladies didn't trust him?'

Again there was the slightest hesitation. 'It might just be the benefit of hindsight because we now know what came after…' said Josephine.

'Frances was too giddy. It made us uneasy,' said Betty.

'And Richard's charm was too practised, too perfect,' said Eliza.

'And yet they threw the most wonderful parties, and Frannie was so sublimely happy…'

'So we kept our reservations to ourselves…'

'Not that it would've done any good to have done otherwise. Frannie wouldn't have a bad word said against him.'

All three nodded at that. Fresh tea and another tray of perfect pastries and *petit fours* that looked like works of art were delivered, momentarily halting the flow of conversation.

'What about my mother?' Callie asked when the waiter had moved away. 'Did she like Richard?'

'Heaven's no! Donna was the only one to openly criticise him. According to Frannie, she called him a liar and a cheat who was only after Frances's money.' Betty bit her lip. 'She told her mother she was making a fool of herself.'

Owen winced. So did Callie.

'It was awful. There was the most enormous row and

Frannie and Donna never spoke again. After that none of us had the courage to speak out against Richard.'

Callie rested her elbows on the table. 'So *that's* what their rift was about. It—' She hastily removed her elbows, as if suddenly remembering her manners. 'It just doesn't seem enough to cause total estrangement, though.'

'I've often thought the same thing,' said Josephine, the quietest of the three older women. 'Your mother was a lovely, bright girl—quick to laugh, but not quick to anger.'

'Frances had a hot temper, though?' asked Callie.

'All I know,' Josephine said, 'is that Donna wasn't at the wedding and Frances never uttered her name again.'

'Donna was a daddy's girl, though. Maybe she couldn't stand the notion of anyone supplanting him in Frannie's affections.'

'That hardly seems likely, Betty. Donna was an adult by then. She never struck me as the kind of girl who would demand something so unreasonable of her mother. No, I just think she saw through Richard and refused to stay quiet about it.'

'Heaven knows, none of us dared ask Frannie for details.'

Owen stared at the older women. He'd known none of this. *None*. It was as if it had happened to someone else, rather than the Frances he'd known.

A tiny smile touched Callie's lips. 'Was Frances such a tyrant, then?'

'Not at all, but she felt things deeply—too deeply, I often thought,' Josephine said. 'It was clear that whatever had passed between her and Donna had hurt her badly. It changed her—not necessarily for the better. It felt wrong to probe—unkind, even. All we could do was offer our silent support and let her know we were there for her. But I never expected their rift to last a lifetime.'

They were all silent for a moment.

'Frannie paid a heavy price for her brief happiness with

Richard...' Eliza sighed. 'They'd only been married for two years when his affairs with other women started. It was a torrid time. The fights!'

'And then what we'd all feared came to light—Richard *had* only married Frannie for her money. And it cost her a pretty penny to extricate herself from the marriage.'

'After that she changed. Became withdrawn. She moved out of her lovely Upper East Side apartment and buried herself in that apartment in Greenwich Village. Don't get me wrong,' Josephine said quickly. 'It's a lovely apartment...'

Betty nodded. 'But nothing like the one she'd been living in.'

'Fabulous location, though...' Eliza sighed.

'Not that she ever took advantage of it. She never left it.'

Here was the woman Owen had known.

'She stopped seeing everyone—all her old friends.'

'She tried to stop seeing us too, only we wouldn't let her. We were very persistent.'

'She eventually stopped being so bloody-minded and let us visit. And she interested herself in the residents of the apartment block. That helped too. But she never regained her zest for life, never recovered her spirits.'

'She once told me she'd broken her own heart—that she'd been wilful and blind and deserved her loneliness and regrets.'

A tiny breath left Callie and snagged at Owen's heart.

'Poor Frances,' she said. 'I'm so glad she had the three of you.'

Owen watched as she rallied, and he sensed the effort it cost her.

'Here's something you might not know. She wrote to my mother—many, many times over the years. My mother returned the letters unopened, but I think it was clear Frances did attempt to reconcile with her.'

Josephine smiled. 'I'm glad. I'm sorry Donna remained

so unforgiving, but I'm very glad Frances tried. Thank you for telling us, Callie.'

Conversation turned to happier times, and although Owen waited for Callie to probe more deeply about her mother, she merely sat amid the splendour of the Russian Tea Room as if in a state of suspended animation.

'Callie is looking for clues as to who her father might be. Would you ladies have any idea where she might start looking?' he said eventually.

Callie started, and then sent him a smile. Beneath the table she briefly clasped his hand in silent thanks. It made his heart double in size.

Eliza's eyes went round. 'You mean Donna was pregnant before she left the States?'

'I was born four months after she arrived in Australia,' said Callie.

'Well, I can't say I recall her dating anyone regularly.' Josephine tapped a finger to her lips. 'Though she must've met a lot of boys at college.'

The three women conferred, but all came up blank.

'Did Donna have any close girlfriends that you can recall?' she asked.

Josephine's face cleared. 'The Ryder girl! She's Hitchcock now. They were thick as thieves. I can text you her details—or, better yet, you could come visit me, Callie. I have albums full of photographs I'm sure you'd be interested in seeing.'

The party broke up with Callie promising to visit each of them.

'Are you okay?' he asked as they made their way outside.

She halted to stare at a display in a shop window, her reflection pensive and troubled, and it was all he could do not to reach out and pull her in close for a hug.

'Frances feels real to me now in a way she didn't before. Her story is so *sad*. I want to cry for her.'

No way was he taking her back to Frances's gloomy apartment just yet. 'Only the final third,' he said. 'The first two-thirds of her life sound pretty damn good if you ask me.'

She blinked.

'And, while she might've become a recluse, her life wasn't totally devoid of pleasure. She had good things even at the end. Don't forget that.'

She reached out and touched his arm. 'I'm really glad she had you and your mother and Lissy and Jack, Owen. Thank you for taking such good care of her.'

'She took good care of us too.'

His throat thickened, but he didn't know if it was grief for Frances rising through him again or the dark troubled depths of Callie's eyes catching him in some unknown but vulnerable spot deep inside.

He forced himself to straighten and smile. 'So, tell me… How much of New York have you seen since you arrived?'

'Um…not a lot. I had an amble along Fifth Avenue, because the New York Public Library is, like, right there. And I went to Times Square because… I mean it's Times Square, right? But I'm not here to sightsee.'

He feigned outrage. 'You're in one of the most vibrant cities in the world! I know you're preparing for that TV job, but you shouldn't squander the chance to experience New York while you're here. What about the Statue of Liberty, the Brooklyn Bridge, the Empire State…the Guggenheim, the High Line? There's so much to see and experience. You should make time for some of that.'

'I suppose you're right. It's just…'

'You've had other things on your mind.' He glanced at her feet. She wore a pair of comfortable-looking boots. 'Are you busy for the rest of the afternoon?'

'What did you have in mind?'

'If those boots are as comfortable as they look, how about a walk through Central Park?'

CHAPTER SIX

'THE PARK IS *HUGE*!'

Callie stared at Bethesda Fountain before moving down the grand sandstone staircase to the terrace below. She felt as if they'd left the city far behind, and some of her earlier sombreness fell away.

'It's *so* beautiful. I'm surrounded by shades of *When Harry Met Sally* and *Home Alone 2* and *Begin Again…*'

'You didn't realise the park was this big?' asked Owen.

She trailed her fingers in the water of the fountain as they strolled around it. 'I knew from looking at a map of Manhattan that it was going to be big. But actually seeing it…' She turned on the spot. 'I feel as if we could be in the country somewhere.'

They strolled for a while, ambling along beautiful paths, and Callie lapped it up, letting it soothe the burn in her chest that had sparked into life during afternoon tea as Eliza, Betty and Josephine had drawn a picture of Frances's life for her. It had been a privileged life. And to think that her mother had grown up in that same privileged world…

It seemed wrong that Callie had known nothing about it. Not that she envied it. While it fascinated her, in many ways her own childhood had been idyllic. But it was part of her beloved mother's history, and it should've become part of Callie's history too—if only by proxy.

The burn in her chest intensified when she recalled all the things Donna had foregone because money had been so tight—pretty clothes, regular visits to the salon, brand-new books…eating out. None of those things were necessities, by any means, but it didn't mean they hadn't been missed.

Her mother had scrimped and saved for the deposit to

buy her modest little house, but Callie recalled one month when they'd fallen behind on the mortgage payments. Donna had pawned her diamond earrings—the only nice jewellery she'd owned—and she could remember listening to her mother cry that night, when she'd thought Callie was asleep. The burn of hot tears that had trickled down her own cheeks had been like the burn that had embedded itself in her chest now.

But her mother's financial hardship would've ceased if she'd only opened one of Frances's letters. Why hadn't she? What had Frances done that had made Donna so determined to shut her out?

Yet she found it impossible to slide Frances into the role of villain. Hearing about her happy marriage to Thomas, and then her disastrous marriage to Richard, had brought Frances to life for her. She'd bled for the older woman—for her heartbreak and grief.

And that made her feel disloyal to Donna.

'Would you like to sit for a bit?'

Owen's voice intruded on her thoughts and she sent him a swift smile. 'Sure.'

They sat on a bench and he gestured in front of them. 'This is Conservatory Water. It's been in lots of movies too. Kids sail model boats here.'

A smile hooked up the right side of his mouth, as if he remembered doing that as a boy, and it made him look young and carefree. Her heart pressed hard against her lungs, making it ridiculously difficult to catch her breath. For a wild moment all she could wonder was what it would be like to press her lips to his.

She dragged her gaze away, her heart pounding. She needed to get over this crazy, stupid crush and be a sensible adult woman again. She focussed her attention on a jogger who moved past them at an easy pace and then realised she was staring at a celebrity.

She grabbed Owen's arm. 'Did you see who that was?'
'I did.'

He didn't sound the slighted bit fazed—as if he saw celebrities all the time. Mind you, this was New York, so maybe he did.

She stared after the celebrity—who'd starred in several of her favourite movies—and shook her head, forcing herself to release Owen's arm. 'You know, I'm not sure anyone needs to see him in bike shorts, though.'

His low chuckle warmed the surface of her skin and helped to ease some of the tension that had her wound so tight.

He turned to her. 'I want to thank you for being so kind to Lissy. She really enjoyed your shopping trip.'

'Kindness had nothing to do with it. It wasn't a chore. I enjoyed it too.' She frowned. 'I don't think you view Lissy as a chore either.'

'Of course I don't. Even if she isn't interested in hanging out with me any more.'

The disconsolate slope of his shoulders was mirrored in the downward droop of his mouth, and it caught at her. This was none of her business, but…

He sent her a smile that twisted her heart. 'Are all teenage girls difficult?'

She dragged in a breath. 'Would you like some advice where Lissy's concerned? I don't have a sister, but I have worked with a lot of young people.'

'Yes.' He said it without hesitation.

'You have to promise not to bite my head off.'

He straightened, his eyes suddenly sharp. 'Cross my heart.'

She pressed her hands together to counter her sudden insane desire to touch him. 'Owen, I honestly think you'd be better served acting like Lissy's fun older brother than…um…'

'A disapproving maiden aunt? That's what she called me on Saturday.'

Which was hardly surprising. She'd watched him. He hadn't tried to hide his disapproval at what Lissy had been wearing. He'd scowled in the most ferocious way whenever Lissy had mentioned the name of any male friend. Lissy had predictably responded with snark and attitude. Callie understood both points of view, but...

'I'd bet a year's salary—' she huffed out a mirthless laugh '—except, of course, I'm not currently earning a salary.'

'But you will be soon.'

His words were clear and sure, and they made her shoulders go back. Of course she would. 'Anyway, I'd bet Lissy only pulls her short skirts out of her wardrobe...and mentions the names of so many boys...just to get a rise out of you. She bought a couple of things on Saturday—items of clothing of which I'm sure you'd wholeheartedly approve. But I doubt she'll wear them if she thinks you're going to see them.'

He stared. 'Why not?'

'And, while boys were certainly mentioned during our shopping day,' she continued, 'they by no means formed the major part of our conversation. We talked about girl-friends and books and movies and so many other things.' Things she'd noticed Lissy hadn't mentioned around Owen.

'So...she's not obsessed with boys?'

'No more than any other sixteen-year-old girl. And I've got to tell you, Owen, you need to ease off a bit or you're going to smother her with disapproval.'

His mouth tightened.

'I know it comes from a good place. From a desire to protect her...'

'Of course I want to protect her! I know how ugly the

world can be. I don't want her ever to suffer the way my mother did.'

Oh, Owen. He hadn't been able to protect his mother so he was determined to protect his little sister.

She blinked hard against the burn in her eyes. 'But Lissy has Margaret and Jack, who both sound smart and savvy. They aren't neglectful, are they? They love her? You trust them, don't you?'

'Of course I do!'

'Then leave the parenting to them.'

His jaw dropped.

'Both you *and* Lissy would be better served if you were the approachable big brother she could confide in without fear of being judged or having her head snapped off.'

He ran a hand over his face. 'You make me sound like the worst of grumps.'

'I know you're not. And deep down Lissy does too. But she's a teenager. At her age everything takes on an added edge that can feel pointed and overwhelming. She thinks you don't trust her.'

His gaze speared to hers and she shrugged.

'Imagine how that makes her feel.'

Very slowly he nodded.

She hesitated, but those grey eyes were on her in a heartbeat, sharpening at whatever they saw in her face.

'There's more?' he asked.

Help! She was about to embark into truly personal territory. 'She mentioned someone called Fiona…'

His head reared back and it took all her courage to continue.

'I got the impression she's an old girlfriend of yours.'

He gave the briefest of nods.

'I also got the impression that something happened between the two of them.'

Everything about him went on high alert. 'Do you know what?'

She shook her head. 'But if you decide to raise the topic—*when* you decide to raise the topic,' she amended, because she could see that he fully intended to do so, 'tread carefully. Instinct tells me she really hurt Lissy's feelings.'

Her stomach churned at his sudden pallor and the self-recrimination reflected in his eyes.

'I expect Fiona didn't mean to cause any harm, but—'

'Then you'd expect wrong.'

The ice in his voice had a chill chasing down her spine.

'Fiona and I were engaged.'

What? To be *married*?

'But she wasn't the woman I thought she was. It never occurred to me she'd take her anger out on Lissy.' His lips twisted. 'Evidently I was too caught up in my own pity party.'

'I'm sorry, Owen. I—'

'You've nothing to apologise for. I appreciate all you've said.' He nodded. 'And I will tread carefully. But I *am* going to fix this.'

He clasped her hands briefly, and she could see something inside him had lightened.

'Thank you.'

She found a smile of her own. 'Well…thank *you* for organising today's meeting. It was great to meet Frances's friends.'

'I was happy to help.' He sobered again, his brow creasing. 'But the woman Josephine, Betty and Eliza described today…the Frances from those earlier years…is a stranger to me. She sounded so vibrant and full of life…'

It hadn't occurred to Callie how her quest might affect him. She didn't want to mar his memory of his godmother. He'd *loved* Frances. She ached to reach out and squeeze his arm in silent sympathy and let him know he wasn't alone. But she hesitated too long and the moment passed.

His frown deepened. 'What happened between her and Richard seemed to break her.'

'I wonder why, though. I know love can be a tricky thing, but…'

His snort told her he considered that an understatement.

'But Frances sounded like a strong woman,' she said.

'Your point being?'

She pressed her hands together, gazing at the column of his throat rather than meeting the misty grey of his eyes.

'Very few of us manage to get through life without making a fool of ourselves romantically at least once, right?'

There was an intriguing sprinkle of hair at the vee of Owen's shirt and— *Stop it!* She deliberately made herself think of Dominic and familiar anger flared in her chest.

'I sure as hell have. And, after what you just said about Fiona, I guess you have too.'

'Yep.'

She swallowed at the way his lips thinned. There was a story there, but she refused to ask about it.

'But most of us don't turn into recluses because of it. Frances made a mistake about Richard—' just as Callie had with Dominic '—but so what?'

Owen blinked.

'I'm not saying that to be callous. I don't doubt he hurt her really badly. But I still don't get it.'

'Josephine said she felt things too deeply. And she *did* marry her mistake. We didn't marry ours, and that has to make a difference.' He stilled. 'At least *I* didn't.'

She shook her head, barely suppressing a shudder. 'Me either.'

'She trusted Richard and he abused that trust. What he did was despicable.'

'You won't get any argument from me about that. It's clear he broke her heart and disillusioned her. But did he break her spirit too? We've just agreed she was a strong woman, and it's clear that she had access to a lot of resources, so why turn herself into a modern-day Miss Havisham?'

'What are you thinking?'

'That thing Betty said about Frances breaking her own heart… What if it wasn't Richard she was referring to?' The thought formed as she spoke. 'What if it was whatever happened between her and my mother?'

He was silent for several long moments. 'If you're right,' he finally said, 'you could be opening a huge can of worms.'

Her heart sank. Maybe she should let sleeping dogs lie.

'You must want this job badly…'

The job! She straightened. Of course she wanted the job. Of course she was going to prise the lids off all cans that needed jemmying.

'So what now?' he asked.

She pulled in a breath to bolster her resolve. 'Josephine is going to text me the details of my mother's friend. As soon as she does I'll arrange a meeting. Hopefully she'll know the truth and will be willing to share it. If not, then maybe she suspects something or can toss me a bone. If she doesn't…' She trailed off.

He leaned his elbows on his knees and stared at the boat pond. Three children were sailing remote-controlled boats and Callie couldn't help thinking it looked like fun.

'You also have the letters, so there's a chance you could find a clue there. Or maybe even the truth.'

Except so far she hadn't had the courage to open them. Dread flooded her every time she picked one up. Callie was an adult now. Her mother didn't get to make decisions for her any more. But there had to be a good reason she'd never told Callie about Frances—and a good reason why she'd never been reconciled with her mother.

Opening them felt disloyal. And a part of her was scared—scared that she'd come to like Frances. And she didn't want to like someone who'd done something awful to her mother. She wanted to find out what had happened between the two women first. She'd relegated reading those letters to being her last course of action.

'You said you wanted to video yourself talking to the camera and explaining how you've traced your family tree from the few seeds you've been thrown?' Owen said.

Glad for the distraction, she nodded.

'Then how's this for a plan? I could rearrange my work schedule, and one day next week we could head up to Ellerslie. The house is currently vacant, but there's a caretaker couple who've worked there for years. We could have a rummage around and maybe film on location there. We'll probably have to stay overnight at a nearby inn, but that shouldn't be a problem.'

Her whole body became electrified at the thought—*visit the family estate?*

'Have you ever been there?' she asked. 'It looks stunning. The photographs are amazing…'

'I had no idea Frances even owned an estate until after her death.'

'It'd be wonderful to do some filming there—it would add a real wow factor. Are you sure we're allowed?'

'I'm the executor of Frances's will. If your mother refuses her inheritance I'm going to have to oversee the sale of the property. At some point I'm going to have to inspect it to see if any work needs to be done.'

'What about your boss? Won't he mind? Can you just take off like that?'

He glanced up into the blue of the sky and she figured he was mentally tallying up his work schedule.

'I can swing it,' he said finally.

To have that kind of leeway and freedom at work had to mean that he was seriously good at his job—that his employer was willing to give him the world in order to keep him. That was what *she* wanted—to be so good at something, so competent, that her job would never be in jeopardy again.

'And you're sure it'd be okay for me to tag along?'

How would her mother feel about Callie visiting Ellerslie?

Owen leaned forward to clasp her hands, as if sensing the tug of war going on inside her. 'As your mother's deputy, I'd have thought you have an obligation to see the house.'

'But my mother hasn't made me her deputy,' honesty forced her to point out.

He hesitated. 'You've kept those letters that Donna returned because you think she needs to read them. In that same spirit you have to see the estate so you can give her… I don't know…a report on it. At least take some photos to send her.'

That made sense. 'You want her to accept her inheritance, don't you?'

He hesitated, and then nodded. Then, 'Can I ask you something? Why consider rejecting your inheritance when Frances has put no conditions on it? I don't understand your reasoning. Why not just accept it and treasure it as the gift it is?'

Callie knew he saw it as his honour-bound duty to ensure Frances's wishes were fulfilled. And in the service of that he'd put pressure on Callie to accept her inheritance. His loyalty belonged to Frances, not her.

She pulled in a breath. 'If something really bad happened between Frances and my mother—and I think it's pretty clear something did—if Frances treated my mother cruelly… Then to accept my inheritance would be…' she searched her mind for the right words '…tacit approval for whatever it was she did. Accepting her money would be like taking a bribe to turn a blind eye to the past.'

If Frances had treated Donna reprehensibly, then she'd show solidarity with her mother. She'd turn her back completely on Frances and her world of wealth and privilege.

'I think both you and your mother have misjudged Frances.'

And after hearing about Frances today… 'A part of me hopes you're right,' she said.

Frances's story had struck a chord with her—maybe because of her own ill-fated love affair—and she felt as if she had a lot in common with the other woman. Just as Frances had thought with Richard, Callie had believed she'd have everything she'd ever wanted—family, children, financial stability, love—with Dominic. Both she and Frances had been cruelly disillusioned.

'It may all turn out to be nothing more than a big misunderstanding,' said Callie. And if that were the case then she might be able to make things right.

'Callie, you have a right to visit the estate. It's your family history too.'

She lifted her chin. It was.

For the time being she'd concentrate on the simplest of her current concerns—the TV job. She had every intention of applying for it, regardless of whatever else happened, and video footage of the estate would add serious drama to her little documentary.

She rubbed her hands together. 'That job is *so* mine. My documentary is going to knock the interview panel's socks off.'

He grinned back. 'Look, I know you're all over this video of yours, but don't forget I'm a tech nerd, with some serious hardware back at my apartment.'

Her heart gave a giant kick. 'You'd help me turn my little home video into something seriously slick?'

He raised his hands skyward. 'I thought you'd never ask.'

'Oh, Owen, thank you!'

Their gazes caught and held in a moment that, for Callie at least, was pure exhilaration. She found herself falling into the warm smoky depths of Owen's eyes.

Very slowly those delectable smiling lips of his sobered at whatever he saw reflected in her face. His gaze lowered to her lips and a tic started up inside her when the smoke darkened to midnight and she recognised his raw hunger.

He wanted her! Owen wanted her every bit as much as she wanted him.

The knowledge lifted her up as if on the crest of a wave—and exhilaration, delight, and the most delicious anticipation thrilled through her, because she knew he was about to kiss her. And she had every intention of meeting that kiss with an enthusiasm that left him in no doubt as to how much she wanted him.

She swayed towards him as his head lowered towards hers. One of her hands landed on his shoulder, the other rested against his chest. His body was absurdly firm, and so throbbing with life that her fingers automatically curled and then flattened in an effort to feel more of him.

And then his lips were on hers and their warmth took her off guard—warmth as in heat, but warmth as in feeling too. He kissed her as if he couldn't think of anything else he'd rather be doing, and she couldn't resist the allure of being so wholly and wholeheartedly relished.

She kissed him back with the same undiluted appreciation and a groan rasped from the back of his throat. That was the moment she lost all sense of herself. Her hands tunnelled through his hair to pull him closer and his hands went around her back, one coming up to cradle her head and hold her still so he could kiss her with a sweeping thoroughness that left her lost to everything except the moment and the rightness of being with him.

She had no idea how long they kissed, but they eventually broke apart to drag air into sawing lungs.

She hung there, suspended between heartbeats…

A shrill and sudden noise intruded on the spring quiet, making her start and Owen freeze. It took her a moment to realise it was her phone, and by the time she'd grabbed it from her handbag Owen had marched across to the pond, his back ramrod-straight.

She stood and pressed the phone to her ear. 'Hello?'

She listened as the voice of the man at the other end explained who he was. She made all the appropriate responses, hoping she didn't sound as shell-shocked and topsy-turvy as she felt, an ocean of need still stampeding through her.

Owen turned to her when she rang off. She didn't know what to make of that kiss, or Owen's reaction now. Was he regretting the interruption? Or was he grateful for it? If it was the latter, she didn't want to be anywhere near him. Not until she had her game face well and truly back into place.

'Callie, that kiss...'

He bent at the waist and braced his hands against his knees. Her heart plummeted, but she refused to let her chin drop.

'Was amazing,' she finished for him.

His gaze speared back to hers and she recognised the wariness in his eyes...and the regret. Acid coated her tongue. But a moment later she shook herself. Of *course* he regretted it. She regretted it too. What on earth had she been thinking? She *hadn't* been thinking!

She swallowed and forced herself to continue. 'But I'm not in the market for anything like that at the moment. I don't want a short-term fling, and anything long-term is just—' she dragged a hand through her hair '—unthinkable. I—'

He straightened. 'You don't need to explain, Callie.'

She didn't?

'I feel the same. Fiona and I broke up eight months ago, but it still feels too soon to start something new.'

Her heart gave a strange little twist. 'That makes perfect sense. You were going to marry her. That takes some...'

Gah, why hadn't she simply stopped at *That makes perfect sense*? 'Some time to readjust,' she finished lamely.

He stared at her. 'So…we're good?'

'Absolutely.' She waved at the bench. 'That was just a blip. One of those "less said, soonest mended" things.'

'Agreed.' His relief was palpable. 'Then we'll just consider it forgotten.'

She had a feeling it wasn't going to be that easy. At least not for her.

Pushing the thought aside, she held up her phone. 'That was Mr Singh. A gentleman who claims he's Barney's owner.'

'Barney's owner?'

'He's in hospital. I said we'd go and visit him.'

He blinked.

'I mean,' she amended hastily, *'I'll* go and visit him, you don't have to come.'

'Of course I'm coming. I've been sharing custody, remember?'

'We should really drop by the apartment to make sure Barney's okay. Maybe take him out for a bit.'

They'd left him in Owen's apartment.

'You walked him this morning. He'll be fine for another couple of hours.'

'Do you think we could smuggle him into the hospital with us? I bet Mr Singh would love to see him and—'

'No.'

But his lips twitched as he said it, and things started to feel more comfortable between them again. Her pulse was slowly returning to normal.

She told him the name of the hospital and he gestured towards the path they should take.

CHAPTER SEVEN

CALLIE WORE THE softest woollen sweater in butter-yellow and a striped scarf in mint-green and orange. She looked like a summer day in spring, but the moment she slid into the car beside Owen he knew something was wrong.

Yeah, idiot, you kissed her!

It was five days since their afternoon tea and their walk in the park. And that kiss. Of course she was going to be stand-offish. She'd made it clear she didn't want a repeat performance.

He gripped the steering wheel so hard his knuckles turned white. What on earth had possessed him to kiss her? He'd asked himself that same question over and over, but still couldn't come up with a satisfactory answer. Nor could he dredge up a satisfactory amount of regret. The kiss itself had been sensational. Not that it could happen again.

Irritatingly, he found he could dredge up more than enough regret about that.

He ground his back molars together. *That* was why he had to play it cool now. After exchanging a brusque greeting with her, he focussed his attention on the traffic and getting out of the city. The family estate of Ellerslie was in Cooperstown, nearly four hours away, and they were aiming to arrive by lunchtime.

Callie made no effort at small talk, and she only turned every now and again to check on Barney, who dozed in his crate on the back seat.

He glanced across when they were finally free of the city, his index fingers tapping on the steering wheel. Was it just that kiss or was something else on her mind?

'I didn't think to ask, but do you get car sick?'

'No.' She hunkered down further in her seat, arms folded. 'Though I still don't know what was wrong with taking the train. I checked, and it would've been fine for us to take Barney.'

'We'll have more freedom with the car.' He fought a frown. 'Besides, Barney will be far more comfortable in the car than he'd be on a train.'

They'd discovered that Mr Singh, Barney's owner, lived a short walk from the apartment block. The elderly man wasn't due out of hospital for another week. They'd assured him they'd be delighted to continue looking after Barney till then.

Owen tried coaxing her out of her odd mood. 'How many times have you been to see Mr Singh this week?'

'Every day,' she answered, as if it were the most stupid question ever asked. 'He needs someone to coax him to go for his twice-daily walks. Anyway, he's good company.'

And Owen wasn't?

He tried to quash that thought. It was pathetic, being jealous of a man who was old enough to be Callie's grandfather. Besides, he wasn't jealous. Mr Singh was minus one kidney. He'd just been through a major operation. With Callie to bear him company, though, Owen didn't doubt Mr Singh would now make great strides forward in his recovery.

Callie might not realise it, but she was a lot like her grandmother. She saw a need and rushed to meet it— whether it involved stray dogs, high school seniors wrestling with math problems, or lonely old men.

'I've dropped in on Mr Singh's neighbour a couple of times too—the one who was supposed to be looking after Barney. She felt so bad about him getting away from her… She'd been scouring the streets for him.'

'Didn't she see the posters?'

'She's seventy-seven. If she wasn't wearing her glasses…

I know what you're doing, you know—you're trying to distract me.'

The collar of his polo shirt—a staid and boring navy—tightened. 'From what?'

'Of you going to the trouble and expense of hiring a car!'

Was that what had been bothering her? 'No trouble. No expense. Callie, this is a company car.'

As he owned the company, he technically owned the car. Not that Callie knew that. He'd made damn sure she had no idea. But the lie was starting to rankle.

He opened his mouth. He closed it again. His financial situation had no bearing on their relationship. Besides, what they had wasn't a relationship. It was an…association. He and Callie had made a deal. As soon as she got this job he'd never see her again. He'd buy the apartment block. And everyone would be happy.

Unbidden, the memory of their kiss rose through him. If he hadn't been driving he'd have closed his eyes to try to shut it out. If she hadn't been sitting beside him, he'd have sworn out loud.

It had just been a kiss—nothing more—a crazy, impulsive moment that had been brief and perfect. He told himself part of its perfection was due to its very transience.

Yet that hadn't stopped the kiss from being on a slow-motion replay in his mind for the last five days. Five days in which he'd barely seen her. Oh, she'd dropped Barney off whenever she went out. And she'd been going out a lot. But she hadn't volunteered to tell him where she was going and he'd refused to ask.

He gripped the steering wheel. He had to stop thinking about that kiss and he needed to get their…*association* back on an even keel.

Before he could come up with a neutral topic of conversation she closed her eyes. He didn't know if she was feigning sleep or not, but he let her be.

Damn! She'd been so excited about filming at the estate and now she could barely stand to look at him.

When she stirred an hour later, he had a question ready for her. 'Hey, sleepy-head, I've been meaning to ask—did you get a chance to meet with your mother's friend? The Ryder woman?'

'Hitchcock now—Melissa Hitchcock.' She stretched and straightened. 'I met with her yesterday. She seems lovely, and was really pleased to see some up-to-date photos of my mother…asked me to send her best, et cetera. But as for shedding any light on my paternity…'

'No luck?' That would explain her low spirits.

'She thought my best bet would be to talk to Richard.'

'Donna hated Richard. Why did Melissa think he could help?'

She pushed her hands through her hair. 'She said he always seemed to know a lot about other people's business.'

Charming.

She was quiet again for a long time. Several times Owen opened his mouth to ask if anything was wrong, but shut it again. If they were friends, he'd ask. If they hadn't kissed, he'd ask. But they weren't, and they had, so he didn't.

'Did you organise those painters?' she finally blurted out. 'Three men showed up before we left this morning, saying they'd been hired to paint the interior of my apartment.'

'Finally!' He feigned exasperation. 'The apartment should've been painted weeks ago. Frances refused to have it done while she was alive—didn't want her peace disturbed. She hated having tradesmen of any kind in the place. I'm sorry, I didn't think to warn you.'

She stared out through the front windscreen, her hands gripping her opposite elbows. 'I rang Mr Dunkley. He knew nothing about it, though he told me the firm was a reputable one that he'd often used and recommended.'

Damn. He hadn't thought to clue the lawyer in.

'Then I rang the firm to find out when they'd been booked, and they told me it was a rush job and they'd only been hired on Monday.'

He grimaced. *Sprung.*

She stared at him. 'So it *was* you. You want to tell me why?'

Things inside him knotted. 'Are you mad at me?'

'I don't know yet.'

Why would she be mad at him? He'd organised it for her benefit.

'The truth is it *should've* been done before you arrived in New York…'

'But you didn't want to change things.' She turned to face him fully. 'That's understandable. You were grieving.'

'But seeing you in the apartment—getting used to seeing you there—has made me realise how damn gloomy the place is. You're spending a lot of time in it—working, living, sleeping there. You deserve something better than a…a dreary brown box.'

He'd been about to say *prison*, but checked himself. It wasn't a prison. And he refused to think of it as a prison for Frances either. It had been a haven.

'Why did you lie about it being something you'd organised ages ago?'

His collar threatened to cut off his air supply. 'I didn't want you feeling it was a nuisance or that I was going to a lot of bother—which I wasn't, by the way.' He glanced at her briefly then back at the road, and swallowed. 'I didn't want you refusing and putting up with all that depressing brown. I didn't want you getting into a funk.'

Something flashed through her eyes and her lips briefly flattened. A bad taste stretched through his mouth.

'I'm sorry. I should've been upfront with you. But it's

been an emotional time and…' His words petered out. 'You're mad.'

'I'm not mad.'

He didn't believe her.

'I'll be glad to be rid of the brown. It was nice of you to think of it.'

All he'd done since Callie had landed in New York was think about her. He stretched his neck, first to the left and then to the right. As soon as she started her new job and her new life things would return to normal.

'But…' she said.

Something in her tone had everything inside him clenching twice as hard.

'Can I ask you not to make any more decisions like that? I know you're Frances's executor, but for the time being at least the apartment belongs to me. I should be the one to make any decisions about it. I mean, what if I'd organised painters myself?'

He stiffened.

She huffed out a laugh. 'Relax! I haven't. It seemed too much trouble to go to when the future is still so uncertain.'

He tapped his fingers against the steering wheel. '*This* is what's been bugging you since you hopped in the car?'

'Technically it's been bugging me since the painters knocked on my door.'

'Why didn't you have this out with me earlier instead of sitting there stewing in silence?'

'If your actions had been mean-spirited, Owen, I'd have raked you over the coals before I even entered the car. But you organising the painters *wasn't* mean-spirited. You were trying to look after me in the same way you do with Lissy.'

'But it's still irked you?'

'Because I'm a grown up! You took a decision *I* should be making out of my hands. You've no right to do that!'

He snorted. 'You *sure* you're not mad?'

Her eyes flashed and he berated himself for poking at her.

'Sorry...'

From the corner of his eye he saw her haul in a deep breath, as if trying to compose herself.

'I'm not long out of a relationship with a man who...'

He found himself gripping the steering wheel too hard again. 'Who what?' He barely recognised his own voice.

'Who tried to rob me of my power. Who almost succeeded.'

He swung to her, appalled. 'I wasn't trying to do that.'

'I know—which is why I'm not mad. I know you're looking out for me because of the obligation you feel towards Frances.'

Except it was starting to feel like a whole lot more than that.

'I'm really sensitive to anyone taking advantage of me or overstepping boundaries at the moment. Normally I'd have let it pass. But after Dominic I swore to myself I'd stop being a doormat.'

He mulled her words over. 'So me going over your head to organise something you were more than capable of organising yourself...?'

'Pushed all my buttons.' She twisted her hands in her lap. 'It's not so easy to slap someone's wrist for overstepping boundaries when the service offered is kindly meant.'

He reached out and clasped her hands. The tension radiating from them told him it had taken courage for her to raise the topic and stick up for herself, to claim her power. But she'd still done it, and he admired her for it.

'You have my sincerest apologies—along with my promise to observe all appropriate boundaries from now on. I've no wish to make you feel less capable or less *anything*, Callie.'

'Thank you.'

The smile she sent him had heat gathering in his veins. He reefed his hand back, hastily reminding himself about appropriate boundaries.

'So…' She shuffled down in her seat, the movement easy and relaxed. 'Did you get my party invitation?'

It had been slipped under his door yesterday afternoon. 'Yes, thank you.'

'It'll be nice to have the apartment looking fresh for that.' She surveyed her fingernails. 'Are you going to come?'

'Wouldn't miss it for the world. Who else have you invited?'

'All the other tenants. I *so* hope they come.'

He made a vow to ensure each and every one of them turned up.

She rattled off three names in quick succession. 'They're the girls you met in the park, plus their parents.'

She'd met their *parents*?

'And I've invited your mother, Jack and Lissy. Mr Dunkley and his wife. As well as Josephine, Eliza and Betty. Melissa Hitchcock and her husband.' She waved a hand in the air. 'And a few other people.'

He started to laugh. 'Who else have you had a chance to meet?'

She gave an exaggerated eye-roll. 'A couple of librarians I became friendly with at the library…the coffee shop manager from that place on the corner.' She rubbed her hands together. 'I love a good party, don't you?'

Not really. Not that he said as much. 'Sure.'

She laughed. 'Liar. I remember—you're an island unto yourself.'

'I'm not! I—'

The gates to the estate had come into view, along with a big brass plaque with the word *Ellerslie* burned into it, and the sight of it had his protest dying in his throat.

Callie gave a funny little hiccup and swung towards him. 'Pull over.'

He did as she asked.

'Remember when we were talking in the park the other day about how you shouldn't let a broken heart turn you into a hermit?'

He remembered every pulse and nuance of their time in the park. And the seriousness of her expression now punched him in the gut.

'Would you react that way if some careless or conniving girl broke your heart?'

It struck him then that that was exactly what he had done when he'd discovered Fiona's duplicity. Not as completely as Frances, admittedly, but he'd definitely cut himself off and shut himself away. And forcing himself out in the service of helping Callie solve her family mystery felt good.

'It might send me to ground for a while—give me a chance to lick my wounds in private,' he said slowly. 'But not for good.'

It felt freeing to know that he meant it.

Callie smiled then—a real, straight-from-the-heart smile that pierced through him, sweet and pure.

'Good. You deserve better than that. We all do. I think we should make a pact in Frances's memory. A pact to never let disappointment in love or a broken heart let our worlds become smaller and narrower.'

His mouth went unaccountably dry. He had to swallow before he could speak. 'Callie, what are you afraid of? What do you think we're going to discover?'

The hand she'd held out for him to shake lowered. She stared at the ornate gates and chafed her arms. 'I don't know. That's what worries me.'

'We don't have to go through with this, you know... Maybe some secrets shouldn't see the light of day.'

'It feels too late to turn back.'

He knew what she meant, but…

She grimaced. 'It feels as if the lid on that can of worms you mentioned has been peeled halfway back already, and I can't pick up all the worms and put them back in.' Her nose wrinkled. 'That's a seriously disgusting analogy. I just mean I'll always have questions now.'

'Callie—'

'No, ignore me.' Shaking her head, she pulled in a breath. 'This is a bout of nerves—nothing more. I'm fine. It's just—' She swung towards him again. 'Owen, whatever we find out, I should hate for it to mar your memory of Frances.'

He reached out and squeezed her hand. 'You don't have to worry about me, Callie. My regard for Frances is steadfast, whatever happens.' He gestured. 'Are you ready?'

She pushed her shoulders back and nodded. 'I'm ready.'

CHAPTER EIGHT

THE DRIVE CURVED around a low hill and the house came into view as they rounded it, nestled neatly in the middle of the rise opposite. Even though Callie had seen photos of the house, coming face to face with it was still awe-inspiring.

Owen let loose a low whistle. 'Now, that's what I call an impressive piece of architecture.'

The house was a late-Georgian mansion, and its white stone gleamed in the spring sunshine, while the surrounding fields were lush with new growth, providing a perfect contrast. Further afield paddocks were neatly ploughed. It all looked fresh and clean and perfect.

He shook his head. 'This must cost a ridiculous amount in upkeep.'

Callie's research came to her rescue, helping to keep the panic from rising up and choking her. 'It pays for itself. Ellerslie has a successful dairy breeding programme. The estate also makes its own cheese. They've not won any national awards—yet—but they've been runners-up. I'm guessing that's all housed over there.'

She gestured to the cluster of large buildings some distance away to their left and then stared about. All of this now belonged to her mother. Had Donna spent a lot of time here as a girl? Did it hold fond memories for her? No memories? Bad memories?

The fact that she had no idea left her feeling bewildered. How could she not know about this part of her mother's life? She rubbed a hand over her chest. What on earth had made Donna turn her back on it so completely?

Owen pulled the car to a halt in the parking area to one

side of the house. He opened her door and stood there waiting patiently. Eventually he held out his hand. 'Callie?'

Forcing in a breath, she placed her hand in his. Warmth flooded her where before she'd felt numb and frozen. Something else flooded her when she found herself almost chest to chest with him—a thread of excitement and a sense of possibility. She didn't know if it was for the estate or the man, but she welcomed it regardless. It was better than being numb with fear and crippled with misgivings.

She glanced up—meant to send him a smile of reassurance—but their eyes locked and everything else receded into the background except the heat in his eyes and the firm promise of his lips... It would be so easy to—

Barney barked his impatience at being confined to the car, and she and Owen snapped away from each other. With hands that shook, she let Barney out. The little dog leapt to the ground and paused, ears alert, before giving a happy yap and running in wide circles on the lawn.

She couldn't help but laugh. 'Looks like Ellerslie has Barney's seal of approval.'

She turned back towards the house, careful not to look at Owen, and found a woman she guessed to be Mrs Dunsmore, the housekeeper, waiting at the top of the steps. The warmth of her smile welcomed them.

'You must be Callie. I'd know Donna's daughter anywhere! You look so much like her when she was a girl.'

'You knew my mother?'

'Oh, bless you, dear, yes—and don't fuss about the dog. Dogs have always been welcome at Ellerslie. Yes, I remember your mother well. She spent a lot of time here with her nan and pop. Those were happy days...back in a time when the house was filled with people. But enough standing here on the doorstep. Come in and make yourselves comfortable. I thought we'd have lunch before touring the house.'

She led them into an impressive entrance hall and

through several large rooms, including the most amazing drawing room filled with gleaming antiques, to a big bright kitchen at the back of the house. From the open back door Callie could see a farmhouse garden.

'I'll hunt up some photo albums for you if you like,' the housekeeper offered.

'I'd love that.'

'Also, the pair of you staying at the inn is nonsense. I've made up a pair of bedrooms for you. Now, don't argue. The young miss here—'

Callie? The young miss? She was twenty-seven!

'—will want to have a good poke about all the places her mother used to like. While you'll be wanting to check that the house and farm accounts are in order, Mr Perry.'

'Owen,' he corrected. 'And I'm sure they're in perfect order, with no need—'

'There's every need. My Pete has been fretting his poor old head about it ever since Mrs Frances died. He'd hate for anyone to think he's been overstepping the mark. There'll be plenty of time for everything if you stay. Besides, it'll be nice to have some young blood in the house again—even if it is only for one night.'

Owen lifted questioning brows at Callie and she nodded. 'We'd love to stay, Mrs Dunsmore. We're sorry to put you to so much trouble, but—'

'No trouble! No trouble at all.'

After a lunch of chicken soup and warmed rolls, she showed them their rooms. 'I gave you your mother's room, Callie. I thought you'd like that.'

Callie loved it.

Owen had the room next door.

After a quick tour, Mrs Dunsmore said, 'Now, I'll leave you to have a mosey around at your own pace. Dinner is at seven o'clock on the dot.'

'It's so grand,' Callie breathed, her head whirling with a million different thoughts.

How could her mother turn her back on all of this?

'The filming opportunities…' Owen said.

She swung around at his words. 'That entrance hall alone!'

'Did you see the portraits on the walls? All forebears of yours, no doubt.'

Her mind raced with possibilities. 'Mrs Dunsmore is bound to know who they all are. I wonder if she'd let me interview her for my video.'

After wandering about for over an hour, they gravitated to a library that looked as if it had come straight from the set of a Jane Austen period drama. There they found an old family bible with the Allbright family tree inside its venerable leather covers. And a bookcase beneath one of the windows that had been given over to estate accounts going back over a hundred years. On another shelf they found the various diaries and journals of different family members who'd lived here.

Callie pounced on one of the journals. 'Look at this! It's Hannah's diary. Hannah and Douglas were Frances's parents—my great-grandparents.' She opened it at random, ran her finger down the page. 'Oh! She's talking about the terrible time after Thomas's death.' She read several paragraphs. 'So sad…'

Owen came to stand behind her, smelling of soap and warm cotton and reassurance. It gave her the courage to flick to the last entries.

'Listen to this. *"Donna came to stay for a few days. She's met someone special. I can't imagine anyone being good enough for my darling granddaughter, of course, but her whole face lights up whenever she speaks of him. It's enough to gladden my heart. She's promised to bring him to visit soon. I can't wait to meet this man who has won her heart.'*'

'It's her final entry,' Owen murmured as Callie turned the page.

'Hannah and Douglas died in a car accident not long after this.'

'So...'

Something in Owen's tone had her glancing up. 'So?'

He rested a finger against the date of the final entry. 'Frances remarried only six months after this. Somewhere between this date and the wedding, Frances and Donna had their big falling out.'

True...

'And neither of them had Hannah or Douglas to turn to,' he said.

She stared as his meaning sank in. 'A lot happened in a short space of time... Both Hannah and Douglas were only children. With them gone, a whole generation of the family was lost.'

'And Frances and Donna lost the benefit of older and wiser heads.'

'You think Hannah and Douglas could've healed the breach?'

He gestured to the journal. 'I bet Hannah would've tried.'

So did Callie.

She traced a finger along the neat handwriting. 'She doesn't mention the name of my mother's beau.'

'Maybe Mrs Dunsmore will be able to shed more light.'

Over dinner that evening, Callie asked her. But, while Mrs Dunsmore clearly recalled Donna's last visit to Ellerslie, she hadn't been aware of any special beau.

'She was a lively girl, and lovely too—which meant she had a lot of admirers. But I don't recall anyone special.'

After dinner Callie returned to the library, to continue

reading Hannah's diary, while Owen hunkered down with Peter Dunsmore to go over the estate's accounts.

Unaccountably restless after only an hour of reading, Callie glanced out of the library's French doors to the huge summerhouse. Its multitude of windows twinkled in the moonlight, and on impulse she pushed through the doors and walked down to it.

The door opened at her touch. Fumbling for a light switch, she blinked as a sudden flood of brilliance blinded her. A series of chandeliers marched down the space, sparkling off the windows and turning the summerhouse into a fairyland. Callie pressed her hands to her chest and drank it in.

Heavenly!

Adjusting the dimmer switch to soften the lights, she walked the length of the pavilion, imagining the space filled with elegant guests and tables groaning under the weight of delectable party fare while a band played on the raised dais at the far end.

This would be the perfect place for a *Great Gatsby*-themed party. Or, better yet, for women in crinolines, their hooped skirts swirling as they waltzed with men in dark tail coats and white cravats.

The picture was so clear in her mind that she found herself pretending to hide her face behind a fan and swaying to imaginary music. 'Could you have this dance? Why, sir, I'd be delighted, I'm sure.'

She swept a curtsey to an imaginary partner, and was about to embark on a waltz when an amused voice in the doorway said, 'I've seen this movie. Julie Andrews in *The Sound of Music*, right?'

Owen. For no reason at all, her pulse picked up speed.

She swung round with a grin, not feeling the least embarrassed. 'Technically it was Liesl, the eldest daughter.

But as you got the movie right I won't hold the details against you.'

He moved the length of the pavilion towards her. There was a light in his eye that made her mouth dry even as his loose-limbed stride had her pulse thrumming.

He stopped in front of her, male appreciation lighting his face as his eyes roved over her. 'Ms Nicholls, you're looking an absolute picture this evening.' He swept a bow. 'Would you do me the honour of dancing with me?'

Oh, this was foolish and reckless. And impossible to resist!

She fluttered that imaginary fan. 'Why, Mr Perry, I thought you'd never ask.'

And then she was in his arms and he was sweeping her around the room as if he'd been born to it. She couldn't recall the last time she'd danced a waltz, but her feet recalled the steps effortlessly. Beneath her hand the latent power of his body came alive and she couldn't help responding to it, her stomach softening and her breasts growing heavy.

'You dance beautifully, Mr Perry.' Heavens, was that breathless voice *hers*?

The expression in his eyes held her prisoner. They continued to spin and twirl, perfectly attuned. 'So do you, Ms Nicholls.' Those grey eyes darkened and his feet slowed. 'You're beautiful…you know that?'

Those last words hadn't been spoken in the formal tones of a bygone era.

Callie desperately tried to think of some flippant quip— a comeback that would break the spell he was weaving around her. There were reasons she should resist it. But her mind had gone blank. Owen and his broad shoulders and his tempting mouth filled her vision and her mind.

They slowed to a halt, staring at each other, breathing hard.

'Callie…?'

She sensed how tightly he held himself, as if afraid that if he unclenched a single muscle he'd not be able to stop himself from sweeping her up in his arms and kissing her senseless. And she wanted that—despite all the reasons she shouldn't. She knew what he tasted like now…knew how he kissed. That was the problem. He was addictive! And she wanted more.

Standing on tiptoe, she met his hot, hungry gaze, her lips drawing closer and closer to his. She maintained eye contact, determined to draw back at his slightest indication, but his eyes dared her, the light flaring in them threatening to consume her. Finally, their lips touched, and a sigh left her as a quiver rippled down Owen's entire length.

Shaping her mouth to his, she threw caution to the wind and pressed closer, demanded more. His answer was swift and immediate. He hauled her close, took control of the kiss so completely her head swam, but she didn't need her head and she didn't need her balance. Owen held her securely and she gave in to the need that consumed her and trusted he would keep her safe.

Tearing the hem of his shirt from his jeans, she ran her hand over the flat planes of his stomach to the defined muscles of his chest. Hot. Firm. Shamelessly seductive.

Owen tore his mouth from hers to emit a low growl that only excited her more. She dragged her fingernails lightly down his chest, back to the waistband of his jeans. His body jerked, making her feel wanton, desirable…powerful.

That was before he dipped her over his arm, pushed her jumper up to her neck and suckled her nipple through the thin silk of her bra. She gasped, currents of pulsing need coursing to her very centre. She found herself almost sobbing with the need for release.

But then he halted and her mind seized up. Forcing heavy eyelids open, she blinked the fog from her eyes to meet his gaze.

'I want you, Callie. I want you more than—' He broke off, his breathing ragged, before righting her and drawing her jumper back down over breasts that throbbed. 'But I need to know this is what you want too.'

The words were an icy wash of cold reality.

He pushed a hand through his hair. 'I can't… We can't… If you're going to regret it tomorrow, then we need to stop now.'

She pressed suddenly cold hands to her overheated cheeks. She'd totally lost her head.

He closed his eyes, before giving a single hard nod. 'The expression on your face says it all.'

She gave a strangled laugh. 'All it can possibly say at the moment is how shocked I am at how completely I just lost control.'

She tottered over to the dais and sat before her legs gave out completely. He hesitated, then joined her.

She glanced at him and then at her hands. 'I've never been reckless when it comes to sex. If anything I've always overthought it…if you know what I mean.'

He nodded.

'But just then…' She covered her face with her hands.

'I lost control too, Callie.'

But he'd found it again. She doubted she'd have come to her senses in time to stop before things had—

Before they'd reached their natural conclusion!

She pulled her hands away. 'I'm horrified at the impression I've given you.'

He bent down so he could look directly into her face. 'You've given me no impression other than the fact that you're warm and lovely.'

'And a mess.' At his raised eyebrows, she continued. 'That ex I told you about—he's the reason my contract wasn't renewed. We worked together. We'd had a fight. A minor one, I thought. But apparently he took exception to

something I said, had a word in the head of faculty's ear…
and my job was suddenly history. I didn't even realise we
were no longer a couple until I was given my marching orders. I guess he wanted to make a big impact.'

Owen's quick hiss of breath told her what he thought
of that.

'So I promised myself that until I had my career back
on track I'd not get involved with anyone.'

He stared at the ceiling for several long moments. 'I
understand, Callie. You don't owe me any explanations.'

But she wanted to give him one all the same. 'I know.
It's just… Even though I'm sorely tempted to blow rasp-
berries at my resolution and start something with you…'
She moistened her lips and did what she could to ignore
the yearning that pounded through her. 'If we were to start
something, and I were then to refuse the legacy Frances has
left me, I can't help feeling that would hurt you.'

'Callie—'

'And I don't want to hurt you.' She tried to find a smile.
'Besides, it was hard sticking up for myself about the painters, but it felt good, and I don't want to start backsliding—
relying on other people instead of myself. Regardless of
how much I want to kiss you, it feels like the wrong time
to be starting something with someone.'

'I'm hearing you. Ever since Fiona I haven't been in the
right headspace to start something new. She lied to me…
used me…and her viciousness once I found her out…' He
shook his head. 'I had a lucky escape.'

A lock of hair fell onto his brow, making him look suddenly young and vulnerable. Her heart turned over in her
chest.

'You once asked me if suspicion was my default setting.
It never used to be before Fiona.'

She couldn't stop herself from reaching out and squeezing his hand. He turned it over in his, lacing his fingers through hers.

'So now I'm going to tell you something I should've told you from the very beginning. The company I work for, the one you think is so eager to keep me... Well, I actually own it.'

She stared at him, trying to work out what he meant.

'I moved back into the apartment building because Frances needed more help than she'd ever admit. I used my break-up with Fiona as an excuse.'

'You were Frances's *carer*?'

'Of sorts. She didn't need full-time care, but it became necessary to check on her every day.'

He was a good man. Most men she knew would've delegated that task to a mother or sister. 'So your company... it's profitable?'

'Very.'

Her mouth went dry as she went over in her mind some of their previous conversations. 'Profitable enough to buy the apartment complex?'

'Several times over.'

She tried to stop her eyes from starting out of her head. 'Are you trying to tell me you're a billionaire?'

He grimaced. 'I guess...'

She gaped at him. 'I have a billionaire living in the basement?' And then she swallowed. 'Oh, Lord. I accused you of using Frances as a meal ticket and resenting the fact you didn't get anything in her will. But of course you didn't *need* anything.'

'I'm sorry. I...'

Why on earth had he let her make such a fool of herself?

She kept her tone light, even as things inside her shrivelled. 'Let me guess—you're self-made, right?' At his nod, she started to laugh. She couldn't help it. 'You know what?

I don't feel guilty any more about dragging you away from your computers or getting you into trouble with your boss.'

'You shouldn't feel guilty about anything! I—'

'Oh, *God*!' She swung to him. 'Fiona only wanted you for your money, didn't she?' The realisation struck her like a bolt from the blue, but she should've seen the connection immediately. 'Oh, Owen, I'm so sorry.' A bad taste coated her tongue. 'You thought I was like her…'

She tried to pull her hand from his, but he wouldn't let her.

'But now I know differently. I know you're not a gold-digger, Callie. And I'm sorry I didn't tell you the truth sooner. At first it didn't seem to matter, but now…' One broad shoulder lifted. 'Now it does. I know our relationship isn't going to develop into anything, but kissing you with that deception hanging over my head…' He stared down at their linked hands. 'It felt like a shabby thing to do. If our positions were reversed, I'd want to know the truth.' He met her gaze. 'I want you to know I trust you. I don't exactly know why, but it seems important that we get at least that much settled.'

Very slowly, she nodded. 'I'm glad I know the truth.' She pulled in a breath. 'After what Fiona did, I can even understand why you kept it from me.'

His lips twisted. 'There's a hardness in me now that never used to be there.'

That perfectly described how she'd felt ever since Dominic had betrayed her trust so badly.

He squeezed her hand. 'And you know what? No woman deserves to deal with that. I need to deal with it myself.'

Ditto, she thought.

She glanced about the summerhouse. 'I'd be lying if I said a part of me isn't disappointed that we're being so sensible, but…there are ghosts here. I can almost feel them. Did my mother dance with my father under these same chandeliers? Did they kiss? Did Frances and Richard dance here?' She swallowed, buttressing her resolve. 'And look what happened to them. It feels like a warning not to follow in their footsteps.'

After several beats he lifted his head, his eyes hooded and unreadable. 'Friends?'

From somewhere she found a smile, and while it didn't ease the burn in her body, it eased the burn in her soul. 'Yes, please.'

CHAPTER NINE

'THIS IS AMAZING!'

Callie beamed at him, and Owen did his best to check the elation her delight sent coursing through him. It was pointless getting all het up. It was pointless wondering what it would be like to make love with her or—

Stop it!

But it didn't matter how often he reminded himself of what she'd said at Ellerslie about not being ready for a relationship, he couldn't get the thought out of his mind. It didn't matter how often he told himself *he* wasn't interested in a relationship either, he couldn't stop from wondering *what if*?

And that spelled trouble.

He dragged in a breath. It had only been five days since they'd returned from Ellerslie. This feeling would fade soon enough. He just had to wait it out.

'You even have the theme music!' She clapped her hands. 'You've stitched all the sequences together so *seamlessly*. Owen, this must've taken you ages!'

'Nah,' he lied. 'I just pulled it together while I was between other jobs. Doing a bit here and there.'

He'd spent a ridiculous amount of time on her video. He'd enjoyed watching her animated face on the screen and the quick, expressive movements that she made with her hands as she explained how she was unravelling the mystery of her family tree.

He'd watched a load of old episodes of the TV series— both the British and Australian versions—so he could get the opening sequence just perfect and adjust the transitions in a way that would highlight Callie's familiarity with the programme, and therefore her suitability for the position she was applying for.

She spun to him now, her hands clasped beneath her chin. 'Thank you *so much*. This is a hundred times better than I could've managed on my own.'

In that moment he didn't begrudge a single second he'd spent on the project. 'It was a pleasure.'

'All that's missing…'

Her sigh had his gut clenching. All that was missing was the identity of her father. He wished he could give her the answer.

'But this—' she gestured to his computer '—is fabulous.' The corners of her mouth turned mock woeful. 'You do know they're going to ask me who put this together and then thank me nicely for applying and come headhunting *you*.'

He laughed. 'They're going to take one look at your video and have you signing on the dotted line before you can say *Mystery Family Trees*. Once you get the job, do you know where you'll—?'

'I've tracked Richard down,' she blurted out.

He fell down into the chair beside her. *'What?'*

'He lives in Larchmont.'

Larchmont was less than an hour's train ride away. 'Have you contacted him?'

'Not yet.'

A hard stone lodged in his chest. 'But you plan to?'

Her eyes implored him to understand. 'It's my last chance.'

He wanted to argue against it—wanted to order her to stay away from the man. Except, of course, he had no right to do any such thing.

'Frances's letters haven't shed any light on the subject?'

Her gaze slid away and her shoulders tensed as she shook her head. He'd be lying if he said he wasn't curious about the contents of those letters, but he refused to pry or force a confidence. On the surface Callie acted bright and breezy and cheerful, not to mention maddeningly capable, but every now and again he glimpsed her bafflement, her hurt, and her worry. It had his every protective instinct roaring to life.

'The man sounds like a real piece of work, Callie. He might not even talk to you.'

'I know. It's just… I feel I have to at least try to follow every possible lead…give myself every possible chance of discovering the truth. Even if it means meeting with people I'm convinced I won't like.'

Her life had been turned on its head when she'd lost her job—and not just her job but her boyfriend too. And then being given the news of her grandmother's death—a grandmother she hadn't known existed…

He understood her need to regain some control, and he admired her for shifting her focus and striving to win her dream job. She was determined to come back bigger, better and stronger. And he wanted to help her.

'He might try to extort money from you in return for information.'

Her nose curled. 'I hadn't considered that.'

He leaned towards her, sandwiching her hands lightly between his. 'Don't go alone. Let me come with you.'

Her relief was palpable. 'I was hoping you'd say that. I'd really appreciate it. I wasn't going to ask…you've done so much already—'

'We're friends, Callie. It's what friends do.'

Just for a moment her gaze caught on his mouth. Her lips parted and her breath hitched and every red-blooded cell in his body fired to life.

She snapped away, slipping her hands from his. 'Oh, is that the time? I need to pop out and grab some bits and pieces for the party.'

She wouldn't meet his eyes as she rattled on about the chores she had to do, and he bit back a curse.

'Is it okay if I leave Barney with you for another couple of hours?'

'Of course. Is there anything I can help with?'

She shook her head, but finally sent him a smile. 'It's mostly under control. Everyone I've invited is coming. You will be there at seven to help me greet everyone, won't you?'

'You bet.' Her party was this coming weekend. He'd even found himself kind of looking forward to it. 'Do you want to have dinner here tonight?' They'd fallen into the habit of her eating with him most evenings. He tried to keep his voice casual. 'It won't be anything fancy—just pasta.'

Her eyes dropped again. 'Thanks, Owen, but not tonight. Barney and I are having a quiet night in. I need to wash my hair.'

It was for the best. He knew it was. But that didn't stop him wishing otherwise or having to fight the urge to change her mind. He—

'Owen?'

He dropped back with a thud. 'Sorry, what were you saying?'

Her smile was gentle. 'Just thanking you again for... that.' She gestured to his computer.

'No problem at all. I'll see you later, Callie.' He pulled his chair across to the computer and opened a work file. He didn't glance at her again. 'You can let yourself out, right?'

'Right,' she echoed.

She was right. They needed to start spending less time together, not more. If he wasn't careful, when Callie left New York he'd find a hole had been left in his life—one he'd never be able to fill—and he wasn't opening himself up to that kind of heartache. Neither he nor Callie needed trouble.

* * *

Owen glanced around Callie's apartment, alive with music and people, chatter and laughter.

'So, after I'd read the letter she slid beneath the door,' Stuart was saying, 'I felt that darned ashamed of myself that I did a whip-around and we bought her that plant as a housewarming gift.'

A large cheese plant in a cheery white pot, with a big yellow polka dot ribbon tied around its base, sat in pride of place on a low table by the front door.

Stu was the third person that evening to tell him about the letter. Apparently Callie had written to each of the residents, informing them of the deal she'd made with Owen in relation to the apartment block, assuring them that nothing would change. She'd done it in plain, unadorned English, without fuss or fanfare, and she couldn't have found a better way to endear herself to the little community.

Stu pointed. 'Look, there's Angus.' He waved over the proprietor of the local bar, The Three Bells.

Owen stared at him. 'How do you know Callie?'

Angus clapped him on the shoulder. 'She's been unofficially tutoring Micah and some of her pals in the afternoons.'

Micah from the park was Angus's daughter? How had he never made the connection?

'And in return I've been plying her with some of New York's finest craft ales.'

That made him laugh. 'You've discovered her fondness for beer?'

'She has a very discerning palate,' he said with a grin, glancing around. 'Micah and her friends should be here somewhere.' He lifted his hand in a wave when he spotted them. 'I promised Lian I wouldn't let them stay out too late.'

Stu and Angus ambled off to top up their drinks. Owen glanced over at Josephine, Eliza and Betty, but they were in animated discussion with Claude and Jilly from downstairs. So he made his way across to Mr Singh, who sat on the sofa with Barney.

'How are you holding up, Mr S?' he asked, lowering himself down beside the older man carefully, so as to not jolt him. It was only his second day out of hospital. Both he and Callie were keeping a close eye on him, not wanting him to wear himself out.

'It's done these old bones good to come out to a party. It's been a long time…' He trailed off. 'She's a grand girl.'

He followed the older man's gaze to where Callie was busy refreshing her guests' drinks. She wore a dark red dress that was neither showy nor racy, but still somehow managed to shout exuberance and good cheer. When she turned too quickly the skirt would flare out, giving beguiling glimpses of her thighs. Owen had spent a significant portion of his evening doing his best not to notice. Likewise, he tried to ignore how the line of buttons that went from the vee of her neckline to mid-thigh made his fingers tingle.

'She's promised to come walking with me and Barney every day.' He ruffled the dog's ears. 'She says she misses him. I know it's just an excuse. She has a kind heart. But she shouldn't be wasting her time on an old man like me.'

'Don't let her hear you saying that. She doesn't consider spending time with you and Barney a hardship. She likes you. You'll be short-changing her and yourself if you think otherwise.'

'Ah, lad, you've a kind heart too. You and Callie are two of a kind.'

Something squeezed tight in Owen's chest—something hot and sweet and intense and gentle and carnal all at the same time.

He glanced at Callie and his mouth went dry. Straightening, he stared about the apartment—really stared. While it couldn't be denied that the new coat of paint had freshened it up, everything else remained the same—the configuration of the furniture, the ornaments and vases and knick-knacks, the pictures on the walls—and yet the apartment seemed completely different. *Transformed.* And that was due to its new occupant. Callie had a life and vitality that infused the place, as well as the people around her.

Yearning drilled through him. Not just the hot edge of desire and attraction, but something quieter and stronger. The pulse in his throat started to pound. The longer he gazed at her, the clearer everything became. Frances had been imprisoned by fear and regret. Wasn't he in danger of making the same mistake?

A woman had betrayed his trust and he'd allowed that one act to cast him adrift on an ocean of suspicion and mistrust. Even though he knew Callie wasn't like Fiona, wasn't after his money or the financial security he could give her, he continued to hold tight to his…his *prejudice*—he couldn't think what else to call it—because it had helped him to feel safe.

His hands clenched and unclenched. Safety hadn't brought Frances happiness.

The hardness he'd been carrying like a ball of concrete inside him melted now, as if it were nothing but wax, spreading warmth and a new sense of possibility through him.

He wanted Callie—and not just for a fling. Finally he had the courage to admit that to himself. He didn't want to lose her when she started her new job. And…wouldn't that job mean she'd be based in the States? Between research trips she'd have to live somewhere, so why not right here, where she'd already formed a community?

He didn't have a crystal ball. He couldn't predict where things between them might lead. But instinct told him that if he didn't fight for Callie now he'd regret it for the rest of his life. He trusted his instincts again now, with a fierceness he refused to dismiss.

Callie glanced up when the apartment door opened and a bubble of something light and happy rose through her when she saw it was Owen, returning after having organised cabs for the last of the partygoers. She'd been aware of him all evening—intensely aware—and her awareness didn't dissipate now, even though the crowd had.

He grinned, and she did her best to keep her feet on the ground and not float up towards the ceiling.

'Your librarian friends are going to have sore heads tomorrow,' he said.

She concentrated on collecting up paper plates to put in the recycling. 'So are a few people in the apartment block. I'll be tiptoeing around in the morning, so I don't disturb Jean below.'

She straightened and pressed her hands into the small of her back. She'd been on her feet all evening, and felt as if she hadn't stopped. Yet when Owen looked at her like that—all warmth and admiration—energy flowed back into her limbs and she swore she could dance till dawn.

'It went well, don't you think? Most people seemed to have a nice time.'

He laughed and started gathering up glasses. 'Callie, it was a major success. Everyone had a ball. I can't remember the last time I was in a room with that many people who all looked happy to be there. How many guests did you have—forty…fifty?'

'Give or take.' She rolled her eyes in mock exasperation. 'When was the last time you were actually in a room with forty or fifty people?'

He paused, consternation chasing across his face.

'Hey…' She almost reached out to touch his arm, but that seemed unwise. 'I was only joking.'

He shook himself. 'It's a long time since I've been to a party.'

'They're not really your thing, huh?' She'd sensed that the moment she'd told him she was throwing one, but he hadn't complained or tried to get out of it. He'd been a good sport.

'I enjoyed this one, though.'

She found herself dangerously happy about that.

They cleaned the apartment in silence for a bit. When she told him he didn't have to help, he waved her protests aside. She didn't protest again. She liked having him here.

'What was the last party you did go to?' she asked eventually.

He tied a knot in the top of the last garbage bag before turning back to face her. 'My engagement party.'

Gah! Talk about putting her foot in it.

His eyebrow lifted. 'You?'

'Oh…um…a few colleagues at the university threw a leaving party for me.' She grimaced. 'It wasn't the best party I've ever been to. I wasn't exactly in a party mood at the time.' She moistened dry lips. 'I'm sorry about your engagement, Owen.' She dug out a smile. 'Would you like a beer?' She'd been careful not to drink too much tonight. 'I think we've earned one.'

'Sure.'

They collapsed on the sofa, side by side, and in unison kicked their shoes off and lifted their feet to the coffee table.

He took the top off her beer and handed it to her. 'The fact I enjoyed tonight's party more than my own engagement party probably tells you all you need to know.'

'Like you said before, at least, unlike Frances, you didn't marry your mistake. And I can't tell you how glad I am I kicked my own mistake to the kerb back in Australia.'

They clinked bottles and drank.

'You want to know something odd? Tonight I realised I wasn't angry any more. Somewhere along the line I've chalked Fiona up to experience.'

She stared at him. *Really?* How had he done that? She was still fuming about Dominic. 'What happened between the two of you?' She held her breath and waited. If he didn't want to talk about it, she wouldn't pursue it.

He stilled, a strange light in his eyes. 'You really want to know?'

With a dry mouth, she nodded. 'But, I mean, if you don't want to talk about it…'

'I'm happy to share the gory details, if you're interested.'

Had she imagined the inflection on the word *interested*?

'It started out much the same as a lot of relationships, I guess. We met through mutual friends and hit it off. She's one of those impossibly beautiful society women—polished, charming, always knows what to say.'

'I hate her already.'

He chuckled.

Callie tried to not stare. His mouth had lost the hard edge it usually wore when he spoke of his ex. 'How did you find her out?'

'I startled her one afternoon. I walked into the apartment we shared and she closed the lid of her laptop a bit too quickly, as if she didn't want me to see what she'd been reading. It sent alarm bells off in my head.' He pursed his lips. 'It wasn't the first time, and I couldn't shake the feeling something was…off. Anyway, the doorbell rang and it was her bridesmaids, and they all went off for a dress fitting. When she was gone, I had a look at her browsing history.'

What on earth had he found that could have damned the other woman so completely? 'What did you find?'

'She'd been researching the best lawyers for divorce settlements.'

Callie's hand flew to her mouth.

'So I waited a couple of days and then told her that my business was in trouble, and as a result we'd have to down-scale both the wedding and where we'd planned to live.'

'How did she take that?'

'Went ballistic and told me if she couldn't have the wedding she'd always dreamed of she wouldn't marry me.'

'Nice to see she was so supportive!'

'I told her then that I knew she'd been researching divorce lawyers and settlements, and that her reaction to my supposed financial woes spoke volumes. That's when it got ugly.' He kinked an eyebrow at Callie. 'She isn't the kind of woman who's used to not getting her own way, and she let me have it with both barrels. Apparently the deal was she'd get my money while I got the satisfaction of marrying up.'

'Marrying...*up*?' Callie spluttered. What was wrong with these entitled people? Her mother had been right!

He rested his head against the back of the sofa. 'Apparently she planned to use my money to save her family's fortune. Once that was done she planned to divorce me—and take me for everything she could get, of course.'

'Of course...' she echoed faintly.

'A child featured in this plan of hers too.' For the briefest of moments his mouth tightened. 'She planned to get pregnant and...'

She'd planned to use their child as a weapon against him? 'Oh, Owen.' No wonder he was so damn gun-shy now when it came to relationships. 'I'm sorry. What a dreadful experience. I—'

'All I can see now, though, is what a lucky escape I had. And you've reminded me that not all women—in fact not even the majority—are out for what they can get. I find myself...weirdly grateful.'

'Which is better than being bitter,' she agreed slowly.

'And I've been meaning to thank you for something else too.'

She took a sip of beer, trying to ignore the latent power of his body that was starting to sing a siren song to her. 'Oh?'

'I had a good talk with Lissy and sorted everything out.'

'I'm so glad!' His half-sister was smart and sassy, and she'd quickly become one of Callie's favourite people. Besides their shopping trip, they'd also spent a day in the city sightseeing, plus had another two dinner-and-movie nights at Owen's.

'She was taken in by Fiona too—totally fooled by her. Until Fiona *"tactfully—"'* he made air quotes '—told Lissy that she was taking up too much of my time, was too demanding, and that maybe it was time for her to grow up a bit and stand on her own two feet.'

Callie's feet slammed to the floor. 'She did *what*? What a complete and utter—'

'I know.'

'I hope you told Lissy that any woman who treats her like that isn't worth your time of day, and is not someone you want to be in a relationship with, and…and…'

He reached out and squeezed her hand. 'I did. We sorted everything out. I've also promised to do my best to stop being such an overbearing, bossy big brother. We're good, Callie.' He squeezed her hand again. 'And that's because of you. Thank you.'

She should pull her hand from his. She should, but she didn't want to.

'So I've been thinking…' he started. 'If you get this job—and I think it's a sure thing given your video—'

'It would help if I could find out who my father is,' she inserted.

'Well, I've been thinking…you'd be based in the States, right?'

She nodded.

'Does that mean you'll stay in New York?'

Something in his tone had her lifting her gaze from the sparkly purple nail polish on her toes to his deep smoky gaze. 'I…I don't know. I haven't thought that far ahead.'

'Tonight I realised that in the month you've been living in this apartment you've built a nice little community here. It'd be a shame to uproot yourself and start over somewhere new.'

She opened her mouth. She closed it again. If she could live in any part of America… 'This tiny bit of New York feels a lot like home,' she said slowly, realising it was true.

With infinite care, he lowered his feet to the rug, something in his gaze darkening and deepening. He set his beer on the coffee table and then took hers and set it beside it. 'Good.'

Her heart tried to beat a path out of her chest. 'Good…?'

One strong hand lifted to trace her cheek, while the other slid beneath her hair to cradle the back of her head.

'It's very good, Callie.'

His thumb traced her bottom lip, sensitising it until her breath hitched and the pulse in her throat fluttered.

'Owen?' His name was nothing more than a breath of a whisper.

'I find I don't want to say goodbye to you, Callie.'

And with that his mouth lowered to hers and she lifted her lips to meet it, helpless to resist the pull between them.

She'd expected the kiss to be slow and sweet, becoming hypnotically drugging as it deepened. It was nothing of the sort. The moment their mouths met they both fired to life—as if a current of pure energy had passed between them. Immediate hunger roared through her. Hunger that demanded satisfaction and release. *Now*.

Her fingers buried themselves in the thickness of his hair as she tried to draw him closer. His hands went to her waist and he lifted her into his lap, so she could straddle him and plaster herself against his chest in a move that felt like utter perfection. The alternative was for him to push her back into the sofa and cover her body with his but, while she hungered for that too, she appreciated the autonomy this move gave her, the sense of control.

Not that she *had* any control!

Drugging kiss after drugging kiss had her losing all sense of time. Owen kissed her with a single-minded focus that undid her completely and had her holding nothing back. She dragged his shirt from the waistband of his jeans to run her fingers across the hot, firm flesh beneath, and he hissed out a breath before raking his nails lightly up her thighs, now exposed as her dress rode high. She had to brace both hands against his ribs as a tremor shook through her.

Growing too impatient with the buttons on his shirt, she tore it open, buttons flying in every direction.

'I like your style.' He grinned at her—a lazy uplift of his lips that momentarily infuriated her because it hinted at a control she could no longer boast.

Lowering her head to one flat male nipple, she grazed it with her teeth, wiping the smirk from his face.

He swore softly, his hips bucking against hers. 'Callie.'

She ignored him to turn her attention to his other nipple until, with another oath, he snaked his hands beneath her dress to cup her buttocks and draw her more firmly against the hard length of him, thrusting up against her. A sob was dragged from her throat as light burst behind her eyelids, and her fingers dug into his biceps to keep her from falling.

'Callie.'

She obeyed the command in his voice to lift her head and meet his gaze. Then he stared at the row of buttons that ran down the length of her dress and his eyes darkened almost to black. Her fingers tightened against his biceps when he licked his lips.

'Undo your buttons.'

His words were part plea, part command, and all sin.

He made her feel powerful and wholly desirable. He made her want to slowly undo each button—to unwrap herself for him—until he was nearly out of his mind with need and greed and impatience. But if she did that there'd be no turning back.

The tips of his fingers had slipped beneath the edge of her panties and they caressed her bare skin, sending ripples of pleasure radiating outwards and making the very centre of her ache with need. She wanted those fingers exploring further, to more intimate places, but…

'I figure you'd be less than impressed if I tore all those buttons off that pretty dress.'

'No tearing,' she panted.

He stilled, as if sensing her hesitation. 'Do you want to stop?'

'No, I just…' She shook her head, trying to clear it. 'I can't help feeling we should think this through more. When we were at Ellerslie we said it was a bad idea…' It didn't feel like a bad idea. It felt like the answer to all her prayers. 'But the minute I—'

She slipped her top button undone. She hadn't meant to, but her fingers, it appeared, had other ideas. Owen swallowed, and she almost tore open the rest of the buttons then and there.

His fingers tightened on her buttocks, as if he were trying to get a grip on his own wayward desires, but in doing so he only fed hers.

'Callie, I have no answers about any of this. I only know I want to keep seeing you. I'm attracted to you—there's no denying that—but I like you too. I trust you. When I'm with you I'm…happy. Knowing you has made me feel hopeful again.'

How could she resist that? How could any woman resist it?

'I know you said this was the wrong time for you to start something new,' he went on, 'but I promise not to stand in the way of your job. I don't want to stand in the way of any of your dreams. But if you're planning to remain in the States then I don't see why we can't keep seeing each other.' He hauled in a breath. '*If* you want to.'

They could…

'We can take things as slowly as you like. I've no desire to rush you. We can stop right now if that's what you want.'

She didn't want to stop. And everything he'd just said sounded perfect.

Her fingers went back to her buttons and she slid each one from its buttonhole with fingers that were suddenly sure. His lips parted with undisguised hunger when she pushed the dress from her shoulders to pool at her waist. If possible, the bulge pressing at the juncture of her thighs grew bigger and harder when she unclasped her bra and dropped it to the floor behind her.

His expression made her feel like the most desirable woman on earth.

'Utter perfection,' he murmured, his gaze caressing her skin before he leaned forward and drew one nipple into the heat of his mouth, suckling hard.

Callie cried out, arching into him, her fingers digging into his shoulders, urging him on.

'I only date exclusively.' He laved her nipple with his tongue, sending a cataclysm of delight dancing across her skin. 'If you can't agree to that then we need to stop before this goes any further.'

When he pulled her other nipple into his mouth, grazing it gently with his teeth with such loving attention, she surrendered utterly. 'When you do that, Owen,' she gasped, 'you can have anything you damn well please.'

* * *

Owen knew the exact moment Callie woke. He registered her sleepy realisation that she wasn't alone, the slight pucker of her brows and then the clearing of her frown. She opened her eyes and her smile came without hesitation.

'Good morning.'

Her husky morning voice could devastate a mere mortal, and Owen felt himself falling hard. Not that he had any intention of saying as much and scaring the living daylights out of her.

Instead he grinned back. 'Good morning.'

And then he kissed her, revelling in her warm sweetness and the way she pulled him closer, as if she couldn't get enough of him. He couldn't stop his hands from roving over her delectable curves. Not that he tried too hard to resist the temptation. They'd made love several times last night, but the way her clever hands touched him—a deliberate boldness and teasing flirtatiousness, mixed with wonder and hunger—undid him.

Nobody had ever touched him like that before—as if his body had been made for her hands alone. And he made love to her again now with a newfound tenderness, losing himself in her breathless sighs and the way she whispered his name. She cried out as she came apart in his arms and light splintered behind his eyelids as he followed her into a kaleidoscope of ecstasy more intense than any he'd ever experienced.

It took a long time for their breathing to return to normal. He turned his head on the pillow to find her curled up on her side, watching him. Late morning sunshine spilled into the room, highlighting the creamy warmth of her skin and the rosy plumpness of her mouth.

'Okay?' he murmured.

'Very okay. You?'

'Never better.'

She frowned, but it wasn't the kind of frown to reach her eyes. 'I'm happy.'

He reached out to trace a finger along her cheek. 'That surprises you?'

'I thought I might wake up this morning with…'

His chest clenched. 'Regrets?' Had he pushed too hard last night? Should he have given her more time?

'Not regrets. I was never going to regret making love with you, Owen.'

He was glad she called it *making love* rather than *sleeping with* or *hooking up* or any of those other less intimate terms. Because what they'd done had felt intimate—not casual or temporary.

'I just thought I might wake worried about the future and wondering if we'd made a mistake or feeling as if we'd rushed into this.'

'But you don't?'

'I just feel…happy.'

It was enough for now.

He forced himself out of bed and reached for his jeans, though he almost launched himself back into bed at the heat in her gaze as it roved over his naked body. Instead he concentrated on drawing his jeans up over his hips without doing himself an injury.

'Do you have plans for the day?'

She shook her head.

'Hungry?'

'Starving.'

'Then let me take you to brunch. Frankie's is the best deli in New York. They do blueberry pancakes that will have you thinking you've died and gone to heaven.'

'Sounds fab.'

'I'll head downstairs for a shower.' He pressed a kiss to her lips. 'Why don't you head on down when—?'

His gaze caught on the stack of letters on Callie's bedside table. Callie's letters from Frances. *Unopened.*

He glanced back at her and she bit her lip, some of the light leaving her eyes. 'I just…' Her fingers pleated the sheet. 'I just haven't been able to.'

A burn started up deep in his chest. She'd had so much to come to terms with in the last few weeks.

'Owen, just for today, can we not talk about it?'

He reached out to touch her face. 'Deal. Today is just about you and me.'

'Thank you.'

Her smile was the only reward he needed. 'I'll see you downstairs whenever you're ready?'

She nodded, her eyes sparkling again.

He hummed all the way down to his basement apartment. And if he sensed his progress being noted by several residents in the block, it didn't perturb him in the slightest.

CHAPTER TEN

'YOU'RE SURE ABOUT THIS?'

Callie glanced across the serving of hot chips lying on greaseproof paper between her and Owen and forced herself to nod. She mightn't have much enthusiasm for this upcoming appointment, but she had every intention of going through with it and meeting Frances's second husband, Richard Bateman.

The last four days had passed in a bubble of exhilaration and bliss. She and Owen had spent most of that time laughing and making love. And he'd shown her all his favourite haunts in Greenwich and the West Village. It had been perfect—as if she'd suddenly remembered how to have fun again after a hundred years of misery and gloom. Which didn't make sense. So little of her life had been either miserable or gloomy.

She stole a glance at him. She couldn't shake a sense of unease—as if this thing between them was too perfect and couldn't possibly last.

Don't be daft! How can anything be too perfect?

She tried to calm the sudden pounding of her heart. She hadn't embarked on this relationship either too quickly or with too little forethought. Why should she have hesitated? Owen was ten times the man Dominic was. She *loved* spending time with him.

'Are you sure you're okay?' he asked. 'You're very quiet.'

She forced herself to smile. 'I'm fine. Just…taking it all in.'

They'd arrived in Larchmont ninety minutes ago, and Owen had driven her around the pretty harbour. They'd walked down the main street, with its assortment of boutiques, bakeries and delis. They'd taken some video footage—just in case. And now they'd settled on the grass in the park with a view of the beach to eat their lunch of what she called chips and he called fries.

The town was lovely—really pretty. The company was great. In fact, the company was the best ever. The sun shone and the air was warmer and more fragrant than she'd so far experienced while she'd been in America. But her appetite had deserted her. And, although he smiled, Owen couldn't hide the concern in his eyes.

An answering anxiety churned in her stomach. 'Look,' she started, 'neither of us is expecting to like Richard, but I can't see what harm he can do us. Besides, what happened between him and Frances took place a long time ago.'

'He could try to charm money out of you.'

'I mean to try to charm information out of him.'

'You think he has any?'

'Probably not.' She pressed her hands together. 'It just feels as if this is my last lead.'

You still have Frances's letters.

She pushed that thought aside. She hadn't been able to overcome her reluctance to read them yet.

'So I have to follow it through.'

'For the job?'

'And my own peace of mind.'

He nodded, and she knew he understood. But questions continued to plague her, and she couldn't help but wonder what would happen when she found out the answers. She wanted to know the identity of her father, and she wouldn't rest now until she discovered it. But just as importantly she wanted to find out what had happened between her mother and her grandmother all those years ago.

If Richard couldn't shed any light on that she'd resolved to ask her mother. How else would she be able to decide whether or not to keep the inheritance Frances had left her?

But… She glanced at Owen. If she didn't keep it, how would he react? He wouldn't be happy—that much was certain. But would it bring their perfect love affair crashing down around their ears? Would he make it a condition—accept Frances's legacy or else he'd break things off between them?

She rubbed a hand across her heart. Surely not. He'd never be that unreasonable. But, no matter how severely she told herself that, a part of her remained unconvinced. Owen had loved Frances as if she'd been his own flesh and blood. Callie couldn't compete with that.

'What if he does know something and you don't like what he has to say? What if he tells you your father is a nasty piece of work?' Owen asked.

They were questions she'd repeatedly asked herself. 'I fully expect my father to be wholly unlikable. Why else would my mother keep his existence a secret? But I'm no longer a child that needs protecting.'

He shook his head again, but his lips lifted and his admiration buoyed her. 'You must want this job really badly.'

She thought of Dominic, and the way he'd gnash his teeth when he found out that she'd landed his dream job. His face, though, was hard to bring to mind.

'*Mystery Family Trees* asks its celebrity guests to do exactly this. I mean the underlying premise of the show is to illustrate history on a personal level, as a kind of living and breathing entity, but it can become extremely personal for the person whose family is being traced. It can be uplifting, but it can also be shocking. What kind of hypocrite would I be if I refused to follow through on my own family tree, just because I might not like the answers I find?'

She pushed her shoulders back.

'I'm doing this for my own curiosity as much as to get the job. I've come too far to turn back. But I understand if you don't want to meet Richard. You can drop me off and I'll text you once I'm ready to leave.'

Owen reached across and took her hand. 'Sweetheart, there's no way I'm leaving you to do this on your own. I'll be with you every step of the way.'

His reassurance and the warmth in his eyes had her chin lifting. With Owen beside her she felt as if she could achieve anything. She was on the cusp of a new life—a new job, living in a new place—and she was falling for the kind of guy she'd only ever dreamed about. It was all there, just waiting for her, and she wasn't going to mess it up.

Half an hour later Owen pulled the car into the driveway of a large and very beautiful house. Callie's pulse thudded. 'It's not exactly a shabby pile of bricks, is it?'

'Larchmont isn't exactly a shabby little town.'

He could say that again—and Richard's house looked as if it might be one of the town's most desirable residences. It was a turn-of-the-century colonial mansion, with stained-glass windows, and a deep front porch that oozed charm and tranquillity. And then she remembered how he'd acquired this home—by taking Frances to the cleaners.

She swung to Owen. 'Remember the plan.'

His lip curled. 'Yeah, yeah. Be charming, be polite, find out what we can. Don't call him names, don't accuse him of anything, don't punch him on the nose.'

'He's in his sixties and you're in your thirties. You can't hit the man. Besides…' she turned to stare at the house again '…it's hard to know what goes on inside other people's marriages. You heard all that Eliza, Betty and Josephine had to say.' She said the words as much for herself as for Owen. 'It's obvious that Frances could be stubborn. She might not have been an easy person to be married to.'

His warm hand closed over hers and the smile he gave

when she met his gaze had her heart turning over in her chest. She was glad he was here with her.

'Do you always try to see the good in other people?' he asked.

'I…' Did she do that? She hoped so. 'Come on. Let's do this before I chicken out. The sooner it's over, the sooner…'

'You can continue your search for your father.'

'The sooner we can go back to your place for the pizza you promised me and stretch out on your sofa and…kick back.'

A wicked gleam lit his eyes. 'Or we could kick back in my bed.'

She sucked her bottom lip into her mouth to stop herself smiling too broadly. 'To…um…*talk*.' But she inflected the word *talk* with so much extra meaning those teasing lips of Owen's widened even further.

'Because I'm such a good communicator,' he agreed.

She started to laugh, and it helped to dispel her nerves.

He slipped a hand beneath her hair and drew her face close to his. 'Hold that thought,' he murmured.

And then he kissed her—a brief, blistering kiss that had her blood pumping and heat rushing into her cheeks.

He eased back, his eyes travelling over her face as if he couldn't get enough of her. He nodded towards the house. 'Ready?'

She pulled in a breath and reluctantly eased away. 'Ready.'

The moment the door opened and she came face to face with Richard she could see why Frances had fallen for him. The man had charisma, and even at sixty-one he was still ridiculously good-looking. His greeting was effusive, and he was all charm, but Callie sensed that his charm was too practised, too calculated…and beneath the glittering cheerfulness in his too-blue eyes she sensed wariness.

When they were seated with coffee and cake in a conservatory that overlooked the canal—a magnificently peaceful view—he turned to Callie. 'So you're Frances's granddaughter?'

She nodded.

'I will confess myself surprised by your email.'

Gut instinct told her to not prevaricate or pretend she didn't know his and Frances's history. 'Because of the way your marriage to Frances ended?'

'Precisely. But what you have to understand, my dear, is that one only experiences that kind of acrimony, that intensity of feeling, when they have loved greatly. And Frances and I did love each other very much.'

Ooh, the man was oily. But two could play this game. She leaned towards him. 'You know, that's what I thought. I saw the photos of your wedding and the two of you looked so happy.'

He pretended to wipe away a tear. 'We were, my dear, we were.'

She made commiserating noises. 'I only learned about Frances when, upon her death, I was informed I'd inherited a substantial fortune. I feel as if I've missed out on so much.'

His eyes gleamed briefly at the mention of Frances's money and she knew she had the man pegged correctly. He was a fortune-hunter, and if he thought there was money to be made from her he'd do all that he could to take advantage of it.

Silently she thanked Owen for insisting on accompanying her. Not that she couldn't have done this on her own. Of course she could. But his support made her feel less vulnerable.

'That's why I'm trying to put together as clear a picture as I can of Frances.'

For an infinitesimal moment, he stilled. 'Your mother never spoke of her?'

'Never.'

He gave a gusty sigh. 'Frannie was never the same after her falling-out with Donna. I believe it's the reason our marriage failed. I'd turned my face towards the future, but Frances couldn't help but keep looking back.'

'That must've been very hard for you,' she said, careful to ooze sympathy rather than call the man any of the names that pressed against the back of her throat. Beside her Owen shifted restlessly, and she put a hand on his knee to temper the frustration she sensed rippling through him.

'It was.'

He shook his head ruefully, but she was aware of the way those practised eyes assessed her.

'Frances froze me out. And I'll be the first to admit I didn't deal with it in the most mature manner possible.'

He could say that again!

She took a hasty sip of coffee. 'These things happen.' She let a pause stretch and then said, 'I know it's a lot to ask of you, Mr—'

'Richard,' he ordered smoothly.

She simpered, but threw up a little bit in her mouth as she did so. 'Richard. It's just…my mother has never spoken about that time at all.' She opened her eyes and knew she looked the absolute picture of naive candour, but she felt no compunction using such tricks on the man. 'I feel as if a whole part of my history is missing.'

'Of course you do, my dear.'

He reached across and patted her hand, and she had to steel herself not to recoil.

'I understand that Donna caused you and Frances a great deal of trouble?' She sent him her most commiserating smile. 'I suspect she never took you into her confidence, but…'

He leaned towards her—all concern and encouragement. She could almost see the dollar signs in his eyes.

'But…?'

'But she never told me who my father was, and I wondered if you…maybe…had any idea…?'

Her voice wobbled as she spoke, and this time it wasn't feigned. That took her off guard. Did she care who this man was on a personal level? Did she have some secret hope of forming a relationship with her unknown father?

As if sensing her inner turmoil, Owen covered her hand with his. She took heart at his silent support.

Richard hesitated. Then, 'Do you mean your father any harm, Callie?'

She followed her gut instinct again. 'Absolutely not! I hope… Well, I hardly know what I hope. But it'd be so very nice to meet him, and maybe even forge some kind of relationship with him.'

'It heartens me to hear you say that.'

Something inside her tightened. 'So you do know who he is?'

'Why, yes, my dear.'

Her head rocked back. Her breathing grew short and shallow.

He spread his arms wide. 'My dear girl, *I'm* your father.'

She froze. So did Owen. She wanted to shout *I don't believe you*, but she couldn't get the words out past the lump in her throat.

He nodded, as if sensing her disbelief. 'It's come as a shock, I see. The thing is, I was dating your mother before I met Frances. In fact, it's through Donna that I met Frances. Of course, once Frannie and I clapped eyes on each other…' He shrugged awkwardly, but beamed as if nothing could make greater sense.

He'd torn her family apart and *that* was all he had to say?

Callie's stomach rebelled at the coffee she'd just drunk and it took all her strength to battle the nausea that threatened to overset her. Richard had used Donna to target

Frances. It was unspoken, but implicit in his words. And Frances… Her head started to pound. Frances had stolen her own daughter's boyfriend.

'I suspect you'll want proof, and I'm happy to undergo a paternity test.'

She didn't want this man as her father!

'But, in the interim, here's a letter from your mother. I dug it out because I thought you might like to see it. I think it'll help dispel your doubts.'

She took the envelope he handed to her. With numb fingers, she pulled out the mercifully brief missive inside.

Richard,
A marriage based on lies is no marriage at all. You know the truth—you know the child I carry is yours. I beg of you, please do the right thing and tell Mother.
*   If you deny your child again, you won't be able to undo the chain of events it will set in motion.*

It was merely signed, *Donna.*

Callie ran her fingers over the words. 'This is my mother's handwriting.'

She passed the letter to Owen. He read it in silence before handing it back.

Richard shook his head when she went to give it back to him. 'You keep it, Callie. Ask your mother about it.'

She folded it and replaced it in its envelope, moistening dry lips, feeling her heart pounding in time with her headache. 'You never told Frances the truth?'

'To my everlasting shame, no.' He actually sounded truly regretful. 'By that stage I was in too deep. I was in love with Frances—'

Liar. He'd been in love with her money.

'And she'd never have spoken to me again if she'd known

the truth. I'd already sworn to her that my relationship with Donna had never become physical.'

Her stomach gave a sick roll. 'Didn't Donna tell her?'

'I said that Donna was lying. And Frances chose to believe me.'

Callie's hands had started to shake. Owen leaned across and took one of them in his. She held on as if he were a lifeline. 'Why are you telling me this, Richard? You have to realise it paints you in a dreadful light.'

'If we're to forge a relationship, my dear, I understand that I have to tell you the truth. I have to be honest with you in a way I was never honest with Frances. I don't want to make the same mistakes that I did in the past. You have to understand that back then I felt I was in a no-win situation. If I'd told Frances the truth she'd have cancelled the wedding. And I knew Donna would never take me back again.'

You think?

'There was everything to lose. What was there to gain in telling the truth?'

'A daughter?'

He sighed a gusty sigh and it was all she could do to suppress a shudder. He hadn't wanted a relationship with her back then and he didn't want one now. He wanted a relationship with her inheritance.

'I'm a reformed character, Callie. I've wondered and thought about you every day. And here's my chance to finally make amends.'

'You're wrong.' She stood. 'I could never have a relationship—any kind of relationship—with a man like you.'

She turned and strode out without a backward glance.

Owen slid a homemade pizza onto the table, along with garlic bread and a green salad, but Callie made no move to put any of it on her plate. Not even so much as a lettuce leaf, though she'd barely eaten a thing at lunch. Her eyes had lost their customary sparkle, her lips drooped at the corners, and her pallor caught at his heart.

He slid into the seat opposite. 'Lissy claims this is the best pizza in all of New York.'

Callie started, and blinked before seizing a slice of pizza and piling salad onto her plate. 'It looks delicious.'

But she didn't start eating.

He grabbed a slice of pizza too. 'Callie, I know Richard's revelation has come as a huge shock, but you need to eat something.'

She shook herself. 'Absolutely.' She speared lettuce with her fork and put it into her mouth, chewed and swallowed. Biting into the pizza, she did the same—chewing and swallowing mechanically—but he doubted she tasted a thing.

She didn't wax lyrical about his pizza-making skills or give him exaggeratedly over-the-top compliments. He didn't need them, of course, but it was out of character, and he watched her in growing concern.

Her shock didn't appear to be easing. In fact, it was as if she had a ticking time bomb inside her, waiting to explode. All he wanted to do was pull her into his arms and tell her everything would be fine.

Except he couldn't guarantee that, could he?

When she realised he was watching her, she pasted on a smile. 'I'm trying to work out how best to frame this revelation in my little documentary.'

He tried to hide his horror. 'You're going to make that revelation public?'

'It'll hardly be public. It's just for the interview. It's not like I'm putting it out there on social media.' She thrust out her jaw. 'Besides, I've done nothing to be ashamed of. Making it public won't hurt me.'

'But what about your mother? What about Frances?'

She shot to her feet, fury suddenly glittering in her eyes.

'Why the hell should I protect Frances? After what she did to my mother…'

She strode away from the table, giving up all pretence of eating, and he did too. He watched her carefully, waiting for her tears to fall; ready to pull her into his arms and give her whatever comfort he could the moment she needed him to. This had been such a shock. It had rocked him to the soles of his feet. And it had to be ten times worse for her.

She stood with her back to him, hugging herself, and his heart went out to her. Before he could move across to pull her against him, she spun around.

'If you still want to buy the apartment block, Owen, then feel free to start proceedings. I'm not accepting anything from that woman.'

That woman being Frances, he presumed.

He did what he could to drag a steadying breath into his lungs. 'Callie, I know you feel betrayed, but can't you see that Frances was as much a victim of Richard's manipulations as your mother?'

'Really?' She folded her arms and stuck out a hip. 'Tell me how you'd feel if this situation ever occurred between your mother and Lissy?'

His head rocked back.

'What? You don't think it could ever happen?'

'Not while Jack's alive,' he croaked.

She glanced away. He saw the way her fingers dug into her upper arms and was afraid she'd leave bruises.

'Callie, both Donna and Frances were wrong about Richard—but, like you said, everyone makes mistakes in love. Frances paid a heavy price for hers.'

'She chose a man over her own daughter—her own flesh and blood. I wouldn't expect my mother to ever forgive her, and what's more I don't blame her. I don't forgive her either.'

'It's not your injury to forgive.'

She blinked.

'The harm was done to your mother, not you. But that's beside the point. I just don't want you making a decision you might come to regret once you've had a chance to mull things over and think about it with a clearer head.'

She slammed her hands to her hips. 'If I follow your logic, I should give Richard the benefit of the doubt too. After all, maybe he just made a mistake as well?'

In her anger, she was twisting his words. 'We both know the man is a predator—' his hands clenched '—a loathsome worm.'

'*Exactly*. And maybe Frances was too!'

With a superhuman effort, he reined in his temper. Callie was in shock and lashing out.

'Until today you'd started to develop a fondness for Frances. You know she wasn't all bad. She was duped by a cad who—' he searched his mind for a way to reach her '—stole her power.'

She pointed a finger at him. 'That's exactly what I'm trying to get back—my power. I refuse to let Frances or Richard or…or anyone else stop me from doing that.'

Including him? Was that what she meant? Was that what she thought he was trying to do?

'Dominic stole my power when he had me fired.'

'You weren't fired!' He didn't know why he yelled the words, knew only that he couldn't help himself. 'Your contract wasn't renewed. There's a difference.'

'A mere technicality!' She hitched up her chin. 'You want to know why he did it?'

She'd gone so suddenly still his mouth went dry. 'Why?'

'He applied for the same job on the Australian version of *Mystery Family Trees* that I'm applying for here in the States.'

He froze, presentiment trailing an icy finger down his spine.

'When he didn't get the job, I tried to cheer him up by

telling him he was an amazing researcher and a wonderful lecturer and that he already had a dream job.' Her lips twisted. 'I didn't realise how much he festered over that. Unbeknownst to me he took it as a sop to his ego, a meaningless banality that proved I didn't understand him. So he took my dream job away from me so I'd know exactly how it felt.'

Nausea rolled through him. 'What a despicable thing to have done. But—'

'When he finds out I've landed the job he coveted...'

Her eyes narrowed in what he assumed was imagined satisfaction, but a moment later she shook herself.

'My application needs to be in by the end of the week. I don't care if you approve or not, Owen, I'm putting what I found out today in my documentary.'

He ignored that. If she wanted to include Richard's shocking revelation that was her business, but... 'The TV job...' acid burned his stomach '...it *isn't* your dream job?'

She frowned. 'I never said it was. I just said I wanted it badly.'

He tried to get his head around what she was telling him. 'I thought...'

Revenge. His stomach dropped. This was all about revenge. She'd told him so in the lawyer's office the first day they'd met. He'd been a fool to forget it.

'So all this effort has been directed at getting back at a man who isn't worth the time of day rather than actually scoring your perfect job?'

She glared at him. 'It's about getting my power back.'

'This isn't about your power! If it was about power you'd be putting your best efforts into finding your *real* dream job—there's more than one university out there.' He felt himself go icy cold. 'This is about getting even. Which means you're hurting yourself more than you'll ever be hurting Dominic.'

Her nostrils flared. 'What do you know about anything? You've known me for a month. That doesn't make you an expert on what I want or need.'

'I know you love spending time with young people and helping them find their way forward, like you have with Lissy and the girls you've been tutoring. I know you like taking Barney for walks in the park because he always picks someone to demand pats from and that gives you an excuse to sit down and chat with a perfect stranger. You like connecting with people, Callie. Sure, you enjoy research. But for heaven's sake, you became best buds with four of the librarians you met at the public library. History is a living, breathing thing for you—not something dry and dusty and impersonal.'

Her mouth opened and closed, but no sound came out. She folded her arms and thrust out her chin, but the martial expression had started to drain from her eyes.

A hard ball lodged beneath his breastbone. 'And if you think you're going to get a chance to indulge your personal touch in this TV job then you're in for a rude awakening. You'll be working months ahead of schedule in heaven only knows what part of the country—probably racing here and there to find out the necessary answers. And as far as the producers are concerned, the juicier those answers are the better. You'll probably never even get to meet the people whose family trees you're tracing. You certainly won't be the one softening the blow of shocking or confrontational news.'

She stared at him, visibly at a loss for words.

His chest cramped, making his breath come hard and sharp. 'Are you still in love with him?'

'With who?' Her eyes widened. 'Dominic? *No!* Why would you even ask such a thing?'

'Because all this effort you're going to—it's as if you're seeking his attention.'

Her lips thinned. 'You couldn't be more wrong if you tried.'

'So it's about pride? He hurt your pride and now you want to get even and hurt his.' Couldn't she see how personally destructive that was?

Her eyes went cold and remote. 'You're starting to sound like just another man who's happy to tell a woman how wrong she is, how she's got her head into a silly little muddle, but never mind he'll fix it all for her—a man who's happy to steal a woman's power!'

He rocked back on his heels, the injustice of her words burning through him. 'If that's what you think, then we have nothing else to discuss.'

She paled, and he immediately regretted the words.

'I didn't mean that. Callie, I…'

She pulled in a breath that made her whole body shudder. 'I know you're not like that.' Some of the steel went out of her. 'Not really.'

What the hell did she mean, *not really*?

'I think you're angry because I refuse to see Frances through the same rose-coloured glasses you do,' she said.

He had to clamp his teeth against an angry retort. He didn't see Frances through rose-coloured glasses. He'd *known* her. And, despite what Callie thought, Frances had been a wonderful woman.

'You're judging Frances based on one mistake. You're not judging the whole woman. You're shutting your mind off to everything else she stood for.'

She gave a harsh laugh. 'You feel it's your duty to see her wishes through, but I'm not the least bit interested in accepting her blood money.'

His jaw started to ache.

'When it comes right down to it, Owen, who would you choose—Frances or me?'

The world felt as if it was suddenly spinning out of control, and he had no hope of preventing the collision that was about to happen. 'Do I have to make a choice? Because I will never be able to hate Frances.' His chest ached. 'So if that's what you're asking of me…'

'It's not.' She stared at him with troubled eyes. 'Yet I won't be able to do anything other than loathe her.'

The ache in his chest radiated outwards.

She pressed her hands together, swallowed and gave a tiny but decisive nod. 'I told you this was a really bad time for me to get involved with anyone.'

'What are you saying?' His words were nothing more than a croak.

Her voice wobbled. 'I'm applying for this job, Owen, whether you approve or not. And I'm not going to accept my inheritance. Can you live with that?'

He opened his mouth to argue with her further.

'One thing I do know for sure, Owen, is that I couldn't live with your silent disapproval and disappointment every time you looked at me. If you can't talk to me about Frances, and I can't talk to you about my work…'

'You're saying we're through?'

Her eyes filled, but her chin remained firm. 'I don't see that there's any other option.'

She didn't? He felt as if he'd been turned to ice.

'There's another option, Callie, but if you don't see it then you're right—there's nothing here worth saving.'

CHAPTER ELEVEN

A KNOCK SOUNDED on her door the following morning and Callie raced to answer it.

Owen.

She stared at him and her heart pounded in her chest like a wild thing. She wanted him to take her in his arms, tell her he was sorry about their fight, and kiss her. She wanted him to tell her there was another way, and that their relationship wasn't doomed before it had even started. She wanted him to tell her he loved her.

The revelation knocked her sideways. Her fingers closed around the frame of the door in a death grip to keep her upright.

He did none of those things. He stood there stiffly, staring back at her with eyes that burned—as if *she'd* dealt *him* a mortal blow when it was *him* who was trying to control *her* and *her* choices. Her eyes stung and her throat ached. She wasn't letting anyone take her power away again, regardless of how much she liked them—*loved* them.

His nostrils flared. 'I came to make sure you're okay after yesterday.'

Of course she wasn't okay! They'd had the worst fight in the history of the world and—

'Finding out Richard is your father must've been the most awful shock.'

Oh, that. Her shoulders ached with the effort of keeping them from crumpling. 'I'm fine.'

He looked far from convinced.

'I never expected to like my father and I was right. I never harboured any secret fantasies that he'd be a good guy. It's just now I know the truth.'

He shoved his hands into his pockets, his shoulders as stiff and uncompromising as the line of his mouth. 'I wanted to let you know that if you need anything you can still rely on me.'

Yeah, like *that* was going to happen. She folded her arms across a chest that felt blown open and shattered. 'Thank you.' She was careful to keep her voice neutral and polite. 'Is there anything else?' If he wasn't going to kiss her, she wanted him gone.

'I'm still the executor of Frances's will, Callie. I thought it only fair to warn you that I've no intention of sanctioning any decisions you make in relation to your inheritance for the next fortnight—to give you time to think things over.'

All the brokenness in her chest filled with anger and it felt good. 'Two things, Owen!'

His mouth whitened at her tone and she told herself she was glad.

'One: you don't get to approve or disapprove of my decisions. You don't have the authority to decide what is and isn't in my best interests. Who the hell do you think you are?'

His head rocked back. His entire body rocked back.

'Two: you have no say in what I do with my inheritance. You don't have an atom of control over it. *End of story.* It's mine to do with as I please and you get zero input in that. As far as my portion of Frances's estate is concerned, you *were* its executor. Past tense.'

It took an effort of will not to slam the door in his face. She wouldn't descend to that kind of rudeness. But, seriously, the hide of the man!

'So, what?' His eyes flashed. 'You're going to sell this building out from beneath me as a form of revenge?' His hands slammed to his hips. 'Because revenge is your MO, right?'

His words sucked the air from her lungs. 'My *what*?'

'Revenge…it's what you do. You're going for the TV job as revenge on Dominic. You're throwing your inheritance away as revenge on Frances.'

'Those things are different. And if you can't see that then you're an idiot—a huge, big, amazingly dumb idiot!' She might be above slamming the door in his face but she wasn't above slinging insults. 'Dominic *deliberately* undermined me—he set out on purpose to hurt me. Frances *betrayed* my mother. And in doing so some could argue she deprived me of my father. Mind you, I'm tempted to thank her for that…but, however you want to view it, what she did was terrible.'

Owen opened his mouth, but she carried on over his protests.

'What happened between us was a love affair gone wrong.'

He stilled.

'Neither of us is winning. Neither of us is getting what they want. We have a difference of opinion that can't be surmounted. *End of story.*' Every word was a knife to her heart. 'I can't help feeling the way I feel, and you can't help feeling the way you feel.'

His eyes burned but he said nothing.

'You're not *deliberately* trying to hurt me and I'm not *deliberately* trying to hurt you. After all, you can't help being a jerk.'

The pulse at the base of his jaw pounded.

'But I made a deal with you and I mean to keep it. If you want to buy this apartment block, it's yours.' Another thought occurred to her. 'Do you want the video footage that you created for me back?'

'No.'

Fine. 'Is there anything else?'

'Yes.'

She raised her eyebrow in *that* way, because she knew he hated it. And because it was better than bursting into tears.

'Your inheritance isn't blood money, Callie, and it's not an apology. It's a gift of love.'

She took a step back. 'Difference. Of. Opinion.'

She was careful to enunciate every word before slamming the door in his face. Because, apparently, she wasn't above that kind of rudeness after all.

Callie didn't clap eyes on Owen for the next two days.

'Which is exactly how I like it,' she muttered, kicking the apartment door shut behind her after returning from her daily visit to Mr Singh.

Dropping her coat to the floor, she unwound her scarf and dropped it to the floor too. It was *freezing* today. The weather in New York made no sense to her. Yesterday had been warm. Today was Arctic.

Ha! Hot and cold. Just like Owen.

Speaking of which…

'I don't care if I never see the jerk ever again.'

Which was a lie. A big fat lie. And pretending otherwise wasn't helping her feel any better.

Her phone pinged as a text came in—her mum, asking if Callie wanted a video chat.

She and her mother had video-called at least once a week since she'd arrived in New York. They'd been careful to skirt around the subject of Frances and the inheritance. Callie had mentioned that she and Owen had taken a trip to Cooperstown, but she hadn't mentioned Ellerslie. She'd chatted away instead about her impressions of New York, and filled her conversation with news of Barney and Mr Singh, the girls she'd been tutoring, Lissy…and Owen.

She'd not spoken with her mother since her visit with Richard.

She hesitated and then texted back.

Just logging on to my computer now.

'Darling,' her mother started the moment she flickered into view on the screen, 'it's so good to see you. I— What's wrong?'

Callie's jaw dropped. 'How do you do that? I haven't even spoken a single word yet. And I'm smiling!'

'Your smile is strained, honey. Besides, the apartment is a mess when normally you're so tidy. What really gives the game away is your coat, lying on the floor as if it's just been dropped there. I know how long it took you to save up for that coat, and how much you love it. So something has to be wrong.'

Callie glanced behind her and with a muttered oath raced across to pick up both her coat and scarf. Shaking the creases out, she hung them on the coat rack before returning to the computer.

'It's nothing,' she tried to say. 'I'm just feeling out of sorts. The weather has turned frigid here and it's making me homesick.'

From ten thousand miles away, she could quite literally see the blood drain from her mother's face.

'You've found out the truth, haven't you?'

That Owen is a jerk, a pompous prat…just another controlling male who—

'You know everything!' Donna's hand flew to her mouth. 'About Frances…about why I left and…*everything*.'

'Oh, that?' Callie waved a dismissive hand through the air. 'I've learned a lot about Frances in the past few weeks. But I visited Richard last weekend and he filled me in on the missing piece I'd been looking for. I mean…you *did* know I was looking, right? I know we never spoke about it, but you know me, and I figured…'

'Oh, God, you *do* know.' Her mother covered her face with her hands.

Callie bit her lip. 'Mum, I'm really sorry about what Frances and Richard put you through. I'm outraged on your behalf, but I'm okay.'

Donna pulled her hands away, her gaze roving over her daughter's face. 'You are?'

'I know it's not a pretty story, but... Hell, there's a part of me that feels Frances took one for the team. I, for one, am glad Richard wasn't part of our lives. We dodged a bullet there.'

Donna's mouth opened and closed. 'Then if that's not the problem,' she said faintly, 'what is?'

Callie folded her arms and glared. 'Do you think I'm a vengeful bitch?'

Donna straightened and her eyes flashed. 'Absolutely not! Who accused you of such a thing?'

'Owen.'

'Owen?'

'Well, he said that revenge is my MO, which comes to the same thing.'

Donna's lips twitched. 'That's not precisely true, honey.'

'Semantics.' She waved that away. 'He claims I only want this TV job to revenge myself on Dominic.'

She'd told her mum about the job with *Mystery Family Trees* weeks ago.

'Dominic is a pathetic excuse of a man who should be dipped in hot tar,' her mother said.

'And that I'm only refusing my inheritance to revenge myself on Frances.'

'You're refusing it?'

Donna's voice had gone faint again and Callie blinked. 'Of course I am. For the same reasons you are. I don't want Frances's blood money—' She broke off to bite her lip. 'The thing is, before I found out the full truth—that she stole your boyfriend and cut you off—I...I was starting to like her.'

She frowned again, remembering every word that Owen had flung at her. 'Owen said it wasn't blood money, but a gift of love…' She tried to push his words away. 'But he sees Frances through rose-coloured glasses, because when he was a boy Frances helped his mother get out of a domestic violence situation.'

'Frances did *what*?'

Callie shrugged. 'She's helped all the tenants here— they range from recovering substance abusers and domestic violence survivors to illegal immigrants from war-torn countries.'

'*Frances* has done all that?'

'The tenants were worried when I first arrived that I might hike up the rents.' Callie found she could smile again. 'But they know better now and we're all friends.'

'Frances left you the apartment block?'

'I know! It's worth a cool sixteen million dollars. Can you believe that? The price of real estate here is mind-blowing. She left me this building, plus five million dollars she had in a trust for me, and she left everything else to you.' She clapped her hands over her mouth the moment the words were out. 'Sorry! That just slipped out. I know you aren't interested in hearing anything about the inheritance.'

Donna stared at her. Callie held her breath, hoping she hadn't upset her.

'Frances helped all of those people?' she finally said.

Callie nodded. 'It appears she changed after discovering Richard's true colours. For the last twenty years she shut herself up in this apartment and never left it.'

Donna blinked.

'And she did good deeds. Though she refused to take any credit for it. She sounds prickly and irascible and…' She trailed off with a shrug.

Donna's face became larger as she leaned closer to her computer screen. 'Callie, tell me everything.'

So Callie did.

When she was done, Donna leaned back in her chair and let out a long breath. 'And all the letters I returned are there? She kept them? And you haven't opened the ones addressed to you?'

'I figured you'd kept them from me for good reason.'

'I love you, honey, and I want to thank you for your lack of resentment towards me…'

'No resentment—I trust you. And I love you too.'

'But I want you to open one of those letters to me—it doesn't matter which one—and hold it up to the screen for me to read.'

Callie did.

When she was finished, Donna blew her nose, dried her eyes and told Callie to put the letter away. 'I should've forgiven her sooner. I turned her into a monster in my mind and bequeathed that resentment to you.'

'Oh, Mum, I—'

'No, honey, let me finish. Hearing you talk about her reminded me of the things I once loved about her—things I'd forgotten. She paid an awful price for the trust she placed in Richard and I'm sorry for that…sorry for how much he must've hurt her. I'm glad she had your Owen and his family to give her some comfort.'

Callie's chest cramped. 'He's not *my* Owen. He's a jerk. Do you know what he said? That he wouldn't *sanction* any decisions I made in relation to the inheritance for the next fortnight. Talk about pompous. Not to mention controlling.'

Donna smiled. 'Do you think I was controlling for keeping Frances's letters from you?'

'No! You were trying to protect me.'

'And I suspect that's what Owen is trying to do as well. He doesn't want you to make a decision you'll regret.'

Her eyes burned and her throat grew too thick for her to speak.

'And after listening to everything you've just told me, I think he's right. I think the inheritance *is* a gift of love. Honey, read your letters and send me mine. Then think long and hard about what will make you happy before you come to any decision.'

Callie swallowed. 'Are you talking about the inheritance, the TV job, or Owen?'

'All of them, darling. I suspect Owen cares about you very deeply. Don't you? What do your instincts tell you?'

She wanted to shake off her mother's words, but she couldn't. She recalled with startling clarity the expression in Owen's gaze after they'd made love—the wonder, the awe…and the hope. It was an expression that had only deepened in the days afterwards, even as their connection had deepened. Yes, Owen cared for her. He cared for her as much as she cared about him.

'Send off your job application, because it won't hurt to apply. You can always withdraw it if you change your mind.' Her mother hesitated. 'I suspect getting your own back on Dominic would feel very satisfying for a brief time, but is it worth turning your whole world on its head?'

The answer came swift and sure and had Callie sagging in her chair. *No.*

She was jobless, she had a ridiculously generous inheritance, and she was free to go in any direction she wanted. The only thing she had to decide was which direction to choose.

She glanced across at the drawer containing Frances's letters. 'We'll talk soon, Mum.'

From his seat on the sofa Owen stared at the wall opposite as the apartment darkened around him, but he couldn't be bothered to get up and switch on a light. The dark suited his mood.

He'd made a rookie mistake with Callie. He'd thought

that just because he'd conquered the hardness inside him and was ready to embark on a new chapter, it meant Callie was ready to start something new too.

Because that was what he'd wanted to believe.

She'd told him it was too soon for her, but he'd refused to listen.

And then to storm in like some authority figure the day after their fight and tell her he wouldn't 'sanction' any decision she made... What the hell had he been thinking?

He ran a hand over his face, trying to dislodge the memory from his mind, but it had been burned there. Could he have been more patronising and superior if he'd tried?

He didn't blame Callie for not wanting to have anything to do with him. Taking her inheritance and the TV job were her decisions to make. He had no right to try to force his will on her or to take those decisions out of her hands.

His chin slumped to his chest. How could he fix this?

What he wanted to do was race upstairs, prostrate himself at her feet and beg her to forgive him. He wanted to pressure her to choose him. But in his heart of hearts he knew that wouldn't be fair. She needed the time and space to work out what she wanted from her life without input from any man.

But the one thing he could do was apologise.

His head lifted. He could send her flowers, with a card wishing her luck with the job application and apologising for being such a jerk. He'd tell her he understood that whatever she chose to do with her inheritance was her decision and hers alone...that he'd overstepped the mark.

He swallowed.

And he'd simply sign it *Love Owen*, and hope she knew he meant it.

CHAPTER TWELVE

OWEN TOOK A seat in Mr Dunkley's office and tried to shift the weight that had settled on his shoulders over the last twenty-five days. Twenty-five days since he'd spoken to Callie. Twenty-five days since he'd messed up completely and alienated her forever. Twenty-five days in which his entire world had turned dark and bleak and the sliver of hope that had taken up residence in his heart had died a slow and painful death.

He wished he'd chosen patience and the long game instead of losing his temper.

He wished he'd had the chance to tell Callie that he loved her—properly and forever.

And he wished to hell he could focus on anything other than the remembered shape of Callie's mouth, the sound of her voice and the fruity scent of her hair.

'Owen?'

'*What?*' He crashed back into the moment, registered the lawyer's wide eyes, and bit back an oath. He had no right to take out his dark mood on the lawyer. 'I'm sorry. I was miles away. A…uh…work issue,' he lied, forcing himself to straighten and look interested. 'What do you want to see me about?'

He had his suspicions. He suspected Callie had had a valuation of the apartment complex completed and that Mr Dunkley had been ordered to put forward a price to Owen. He'd pay it. Whatever price she wanted, he'd pay it.

Mr Dunkley glanced at the clock. 'It's just that…well—'

The door burst open. 'Sorry I'm late!'

Owen blinked as Callie burst in, wearing her raspberry coat and shaking droplets of water from her hair as she dropped both her coat and scarf onto a spare chair. Everything inside him fired into sudden and furious life.

She threw herself down into the seat beside him, and the scent of her hair engulfed him.

'What is it with New York and the weather? You can't call this spring. I swear it feels as if it should be snowing out there.'

He couldn't stop himself smiling, even as his heart ached with need and want. 'You should see what it's like in the dead of winter.'

She gave a theatrical shudder, but laughed as she did so.

His pulse pounded. He stared at her the way a starving man stared at a loaf of bread. He couldn't help it. In the same way she couldn't help walking into a room and filling it with warmth and laughter and goodwill.

He couldn't get enough of her. And seeing her freed him and oppressed him in equal measure.

Freed him because to see her was a balm to his soul. Oppressed him because he wanted her. He wanted to hold her, kiss her and tell her he loved her.

But she wanted none of that.

She didn't want *him*.

It took all his strength to drag his gaze back to Mr Dunkley.

The lawyer cleared his throat. 'Ms Nicholls requested that I set up this meeting to table a proposition—one I have every expectation you'll endorse, Mr Perry. It's an enterprise that will amalgamate a variety of initiatives—'

'Oh, for heaven's sake, Gerry, could you be more ponderous if you tried?' Callie broke in, rolling her eyes even though her lips curved upwards.

Ever since Mrs Dunkley had drunk too freely of the punch at Callie's party and forced her husband to dance up a storm on the dance floor, Callie and the lawyer had been on first-name terms.

'Callie, this is a business meeting, and as such certain formalities should be observed.'

'Tosh,' she said cheerfully, turning to Owen. 'Let me cut to the chase. I—'

When her eyes finally met his, her words stuttered to a halt. Her throat bobbed as she swallowed. 'Thank you for the flowers and the card. They were lovely.'

She'd thanked him already, via text message.

'You're welcome.'

They hadn't had the desired effect, though. They hadn't had her rushing to his door and throwing herself in his arms.

'Have you heard back yet?' he asked. 'Did they offer you the job?'

'Of course they did. The video you made for me blew them away!' She shook her head and waved her hands between them, as if trying to clear her head. 'But that's all by the by, and it's not why I asked you to meet with me today.'

She didn't want to talk to him about the job because she thought he disapproved. The thought was a knife to his heart. 'Congratulations, Callie—I mean it. I'm happy for you. You've worked really hard and you deserve your success.'

She stared at him and frowned, as if she could sense the hollowness in his heart.

He straightened. 'So what kind of *initiative* and *strategic vision* did you want to *table* today?'

Her lips twitched and her eyes danced, but she straightened too, folding her hands neatly in her lap. 'Owen, I'm setting up a foundation. I'm calling it the Frances Foundation—because I like alliteration, don't you?— and as Frances's godson, and someone who loved Frances dearly, I thought you might like to be involved and become a trustee.'

Her words made no sense. A foundation bearing Frances's name? You only did that to honour someone, and Callie didn't want to honour Frances. She loathed her.

He leaned towards her. 'What about your TV job?'

Setting up a foundation and running it took a lot of time and…commitment.

Callie couldn't stop the nerves from fluttering up into her throat, making her heart race and making it increasingly difficult to catch her breath. She'd spent the best part of the last month asking herself all the hard questions—what kind of person did she want to be? What did she want to do with her life? What gave her joy? Where did she want to live?

And, most importantly of all, who did she want to share that life with?

She'd discovered the answers to all those questions and she'd found a way forward—one she could be proud of. But it hadn't happened overnight. It had taken a lot of soul-searching, a lot of honesty, and that had taken time. Too much time? She dragged in a breath. Please, please, please let there still be a chance for them. She couldn't bear it if she'd lost all hope of winning Owen's heart.

'I turned down the TV job.'

He stared at her. He had dark circles under his eyes and his hair looked in serious need of a cut. But the swift keenness in his gaze told her she had his full attention.

'You did *what*?'

His lips—lean and firm—reminded her of all the ways he'd taken her to heaven, and the memories tugged at places inside her with insistent hunger. It took all her strength to focus on his words and not to reach across and press her lips to his.

'I've decided to do something different. Something I think I'll find more fulfilling. I mean, the TV job would've been interesting in the short term.' She could feel her lips twist. 'But when I examined my reasons for applying for the job I came to the conclusion that they were less than ideal.'

He didn't say anything, so she continued.

'On top of that, there was a lot of travel involved—as I expected there would be—but no time to really explore the places that I'd be travelling to. So, basically, I'd be living out of a suitcase and...' She shrugged. 'That's not how I want to live my life. The time pressures and turnarounds were going to be tight, and I couldn't see that there would be much of a chance for me to develop relationships with anyone. And, as my career counsellor pointed out, I'm a relationship-builder, so...'

She let the words trail off, feeling she might be babbling and getting off course. But the way Owen stared at her, as if he'd hung on her every word, had her heart crashing about in her chest.

He leaned towards her, bringing those tempting lips even closer. *Breathe*, she ordered herself. *Breathe*.

'You've been seeing a career counsellor?'

'I had some big decisions to make and I needed all the help I could get. She was great too—really helped me sort out my priorities.'

He stared at her for a long time and she found herself holding her breath.

'Tell me about the Frances Foundation,' he said.

She let the breath out slowly. 'Well, we know that Frances championed the underdog, and—'

'You don't loathe Frances any more?'

'No.'

The light in his eyes deepened. 'Go on.'

Her heart raced. 'With which part?' She'd tell him whatever he wanted to know in whatever order he wanted to hear it.

From the corner of her eye she saw Gerry Dunkley get

to his feet and leave the room, but she didn't bother calling him back. Owen didn't either.

'The Foundation or not loathing Frances any more?'

'Tell me about the Foundation.'

So she did. She told him how it would be set up to help unemployed youths find jobs or develop the skills they needed to break into the kind of work they hoped to find. She had plans to create industry links for scholarships and internships. With her mother's blessing, she was going to turn the family estate of Ellerslie into a retreat-cum-training centre.

'Your mother has agreed to this?'

His incredulity made her smile. 'Absolutely.'

'I… This—' He shook himself, as if to gather his thoughts.

She wanted to kiss him so badly it hurt.

'Okay, first things first,' he said.

He hauled in a breath and she had a feeling he was mentally counting to ten.

'What do you see as my role in the foundation? Obviously you want a financial investment, but—'

'I don't want your money, Owen!' *Oops.* 'I mean,' she amended, 'the *foundation* doesn't want your money. Obviously donations are always welcome, but that's not what this is about. I want… I mean the *foundation* wants,' she corrected herself again, 'your vision. You're the person who loved and knew Frances best. We want your knowledge of Frances to help us determine the direction of the foundation—to help us decide what programmes to offer, what strategies to take. There'll be a board made up of my mother, Mr Dunkley and myself, and we're hoping you'll join us.'

He didn't say anything and her chest clenched up tight. It was entirely possible he wanted nothing to do with her, regardless of the fact that she now wanted to honour Frances's memory.

'I understand you might want to take some time to think about it. Mr Dunkley has drawn up some documents that you'll want to read over before coming to a decision. I'll call him back in and—'

'Don't call him back in.'

She swore her heart stopped—before beating even harder and faster.

'This is so far from what I was expecting it's making me slow to respond. But it's unexpected in a good way.' He reached out to briefly squeeze her hand. 'A very good way.'

His words unfroze something small but vital inside her, and she found that she could smile again. 'What were you expecting?'

'For Mr Dunkley to name the price you wanted for the apartment block.'

'Ah, about that…'

Owen sat back and waited.

She moistened her lips. 'I'm not actually planning on selling the apartment block in its entirety. I want to keep the upstairs apartment—Frances's apartment—for myself. But that still means the other seven apartments are yours if you want them. The proceeds of the sale, plus the trust fund Frances left me, will be going towards setting up the foundation.'

He frowned and she winced.

'You hate the idea, don't you? It's just, if I don't have to pay rent then I can afford to continue living in Greenwich Village.'

The apartment was the only part of Frances's legacy she was keeping for herself.

'I think it's a great idea! What concerns me…' his frown deepened '…is how you will support yourself. Callie, you'll need an income.'

'Besides giving Ellerslie over to the foundation, my mother is investing a generous sum to cover, among other things, my wages.' She folded her arms. 'Though we're currently in discussion about what that wage should be. She thinks it should be commensurate with my university salary, but I don't need much and—'

'She's right.'

Glancing up at the deadly serious note in Owen's voice, she found herself swallowing at his almost-glare.

'You can't short-change yourself, Callie. I can already see how much time and effort you're going to put into those youth programmes—your research skills are going to be well utilised. Additionally, if you were to eventually hire someone else, because demand required it, would you pay them a pittance to do the same work you'd be doing?'

'Of course not. But at the moment this is all a risk. It's possible we could lose everything—'

'You need to trust your board to have the competence to judge the programmes you propose, as well as your abilities to implement them. You deserve to earn a wage that reflects that.'

She opened her mouth, but he held up a finger to forestall her.

'Also, I will never lie to you. If I think one of your programmes is too ambitious, or won't fly, or has issues that need to be ironed out before it can proceed, I'm going to say as much.' He smiled briefly. 'I don't doubt there'll be days when you feel you're working very hard for your wage.'

She couldn't speak as she allowed his words to sink in. Hope tightened her chest. 'Does that mean you're on board?'

He nodded. 'I'm honoured to be asked.'

She smiled then too. 'I can't tell you how glad I am.'

She did what she could not to get lost in his answering smile, tried to force her mind back to matters of business.

'I'm sure you must have a lot of questions, and I'm not actually sure I'm qualified to answer them, so we should probably get Gerry back in here to—'

'You're the only person who can answer the questions I want to ask at the moment.'

Her breathing went erratic. 'Oh…?'

He stood, but her legs had gone to jelly at the expression in his eyes and she doubted they'd support her if her life depended on it. She remained seated, staring up at him.

'Can I take you out to dinner soon?' he asked.

'I'm free tonight.'

The words were out of her mouth before she could think better of them, but she didn't care. She wasn't interested in hiding how she felt.

'Perfect.'

He leaned down, his hands going to the arms of her chair, bracketing her in.

'Can I kiss you?'

'I think I'll die if you don't.'

His lips descended with a speed that made her head reel, but those lips—sure and tantalising, full of hunger and tenderness in equal measure—had her finding the balance she'd been lacking ever since she'd slammed her apartment door in his face twenty-five days ago, and she kissed him back with every ounce of yearning and need in her soul.

A short while later she found herself in Owen's lap on Mr Dunkley's Chesterfield sofa. She lifted her head and sucked in a breath, tried to cool the heat rampaging through her veins.

'Owen, we can't make out on Gerry's sofa.'

He sucked in a breath too, staring up at the ceiling for a moment as if trying to gather himself. He glanced at her, started to speak, but broke off whatever it was he'd started to say.

He grinned at her instead. 'Marry me.'

A laugh pressed against the back of her throat. 'Careful, Owen, you almost sound serious.'

'Because I almost am.'

She glanced back at him to find he'd sobered. Those intense grey eyes stared at her as if she were a miracle.

'I love you, Callie. These last twenty-five days without you have been hell.'

He'd been counting the days too?

'I never want to lose you again. I'm sorry about our fight. I'm sorry I overstepped the mark like I did. I panicked, and I know it's no excuse, but—'

She pressed her fingers to his mouth to stem the flow of his words. 'I'm sorry about our fight too. But you were right in what you said to me. I'd become too focussed on how people had done me wrong and on getting my own back. You held up a mirror and I didn't like what I saw. I didn't want to be that vengeful person.'

'Both Frances and Dominic injured you and—'

'And both of them are more than that single act. And in Frances's case she paid so heavily for her mistake and regretted it so much.' She pulled in a breath. 'I finally read her letters. She didn't reveal the identity of my father in them—she respected my mother's wishes on that—but through those letters I've come to know the woman you loved. And I've discovered that I like her.'

His hands cradled her face. 'I'm glad.'

'And in helping me sort through my own emotions, my mother has been on a similar journey. It's been good for the both of us.'

'I hardly know what to say.'

She smiled at him, love welling inside her. 'You've said enough for the moment. You need to listen to me for a little while instead.'

She straightened in his lap until they were eye to eye.

'I'm sorry it took me so long to work things out. Every

night I wanted to race downstairs and climb into your bed—I missed you every waking second.' She grimaced. 'Every sleeping second too.'

His arms tightened about her, and it gave her the courage to continue.

'But I knew it wasn't fair to come to you without a plan. I needed to sort my life out before I did that, and I couldn't ask anybody else to do it for me. I had to do it on my own.'

'I understand, Callie.'

'I have my work—my vocation—all sorted out now. I'm so excited about the Frances Foundation. And I know where I want to live—and that's here in the Village. You're right. I've built a community here, even in such a short time. It probably sounds crazy, but this place feels like home.'

'It's where you belong.'

'And I know who I want to spend my life with—and that's you, Owen. I love you.' Her smile widened at the awe and amazement that spread through his eyes. 'I love you and I want to build a life with you.'

His lips slammed to hers and he kissed her with a possessive thoroughness that left her giddy and breathless.

He lifted his head, breathing hard, his eyes dark, but a hint of humour lightened the corners of his mouth. 'I can't promise that I'll never be a jerk again.'

'That's okay. I'll love you even when you're being a jerk.' She sobered. 'I know that what you saw when you were a little boy—your father's violence—has affected you. I know that as a result you try to protect every woman in your circle. It's an admirable trait.'

'But I take it too far sometimes.'

'Owen, we're both works in progress. We'll work on it together.' He smiled, and a bubble of lightness and fizz built at the centre of her. 'You need to know that I'm never going to like baseball.'

'You don't have to like baseball.'

'But you love it more than life itself. You said so.'

'I love you more.'

She couldn't wipe the grin from her face, but a thought had her sobering. 'In terms of money, I'm not ever going to be rich. I'm sorry if that's not what you think Frances wanted. But in my heart I feel this is the right thing to do. I'm simply taking what she started and building on it.'

'I think what you're doing is perfect.'

She released a pent-up breath. 'So you don't care that I'm not going to be rich? And you know that I'm not after your money, right?'

'I know you're not after my money, sweetheart. Besides, you're already rich in all the ways that matter.' His hand snaked beneath her hair to cradle her skull. 'And I'm going to cherish you every single day of your life.'

'You are too, you know—rich in all the ways that matter. I don't want you ever doubting that.' She cupped his face. 'I want you to know that if you were to lose your fortune overnight it wouldn't make any difference to the way I feel about you.' She pressed a hand to his heart. 'It's the man you are, and your heart, that I love. And I promise you I mean to take very good care of it.'

'I know you will.' His grin hooked up one corner of his mouth. 'Does that mean you'll marry me?'

She had every intention of marrying him. But she wanted him to be one hundred per cent certain before she gave him an answer.

She stuck her nose in the air. 'Do you have a ring?'

'Not yet.'

'Ask me again when you have a ring.'

He immediately set her on her feet. 'Right, let's go buy you a ring.'

Her laugh bubbled up from the very centre of her. 'I'd rather stay here and make out.'

She found herself back in his lap on the sofa again.

'Good idea.'

'Though Gerry is bound to want his office back soon.'

'Nope, he took the rest of the day off—mumbled something about having to go home and kiss his wife.'

'Aw…he's a romantic at heart.'

'So it appears.'

She wrapped her arms around his neck. 'The answer is yes, Owen. I have every intention of marrying you. But this has happened so fast and I want you to be sure.'

He traced a finger across her cheek, his eyes filling with warmth and jubilation. 'I've never been surer of anything in my life. But I can see why you might think this has been a whirlwind affair. If it'll help set your mind at rest, you can choose the date of our wedding. I won't pressure you, Callie. I want you to be happy.'

'Hmm…' She pretended to think about it. 'I've always fancied being a spring bride. Do you have a spare slot in your diary next week?'

He laughed. 'For you, I'll find one.' And then he kissed her.

* * * * *

HIS FOREVER
TEXAS ROSE

STELLA BAGWELL

To my great friends, Pam and Roy Cox,
with love and best wishes, always!

Chapter One

"Doc! There's a problem up at the barn with Frank Whitmore's heifers! The old man is gonna be raising hell!" Trey Lasseter announced as he strode into the veterinarian's office inside Hollister Animal Clinic. "I don't—"

His boots skidded to a stop, along with the rest of his words, as he spotted the attractive young woman standing in front of Chandler Hollister's desk. "Oh—uh, pardon me. I didn't know you were busy with a client. I'll—uh—come back later."

He started backing his way out of the office only to have the veterinarian order him to stop.

"Trey, come back here! Nicci isn't a client. She's

our new receptionist. We were just going over today's schedule before things start hopping."

Receptionist? This woman? She was too refined and delicate to be working in this dusty animal clinic. Was he dreaming, or had Chandler finally cracked beneath his heavy workload?

Trey moved closer as he dared a second glance at the woman. Straight strawberry-blond hair hung all the way to her waist while a pair of silver-gray eyes were staring at him with a mixture of amusement and disbelief. Where in the world had Chandler found *her*? In a high-rise office in Phoenix? She definitely came across as a city girl.

"I was going to introduce you yesterday. But we got called away from the clinic." Chandler gestured toward the woman. "This is Nicole Nelson, but she goes by Nicci. She only arrived in Wickenburg last week, so she's trying to get acclimated to Arizona and working here at the clinic at the same time."

Trey ordered his gaze to remain fixed on her face, but it blatantly disobeyed by slipping up and down the length of her petite figure. A pale pink dress, belted at her tiny waist, stopped just above her knees. Her tanned legs were bare and just as perfectly curved as the rest of her body. It was her choice of footwear, however, that caught the majority of his attention. The nude high heels had extremely pointed toes and straps that crisscrossed atop the foot and fastened around the ankle.

He had to admit the fancy footwear was as sexy as all get-out. But hell, what kind of woman would wear such shoes to work in a small-town animal clinic? The vain kind, or one that lacked good sense?

Trey extended his hand to Nicole Nelson, while worry for his boss was growing in leaps and bounds. This wasn't like Chandler, he thought. No. The man was as practical as the day was long. What had possessed him to hire a woman who looked like she'd never dealt with a sick or wounded animal before. As the receptionist at Hollister Animal Clinic she needed to be prepared to see many.

"My pleasure, ma'am. I'm Trey Lasseter," he introduced himself. "Doc's other right hand."

She arched a skeptical brow at Trey, which promptly caused Chandler to chuckle.

"As much as I hate to admit it, I couldn't run this place without Trey," Chandler told her. "He's a vet technician and has worked with me for more than eleven years now. Most of the time he gives me a headache, but I've learned to live with the pain."

Stepping closer, she placed her small hand in Trey's and bestowed on him a smile that made the Arizona sun appear dim in comparison.

"I'm happy to meet you, Mr. Lasseter. I was just telling Chandler that I hope everyone on the staff will have patience with me while I get the hang of how things are run here in the clinic."

If Trey ever had the chance to touch an angel's

wing, he figured it would feel like Nicole Nelson's hand. All soft and smooth and delicate.

"I'm sure you'll do a fine job," he said, then immediately kicked himself for lying. She'd probably do well to last two weeks here before she went running back to wherever she'd come from. But in this case, telling a fib for the sake of politeness was better than cutting her down with honesty.

"If you're wondering about Nicole's Texas twang, she's from Fort Worth," Chandler spoke up. "She and Roslyn have been close friends for many years."

Oh, so that explained everything, Trey thought. Chandler had hired Nicole because of his wife. Well, at least he could breathe easy knowing that the vet wasn't cracking up.

"That's nice," Trey said inanely. "I mean, that you and Ros will be working together. Doc and I are friends, too. We go way back."

The woman's silver gaze dropped to the front of his shirt where moist green cow manure had splattered a wide swath across his chest and down his left sleeve. The smell was second nature to him, but he figured that was the reason her dainty nostrils were flared in protest. Or maybe it was the fact that he was still holding on to her hand. Either way, he realized it was time for him to move away from the Texas beauty.

Clearing his throat, he dropped her fingers and

inched himself backward until his hip rammed into the edge of Chandler's desk.

A faint smile curved her lips. "I hear the door buzzer," she said. "I need to get back to my desk. Nice meeting you, Mr. Lasseter."

Before he could invite her to call him Trey, she hurried out the door and left him staring after her.

"What were you saying about Frank's heifers?"

"What?"

Chandler's chair squeaked, and Trey glanced around to see the veterinarian reaching for his cowboy hat.

"Frank is going to be raising hell—that's what you said." Chandler levered the brown felt hat onto his head. "What's wrong?"

Trey did his best to push the image of Nicole Nelson from his mind and focus on the problem at hand. "Oh, uh—about a third of the heifers are empty. No calves on the way."

Chandler frowned. "Out of the whole hundred head?"

"That's right. I've written down the tally, but I've not finished the paperwork," Trey told him. "Jimmy is up at the barn right now marking the barren ones."

Chandler whistled under his breath. "You're right. Frank is not going to be happy about this. But he can't rail at us about it. We're just the messenger."

"It's a cinch his bull isn't getting the job done. Think he'll want us to AI the barren heifers."

Chandler said, "Not now. It's February. He won't want babies arriving at the beginning of winter."

"That might be better than no babies at all," Trey pointed out.

"Not if bad weather hits." Chandler shouldered on a worn jean jacket. "Let's go to the barns. I want to look at these heifers myself. We might need to pull blood on them."

Trey snorted. "Frank isn't going to want to pay for that extra expense. He'll accuse you of using him to make an extra dollar."

"He can always get a vet out of Phoenix or Prescott if he doesn't want to use my services."

"Ha! That's not going to happen." He followed Chandler to the door of the office. "Uh, Doc, what's with the Texas lady? Couldn't you find a local to take Violet's place?"

Pausing, Chandler glanced over his shoulder and scowled at Trey. "I probably could've found a local. But Nicole needed a job, and she has plenty of office experience. She's perfectly qualified for the job."

"And she's Roslyn's good friend," Trey dared to add.

Chandler's frown deepened. "That's hardly her fault, Trey. Roslyn has been after Nicole for a long time to move here to Arizona. The job helped make up her mind. If you think that's favoritism, I'm sorry. You'll just have to get over it."

Trey gruffly cleared his throat. "Sorry, Doc. It's

none of my business who you hire to work here. I—well, I'm just a little shocked, that's all. Miss Nelson—uh—she is a *miss*, isn't she?"

Chandler rolled his eyes. "Nicole is single. But knowing you, I'm sure you scoped out her ring finger before she left the room."

"Aw, Doc, I wasn't looking at her *that* close. She just has that unconnected look. You know what I'm talking about."

"Not exactly," Chandler said dryly. "Unless you mean she doesn't look overly stressed and matronly."

Annoyed with himself for bringing up the subject of Nicole Nelson in the first place, he said, "Well, she just hardly seems the type to work in a place like this."

Chandler's brows very nearly disappeared beneath the brim of his hat. "A place like this?"

Trey smirked. "Hell, Doc, cow and horse manure, dust and animal hair, gory wounds and blood—you've been around all that stuff for so long you forget how it might look to someone like her."

"Working at the front office, Nicole won't see too much of that," Chandler replied. "Besides, I believe you're going to find she has a stronger constitution than you think."

She was going to need a whole lot more than a strong constitution to work around here, Trey thought, as he followed his boss to an exit at the back of the building. He seriously doubted the strawberry blonde had the fortitude to stick around this little cowboy town any more than a month, or six weeks tops. But he was going to keep that opinion to himself. Like he'd told Chandler, Nicole Nelson was none of his business.

The sun was incredibly warm for the third week of February, and Nicole had planned to soak up a bit of the sunshine on her lunch break, but just as she was about to carry a sandwich outside, her cell rang.

When she spotted her mother's name on the ID, she released a heavy sigh. Her parents were having a hard time accepting their daughter's decision to move to Arizona, and for the past week and a half, her mother had called at least three times a day.

"Hello, honey. How are you?"

The tone of her mother's voice made it sound as though Nicole had been critically ill instead of moving to Arizona and starting a new job. Biting back a groan, she said, "I'm at work, Mom. I'm on my lunch break."

"I'm aware of the time," Angela Nelson replied. "I purposely waited for your break before I called. Aren't you proud of me for not interrupting?"

Putting her plan to go outside on temporary hold, Nicole sank into one of the gray metal chairs grouped around a long utility table inside the break room. "I need to use these few minutes to eat, Mom. Before I have to go back to my desk."

A short pause came back to her and then a sniff. "Well, pardon me for wanting to make sure my daughter is okay—way out there in the godforsaken desert—miles away from home."

"Is that violin music I hear in the background?" Nicole asked dryly. "If it is, it's not working. I'm well and happy." At least, she would be, she thought, if her parents would allow her to move forward instead of trying to pull her back to a time and place that she wanted to forget.

"All right, Nicci, you've made your point. So, there's no use in me trying to be subtle."

Nicole rolled her eyes at the idea of her mother being subtle. It wasn't possible.

"Your father and I want you to come home," Angela continued. "Where you belong. As of yesterday, he's been promoted—again. And his salary is going through the roof. He wants to help you financially—buy a new home, car, whatever you want."

"That's nice, Mom. Really, it is. But I still have plenty in the trust fund you and Dad set up for me years ago. I don't want or need financial help." Especially from her parents at this stage, she thought ruefully. Two years ago, Mike Nelson had divorced Angela for another woman and left Fort Worth entirely. His adultery had wrecked the whole family. Angela had suffered a mental breakdown, and Nicole had been left to help her mother pick up the shattered pieces of her life. Then a few months ago, Mike had

returned, begging Angela for another chance. Ultimately, her mother had forgiven him, and her parents remarried. But Nicole was far from forgetting
or forgiving the upheaval the ordeal had caused in
her own life. "I'm doing fine on my own. And we've
hashed this out a thousand times already. I have no
desire to move back to Fort Worth."

"Well, there's always Dallas."

If Nicole hadn't been so frustrated, she would've
laughed. "Is there any difference? Other than about
thirty miles?"

Her mother released a short, mocking laugh. "We
could have a long debate about the differences of the
two cities. But your parents would be perfectly happy
for you to live in Dallas. At least, you'd be near us.
Not way out there—among strangers."

"I'm already making plenty of new friends. And
I'm liking it here." She added, "Very much."

"You would say that. Even if you are miserable,
you'd be too stubborn to admit it. But anyway, Leah
Towbridge—you know, she's good friends with Randy's mother—told me that Randy hasn't gotten over
you. That he'll be coming back to Texas soon and
wants to connect with you again. That should be
enough to get you back here."

Furious that her mother would stoop to using that
kind of emotional extortion, Nicole muttered, "I'm
sorry, Mom. I have to get off now."

She punched the face of the phone to end the call,

then turned off the sound so she couldn't hear the ringer in case Angela did call back.

Nicole's hands shook as she dropped the phone into a pocket on her skirt and reached for her sandwich. Damn it, she'd moved hundreds of miles to get away from her mother's smothering attention, her father's betrayal and the regretful choices she'd made regarding her ex-boyfriend. She couldn't allow those things to creep in and shadow the new life she wanted to create here in Arizona.

She started to remove the plastic wrap from the sandwich, but tears suddenly blurred her vision, making it impossible to do anything but bend her head and try to sniff them away.

"Miss Nelson, are you okay?"

The unexpected sound of Trey Lasseter's voice caused Nicole to outwardly flinch and hurriedly wipe at her eyes. "Oh! I didn't know you were there."

"Sorry, again," he said. "This must be my day for interruptions."

Nicole swallowed and straightened her shoulders. "Please, you shouldn't apologize. This break room is for everyone. And I—I'm fine—really."

She glanced up to see the man was looking at her with those dark green eyes that she remembered from their earlier meeting. At the moment they were regarding her with gentle concern, which surprised Nicole greatly. He looked like a man who wrestled a steer by the horns just for the fun of it, hardly the type to notice a woman's tears.

"Well, if anybody gives you a bad time up at the front desk, you just let me know. I'll take care of it."

"Oh, it's nothing like that. So far everyone has been very nice and understanding."

He smiled at her as he crossed the room and pulled a small bottle of water from the refrigerator. "That's good to hear. But sometimes folks can get irate and start making threats. Especially if they think they've waited too long, or don't get the appointment they want."

She watched him twist the cap off the bottle and down half the contents before he lowered it away from his mouth. A very nice mouth, too, Nicole thought, as her gaze slid over the set of chiseled lips. The bottom was just plump enough to make for a nice kiss, while the top was a thin, masculine shape that matched his hooded brows.

Clearing her throat, she said, "I've worked in a public job for several years. I'm used to people being rude and impatient."

He gave her a little half smile, which created a pair of charming dimples in both cheeks. The sight had her drawing in a long breath and letting it out. What in the heck was wrong with her? Why was she looking at this man like she was sexually starved, or worse? Was the high altitude of the desert affecting her brain?

"That's good," he said. "I mean—at least it won't be a shock when a rude one does walk through the door."

He was still wearing the same splotched denim shirt he'd been wearing earlier this morning when he'd walked into Chandler's office. The manure appeared to have dried and the process had apparently taken away most of the odor. Now he smelled more like alfalfa hay, dust and sunshine. The triple combination was totally masculine and not at all unpleasant, Nicole decided.

She began to unwrap her sandwich, more to give her hands something to do, not because she was hungry. Her appetite had vanished the moment she'd answered her mother's call. "Have you already eaten your lunch?" she asked.

"No. I usually just eat twice a day. Once before work begins and then when we quit—whenever that might be." He gestured to the bottle in his hand. "Would you like a water? Or soda? Doc keeps the fridge stuffed for the staff. Guess you've already noticed that, though."

"Yes, I noticed. Chandler is not only nice, but he's thoughtful, too." She put down her sandwich and rose from the chair. "I think I'd rather have coffee right now. Would you like to have a cup with me? Or do you have time?"

Nicole didn't know exactly why she was inviting Trey Lasseter to join her. Except that he was a coworker and she wanted to have a friendly relationship with everyone on the staff at Hollister Animal Clinic. Besides, he was nice to look at and easy to talk to. And anything to divert her thoughts away from Fort Worth was welcome.

He shoved back the cuff of his Western shirt to peer at a square silver watch on a brown leather band. "Sure. That would be nice," he told her. "You just sit back down. I'll get the coffee. I bet you like cream and sugar."

Nicole hardly expected him to serve her, but since he seemed to want to deal with the chore, she wasn't going to argue. "I do. How did you guess?"

"Oh, most girls seem to like things softer." He poured two foam cups full of coffee and added sugar and cream to one of them. As he carried the drinks over to the table, he said, "I have to be back at the barns in ten minutes. Jewell Martin is bringing a load of goats to be vaccinated. She's getting a little long in the tooth to be doing the job herself. I told her I could drive out to her place in a couple of days and take care of the goats there, but she didn't want to wait. Those goats are her babies."

He handed her the coffee before taking a seat in a chair kitty-corner to Nicole's.

"Long in the tooth?" she asked with a confused frown. "You mean she's an older lady?"

He laughed, but then seeing the blank look on her face, he immediately apologized. "Sorry, Nicole. I wasn't laughing at you. Jewell is an older lady, but she does have a mouth problem, too. It's the same problem I have with mine. It's always running off when it shouldn't be."

He gave her a full-blown grin, and the expression caused those adorable dimples near his mouth to deepen even more. Nicole found herself staring at him and forgetting all about her sandwich.

"Oh, I see. Because Jewell is older she needs a little extra help from you?"

He nodded. "And sometimes goats can get rowdy as hell—uh, I mean heck. Especially when you're jabbing them with a needle or squirting meds into their mouth."

"Ouch. That sounds awful," she remarked. "But I guess it's necessary to keep them healthy."

"Aw, it's not that bad. About like giving a person a flu shot." He sipped his coffee, then leveled a curious gaze at her. "How are you and Arizona getting along?"

After taking a cautious sip of coffee, she answered, "Good. It's beautiful here, and the weather is especially lovely."

"This time of the year is spring for us. You've come at the right time to get acclimatized. A few more weeks and it'll be as hot as he—heck. But you'll get used to it—after a while."

After a while. Yes, she would get used to her new home. If her parents would respect her independence and understand that she needed a change in her life, Nicole thought ruefully.

"Fort Worth can be sizzling in the summer, plus the humidity. I don't think I'll have any problem adapting to this drier climate. Actually, I'm still working to get everything unpacked," she admitted. "I didn't realize I brought so many things from Texas with me until I took a look at all the boxes stacked around the house."

"The first four years after I graduated high school, I lived in the bunkhouse on the Johnson Ranch. Bunking with a bunch of cowboys doesn't give a guy much room to collect very many things. When I moved closer to Wickenburg, I didn't have much to box up. But that's been years ago, and I've lived in the same house ever since. I'd hate to think of packing all the junk I've collected." He grinned at her. "I'm too sentimental to get rid of things. I still have the first pair of spurs I ever bought. They're cheap ones and falling to pieces now, but I wouldn't part with them. I'll bet you have things like that, too."

She laughed softly, and it dawned on her that Trey had already managed to lift her spirits. Which was surprising. Especially since she'd met him not more than two hours ago. But he seemed warm and friendly. And God only knew how much she needed a kind, encouraging word.

"I do," she told him. "I still have the first doll Santa brought me for Christmas. She's practically bald now, but I couldn't part with her." She eyed him curiously as she sipped her coffee. "You worked on a ranch before you hired on for Chandler?"

He nodded. "The Johnson. I went to work there as soon as I graduated high school. See, my dad is a cowboy, but he moved to Montana when I was just a kid. I didn't want to live up there, so I stayed here with my mom—until she left for New Mexico. That's why I ended up bunking on the Johnson. And that's how I ended up being a veterinary assistant at first and then later I went to college and earned a tech certificate. Mr. Johnson, the owner, said I had a knack for healing animals."

When Nicole had first started dating Randy Dryer, she was drawn to him because he'd had a serious, no-nonsense personality. She'd been looking for a man who didn't view life as a joke, who was disciplined about what he wanted for himself and his future. Roslyn had called him a stuffed shirt, and if Nicole was being honest, she could admit he'd probably been a bit dry at times, even boring. But he'd been safe and trustworthy. If anything, Trey Lasseter appeared to be the exact opposite. A happy, laid-back kind of guy, who smiled his way through whatever life threw at him. And wonder of wonders, he made her want to smile, too.

She said, "That's good—that he helped you find your calling. I get the impression you like your work."

His grin deepened. "I'd be lost without it. What about you? Are you an animal person?" he asked, then chuckled. "I guess that was kind of a stupid question—with you working in an animal hospital, I mean."

His question was pertinent and certainly nothing to blush about, but Nicole felt a sting of color creep over her cheeks. "Your question wasn't stupid. But I feel sort of stupid answering it. You see, I haven't been around animals all that much. My brother— he's older than me—had a dog when we were little kids, and a few of my friends back in Fort Worth had small pets. But I don't know anything about cows and horses and goats or any kind of livestock."

He reached over and gave her forearm a reassuring pat. "Don't worry a bit, Miss Nelson. After you're here awhile, you'll learn more about animals than you probably want to know."

Rising from the chair, he tossed his cup into a trash basket. As Nicole watched him walk to the open doorway of the break room, she realized she was disappointed to see him go.

"There's no need for you to call me Miss Nelson," she told him. "Nicci will do just fine."

Pausing with a hand on the door facing, he glanced back at her. "Okay, Nicci. And you be sure and call me Trey. That's the only name I know how to answer to. Unless Doc gets mad and calls me something worse," he added in a teasing voice.

"Okay, Trey. Thank you for the company."

Her remark appeared to catch him off guard for a moment, and then he winked and pointed to the sandwich lying on the table. "Better eat your lunch. We have a long day ahead of us."

He disappeared out the door, and Nicole thoughtfully picked up the sandwich and began to eat.

We. Strange how Trey's one word made her feel as though she belonged, as though she was a part of something meaningful.

The idea made her smile, and for the remainder of the day, she didn't allow herself to think about her parents, or Randy Dryer or any other miserable thing she'd left behind her. Instead, her thoughts kept returning to the twinkle in Trey's green eyes and the way those mischievous dimples carved his cheeks.

He was a happy guy. And Nicole needed some happiness in her life in the worst kind of way.

Chapter Two

"Ros, just tell me if you don't have time to talk. I realize it's probably getting close to the kids' bedtime," Nicole said as she sat curled up on one end of her couch with the phone pressed to her ear.

"I still have a few minutes before their bath times," Roslyn told her. "What's up?"

With a husband, two babies and a part-time job at Hollister Animal Clinic, Roslyn Hollister was a very busy woman and nothing like the young woman who'd left behind her plush life in Fort Worth more than three years ago. When her friend had first fled to Arizona, Nicole had been more than upset with her—she'd been downright angry. She'd believed Roslyn was crazy for leaving the security of her father's wealthy home. But now Nicole could see that Roslyn had been the sane one all along. The woman had followed her heart and ultimately found love and happiness. If only Nicole could be that brave and make the same wise choices her friend had made, she thought.

"Nothing, really. I'm still trying to find a place for all this stuff I packed in the U-Haul. I must have been crazy. Half of it I could do without. In fact, I think some of it I'm not going to bother unpacking— I'm going to donate it to charity."

Roslyn chuckled. "And I'm sure most of it is high heels, handbags and fashion jewelry."

Nicole laughed along with her friend. "Well, a girl has to accessorize, you know."

"Hmm. Yes, and you do it so well. But think about it, Nicci—where are you going to wear all those things around here?"

"I don't know," she said, then let out a wistful sigh.

Roslyn groaned. "Oh Lord, don't tell me you're already homesick and that you think you've made a mistake by moving out here. I do *not* want to hear it, Nicci! I—"

Grimacing, Nicole interrupted, "Do you think I'm really that wishy-washy and shallow, Ros?"

"Well, not exactly, but you sound—"

"Forget about the way I sound! I'm tired, that's

all. And anyway, what I'm actually calling you about is—Trey Lasseter."

"Trey Lasseter," her friend repeated in a blank voice. "What does he have to do with anything? Uh—unless—did you two have a run-in or something at the clinic? Did he insult you?"

"Oh, great day, no! Quite the opposite," Nicole assured her. "I only met him this morning. And—well—I'm curious about the guy."

There was a long pause before Roslyn asked slyly, "What kind of curious? Like is he a good employee or is he married?"

Nicole let out a soft, knowing chuckle. "Listen, if Chandler keeps someone around as his right-hand assistant for eleven years, I don't have to ask if he's a good employee. I'm just—well, yes, is he married?"

"No. He's never been married. As far as I know, he's never been engaged. Chandler mentioned that he had a steady girlfriend once or twice, but that was years before I moved out here. I think now Trey just has women friends. You know what I mean? He dates, but none of those dates are serious."

Nicole pushed a hand through her hair as she tried to picture him with his arm around a woman's waist and giving her the same charming smile that he'd given Nicole. It wasn't exactly an image she liked. "Oh. Well, I was just curious. He's really cute."

"He's also really not your type."

Nicole's lips pursed into a disapproving line. "How do you know that?"

"Because Trey is country. His life is simple, and that's the way he likes it. You, on the other hand, love bright lights, big city, shopping, traveling—"

Nicole interrupted with an annoyed groan. "There's nothing wrong with a girl enjoying those things. And I hardly see what Trey has to do with any of that."

"Well, if you can't see what kind of problems that might create, then I can hardly point them out to you."

Scowling, Nicole asked, "Why are you bringing up that sort of thing, anyway? None of that was ever an issue between me and Randy. He was a city guy— totally different than Trey."

There was a long pause before Roslyn finally said, "You're certainly right about that. The two men are nothing alike. And the way I remember, there never was much of anything between the two of you— other than boring acceptance. Maybe now that he's finally out of your life, you'll realize you need some sparks. A man that will remind you that you're a woman."

Nicole stifled a gasp. "Ros! Randy was dependable, thoughtful, responsible. I could count on him to—well, not make a mess of my life." The way her father had made a mess of her mother's life, the way he'd ruined any and all chances for Nicole to make a future with Randy.

Oh Lord, she didn't want to think of that now or ever again.

Roslyn's voice broke into her gloomy thoughts. "Randy was boring. And more interested in keeping his muscles bulked up than making you happy. Be glad you didn't follow him to California. You made a great escape."

"That's easy for you to say, Ros. You have a husband who's insanely in love with you and two beautiful kids. You have a wonderful family—your future is all mapped out. Mine is—"

"Yours will take shape if you let it," Roslyn finished for her. "But it won't if you keep looking backward, nursing your regrets. Frankly, Nicci, that would be another huge issue between you and Trey. He's a happy-go-lucky guy. Your negative outlook would turn him off."

Nicole started to argue that point but quickly bit back the retort. She'd not thought she'd turned into a negative person, but she could admit to herself, at least, that the past year and a half had changed her. And not in the best of ways.

She let out a weary sigh. "Am I really that bitter, Ros? Give me an honest answer instead of this syrupy stuff my mom throws at me."

There was another pause before Roslyn said,

"Okay, I wouldn't call you bitter, Nicci. But you're not the fun girl I knew back in Fort Worth. Before—"

"Before the divorce and Mom's breakdown," Nicole finished the sentence. "Before Dad twisted off and ruined our family."

This time her friend was the one who let out a long sigh. "Listen, Nicci, take it from me. Blaming your dad for your misery isn't a good thing. Nor is it right. I learned that the hard way."

Even though her friend couldn't see her, Nicole shook her head. "Your father was an ogre, Ros. He made your life a living hell. You had every right to blame him."

"No. He made my life hell because I allowed him to. When I finally realized I was strong—that I could stand on my own—my life changed for the better. And thankfully it opened his eyes, too. It hasn't been easy, but we finally have a meaningful relationship."

"Yes, everything has worked out for you," Nicole replied. "And I'm glad. But it's different with me. I've made all kinds of silly mistakes. Not to mention my parents divorcing and then remarrying. They act like they're deliriously in love now, but I can't help but hold my breath. I often worry this newfound happiness with them is all an act and that it can't last."

"You have to quit worrying about your parents and think about your own future. You've taken the first step by moving out here and away from them. Now get a backbone and make the most of it."

Nicole leaned her head against the back of the couch and stared blindly at the whirring blades of the ceiling fan. "I called to ask you about Trey and end up getting a lecture on life. But I suppose I needed it. Has anyone mentioned that you've turned into quite the psychologist?"

"That's what having kids does to a woman," she said with a chuckle. "As for Trey, he's an extremely hard worker, a bit of a motormouth and too kind-hearted for his own good."

"Hmm. Well, this afternoon we had a cup of coffee together in the break room. Uh—just for a few minutes. I liked him." Actually, she'd more than liked him. She'd been taken by his rugged looks and warm smile. More than that, he'd had her thinking she could actually be a happy person again. "But you're probably right. We're too opposite to ever be more than friends."

"Nothing wrong with having a friend," Roslyn suggested. "And Trey is the best kind of friend a person can have. If you need help, he's there. If you need cheering or comforting, he's there. He thinks of everyone else before himself. Throughout those dark days after Joel was killed, Trey was a great support to Chandler. He was someone outside of the family that Chandler could talk to about the loss of his father. Their friendship is as strong as an oak. It always will be."

After Roslyn had met and married Chandler, she'd

told Nicole about the tragic death of Joel, the patriarch of the Hollister family. From the way her friend had told the story, the rancher had ridden out to check on a herd of cattle, but later, a pair of ranch hands had found him dead; dangling head first from his horse. Since his boot was still wedged in the stirrup, it had first been believed the incident was an accident. For some reason the horse had spooked and drug Joel to his death. Even the Yavapai County Sheriff had closed the case. But over the long years since, certain clues had come to light that the man could've possibly been murdered.

"Speaking of your late, father-in-law, has progress been made about finding the truth about his death?"

Roslyn said, "Chandler and his brothers believe they're getting close to discovering what really happened. But nothing definitive yet."

"I'll be wishing them luck," Nicole said, knowing how much solving the case would mean to the family. "Now, back to Trey, I was going to say you make him sound like a saint."

Roslyn let out a short laugh. "Not really. Trey has his wild side, too. But you'll have to hear about that from him."

Nicole would have loved to prod her friend further about the man, but a glance at her wristwatch reminded her that she'd already kept Roslyn on the phone longer than she'd intended. "Okay, it's getting late, and I'm sure you need to be getting the kiddos ready for bed. And I need to get busy with more unpacking."

"Billy is quiet for the moment. I'm almost afraid to see what he and Chandler have gotten into," she said with a laugh. "Good night, Nicci. I'll see you at work tomorrow. And I expect your chin to be up and a smile on your face. Got it?"

"I'll do my best. Good night, Ros."

After ending the connection, Nicole placed the phone on the coffee table, but instead of leaving the couch, she scooted to the edge of the cushion and gazed around the spacious living room. It was beginning to take shape, but the remainder of the rooms were still in a bit of chaos with all sorts of boxes and containers sitting around, waiting to be opened and the contents organized.

Nicole had purchased the house sight unseen, but not before Roslyn had sent her tons of pictures and Chandler had checked out the major parts of the structure like the roof, foundation and plumbing. Once Nicole had arrived in Wickenburg, she'd been more than happy with her new residence. The house was old but full of character, with little hidden alcoves and plenty of shelves to hold all her books and whatnots. She especially loved the oak floors, the varnished pine cabinets and open arched doorways. Outside, the street was quiet, and her fenced yard possessed two large shade trees. There was even a large covered porch that stretched across the front of the house and a smaller one to shelter the back entrance.

A year and a half ago, she'd been living in a modern second-floor apartment with a partial view of downtown Fort Worth. At that time, she'd not given much thought to the noise of the traffic or the neighbors on either side of her. Nor to having a yard of her own, or a cat or dog for company. She'd been too busy with her job at the travel agency and dating Randy to think about much else.

But all that had changed when her father, Mike, had confessed to an ongoing affair and his wish for a divorce. Angela turned into a shattered mess, and Nicole had been forced to give up her apartment and move back in with her mother just to help her deal with the daily chores of living.

For the longest, Nicole had believed she was going to be forever trapped with her emotionally crippled mother. She'd had to let Randy move on without her, and during that nightmarish interval, she'd wondered how long she'd have to go on sacrificing and paying for her father's betrayal. To be fair, her older brother, Trace, who lived in Louisiana and worked in offshore drilling, had offered to come help care for their mother, but Nicole had put him off, convincing him that there wasn't any point in both of them disrupting their lives.

Now Nicole needed to follow Roslyn's advice.

She had to quit dwelling on the past and start living for the future.

With that thought in mind, Nicole left the couch and walked through the house to the master bedroom, where boxes of her clothing were waiting to be hung or put away in drawers.

At the foot of the bed, she opened one of the larger boxes and pulled out a red sequined dress she'd worn for a company Valentine party. The compliments she'd received had assured her the dress had been perfect for the occasion. But now the notion of glamming herself up and walking down the streets of Wickenburg seemed ludicrous.

Trey is country. His life is simple.

Nicole and Trey probably were complete opposites, she thought. But hadn't Roslyn ever heard of the old adage that opposites attract?

Smiling to herself, she put the sequined dress back into the box with the other party dresses and carried the whole thing to the closet, where it was going to remain out of sight and out of mind.

Tomorrow Nicole was going to go shopping for a whole new wardrobe, and she would make sure it didn't involve high heels or sequins.

The next evening the last bit of sunlight was slipping behind a ridge of bald desert mountains when Trey knocked on the front door of his grandmother's house. It wasn't often that work took him this far from the clinic and over into Maricopa County, but he'd spent the better part of the afternoon helping a nearby rancher treat a herd of sick cattle. Afterward, he'd decided to take advantage of the close proximity to the one and only relative he had living in the area.

When his grandmother failed to answer his knock, Trey entered the unlocked house and passed through the rooms calling her name. In the kitchen, he found a transistor radio playing on the cabinet counter and a pot of charro beans cooking on the stove, but Virginia Lasseter was nowhere in sight.

When he'd braked to a stop in the driveway, he noticed her car was parked beneath the carport. She had to be close by, he thought, as he stepped onto the back porch. As he peered across the lawn to a small vegetable garden, he spotted her hoeing between rows of leaf lettuce.

"Granny, you have company!"

She looked around and instantly squealed with delight. "Trey! Wait right there! I'm coming!"

She dropped the hoe, then brushed the dirt from her jeans and shirt and trotted over to the porch.

"You don't need to bother tidying yourself up," Trey said with a grin. "I'm dirtier than you are."

Laughing, she climbed the steps and gave him a fierce hug. "I don't care how nasty you are. You look great to your old grandmother."

"Old? Hah! You're only seventy. That's still a young chick."

With another laugh, she pointed to the ponytail hanging over one shoulder. "I found a few more gray hairs yesterday. At the rate I'm going, I'll be silver pretty soon instead of black."

"And you'll still be just as pretty," he said as he smacked a kiss on her cheek. "Need help with the garden?"

"No. Everything is growing. All I need is hot sun and the water hose." Snaking an arm around the back of his waist, she urged him toward the house. "Come on. I'll feed you some beans."

"I didn't stop by to mooch a meal. But I'll accept if you're offering. Are they done?"

"They're done. Been simmering for hours. Are you hungry?"

He opened the door and allowed her to enter the house ahead of him. "For your cooking, Granny, I'm always hungry."

Inside the small kitchen, she didn't waste time pulling out dishes and silverware.

"Want some help setting the table?" he offered.

"No. You go on and wash up. I'll have it ready by the time you get back here."

Five minutes later Trey was sitting across from his grandmother eating the spicy beans with warm flour tortillas on the side.

"What are you doing this far west?" she asked, as she lifted a spoonful of beans toward her mouth. "Working, or did you drive out here just to see me?"

Virginia, or Virgie, as most everyone called her, had been widowed more than fifteen years ago when James, her husband and Trey's grandfather, was killed in a freak tractor accident. Since then, a few of the single men in the area had tried to talk Virgie into marriage, but none had succeeded. She liked her independence.

Chuckling, he said, "You know, I should lie and say I drove out just to see my precious grandmother. But you taught me that lying isn't good, so I won't. I've been helping a rancher, Hoyt Anderson, with some sick cattle today. After we finished with all the doctoring, I decided I was so close to Aguila that I'd drop by to see you before I drove home."

She smiled at him. "I'm glad you did. Doc didn't come with you?"

"No. He had too much to do at the clinic today. He sent me to do this job alone. And it wasn't easy. I didn't bring any of my own horses. I rode one of Hoyt's, and he was a stargazer. I wore myself out just trying to keep him under control."

She nodded knowingly. "I'm acquainted with Hoyt. He comes into Yellow Boot fairly often. I've heard he's a cheapskate."

Virgie worked as a waitress in a café called the Yellow Boot, located less than a mile away in the tiny community of Aguila. Along with needing the income, she loved being around people. Trey was just thankful she was very healthy and didn't have any problem keeping up with the physically demanding job.

"Yeah, he uses baling wire to keep the tailgate from falling off his truck. But he takes good care of his animals, and that's the most important thing."

"Well, he can't take good care of his wife because she up and left him. Guess you knew that, though. Word was that she took off to Reno with some guy who'd just happened to be driving through town. Guess he wasn't as cheap as Hoyt."

"Poor man," Trey muttered.

"Which one?"

Trey laughed at her question, then promptly shook his head. "Granny, you're terrible. We shouldn't be joking about Hoyt's troubles. And anyway, I'm beginning to think no one values marriage anymore. Every time you turn around, someone is getting divorced. Hell, my own parents couldn't even stay together. I'm lucky to be single, Granny. Damned lucky."

Cutting a brown eye in his direction, she leaned back in her chair. "You think so?"

"Damned right," he repeated. "I don't have to worry about a wife running off or cheating or spending every dime I've busted my butt making. Who needs that?"

She tore off a piece of tortilla and ate it before she asked in a sage voice, "Is that how things are with Doc and his wife?"

Trey grimaced before he finally admitted, "Okay. It's not that way with everyone. But Doc and his siblings are a rarity nowadays."

"I see. You're thinking you'd end up in the miserable majority."

"Pretty much."

"Well, when the right woman comes along, you'll see different."

As Trey watched his grandmother's focus return to her food, he couldn't help but think about Nicole.

"Doc hired a new receptionist. Violet had to quit—for family reasons."

She cocked a brow at him, and Trey thought how pretty and youthful she looked in spite of living for seventy years. Her complexion was freckled and wrinkled a bit from too much sun, but the clarity in her eyes suggested she was definitely young at heart.

"Do I know the new girl?" she asked.

"No. She just moved here from Texas. She's an old friend of Roslyn's."

"I see. How's she working out?"

For the past couple of days, Trey had been surprised at how often his thoughts had drifted to Nicole and how much he'd wondered about her. But he wasn't about to admit such silliness to his grandmother. He was way past the age to be daydreaming about a woman. "I guess okay," he answered with a shrug. "I've only talked to her once."

"Does she have a family?"

"If you mean a husband or kids, no. She's fairly young. I'd say no more than twenty-five."

"Oh. That's interesting. What's she like?"

Trey kept his gaze on the bowl of beans in front of him. "She's one of those delicate types. Slender and fine boned with soft skin and long hair that's kind of reddish blond."

"You're telling me what she looks like. I wanted to know what kind of person she is."

"Heck, Granny, she'd have to be trustworthy for Doc to put her on staff. Anything else, I couldn't say. She seems nice enough. And before those little wheels in your head start turning, she's way too nice for me. She wears high heels and smells like some sort of exotic flower."

"What's wrong with that? Women like being women. Even me."

He let out an amused grunt, then reached over and patted the top of her leathery tanned hand. "Yeah, but you're a combination of pretty and tough. If I ever find a woman for myself, that's the kind I need. Especially if I ever get to have my own ranch. She'll need to be rough and strong."

"In other words, you need a ranch hand. Not a soft little thing to hug and kiss and make you feel like a man."

Trey groaned. "Granny, look at Mom and Dad. They couldn't even stay together until I got out of elementary school."

"No. But they're better off apart," Virginia said. "They just didn't fit together, and they both had sense enough to realize it."

Trey gave his grandmother a wry smile. "I guess I should be grateful they fit together long enough to have me."

"That's right." She lifted a pitcher of sweet tea and topped off Trey's glass. "And if you're happy with the way things are now, that's all that matters."

His grandmother had never pushed or nagged him about his private life. If he asked for her advice, she'd give it, then step back and let him make up his own mind about things. It was one of the many reasons he loved her and enjoyed her company.

"If I got any happier than I am right now, I couldn't stand myself," he said, then leveled a pointed look at her. "And speaking of happy, how many marriage proposals have you received so far this week?"

She slanted him a coy look. "Four, I think. But only two of them were serious."

He playfully clicked his tongue. "Only half of them. That's downright terrible. What's wrong with the hold-out guys?"

She snorted. "Nothing. They're just smart enough to know I'm not about to sit around and take care of an old man who's too shiftless to take care of himself."

"And what about the other two? Will you ever say yes to one of them?" he asked.

Her expression turned a bit wistful. "After sleeping with your grandfather for thirty-seven years, it would take a mighty special man to make that happen."

Trey reached over and squeezed her hand. "Guess I can quit worrying about you eloping with one of those old men."

She shot him another coy look. "I didn't say they were all old. One of those marriage proposals came from a fifty-seven-year-old guy. Pretty good-looking, too, if I say so myself."

Trey sat straight up in his chair and stared at her. "Who? Are you kidding me, Granny?"

Clearly amused by his stunned look, she laughed. "No. Why do you look so surprised. You just said I was still a young chick. Apparently, Harley Hutchison thinks so, too."

"Harley! Why, I ought to go beat the snot out of him," he muttered, then on second thought, he arched a questioning brow at her. "Or was he in the nonserious half of that group of proposals?"

"No, Harley was serious." Sighing, she stirred the beans left in her bowl. "I keep telling him he needs a woman young enough to give him children. He says he doesn't want children. He wants me."

Trey was incensed. "The hell he does. What's gotten into him, anyway? I always thought he was a good man."

She scowled at him. "Harley is a good man. And I think you need to stop and listen to yourself."

Trey's mouth fell open. "What does that mean?"

"Just that you're making me sound like I'm a shriveled old prune of a woman that no worthwhile man would take a second look at. Well, for your information, I might not be a raving beauty, but I can still be sexy!"

Her sassy retort caused Trey to put down his spoon and study his grandmother with sudden dawning. "Granny, are you—why, I'm getting the impression that you might have some feelings for Harley. Do you?"

She cleared her throat and reached for her tea. "I guess I do. In a way. He makes me feel young and pretty and worthwhile. But—I believe he's mixed up about wanting to marry me. And anyway, I need to think on it some more before I say yay nor nay."

Trey didn't know what to say or think. Frankly, she'd shocked him. Asking her about the marriage proposals she got every week was something he'd always done out of fun. But this time she'd thrown him a real curve, and he recognized with a bit of guilt that he was jealous of the idea of Harley, a brawny and virile farmer, loving his grandmother. She was the only relative Trey had that lived close to him. And the only one who'd ever really shown him much affection and love. He resented the idea of having to share her company with anyone else.

"I'm sorry, Granny. I didn't mean anything like that. Hell, you could pass for sixty easy. Probably even pass for Harley's age," he told her.

Smiling wanly, she waved a dismissive hand at him and rose to her feet. "You don't have to spread it on, Trey. I'm not angry with you. In fact, as soon as you finish those beans, I'm going to give you a big piece of chocolate sheet cake."

He watched her go over to a row of cabinets she'd painted a sunny yellow color, and as she gathered makings for coffee, he was reminded of exactly how long she'd been living without a husband. He thought, too, of how much fuller her life would be with Harley.

Yours would be a heck of a lot fuller, too, if you'd find a good woman to love.

The voice drifting through his head came out of nowhere, and before Trey could stop it, Nicole's image followed the unnerving words.

Cursing under his breath, he left the table and went to stand next to his grandmother. "You go sit down, Granny. Let me do this. I know where to find everything."

For a moment she looked as though she wanted to argue with him, but then she smiled and patted a hand against his chest. "All right, I'll go sit and you can tell me a bit more about this new receptionist. I might just have to bring one of my dominickers over to the clinic to check on her. The hen, that is," she added slyly.

He rolled his eyes and shook his head. "Granny, you and me both know that there's not a thing wrong with any of your hens or you would've already had them over to see Doc. And I've never known of you to want to spy before. What's come over you?"

With a knowing chuckle she headed back to the table. "Spring is in the air, Trey. It makes a woman start dreaming and a man start thinking."

He'd been doing plenty of that these past couple of days, Trey thought, as he opened a can of coffee and spooned a hefty amount into the brewing machine. And it had all revolved around a strawberry blonde with silver-gray eyes and a smile that could wither the sun.

Chapter Three

By the time Friday arrived, Nicole was getting more into the swing of her job. Nothing was hard about answering the phone, or writing down names, dates and times. The difficult part was trying to figure out which cases to put on Dr. Hollister's priority waiting list and which ones weren't quite so urgent. When it came to their pets, some people were very persnickety. Like Mrs. Daniels, who was standing in front of a long counter that separated Nicole's desk from the customers. The black-and-white Boston terrier was far too large to be holding in her arms, but the middle-aged woman with frizzed blond hair didn't appear to mind the extra weight, or the loud barks directed at her face.

"The only opening I have is at four thirty this evening, Mrs. Daniels. Or you can try your luck as a walk-in, but as you can see, the waiting room is full and you might be sitting for a few hours."

The woman pursed her lips in disapproval. "Nicole, I realize you're new here and don't understand the situation, but I am one of Dr. Hollister's long-running customers. I'm here frequently, and I know if you were to go tell him the dire situation that my darling little Susie is in right now, he'd want to check her out immediately. She won't eat a bite. Not even a scrap of sirloin! This is an emergency!"

Nicole was hardly an expert on dogs, or any kind of animal for that matter, but it seemed to her that the only thing the squirming, barking Susie needed was to be on her own four feet and left alone to do what dogs love to do.

"Uh, Mrs. Daniels, when was the last time Susie ate anything?"

The woman looked properly offended that Nicole had even asked such a question. Dear Lord, where did Chandler find the patience to deal with these types of pet owners?

"Last night, before bedtime," the woman answered. "I gave her a plate of macaroni and cheese and frankfurters. She loves it and I was treating her for her birthday. You see, she turned three yesterday. And don't try to tell me that the table scraps have upset her tummy. There's something else wrong with her!"

Nicole was trying to decide the best way to deal with Susie, and her owner, when another woman walked up carrying a pet carrier with a yellow striped cat inside. The animal was emitting a loud, hoarse meow, which caused Susie's barking to grow downright ferocious.

Just as Mrs. Daniels turned to give the cat owner a withering glare, Nicole heard a door behind her open and close. Glancing over her shoulder, the sight of Trey entering her workspace left her weak with relief.

Turning her back to the waiting customers, she mouthed the word *help* to him. Nodding that he understood, he ambled over to her as though he had all the time in the world.

Mrs. Daniels instantly directed her ire at him. "Mr. Lasseter, will you tell this woman that Dr. Hollister is—"

"I'm sorry you've had to wait, Mrs. Daniels, but it can't be helped. Dr. Hollister had to leave on an emergency call. He probably won't be back until much later this afternoon. If you'd like, I can show you and your dog back to a treatment room and I'll see if I can figure out what's wrong with her. Then Dr. Hollister can treat Susie whenever he returns."

Somewhat mollified, the woman sniffed and lifted

her chin to a proud angle before she shot Nicole an I-told-you-so glare. "Thank you, Mr. Lasseter."

"I'll be right with you," he told the woman, then taking Nicole by the arm, he led her away from the counter and out of earshot from the crowd in the waiting room.

"Has Doc really been called away?" she asked, while trying to ignore the way the warmth of his hand was sending tingles up and down her arm.

Trey nodded. "An emergency C-section for a mare on a ranch about twenty miles from here. He'll be tied up for a while. He took Jimmy to help him because I have a little more experience with handling small animals and I'm needed here in the clinic to do whatever I can."

Surprised, she asked, "You mean you're going to stand in for Chandler here in the clinic?"

Grinning, he patted the side of her arm. "Not exactly. No one can stand in for Doc. But don't look so worried. I can handle simple things like fleas or ear mites. Just don't schedule any delicate operations for me to perform," he joked.

"What do I tell the people who are sitting out there waiting and expecting to see the doctor?"

"Most of the clients are accustomed to Doc being called away from the office. The ones that have animals with a serious problem will reschedule their appointments." He winked at her, then added in a teasing voice, "Right now, I'd better see if I can smooth Mrs. Daniels feathers."

She watched him slowly saunter out of the room, while wondering if his laid-back style of dealing with things stemmed from an uncaring attitude or an overabundance of confidence. It had to be the latter, she decided. From what she'd seen so far this week at the clinic, the man worked too hard and cared too much.

In any case, Trey had come along and rescued her when she'd desperately needed help. And once this trying day was over, she was going to make sure he knew how much she appreciated him.

Trey was washing up after treating the last patient, a dog with a flea infestation, when the door to the treatment room opened and Nicole stepped inside.

"Knock, knock," she said, her pretty face peering around the edge of the door. "Is it safe to come in?"

He grinned at her. "Sure. I won't try to stitch up your ear or give you a shot for heartworms."

She stepped into the room. "The waiting room is empty. And everyone left happy—I don't know how you managed it."

He sprayed down the long treatment table with disinfectant and wiped it dry. "One animal at a time. It wasn't that bad. Thankfully, all the problems were simple today and I could deal with them."

She smiled at him. "I guess you've learned a lot from Chandler over the years."

He nodded. "Normally, I just assist Doc with large-animals. That's what I enjoy the most. But in the beginning when Doc first opened the clinic, I had to help him with the small patients, too. Nothing better than watching firsthand. And Doc is a genius. He hates it when I say that, but it's the truth."

"He's a humble man."

She pushed back a strand of hair that had fallen over one breast, and Trey found himself watching the graceful movement of her hand and how the silky hair slipped through her fingers. It was the same color of the mane and tale on his sorrel mare, Lucy. Sort of blond and red with a bit of gold in between. Except that Nicole's hair would be much finer and softer than Lucy's, he thought.

Clearing his throat, he asked, "Did you need me for something?"

A pretty pink color seeped into her cheeks, and like a fool, Trey couldn't help but notice that the blush matched the color of the flowers on her cotton dress.

"Actually, I came back here to thank you. Before you walked up, I wasn't sure who was going to have a meltdown first. Me or Mrs. Daniels."

He chuckled. "Yeah, she can be worse than demanding. It wasn't exactly fair of me to take her ahead of the others, but she can get so overbear-

ing that it's upsetting to the other clients. The way
I look at things, it's better to get her taken care of
and out of the building than to have an uproar in
the waiting room."

"Well, I really appreciate you rescuing me."

"You were doing fine on your own."

She chuckled. "Not if her dog had gotten loose.
I expect she would've terrorized the whole waiting
area."

"That's happened before. Mrs. Daniels used to
have a Doberman and he got loose once. It took about
fifteen seconds for the waiting room to empty."

"Oh my," she said with another laugh. "I thought
this job was going to be much quieter than the one
I had at the travel agency. I arranged and booked
travels for corporate groups. It could sometimes get
hectic. But this can get a little stressful."

He leveled a meaningful look at her. "Changing
your mind about hanging around here?"

Her lips parted at the same time her brows disappeared beneath the bangs covering her forehead.
"You mean quit? Leave?"

He nodded and then, with a sheepish shake of his
head, said, "Sorry, I shouldn't have thrown a question like that at you."

Frowning slightly, she said, "No need to apologize. Your question didn't offend me, but it did catch
me by surprise. I'm curious—do you think I look
like a quitter?"

He'd certainly held that opinion of her a few days ago and even voiced those thoughts to Chandler. But nearly a whole work week had gone by since then, and she'd continued to prove Trey's prediction wrong.

"Not exactly a quitter. I was only thinking this job might not be what you expected. Not anyone on staff has it easy around here, including you. In fact, I wouldn't trade places with you for a million bucks. It wouldn't be worth it to have to deal with people like Mrs. Daniels."

She shrugged. "My job at the travel agency could get crazy. Companies planning travel trips for employees were often changing their minds, canceling at the last minute, demanding their money be returned or threatening lawsuits because the trips ended up being less than pleasant. I'm used to demanding people. But here it's different because of the animals. They are what's really important. As for me hanging around—I'm here to stay. I hope that doesn't disappoint you."

Disappoint him? It scared the hell out of him. Even though he'd scarcely crossed paths with her since the day he'd met her, she was constantly in his thoughts. The longer she was here, the bigger the chance of him making a fool of himself over her.

"Not at all." He cleared his throat and glanced away. "I'm glad you plan to stay."

She let out a sigh, and he looked up to see an impish smile curving her lips.

"I'm going to make a confession," she said. "I'm a terrible cook. So if you know a good restaurant in Wickenburg, I'd love to take you out to dinner. That is, if you'd like to go and you don't have anything better planned. It's the least I can do after the way you saved me from Mrs. Daniels."

Trey figured if he caught a glimpse of his image in the mirror right now, he'd be looking at a mighty goofy expression. Aside from working together here at Hollister Animal Clinic, he'd never imagined this woman wanting to spend a minute with him.

"Aw, Nicci, you don't need to do anything for me. That's just a part of the job."

"Listen, Trey, you'd be doing me a favor by joining me for dinner. You can give me advice about which dining spots in town are good or should be avoided."

Join her for dinner? He wondered if, somewhere between the cat with the abscess and the dog with the torn ear, he'd stepped into another dimension.

He tried to chuckle, but it came out sounding like a strangled bullfrog. "You might not like the food that I do," he said.

She laughed, and he decided this Nicole was a totally different woman from the one he'd found a few days ago sniffing back tears in the break room.

"I'm not a picky eater. What do you say? Are you

free tonight? I realize it's Friday night and you might already have a date. If that's the case, just tell me. We can always go at a later time."

He hesitated as his stunned brain tried to assemble a response. If he had any sense at all, he'd thank her for the invitation and tell her he was too busy to go to dinner, or anywhere else with her. Ever. But when it came to women, Doc had always insisted Trey lost his mind.

"Naw. I don't have a date. I—uh, don't have a thing to do except wash a sink full of dishes."

Hell, he might as well have told her his house stayed in a mess. And she probably didn't like messy men. Yet the wide smile that was slowly spreading across her face said otherwise.

"Great. I'll pick you up around seven. How's that?"

She'd pick him up? Lord, he couldn't believe this was happening. "Uh—sounds perfect." He proceeded to give her directions on how to find his place north of town. "If you get on the wrong road or can't find me, just call."

Nodding, she pulled a blank appointment card from a pocket on her skirt and handed it to him. "Better write your cell number on that—I'll enter in my phone later. Just in case I take a wrong turn."

He scribbled down the number and gave it back to her, then on second thought, he asked in a bewildered voice, "Are you sure about this?"

"Sure, I'm sure," she said on her way out the door. "Be ready. I'm always starving."

Trey was still staring in wonder at the empty doorway when Cybil, a tall middle-aged woman with a head full of frizzy blond curls, walked into the room.

"What's wrong?" the vet assistant asked. "I just saw Nicci hurrying back down the hallway, and there's a sheepish look on your face. Did you say something awful to her?"

Only that he'd have dinner with her, he thought wryly.

Turning back to the work counter, he dropped the instruments he'd used to treat the dog into a jar of disinfectant. "Not hardly. Why would I?"

"You wouldn't intentionally. But you open your mouth before you think. And Nicci's a sweet girl. She's not like those girls you dance with at the Fandango."

Cybil was a good friend and a dependable assistant with the small-animal patients, but that didn't mean Trey appreciated her nosiness, especially when it came to his love life, or lack of one.

"I never thought she was," he said flatly.

Cybil shot him a look of warning as she pulled a trash bag from a basket and fastened the top with a tie. "I just think it would be a shame if you ended up breaking her heart."

Trey's short laugh was incredulous. "Me break

Nicci's heart? That's funny, Cybil. You ought to do a comedy act."

Cybil shook her head. "I'm serious. I can tell that Nicci likes you a lot. And I'd hate to see you take advantage of that."

Nicci liked him a lot? Not in the way Cybil was thinking.

"Don't worry. The only thing Nicci will ever be to me is a friend."

Later that evening, Nicole tossed a piece of clothing onto the pile she'd already tried on and dismissed. Darn it, she wanted to look nice, but not overly so. And sexy, but only in a subtle way. A pair of tight jeans might give her the right sort of country flavor, but she had no idea where Trey might want to eat. Jeans might not be dressy enough. On the other hand, he might want fast food, and a fancy dress would look ridiculous.

You're behaving like a silly schoolgirl, Nicole. It's not going to matter what you wear tonight. Trey Lasseter isn't going to look at you in a romantic way. And you should've never been so forward to ask him out in the first place.

Nicole grimaced at her image in the dresser mirror. Maybe she had been a little forward to ask Trey to dinner. But for the past few years everything she'd done had been for someone else, never for herself. It was time she changed.

Seeing that the hands on the clock were fast ticking away, she finally grabbed a mint-green dress with narrow straps over the shoulders, a close-fitting bodice and a straight skirt that belted at the waist. The summer garment was cool and casual, but nice enough, she decided.

Minutes later, she was walking to her car when her cell phone rang, and thinking it could possibly be Trey, she paused to dig the phone from her purse.

The moment she spotted her mother's number on the caller ID, she promptly dropped it back into the side pocket inside her purse and walked on to the car. She wasn't going to deal with her mother's emotional edicts tonight. Instead, she was going to enjoy Trey's company and hope that he enjoyed hers.

Did women prefer striped shirts or plaid? Or would he make a better impression if he wore a solid color, like light blue or gray? Trey considered calling his grandmother for advice on the matter, but then he'd have to explain that he was going out to dinner with the new receptionist, and then she'd really dig into him. Trey wasn't ready for that. No more than he'd been ready to hear Harley wanted to marry Virgie.

Damned man, who did Harley think he was? And why hadn't his grandmother turned him down flat?

Because she's lonely, Trey. Because she might need to feel a man's loving arms around her. Be-

cause she needs something more in life than waiting on diners in a dusty café. Just like you need more than treating a sick cow or horse and coming home to an empty house.

Frowning, he poured aftershave into the palm of his hand and slapped both cheeks in hopes of slapping away the taunting voice going off in his head. He didn't want to hear that kind of nonsense tonight. For the first time in his life, a woman had asked him out. And not just any woman. She was educated and pretty and had real manners. She wasn't the type who swigged down half a beer and then wiped her mouth on the back of her hand. No, Nicole was a lady. A real Texas rose. And he wanted to enjoy tonight. Because he was pretty damned sure it would be the first and last time that he'd get to go out with her.

After slipping on a blue-and-white paisley Western shirt and tucking the tails inside his jeans, he turned out the light in the bathroom and walked to the living room. Earlier this evening, after he'd arrived home from work, he'd hurriedly tried to pick up the worst of the clutter. Even so, dust was everywhere and the floor needed to be swept and mopped, but most nights Trey did well to find time to eat and sleep, much less do housekeeping chores.

He was trying to brush some of the grime from the brim of his brown cowboy hat when he heard a car pull to a stop behind his truck.

As Trey walked outside to greet her, the last of the

day's sunlight was rapidly sliding behind the hills to the west of his house, sending wide swaths of shadows across the porch and the small front yard cordoned off by a fence of cedar post and barbéd wire.

She'd nearly reached the yard gate when she gave him a cheery wave. "Hi! I found your place with no problem at all."

"I'd like to say it was my good directions that got you here without a snag, but I'm betting it was your navigating skills."

She laughed. "Oh, if you only knew how easily I get lost. I'm still having trouble remembering the route from my house to Conchita's coffee shop. And that's only a few streets away!"

As she stood beside him at the gate, it was all Trey could do not to gape at her. She was so pretty and soft, and the smile on her face made him feel a whole foot taller than his six feet and three inches.

"That's only because you're new around here. After a bit you'll remember the layout." He gestured to the front of the house. "Would you like to go in? Except for getting my keys and wallet, I'm ready."

"I'd love to go in." She casually wrapped her arm around his, and they walked along the row of stepping-stones that led up to the porch. "But you really don't need to bother about your wallet or keys. I'm going to drive and I'll be paying for dinner, too."

Trey very nearly stumbled. "Uh—that's not the cowboy way," he told her. "We buy a lady's dinner."

She slanted him a cheeky smile. "Well, that's not the Nicci Nelson way. I invited you tonight, so I'll get the bill. You can take care of the next one."

He came close to stumbling a second time. The next one? That had to be a figure of speech, he thought. There wouldn't be a second time. Not with him and her. After tonight she'd have more than her fill of Hayseed Trey.

"Uh—I guess—well, Granny always taught me to never argue with a lady, so I won't."

He glanced over to see her smile had turned soft, and Trey suddenly wondered if it was possible for a man to continue to walk upright after his bones melted. He was still standing and moving one foot in front of the other, but as they climbed the steps and crossed the porch, he didn't feel anywhere close to normal. In fact, he hadn't felt this shaky or breathless since a bull had rammed a horn into his rib cage and punctured a lung.

"Good," she said. "Your grandmother sounds like a woman I'd like to know. Does she live close by?"

"Not really. She lives near Aguila. About twenty-five miles west of here."

He pushed open the door, and after motioning for her to precede him, he followed her inside. "It probably feels hot in here," he said. "Since I knew I'd be leaving, I didn't bother turning on the air conditioner."

She shook her head. "It feels fine. Actually, I'm

learning how quickly it cools out here in Arizona after the sun goes down. In another hour's time I'll probably need a sweater."

Trey hoped not. The dress she was wearing exposed her bare creamy shoulders, toned arms and a hint of cleavage above the V neckline. Covering up all that beauty would be an awful shame, he thought.

"I'll get my things from the bedroom," he told her and gestured toward a couch and two armchairs grouped in a U shape in the middle of the room. "Have a seat."

"Thanks," she told him as she sank gracefully into one of the armchairs. "And take your time. There's no hurry. Unless you have to be up early to work in the morning. I didn't schedule anything early for you and Chandler, but I'm learning that he agrees to jobs on his own and forgets to tell me to put them down on the appointment book."

Trey chuckled. "That's Doc. But no, for the first Saturday in a long while, we're not making a house call, or opening the clinic for a special reason. It's foaling time at Three Rivers Ranch, and Holt needs him."

He fetched the keys and wallet from the bedroom and returned to the living room. The moment she heard his footsteps on the wooden floor, she looked around and smiled at him.

"I was just thinking you have a nice place here. Have you lived here long?"

"About nine years. It's an old house, but it's solid." He made a circular gesture with his hand. "I hope you'll overlook the messiness. I'm not much on house cleaning. And I—well, I hardly ever have company. Unless it's just one of the guys—like Jimmy or somebody like that."

The corners of her mouth tilted upward in an impish smile. "No female guests?"

A hot blush climbed up his neck and over his face. "Me? Shoot, I'll be honest, Nicci, you're the first woman who's ever been here. Uh—I mean, other than Granny. And Roslyn. She and Doc have stopped by together. Back when I had girlfriends—the steady kind, that is—I didn't live here in this house."

Her expression sobered as though she'd suddenly been struck by a sad thought. Either that, or she felt terribly sorry for him.

"I see. Well, I'll be honest with you, Trey. I'm not much on house cleaning, either. This all looks nice and neat. Would you care to show me the rest of the house?"

Something had gone haywire with his lungs, he decided. He couldn't seem to suck in enough air or push it out. Still, he forced himself to walk over to where she was sitting. "I don't mind. But then you're going to see where I piled all the junk that was here in the living room so that you wouldn't see it."

She suddenly laughed, and Trey was relieved to see a smile back on her face.

"You shouldn't have bothered. Not for me. I've only been in Wickenburg a little more than two weeks and I had to start to work right away. So my house is still piled with moving boxes," she assured him.

He reached down and gave her a helping hand up from the chair. "That makes me feel better."

Expecting her to pull her hand away as soon as she was on her feet, he was more than surprised when her fingers tightened around his. Since when had a woman wanted to hold his hand just for the sake of holding it? He tried to remember but couldn't come up with one single time. Unless he went way back to when Lacey still lived in town. But that was several years ago, and he didn't want to think about her or any of the fruitless relationships he'd had in his younger years.

"Lead on," she told him.

With the warmth of her hand wrapped in his, Trey led her through a short hallway and into the kitchen.

"Next to the bedroom, I use this room the most. That's why it's messy," he said sheepishly. "Guess you can see I haven't gotten around to that sink full of dishes yet."

She smiled up at him, and Trey was surprised to see a twinkle in the silver-gray depths. "Don't feel bad. I haven't gotten around to mine, either."

Gesturing toward the cabinets, she said, "These are nice. Did you build them?"

The mere fact that she considered him to be a man with enough skill to do such intricate carpentry work was a huge shot to his ego. Yet at the same time it puzzled him. It was as though the woman looked at him with different eyes from everyone else. And that could only end up causing problems. Because sooner rather than later, she'd see the real Trey. The goof-ball who was good at doctoring animals but inept at most everything else.

"Do I look like I could do carpenter work?"

She stepped back as she swept her gaze over him. "Yes, you do. Can you?"

He gave her a lopsided grin. "I can build a barn and do simple repairs. That's about it. I didn't make these cabinets. They were already together when I got them. But I did tear the old ones out and put these in."

She beamed a smile at him. "See, I was right. You can do carpenter work."

"I wouldn't go so far as to say that," he said.

"Oh, I would. My father can't hammer a nail in straight. And probably wouldn't even if he could."

"What kind of work does he do?"

Turning her back to him, she walked over to the cabinet counter and ran a hand over the marble-like top. "He's an oil and gas consultant."

Trey whistled under his breath. "Guess he makes plenty of money."

"Plenty," she said flatly. "He's not nearly as

wealthy as Roslyn's father, but he's like him in some ways."

"I'm sorry to hear that. Old man DuBose isn't the most likable person. Although he's a heck of a lot nicer than he used to be."

She turned back to him, and Trey noticed there was a wan smile on her face that hinted all wasn't right with her and her father.

"His personality isn't like Mr. DuBose's, thank God, but his drive for money is," she said. "Both men have made tons of it, but neither man has ever been content."

Trey chuckled. "Boy, am I ever safe," he said. "There's no danger in me becoming rich."

She laughed, and he motioned for her to follow him out of the room. "Come on and I'll show you the rest of the house."

She walked over and clasped a hold on his upper arm and the two of them ambled down a short hallway, where he pointed out two spare bedrooms, a bathroom and finally the master bedroom, where he slept.

"Do you have property with this place?" she asked as she stepped inside the room.

For a moment Trey's brain didn't register her question. He was too busy imagining himself lifting her onto the rumpled bedcovers and slowly removing that pretty green dress.

He rubbed a hand over his eyes in an effort to

push the erotic image away. "I'm sorry, what did you say?"

She walked over to the window and peered past the curtain. "I asked if you have any property with the house."

"Oh. Yes. Ten acres. I have three horses. They're necessary for my job—when we do ranch calls. Would you like to look out back?" he asked, while thinking he had to get her out of the bedroom before he said or did something that would make him look like a total idiot.

Nodding, she walked back over to where he stood. "I'd love to."

She latched onto his arm once again, and Trey led her to the kitchen, where they exited the house through a back door.

"The house really needs a porch here, too. But I hate to go to the expense of building one. Especially since I don't always plan to live here. I'm saving my money to buy a ranch," he told her.

She glanced at him with surprise, and Trey figured she was wondering where a guy like him would ever get enough money to buy land, much less the livestock to put on it.

"That sounds like an ambitious plan. Is that something you've always wanted?" she asked as he guided her down the set of wooden steps.

"It is. I'll probably have to work a long time to make the dream come true, but that's okay. The harder a guy has to work for something, the more he appreciates it when he does finally reach his goals. You know what I mean?"

Nodding, she squeezed his arm. "That's one of the reasons I moved here to Arizona. So that I could work for my own home, my own goals."

Did those goals include a man? He wanted to ask her, but he told himself her private plans were none of his business. Like he'd told Cybil, the only thing he could ever be to Nicole was a friend.

Chapter Four

The restaurant Trey suggested for plain, downhome cooking was the Wagon Wheel, an older establishment located in the main part of town. The long, narrow dining room consisted of several small square wooden tables in the front area near the windows and booths lining the back walls.

Authentic wooden wagon wheels holding hurricane lamps hung from the tall ceiling, while the pale green walls were decorated with large photos and paintings depicting the town in its earlier heyday of gold and silver mining. Near the table where Nicole and Trey chose to sit, she noticed a small wall mural depicting a grizzled prospector leading a burro loaded down with packs of supplies.

"This is a neat place, Trey," she said as he helped her into one of the wooden chairs. "Do you come here often?"

"When I'm lucky enough to have the time." He eased into the chair across from her, and after pulling off his hat, he raked a hand through his blond hair. "Usually it's so late when Doc and I finish up the day that I just go home and scrounge up something. Like a fried bologna sandwich."

She laughed. "You can make those?"

"Sure. I have a steady diet of them. Sometimes I change it up and fry salami instead, but it's not as good as bologna."

"Sorry, Trey, you're not going to get bologna in here. But we do have grilled cheese if you're that set on having a sandwich."

Nicole looked up to see that a young waitress with long black hair pulled into a low ponytail had arrived with two glasses of ice water and a pair of menus. Between the smiles she was directing at Trey, she eyed Nicole with open curiosity.

"Hi, Linda. And I don't want a sandwich. I'm going all out tonight. Nicci is buying."

The woman's brows arched skeptically as she settled her gaze on Nicole. "How nice of you to treat Trey. He's solid gold."

Trey's laugh was more like an embarrassed cough. "Yeah, just melt me down and I'd be worth millions," he joked, then gestured to Nicole. "Linda, this is Nicci Nelson, our new receptionist at the clinic."

"Hi there," the waitress said politely. "I'm Linda Barstow. I've been friends with Trey for years and years."

Nicole thrust her hand out to the woman. "I'm happy to meet you, Linda. I'm new in town, and Trey has been telling me this is one of the best places to eat."

The waitress shook her hand. "Nice to meet you, too, Nicole." She looked at Trey and then back to Nicole. "Er—did you two know each other before you came to Wickenburg?"

Nicole answered, "No. I'm from Texas."

"But she's rooting down here," Trey added. "That's what she's planning to do."

"That's nice," the waitress said, then glanced over her shoulder as a bell above the door announced more patrons entering the restaurant. "Well, I'd better take your drink orders. I'm the only waitress working tonight, and it looks like we're going to get busy."

After Trey ordered a beer and Nicole a glass of ice tea, Linda hurried away.

As Nicole began to study the menu, Trey said, "Linda went through hell a few years ago. Her parents were killed in an auto accident down in Phoenix and then she lost her little sister to a blood disease."

Lowering the menu, Nicole looked at him with

dismay. "How awful. Does she have other siblings or family around?"

"No," Trey replied. "She's all that's left of the Barstows. I believe she has distant relatives somewhere in Nevada. But I don't think they get along."

Nicole grimaced. "Relatives can be well-meaning, but they can be smothering, too."

He let out a dry laugh. "That's one thing I don't have to worry about."

Nicole wondered what he meant by the remark, but before she had the chance to ask, Linda arrived with their drinks.

Once the waitress had jotted down their orders and moved on to a nearby table, Nicole turned her attention back to Trey.

"I'm interested to hear more about this ranch you'd like to have," she told him as she pushed a straw into her ice tea. "Have you already chosen a place you want to purchase?"

Nodding, he twisted off the cap on the beer bottle. "Yes. Except that the owner doesn't want to sell. At least, not now. I'm hoping that by the time I'm financially able to offer him a price, he'll change his mind. It's a long shot, but I'm like the little engine that could—I think I can, I think I can," he added with a grin.

She chuckled at his self-description. "This property must be your dream spot."

A wistful look spread over his face. "It is. Part

of the property runs along a tributary of the Has-sayampa River. It's lush and beautiful land. A man could raise some fine cattle there."

"Is the owner using it to raise cattle now?"

He frowned. "No. The man's too old and feeble to do outside work anymore. He mostly just sits on his porch and looks out over the land."

"Aw, that's sad," she said. "I guess holding on to the property brings him a measure of comfort. But that doesn't replace being young and virile and able to do the things he used to do."

"Age is a thief," he agreed, then grinned at her. "But it'll be a long, long time before you have to worry about aging."

"I'm twenty-six." She leveled a curious look at him. "How old are you?"

"Thirty-one. Compared to you, I'm ancient."

"Hmm. You do look ready for a rocking chair," she teased.

He chuckled. "You didn't look close enough. I have two rocking chairs on my front porch."

"One for you and one for a lady friend." Her expression sobered as she thoughtfully studied his rugged face. "I'm very curious about something, Trey. Why don't you have a wife and kids?"

From the incredulous look on his face, it seemed he considered being a husband and father as far-fetched as becoming a brain surgeon.

"Me? With a family? That's—uh—funny, Nicci."

"Why?"

He shrugged. "I'm just not cut out for that kind of life. And the women around here know I'm just a confirmed bachelor. That's why—well, I don't have women knocking on my door."

Intrigued by his response, she said, "Frankly, you look like a family man to me. You don't like women or children?"

His short chuckle was awkward. "I like both— plenty enough. Kids are great. So are women."

"Ah—so, you just don't want one on a permanent basis. Is that it?" She didn't know why she was persisting on the subject. She wasn't interested in husband hunting. Her chance for that went out the window with her mother's nervous breakdown. Besides, she and Trey were completely opposite. They'd never be a match. That's what Roslyn had said. And yet, each time Nicole gazed at Trey's warm smile, she wanted to believe they'd be perfect together.

He coughed and reached for his beer. After a long swig, he let out a long breath and shifted around in his chair.

Seeing that he was terribly uncomfortable, she took pity on him. "I'm sorry, Trey. I'm being nosey. You don't have to answer that if you'd rather not."

A little half grin creased a dimple in one of his cheeks, and Nicole found herself mesmerized by the endearing expression on his face.

"You're not being too nosey. I just don't know

how to answer your question. Except that women like me for a friend. But they don't give me a serious thought."

She found that hard to believe. He was a good-looking man. No, he was more than that, she thought. He was very sexy in a rugged, earthy way. Plus, he was nice and easy to talk to. There had to be women around here who found him attractive. Which made her wonder if he deliberately ignored most of them.

"Maybe that's because all you want is to be their friend," she suggested. "Maybe you're not encouraging any of these women to be more."

He let out another long breath. "You could be right. I've been told that I put out some weird vibes."

Different perhaps, but not weird, she decided.

After a sip of tea, she leaned slightly forward. "What would you do if a woman wanted to get serious with you?"

He laughed, but Nicole could tell it was a nervous reaction more than a sound of humor.

"Probably run like hell. Later on, she'd be glad that I did."

Her gaze met his, and as she studied the green depths, she saw flickering shadows. The kind of darkness that was born of deep disappointments and lost trust. He'd been hurt in the past, she realized, yet he hid it all behind a beguiling smile.

Deciding it was time to change the subject, she

gestured to the mural next to their table. "I've learned that mining played a big part in founding this town."

"Mostly gold. And some silver," he replied. "You might not know it, but there's still quite a few mine claims around here."

Surprised, she asked, "For real? Is any gold actually found?"

"I couldn't say. I've heard of some being unearthed, but I don't think any major veins have been discovered. Thank God for that. I'd really hate to see a modern-day gold rush hit around here."

Nicole said, "Speaking of gold rushes, Roslyn was having a fit for me to move out here a week earlier than I did. The Gold Rush Days festival was going on, and she wanted me to be here to enjoy some of it. Unfortunately, I couldn't get everything packed by then, so I missed the celebration. She says it's a very big deal. Her mother-in-law, Maureen, always throws a big party at Three Rivers Ranch, and the town is always loaded with people and fun things to do."

"Doc always insists that I go to the party at Three Rivers. This last one was a doozy. I think there were at least a hundred people there, and I ate so much I thought I was going to be sick. As for here in town, thousands of people come to the festival every year. Booths and special events are set up on the streets. And there's always the big rodeo and music concerts."

"Did you go to any of the events?" she asked curiously.

"One night of the rodeo. That's about all I could make room for in my schedule. Foaling and calving time is always a busy time for me and Doc." He gestured to the mural of the prospector. "Did you know that Loretta often pans for gold?"

Nicole looked at him with surprise. "You're talking about Loretta at the clinic? The girl who does the bookkeeping and billing?"

"Yeah. She lives up by Congress. It was a big gold-mining town back in the 1880s. Now the area is mostly a ghost town, but there's still a small community of folks around there. Loretta likes to hike the canyons and pan a little."

"That sounds like fun to me. Has she ever found gold?"

"I think she's found a few tiny nuggets. She's stashing them away until she gets enough to make a down payment on a house."

"That doesn't surprise me that she's saving her finds. Loretta seems very down-to-earth and responsible. I wonder if she'd show us how to do it? Or maybe you already know how?"

His thick brows lifted with uncertainty. "Do it? Uh—you mean pan?"

Nicole laughed. "What else would I mean?"

With an awkward chuckle, he shifted around on his seat. "Well, uh—show us how to save money?

She has a degree in business. But yeah, I figure she'd be happy to show you how to pan."

"Us," Nicole corrected. "Me and you. I wouldn't want to go without you."

The look on his face was a mixture of disbelief and bewilderment. "Oh—I don't think, uh—you'd want me along."

"Why not? You're an outdoor guy. Me, I've always been a city girl. But now that I've moved out here, I'd like to learn how to be more of an outdoor girl."

He leveled a thoughtful glance at her. "Guess you don't have much to do around here. Not like what you were used to in Fort Worth with all the fancy shopping places and theaters and things like that."

This wasn't the first time he'd suggested she might be bored by small-town living, and Nicole resented his way of thinking. It was too much like her parents, who continued to insist she'd soon grow bored and want to return to her old home.

Frowning, she tried not to sound annoyed, but frustration wrapped around her words anyway. "From what I understand, Phoenix has all those things, and it's not that far away. But contrary to what you may think, I'm not overwhelmed with the urge to see city lights. I don't have a craving to run to a shopping mall or theater, or concert!"

A look of mild surprise came over his face. "Pardon me, Nicci, I guess I hit a sore spot."

She heaved out a long breath. "I guess you did. A

very sore spot. You sound just like my parents. And I moved a thousand miles away so I wouldn't have to hear them tell me what I needed or wanted to make me happy. I prefer to decide those things for myself."

A wide grin suddenly curved his lips. "I knew there had to be some fire to go with all that red hair. Do you always look so darned pretty when you're— uh, fired up?"

Her mouth fell open, and then she rolled her eyes and chuckled. "I don't know. I've never bothered to look in the mirror when I'm fired up," she admitted, then feeling more than foolish, she reached across the table and placed her hand over his. "Forgive me, Trey. I shouldn't be so touchy. You were just making a reasonable assumption, and I went off like a shrew. I'm not really one of those. It's just that— before I moved out here, things were a little rough back in Texas. I think it's going to take me a while to get past them."

The grin on his face gentled to an expression of understanding, and Nicci felt something inside her go as soft and gooey as melted candy.

"Aw, you don't ever have to apologize to me. I've got a tough hide. You could shoot an arrow right at me and it would just bounce right off."

"Especially if it's a cupid's arrow," Linda remarked as she arrived carrying a tray with plates of steaming food. "If you tried to shoot one of those into him, it would probably break the arrow."

Trey scowled at the waitress while Nicole studied her with amused curiosity.

"You say that like you know him," Nicole said impishly. "I've never seen him without his shirt. Does he wear metal armor under there?"

Linda laughed as she carefully placed the plates on the table. "Well, I confess, I haven't seen him shirtless, either. But I figure there's a bunch of barbed wire under there. To keep all the women at a safe distance."

"Oh, now Linda, you know I use a big stick to keep the females away. Not barbed wire," Trey joked.

Linda looked at Nicole and winked. "Don't believe anything he says. He tells stories. But he's a superman with animals."

Nicole glanced over the table to see that a ruddy color had appeared on his neck and jaws.

"A superman with animals, huh? That's quite a compliment."

Trey laughed. "Talk about telling stories—Linda's really telling one now."

The waitress poured more ice and tea into Nicole's glass and then placed a fresh bottle of beer in front of Trey's plate.

"Remember, Trey, you rushed my sister's cat to the animal clinic, after a stray dog tore a hunk from her side. Doc Chandler sewed her up and it never even left a scar. And she loved you for that."

"Oh yeah, I remember her. She was an orange

tabby," Trey said. "But I'm not surprised that she loved me. Most cats take right up with me."

Groaning, the waitress rolled her eyes toward the ceiling. "Janna loved you, silly! Not Annabelle."

His grin was suddenly replaced with a somber nod. "I loved Janna, too. I'm glad I made her happy by saving her cat."

Linda cleared her throat and took a step back from the table. "Yeah, well, if you two have everything you need, I'll let you get on with your meal."

The waitress walked off, and Nicole thoughtfully watched the young woman until she disappeared through a pair of swinging doors at the back of the room.

Picking up her fork, she looked over at Trey. "You know, I'm very glad you suggested we come to this restaurant tonight. I've learned something important from your friend."

His lips twisted to a wry slant as he sliced into a chicken-fried steak covered with gravy. "That I wear barbed wire and can help care for an injured cat? Nothing important about that."

Smiling faintly, she said, "Those are nice things to know. But I was thinking more about the suffering Linda has endured. It reminds me to focus on the important things. And you know what I've decided? That you and me sitting here enjoying dinner together is one of them."

His fork stopped midway to his mouth as he

looked at her in wonder. "Gosh, Nicci, that's a nice thing to say. It feels pretty important to me, too."

No glib words to try to impress her. No pretending to be anything more than a simple, hardworking guy. Nicole liked his unassuming manner. In fact, she was beginning to like everything about the man. And whether that was foolish or smart, she figured only time would tell.

Normally, Trey was never at a loss for words. But as Nicole drove the two of them back to his place, he couldn't think of a sensible thing to say.

Maybe because his brain was too busy trying to figure out her motive for spending this evening with him. Any idiot could see she didn't need *him* for company. And there sure wasn't any need for her to act as though she liked him. Not really like him in a romantic way.

Where did you get the idea she's thinking of you in that way, Trey? Just because she was nice enough to invite you out? You're a fool if you let yourself start imagining her as a girlfriend. She's just a coworker. Nothing more.

"From the scowl on your face you must be miserable," Nicole said as she turned the car off the main highway and onto the dirt road leading to his house. "I'm sorry, Trey, if the evening has bored you. Hopefully, as time passes, I'll learn more about the clinic and the animals you treat. Then I'll be able to talk shop without sounding too ignorant."

Still frowning, he glanced at her. "I'm not miserable."

She said, "Then you must be feeling ill. You haven't said more than ten words in the past fifteen minutes."

Doc would be splitting his sides laughing at the mere idea that Trey could stay quiet for five minutes, much less fifteen. "Sorry, Nicci. I guess I've been thinking. That's all." He glanced over at her lovely profile illuminated by the lights on the dash panel. "And you don't sound ignorant about anything. You've been great company. Just great."

He could hear her release a long breath, and the sound had him wondering what she could possibly be thinking. That this was the first and last time she'd ever waste an evening on him? No. She couldn't be thinking along those lines, he decided. During dinner, she'd asked him to go panning with her. That didn't sound like she intended to end their friendship—or whatever it was.

"I'm glad," she said. "I didn't invite you out tonight to bore you silly."

Bored? Trey could've told her that he'd never been so wide-awake in his life. Every cell in his body was standing at attention, every nerve was humming like a high-voltage wire.

Instead, he said, "Don't worry. I'm not about to go to sleep."

Less than five minutes later, she was turning into his driveway and parking behind his truck.

Once she switched off the engine, he nervously swiped his palms down the thighs of his jeans. If Candy Anderson, or any of the other girls he often danced with at the Fandango, had been sitting behind the steering wheel instead of Nicole, he wouldn't be at a loss for words. He wouldn't be floundering around wondering what might be the right or wrong thing to say or do.

She turned slightly toward him and smiled. "This has been nice. The meal was delicious."

Her lips reminded him of pink rose petals, and he figured if he ever had the good fortune to kiss them, they would feel just as soft and smooth. "Good. Homestyle cooking is hard to beat," he said, then made a backhanded gesture toward the house. "Would you, uh, like to go in or sit on the porch? I can make coffee."

"Oh, I'm too full for coffee, but I'd love to sit on the porch," she told him.

He'd not expected her to accept his invitation. The fact that she did, and so readily, caused his spirits to soar.

"Great!" He practically jumped out of the car and hurried around to help her out. "I'll show you my rockers."

Laughing, she placed her hand in his and stepped onto the ground. "Okay. But I think I'd better get my jacket first."

He released her hand, and Nicole opened the back door of the car and collected a jean jacket lying on the seat.

"Let me help you with that," he said.

He took the jacket from her and held it open so that she could easily slip her arms into the sleeves. The gentlemanly gesture was unexpected and so was the way her heart fluttered as his hands smoothed the fabric over the back of her shoulders.

"Thanks. I won't shiver now." Not from the chilly air, she thought. But the way her body was reacting to his nearness, she was definitely having to fight off the trembles.

"We wouldn't want that." He gently rested a hand at the small of her back and urged in the direction of the house. "Maybe we should go inside where it's warmer and forget about the porch."

"Oh, I'm not that fragile." She glanced up at him. "But it's nice of you to be so thoughtful."

As they walked through the short gate and down the stepping stones that led to the porch, he said, "I have a feeling you're being extra polite. I'm kind of rusty when it comes to entertaining a woman. And to be honest, I don't know any women like you. I mean,

I'm friends with Roslyn and acquainted with all the Hollister women, but you're different."

"How am I different? Because I'm not from this area?"

"I—that's part of it," he said. "And you're—well, more refined—is what I'm trying to say."

Nicole realized he meant that as a compliment more than anything else, but somehow it didn't feel that way. Rather, it made her feel like he'd lifted her up and set her several feet apart from him. She didn't want to be different from him. She wanted to fit into his life.

She cast him a doleful glance. "Don't put me on a pedestal, Trey. I'm just a regular person. Like you."

"Aw hell, Nicci, no one is like me," he said with an emphatic shake of his head. "Or I should say, no one would want to be like me."

Nicole couldn't stop herself from laughing. "Well, you are a little unique. But that's what makes you special."

They stepped onto the porch, and Trey's arm settled across the back of her shoulders. The weight of it was a warm reminder of just how long it had been since she'd had any sort of physical contact with a man. So long, in fact, that she'd forgotten how it felt to feel a spark of attraction.

A spark? Who are you kidding, Nicole? From the moment this evening with Trey started, you've been experiencing an explosion of thoughts and urges that could only be described as hot and bothersome.

He said, "Come over here and try out one of the rockers. I'll let you sit in Granny's. She's the reason I have two. When she comes for a visit, she likes to sit out here on the porch."

The yard lamp situated on a pole at one corner of the lawn illuminated the wooden rockers. Both chairs were painted hunter green and possessed tall backs. A padded cushion covered in yellow print calico was in one of the seats, and Nicole didn't have to guess that this particular chair was his grandmother's.

He gestured toward the one with the cushion. "You take that one," he said. "It's Granny's."

She sank into the rocker and immediately set it into motion. "I feel ten years older already," she joked. "I hope I don't look it."

He laughed as he took a seat in the nearby chair. "Rockers aren't just for old people. They're good for everybody. The back and forth kind of takes your troubles away and eases your mind."

Maybe she should've gotten her mother a rocker back when her father flew the coop, Nicole thought ruefully. It would've been a heck of a lot better than Angela lying in bed, expecting an anxiety pill to change her life for the better.

She looked over to see he'd stretched his long legs out in front of him and crossed his boots at the ankles. In spite of his tall, muscular frame, he had a litheness about him that made his movements very sensual. Although, she expected he would laugh at that notion. He'd intimated through his conversation that he considered himself a clumsy oaf in lots of ways, and she didn't know why. He actually seemed the opposite.

"Does your grandmother stop by often?" she asked.

"She drives over to see me at least once a month."

"Oh, she drives?"

He chuckled. "An old ton Ford pickup with a floor shift and dually wheels."

"Wow! Exactly how old is your grandmother, anyway?"

"Seventy. But she'd pass for years younger. She's a widow—Granddad died about fifteen years ago. Now she works as a waitress in a little café over in Aguila. That's a community west of here in Maricopa County."

Intrigued, she asked, "She still works?"

He nodded. "She still does *everything.* In fact, I just learned she has a fifty-seven-year-old boyfriend who wants to marry her," he added with a touch of sarcasm.

She glanced at him. "You look and sound sulky. I take it that you don't approve."

He wiped a hand over his face. "Oh, I wouldn't say I disapprove. I just don't want her to lose her head and get hurt."

Nicole couldn't help but chuckle. "If your grandmother has been single for the past fifteen years, she hardly sounds like the type to lose her head."

"Well, no. She's very sensible. I guess that's why I'm a little concerned. Since Granddad died, this is the first time she's ever acted serious about a man. And Harley—he's—I guess most women would see him as a virile, good-looking guy."

"Is that supposed to be a problem?"

The smirk on his face very nearly made Nicole laugh out loud.

"Not exactly."

"Then what's wrong? Is he a deadbeat? A jerk or something along those lines?"

Shaking his head, he looked out over the shadowy yard. "He's hardly a deadbeat. He's a farmer and works hard at it, too. He owns plenty of land and a nice old farmhouse. Lots nicer than the house Granny lives in. And he's not a jerk—I—hell, I guess it just gets to me when I think about my grandmother with a guy like him."

"Not a bit jealous, are you?" she asked, unable to keep a teasing note from her voice.

He slanted a sheepish glance at her. "Okay. I'm guilty. But dang it, for the past fifteen years she's been more like my mother than my grandmother, and she's the only relative I have around here. Guess you think I'm acting like a child."

"No. You're acting like a typical man."

His grunt was full of amusement. "Granny says they're one and the same."

She chuckled and then sat back to study him thoughtfully. "You say your grandmother was more like a mother for the past fifteen years. Did your mother pass away?"

"No. Mom is well and happy. See, my parents divorced when I was a kid. After Dad moved to Montana, Mom stayed here and took care of me. As soon as I graduated high school, she remarried and moved to New Mexico, where a lot of her side of the family still lives. But it wasn't long after Mom left that Grandpa was killed in a tractor accident. So that left just me and Granny. We're the only two Lasseters still around here."

From Trey's happy-go-lucky attitude it was hard to imagine that he'd come from a broken home. She needed to take lessons from him.

"I can understand why you feel a bit overly protective of your grandmother," she told him. "But on the other hand, you ought to be happy for her. I'm sure she gets lonely. And we all need to feel loved."

He darted a hasty glance at her before he turned his gaze on the darkened landscape beyond the house. "Yeah. You're right. And Granny would never quit loving me. No matter what," he murmured.

They both went quiet after that, and just as Nicole had decided it was time she start for home, he turned to look at her.

"Do you need to feel loved, Nicci?"

Her heart thudded like a slow, heavy drumbeat. "Sure, I do. Don't you?"

He looked away from her and made an issue of clearing his throat. The awkward reaction made Nicole wonder if he'd ever talked about the emotion to anyone before now. Had he ever loved a woman? Really loved her with all his heart? If so, it obviously hadn't lasted.

He said, "Sometimes I think about Doc and his family. Roslyn is nuts about him. And he feels the same way about her. But a guy like me doesn't need that much love. What would I do with it?"

How could she answer his question? She'd never been on the receiving end of that much love, either. And if she wanted to be completely honest about it, she'd never given that much of her heart to anyone. Not even Randy. Funny how she was beginning to see that now.

Doing her best to put a teasing note in her voice, she said, "Oh, I don't know. Lock it away in a drawer and take it out whenever you get lonely."

He grunted with amusement, then looked at her and grinned. "Heck, I don't have time to be lonely."

She was wondering how to respond to that when he suddenly rose to his feet.

"I'm a bad host," he said. "Would you like to go in where it's warmer? I can still make coffee?"

Her heart was already hopping around like a

bunny on steroids; the last thing she needed was a dose of caffeine. "Thanks for the offer, but I think I'd better be going."

Leaving the rocker, she closed the short span of distance between them and reached for his hand. His fingers immediately wrapped snugly around hers, and the warmth that emanated from his hand radiated through her whole body.

"This has been such a lovely evening, Trey. Thank you for being nice enough to share your time with me."

The odd expression that swept over his features told her he'd not been expecting such a declaration from her. And she suddenly realized that he was clueless to the effect he was having on her. He had no idea that she was attracted to him, or how much she longed to be close to him.

"It's been my pleasure. Thank you for inviting me."

She continued to stand there gazing up at him, hoping he could read the wanting on her face. When he failed to respond, she let out a long, exasperated breath.

"Am I going to have to bop you over the head?"

His eyes widened. "Have I done something wrong?"

"You haven't done *anything*. That's the problem. I thought you might show your gratitude for dinner by giving me a kiss. Or was it not worth that much to you?"

His features twisted with comical confusion. "A kiss? From me?"

She didn't know whether to laugh or groan. Instead of doing either, she gestured to the darkness around them. "I don't see anyone else around here."

"No. But—uh—have you forgotten who I am?"

"Not hardly. You're Trey. Doc's other right hand. The guy who can sew up a cat better than a neurosurgeon. I think I remember you, all right." She rose up on the tips of her toes and pressed her lips to his lean cheek. "Except that tonight you don't smell like cow manure."

His hand came up to cradle the side of her face, and she closed her eyes as the gentle touch washed over her.

"That's because I spent most of my day with cats and dogs."

Opening her eyes, she found herself staring at his lips. The alluring curve of the bottom one, the fine vertical lines running through both and the chiseled corners guarded by a pair of irresistible dimples.

"The only thing you smell like right now is—a man," she murmured.

His hand slipped into her hair, and with his fingers against her scalp, he tilted her face up to his.

Barely breathing, Nicole waited for his lips to settle over hers. By the time the intimate contact was made, her legs were trembling, and she flattened her hands against his chest in order to support herself.

His kiss was everything she'd imagined and much, much more. Like a double shot of bourbon, the masculine taste of him went straight to her head, numbing her senses to everything but the pleasure he was giving her.

With an unwitting groan, she wound her arms around his neck and opened her lips to his. This time she didn't have to tell him what she wanted; he instinctively knew that she was craving his nearness, that she was hungry for the connection of his mouth upon hers.

Even if a clock had been ticking away the seconds in her ear, she wouldn't have registered how long she continued to kiss him, or how much time had passed since she'd pressed the front of her body against the hard length of his. All she knew was that she felt warm and alive and wanted.

It wasn't until the distant sound of a dog's bark broke through her foggy senses that she realized she'd lost complete control of herself. The reality caused her to quickly step back.

With her gaze glued to the floor, she sucked in a long, ragged breath. "Oh, Trey, I'm sorry! I don't know what happened to me. You must think I'm awful or—worse."

When he didn't immediately respond, she looked up to find a serious expression on his face. The sight of it rattled her almost as much as the kiss they'd just shared.

"Nicci, I—why are you sorry? Because you regret kissing me?"

"No! Nothing like that—" She swallowed hard, and then because she just had to touch him, she stepped forward and rested a hand against the middle of his chest. It was like touching a rock wall, hot from the baking rays of an afternoon sun. And the urge to slip her fingers between the snaps on his shirt and touch his bare skin was so strong it was all she could do to resist.

"I don't regret kissing you. It's just that I've probably given you the idea that I'm—cheap or on the prowl. That's not the way it is, Trey. Not at all."

A little half grin lifted one corner of his mouth. "I could never think such things about you. If you want the truth, I feel darned flattered. In fact, I doubt I'll be able to get my hat on tomorrow. You've just caused my head to grow about two sizes bigger."

His sweetness made tears prick the back of her eyes. "You're so nice to me. Too nice, really," she said huskily. "I hope I haven't scared you off. I hope you'd like for us to spend more time together. Because I'd like it—very much."

His green eyes connected with hers, and in that moment, Nicole decided that everything she'd ever believed about herself, every plan she'd held for her future had suddenly changed.

How could her life shift so drastically in just one short evening? After one sweet kiss?

He suddenly grinned and tugged playfully on a strand of her hair. "Okay. You said you'd like for us to go panning. We'll do that Sunday. Just the two of us—like prospectors in the old, Wild West days. How does that sound to you?"

Like heaven to her ears, she thought, then very nearly laughed at the idea of her hiking a gulch. "I think I'd better go buy myself some sturdy boots."

"And a hat," he added with a wink. "You don't want to burn your pretty face."

Amazed at the joy and excitement she felt at the notion of going out with him again, she laughed.

"Okay, a hat, too," she said, then momentarily pressed her cheek against his. "We'll have fun."

"Sure, we will," he murmured against her hair.

Knowing if she stayed close to him much longer, she'd end up making a fool of herself, she eased away from him and started toward the steps.

"I think I'd better be going. Good night, Trey."

He lifted a hand in farewell. "Good night, Nicci."

She flashed him a smile and then hurried out to her car before she could do an about-face and run straight back to his arms.

Chapter Five

Barring emergencies, the clinic was normally closed on Saturdays, but that rarely meant Trey would get the day off. Chandler used most Saturdays to make remote calls to outlying ranches, so Trey was hardly surprised when he called at five thirty the next morning with two jobs scheduled for the day.

Now it was five in the evening and they were finally driving away from the Flying W to head back to the clinic at Wickenburg.

"I didn't ask you this morning if you had plans for today," Chandler said as he slumped tiredly back in the passenger seat of the truck. "If you did, they're ruined."

Trey chuckled. "Make plans for Saturday? I know you better than to do something like that."

Chandler let out a tired sigh. "I always start out with the intentions of taking the day off, but then the phone rings and I can't refuse."

Trey took his eyes off the highway long enough to glance at his boss and longtime friend. Sometimes he really worried about Chandler's health. Not that the man was ever sick. But he worked himself to the point of exhaustion. Not only at the clinic and with remote calls, but he also handled most of the veterinary work for Three Rivers Ranch, which in itself was a major job.

"Tomorrow is Sunday. You need to rest, Doc. Have breakfast in bed. Let Roslyn spoil you a little."

He let out an amused grunt. "That's not my style. Besides, Evelyn and Billy are always up early. Those two would have my breakfast scattered all over the bed. As for me needing rest, I've figured out how to lighten my workload. It's something I've been thinking about for a long time now."

Trey frowned as he pressed hard on the accelerator and shot past a rattletrap car chugging smoke from the tailpipe.

"How's that? Close the clinic and just work at the ranch?"

"Hell! That won't ever happen. Having the clinic was always my dream." He straightened up in the seat and looked at Trey. "No, the way I figure how to fix this problem is to have another veterinarian working with me. And I don't mean hire some stranger. I want to have someone I've known for years working with me. Someone I can trust. I'm talking about you."

Trey's head whipped around so fast the bones in his neck made a cracking noise. "What? Damn, Doc, I'm no vet. I'm just an assistant."

He swatted a hand through the air. "You're more than an assistant. You've been more than that for years now. All you need is a bit more experience with surgeries and a few more years of college and vet school to get a diploma to certify you're a veterinarian."

"You're helping me get experience by watching you do surgeries. But the diploma is a whole different matter. What are you thinking? That you'll pay some underworld person to make a fake diploma for me? Won't work, Doc. Everybody around here would know it was a forgery."

Chandler groaned. "I ought to knock you in the head."

"You're not the only one who's told me that," Trey said, his mind replaying every word, every touch he'd exchanged with Nicole as they'd stood on his porch last night. He'd never been so stunned in his life when she'd told him she wanted to bop him over the head because he hadn't made a move to kiss her. Him, kissing a woman like her? A part of him still couldn't believe any of those moments had happened, while the other part was finding them impossible to forget.

"I don't do fraudulent things, Trey. And I wouldn't buy you a diploma in veterinary medicine even if I could. I want you to earn it the old-fashioned way. With that nose of yours in a book."

Trey's short cackle was full of disbelief, and then he began to laugh in earnest. "Oh, Doc, sometimes you're hilarious. And the funny thing about it, you're not even trying to be."

Chandler muttered a few curse words under his breath. "What's so funny about you setting goals for yourself?"

Trey grimaced. "I have goals. You know about them. I'm saving up for a ranch of my own. It might take me a while, but I'll get it."

"Who says you can't have the ranch and the diploma? I'll tell you one thing, Trey, you could get a heck of a lot more ranch if you made the money of a veterinarian."

"Well, yeah. But that's a whole lot of schooling, and I'm not smart enough to be a vet."

"The hell you aren't," Chandler shot back at him. "You already have an associate's degree in vet tech. All you need to do is plow forward and get the rest."

Trey smirked. "Sure, Doc. Two more years of undergraduate studies and then four years of veterinary school. In the meantime, I have to make a living. No, you need to find a practicing vet who'd be willing to move here. Or better yet, talk Roslyn into becoming a vet. She's smart and loves animals. And she has a special touch with the small ones."

"Hmm. It's true that Roslyn enjoys working at the clinic, but she loves being a mother to our children, thank God. That's more than enough to keep her busy. Besides, you don't need to be worried about making a living while you're studying. I can take care of that problem."

Trey had no doubt that Chandler could take care of him financially. The Hollister family was one of the richest in Arizona. And for more than a decade now Chandler had added enormously to his wealth from the income of the clinic. Still, Trey had always paid his own way. In fact, as a teenager he'd worked to help his mother put food on the table for both of them. He wasn't about to start taking handouts now.

"You're a good man, Doc. And way too generous—especially where I'm concerned." He shook his head. "Me being a real, certified vet? Your dog is sniffing the wrong trail."

"We'll see," he said, then slanted a sly look in Trey's direction. "I heard you went on a date last night. How did that go?"

Trey eased off the gas as the Hollister Animal Clinic, a large brick building with a spacious parking area, finally appeared on the left-hand side of the highway. "Where did you hear that?"

"Roslyn invited Nicci out to the ranch last night for dinner. Nicci told her she couldn't make it because she was taking you out to dinner." Chandler chuckled. "How did you manage that, ole pal?"

Trey let out an uncomfortable laugh. It wasn't often that Chandler questioned him about his social life. Mostly because Trey didn't have one. Not the romantic kind.

"To tell you the truth, Doc, I'm still trying to figure it out myself. I didn't do anything. Nicci's invitation just kinda came out of the blue. And I couldn't turn her down and hurt her feelings. Seeing how she's new around here and doesn't know a lot of people yet."

"Yeah, I'm sure it was a real pain forcing yourself to go," he said dryly.

"Okay, go ahead and make jokes about it," Trey shot back at him. "But it was nice. Really nice. And we're going out again tomorrow. So there."

Chandler sat straight up in his seat. "Seriously? She agreed to another date with you?"

Trey scowled as he flipped on the blinker and steered the work truck into the clinic parking lot. "She suggested it. And I didn't want to disappoint her," he said, then relented just a bit. "Actually, I'm looking forward to it. We're going panning."

Chandler was clearly floored. "Panning for gold?"

Trey parked the truck near one of the treatment barns and cut the motor. "Yeah, that yellow stuff that makes men crazy," he joked, then added in a more serious tone, "It was her idea, but I think it might be fun. I have a friend who owns some land up near Congress. He's always told me I could pan there anytime I like. I just never took him up on the offer."

Chandler tugged the brim of his hat down on his forehead. "Hmm. On second thought, you might just find yourself a fortune."

"Doc, now I know you've been working too hard. We both know that finding gold, even a tiny nugget of it, would be one chance in a million."

Chuckling, Chandler reached for his medical bag and opened the truck door. "I'm not talking about gold, Trey. There are other kinds of fortunes a man can find."

"Well, there might still be some veins of copper and silver around here, but that's not something you can pick up and put in your pocket." Trey pulled out the truck keys and tossed them to Chandler. "Nicci and I aren't hunting a fortune. We're just going on a little excursion, that's all."

Shaking his head, Chandler climbed to the ground. "I'm not talking about the kind of fortune you put in your pocket."

Trey looked at him with sudden dawning. "Oh, guess you're talking about Roslyn and the kids now."

A clever smile crossed Chandler's tired face. "That's exactly what I'm talking about. And right now, I'm going home to Three Rivers. Good luck on the panning expedition."

"Thanks, Doc. I'll lock everything up here. See you Monday morning."

The veterinarian lifted a hand in farewell and then walked across the parking area to where he'd left his personal truck beneath the shade of a mesquite tree.

Trey was busy unloading the equipment from the bed of the work truck when he looked up to see Chandler driving away. For a moment he thoughtfully watched the vehicle until it disappeared on down the highway.

There are other kinds of fortunes a man can find.

Surely, Chandler hadn't been talking about a man finding himself love, or a family. That would be crazy. Trey had known Nicole only a few short days. Besides, Trey wasn't looking for that kind of fortune. He figured his life was already rich enough. When a man started being greedy, he was deliberately asking for trouble. And Trey didn't need trouble. Not even the kind with strawberry-blond hair and big gray eyes.

Early the next morning, Nicole was hurriedly downing a light breakfast of coffee and toast when her cell phone rang. As soon as she spotted her mother's number on the ID, she cringed with dread and guilt.

For more than two years, she had basically been her mother's caregiver. Now that Angela was well and supposedly happy again, Nicole needed a break. She needed time for herself. Time to deal with the changes her parents' divorce and subsequent remarriage had brought to her life.

Sighing, she punched the accept button and lifted the phone to her ear.

"Good morning, darlin'," Angela spoke cheerfully. "I thought I'd call early before you started getting ready for church."

"I just got home from early Mass. I'm having breakfast now."

"My goodness, you're energetic this morning," she said. "Your father is still asleep, and I'm having my first cup of coffee. You must have big plans for today."

Ignoring the last bite of toast on her plate, she said, "Actually, I'm going out—with a friend."

"Oh, I'll bet you're heading to Phoenix on a shopping trip. I almost wish I were there to go with you."

Oh Lord, spare me that, Nicole prayed. "I'm not going shopping, Mother. Or to Phoenix. We're going out in the countryside."

There was a short pause before Angela's skeptical laugh sounded in her ear. "Really, Nicci, I understand you think you like this new job at an animal hospital, but that doesn't mean you've turned into the farmer's daughter."

Trying to keep from grinding her teeth, Nicole rose from the little breakfast table and carried her plate over to the sink. "I don't just like my job, Mother. I love my job. And why should it surprise you that I might do something outdoors? When Roslyn still lived in Fort Worth, she and I would picnic at the lake. And during the workweek, I often ate my lunch at the park. I'm not afraid of fresh air and sunshine."

"No. But you live in the desert now. It's probably full of rattlesnakes and scorpions and all sorts of things that sting and bite."

"You mean like all those snakes and things in Texas," Nicole attempted to joke.

"Yes, but we're more civilized here in the city," she argued. "I imagine you have to drive miles before you can find a shade tree."

Rolling her eyes, Nicole was thinking how to reply to that absurd comment, when her mother spoke again.

"Are you and Roslyn doing something at the ranch today?"

Knowing her mother was on a fishing expedition, Nicole said, "No. This is Chandler's only day off, and Roslyn always spends it with him and their children. I'm going out with a friend at work. And time is ticking on, Mother. I need to finish getting ready or I'm going to be late. I'll talk to you later."

There was a long, pregnant pause before she finally said, "Well, I get the message—all right, goodbye, Nicci."

The connection went dead, and Nicole didn't

waste time agonizing over her mother's call. She hurried to the bedroom and reached for a pair of jeans and a yellow T-shirt. As she changed into the casual clothing, she thought about all the plans she'd made before she moved to Arizona. None of them had included a man, or giving her heart away. But all of those well-meaning intentions had flown out of her head the moment she'd kissed Trey.

Or had he kissed her? True, she'd initiated the embrace, but he'd definitely followed through and in the most mind-bending way. Since then she'd not been able to get him, or the kiss, out of her thoughts. What did it mean? That she was starved for physical affection, or that she'd finally met the man of her dreams? One way or the other, she was determined to find the answer.

When Nicole arrived at Trey's place, he met her at the yard gate, and she promptly stood on her tiptoes to press a light kiss to his cheek.

"Good morning." She stepped back and gave him a wide smile. "I hope you're feeling like a prospector today."

Beneath the brim of his brown hat, she could see a twinkle in his green eyes. The sight of it made the morning sun behind his shoulder seem even brighter.

"I don't have a burro and pickax," he said with a chuckle. "But I'm ready to try my hand at finding gold—or something."

Worn faded blue jeans encased his narrow hips and long, muscular legs while a khaki Western shirt covered his broad shoulders. He looked so rugged and masculine and so very endearing that she wanted to glue herself to the front of his body and kiss him until they both forgot everything but each other.

The reckless thought warmed her cheeks and made her laugh sound a bit breathless. "I don't have a pickax or burro, either. But I did pick up two pans and a shovel yesterday at the local hardware store. And a few things from the deli for our lunch."

"I hope you know that we'll be lucky if we find one flake of gold, much less a nugget."

His warning was softened with a lopsided grin, and Nicole realized it wouldn't matter to her if they found only worthless rocks.

"No worries. I liken it to fishing. The fun is in the trying. At least, that's what I'm told. I've never really fished," she added jokingly. "But then, I've never panned, either. So this is a learning experience."

"For me, too." He gestured toward his truck. "Let's get everything loaded and be on our way."

It took only a minute or two to move the equipment from her car to his truck. Once they'd finished, Trey said, "I'd better go fetch a jacket. Just in case a cold wind blows in. You might want to come along and visit the restroom before we leave. The trip is long and bumpy."

"Thanks for the warning," she said as she fell into step beside him.

As they walked past the rocking chairs, Nicole decided she probably had been a bit forward for daring him to kiss her. But she didn't regret it.

From the moment she'd met Trey, she'd sensed a gentle innocence about him. Given the fact the man was thirty-one and had probably enjoyed a few girlfriends in his time, the notion seemed laughable. But the innocence she perceived in him had nothing to do with sex. It was something precious and untouched, something that came straight from his heart. And that simplicity was the very thing that drew her to him.

"Come on in," he invited, as he held the door open for her to enter. "Guess you can tell I haven't cleaned anything since you were here the other night. Doc kept me working all day yesterday. But that's not really an excuse. I hate doing housework."

She laughed lightly. "Most people do. Including me. One of these days I might get around to unpacking everything I brought from Fort Worth. I honestly moved too many things out here with me. And I've hardly had time to turn around."

At best, the look he gave her was skeptical. "Why? Are you thinking you might not want to stay here— in Arizona?"

He'd intimated before that she might soon want

to leave and go back to Texas. Did he see her as that flighty and unpredictable? The idea frustrated her.

"Darn it, Trey, do you think I moved over a thousand miles just to turn around and go back?"

He shrugged. "I guess I have been wondering if you might. People do change their minds."

She grimaced. "My parents wish I would change my mind. But believe me, Fort Worth isn't on my radar. It's totally off the map. Now, if you'll excuse me, I won't be long."

Short minutes later, she returned from the bathroom to find him waiting near the door. A faded jean jacket with a ragged collar and cuffs was thrown over one arm. The relaxed expression on his face suggested he'd already forgotten the stilted exchange they'd had moments ago.

"Ready?" he asked.

"All ready," she told him.

Outside, he helped her into his two-seater truck and, after slipping on a pair of aviator sunglasses, steered the vehicle onto the dirt road that led to the main highway.

Once they were traveling northwestward across the desert floor, Nicole could hardly contain her excitement. Not only was she going on an adventurous trek; she was making the trip with Trey.

"Have you noticed my new boots?" She turned slightly around in the seat so that she was facing him.

He glanced down at the scuffed and worn red

cowboy boots on her feet. "If you bought those as new boots, Nicci, someone sure did cheat you."

Laughing, she said, "They're a pair of Roslyn's old boots. We wear the same size, and she kindly dropped them by my house yesterday. She even said I could keep them." Nicole pulled up one leg of her jeans in order for him to see the fancy inlays on the shaft. "Look at this. Thunderbirds on the front and back. Aren't they fabulous?"

After casting another quick glance at the boot, he gave her an indulgent grin. "Just your style."

She tugged her jean leg back in place. "You're laughing at me now."

He shook his head. "No. I'm serious. They're cute and sexy. Just like you."

Liking the definition of his compliment, she flashed him a smile. "I'm sure Roslyn paid a small fortune for them when they were new. I tried to tell her I would just borrow them, but she says they're on their last leg and need new soles. So my plan is to get them resoled and keep them."

"Roslyn is as generous as Doc." He shrugged one shoulder. "Sure, some would argue that the couple has money to burn. But I figure they'd be just as charitable even if they were poor."

"That's true," Nicole agreed. "Roslyn's father has always been rolling in money. When we were just little girls, I remember how he bought her anything and everything. Trouble was, she didn't want three-fourths of the things he bought for her. The majority of the stuff, she gave to me or her other friends."

"Hmm. Why did she give it away? To spite him?"

"Not spite, exactly. She considered her father's lavish gifts as bribes. To make up for not spending time with her and her mother. Ros didn't want to be—well, bought off by her father. You know what I'm trying to say?"

Trey nodded. "I'll never forget when Ros first showed up in Wickenburg. She was very pregnant and so alone. If Doc hadn't helped her, I think she would've just kept on running—to get away from her father. Thank God that's all behind them now. And her old man is actually acting like a decent human being."

Nicole wished she could believe the bad times she'd gone through with her family were behind her once and for all. If her mother backslid emotionally, or her father had another affair, she hated to think what would happen. Most likely, Angela would probably fly straight here to Arizona and expect her daughter to become her 24/7 caretaker all over again.

Pushing that horrifying idea out of her mind, Nicole changed the subject to something pleasanter. "Ros is going to help me learn to ride a horse. Well, actually Maureen and Isabelle will be my teachers. Ros says they're the experts on riding. I'm excited about it. I figure if I'm going to live around cowboys and ranchers, then I need to learn how to ride like a real cowgirl."

"Have you ever ridden before?" he asked.

"Only a few times. Years ago, on a docile, stable pony," she admitted. "But that's not the same as what you guys ride when you're working on ranches."

"No. Our mounts are a bit more spirited." His lips took on a wry slant. "You're not afraid to get on a big horse?"

"Not really. I trust Chandler's mother, Maureen, not to put me on a bucking bronc."

He chuckled. "I'd really like to see your first lesson."

She shot him a playful smirk. "You say that like you think you're going to see a rodeo with me doing the trick riding—accidently."

"I'm teasing," he said. "I think it's good you're going to learn how to ride. Maybe we can go riding together sometime and take our mining pans with us. Doc says there's some old mine diggings not far from his great-great-great-grandparents' first ranch house. Might be interesting to ride over there."

The idea that he was already thinking of going out with her again was enough to send her spirits soaring. "You think the Hollisters wouldn't mind?"

"Gosh, no. Doc's always inviting me to come over and ride anytime I want. There are some really spectacular places to see on Three Rivers. And given the ranch goes for miles and miles, we wouldn't get in anyone's way."

"That would be interesting," she replied. "Did you say great-great-great-grandparents? Three times great?"

He nodded. "From what Doc has told me, Edmond Hollister built the first ranch house back in 1845. He and his wife, Helena, lived there until the big house was built some years later—the one the Hollisters live in now. The original family and their part in settling Yavapai County is in historical records at the library in Prescott if you'd like to read about them."

"I would. I love history." Nicole thoughtfully repeated, "Hmm, 1845. If I'm remembering what little I've learned about Wickenburg's history, the big gold strike there didn't happen until 1863. So that means the Hollisters settled in the area before the rush."

"The Hollister family arrived in Arizona long before the big Vulture Mine was discovered. Doc and his brothers have a theory that Edmond originally came to Yavapai County to look for gold or silver."

"Did he find any?" Nicole asked.

"Doc says, from what they've gathered from old family documents, the man found some of both and used the money to invest in cattle and horses. So that's how the ranch got started."

"That's how it is sometimes," Nicole said thoughtfully. "A person starts out with a certain plan, but halfway there something comes along to change it. Usually for the better."

"Yeah, just like the old saying goes. When one door closes, a better one will open."

She studied his profile. "I believe you've already walked through your better door, Trey. You've found the spot in life where you want to be."

He grunted. "Funny you should say that. Only last evening, Doc implied that I should get more ambitious."

Nicole's jaw dropped. "Ambitious? I can't believe Chandler would say such a thing to you! You work so hard. How could he expect more from you?"

He shook his head. "Doc doesn't think I'm lazy. He says I do the work of two men. I don't think so, but anyway, he—uh—well, this sounds ridiculous, but he wants me to go back to college to add on to my associate degree in veterinary tech and get a veterinary degree. Imagine. Me being a vet? Funny, isn't it? You can go ahead and laugh. It won't bother me."

Nicole had to admit she was surprised by the suggestion, but she hardly found it amusing. "Why would I laugh? You should be flattered he has that much faith in you."

He laughed, but the sound was hollow. "Like I could pass all those chemistry and anatomy classes."

"Why not? You have a brain. All you have to do is make it work. The real question is whether you *want* to be a vet, rather than *can* you become one."

Frowning, he shoved the brim of his hat back off his forehead. "Well sure, why wouldn't I want to be a vet and make big money?"

"The heavy workload, the emergency calls at all hours of the night, the responsibility, not only for the welfare of the animals, but to the owners. And that's just for starters," she answered.

He pulled his hat back onto his forehead. "Doc wants me to be his partner. Which I guess I am in a working sense, just not on the business side of things."

"That's quite an honor."

He looked at her and frowned. "Yes, it is. But I wish he'd never said any of this to me. It's got me feeling mixed-up and guilty. I don't want to let my buddy down."

Nicole could hear a wistful note in Trey's voice. He wanted to dream, even believe that one day he could be a doctor of veterinary medicine. And she wanted to believe it for him.

"Whether you choose to remain Chandler's assistant or become a veterinary partner, he would never think you let him down. I seriously doubt you've ever let anyone down," she said gently.

He cast her a wry glance. "I'm human, Nicci. I've disappointed a few people over the years. We all have—even you."

His honest reply hit her hard, and she turned her gaze out the passenger window. The desert hills they were traveling through were beautiful, but at the moment she wasn't seeing them. She was back in Texas and faced with the choice of letting her mother down, or ending Randy's future plans.

"Yes. I'm guilty, too," she said quietly.

There was a stretch of silence and then he asked, "A man?"

She stifled a sigh. Not for anything did she want him to think she was still pining for a lost love. That part of her life was long over.

"Yes. He's a marine now. I turned down his marriage proposal and he was disappointed. But I made the right choice—for both of us."

Even though she was staring straight ahead, she could feel his gaze traveling over the side of her face. What was he thinking? That she'd callously tossed her boyfriend aside? That she cared only about her own happiness? She could try to explain what had happened with her family and with Randy. She could tell him how her mother had suffered an emotional and physical breakdown after her parents had divorced. Therapy and medication hadn't helped Angela Nelson recover from the loss. The only thing that had seem to help was having Nicole constantly at her side. In the end, when Randy had announced he was leaving for California for military boot camp, Nicole couldn't abandon her sick mother and join him. But spoken words weren't always enough, she thought. Trey needed to discover for himself that she wasn't a self-absorbed person.

"You're saying you'd make the same choice all over again?"

For a long time, she'd regretted letting Randy out of her life. But that was before she'd come to realize that she'd never really loved him. He'd been like a comfortable pair of shoes she'd not wanted to give up. That was hardly the basis for a lasting marriage.

Smiling, she reached for his hand lying on the console between them. "Most definitely."

His hand turned over and wrapped around hers. "I hope I don't ever let you down, Nicci," he said gently, then slanted a grin in her direction. "But what are you going to think if we don't find any gold?"

Laughing softly, she could only think she'd already found her gold in the form of a long, tall cowboy with sparkling green eyes and a smile that made her heart sing.

"That the fun is in the trying."

Chapter Six

Nicole had turned down a marriage proposal. A man back in Texas had loved her enough to want to marry her.

For the remainder of the drive to Congress, Trey tried to push those realities from his head, but the tormenting images of Nicole making love to another man refused to budge from his brain.

He was reacting like fool. Her love life, past or present, was really none of his business. Or was it? Hadn't that kiss they'd shared on the porch made it his business?

It could be your business if you wanted to make it yours, Trey. But you're not a family man. Don't be stupid and let yourself get mushy over Nicole.

Trey was fighting to push the annoying voice out of his head when he spotted the turnoff to his friend's property and steered the truck onto a hard-packed dirt road.

As the vehicle rattled across a pair of cattle guards, Nicole leaned up in the seat and peered out the windshield. "I'm going to make a guess and say this isn't the road to Congress."

"No, it's up the highway," he told her. "This is a friend's land. He raises cattle—that's the reason for the cattle guard."

"Has he ever looked for gold on this land?" she asked.

"He's had several mining companies offer to buy it. But he considers cattle to be his wealth."

"Must be a man who bets on a sure winner," she replied.

"Nothing is a sure winner. All sorts of things can happen to deplete a herd of cattle. The weather, disease, predators, and then there's the market value that can drop on a whimsy."

"I guess there are risks to most everything," she remarked.

Especially when a simple man like himself becomes involved with a beautiful woman, Trey thought. But who said he was involved, anyway? Just because he'd gotten lost in her kiss didn't mean he was about to fall in love with her. No, indeed.

"That ridge of mountains over there looks fairly close. Are we going that far?"

Her question interrupted his thoughts and he followed the direction of her gaze. "No. Those mountains are probably thirty or more miles away. Why do you ask? Are you ready to get out and stretch your legs?"

"I'm fine. And the scenery is gorgeous."

She looked at him and smiled, and Trey wondered for the umpteenth time why she'd invited him to kiss her. Was she one of those women who liked to tease a man? Is that why she turned down the marriage proposal? Because she never intended to have a serious relationship? The idea should give him a measure of relief, but it bothered him to think she might be just playing him along.

Another three miles passed before Trey finally braked the truck to a halt a short distance away from the edge of a gravelly wash.

"This is probably as far as we should take the truck," he told her. "If we walk on up the wash, I believe we'll find a bit of water in this little stream. It would probably make panning easier. Are you up for a hike?"

"Sure," she replied as she peered out at a rocky shelf shading the west side of the wash. "It's so beautiful here. I can't wait to see more."

After he helped her out of the truck, they gathered their equipment and lunch fixings, and Trey loaded everything into a canvas duffel bag that he'd brought along to use as a carryall.

As he shouldered the bag, she said, "That's a lot for you to carry. We could leave our lunch here at the truck and walk back later when we get hungry."

"It's not that heavy," he assured her. "Besides, once we get to where we're going, we might not want to leave for a while."

"Sounds logical. But how will we know when we get to where we're going?" she asked.

Trey laughed. "Good question. Let's just play it by ear. When you start getting good vibes about a place, we'll stop."

"Okay. I'll put out my ESP antenna," she joked.

They took off hiking up the shallow arroyo, and Trey remained close to Nicole's side just in case she tripped over any of the small boulders embedded in the dry creek. Because she was unaccustomed to wearing cowboy boots, he'd not expected her to navigate the rough terrain all that well. But the farther they hiked, the more she impressed him with her sure-footedness.

"Look at all the blooming sage!" she exclaimed as they passed a thick patch of the bushes covered in tiny purple flowers. "It's beautiful. And what are those trees with the yellow and pink blooms? Those are very pretty, too."

"That's salt cedar," he explained. "Most of the

farmers and ranchers here in the southwest call it a monster."

She looked at him with surprise. "Why a monster? It's lovely."

"It's invasive and sucks up an enormous amount of water that's needed for grasses and other useful vegetation," he explained. "And salt cedar trees are very difficult to clear away. But in recent years the pros and cons of the plant are becoming more debated. Because the trees provide a nesting place for birds and that sort of thing."

She paused to gaze at one of the trees. The long feather-like leaves were covered with yellow blooms and a mass of buzzing honeybees.

"Being a city girl and studying business in college, I never learned much about the environment. I didn't realize it was so fascinating until I moved out here and started experiencing it firsthand." She glanced around at him, then promptly asked, "What's wrong? You're looking at me like I'm strange, or something."

He shook his head. "Nothing is wrong. I was just thinking back to when I first met you. Those high heels you were wearing—well, you looked darn pretty, but I was worried."

A knowing smile curved her lips. "Worried? That I might be out of place?"

"A little." Placing a hand on her elbow, he urged

her forward. "Come on. Let's walk on before the bees decide they want us, too."

They walked about a quarter mile on up the creek before a few shallow pools of water began to appear. When they finally reached a spot where a larger pool was partially shaded by willows, Nicole paused and looked around her.

"What do you think about this spot, Trey? Might not be any gold nuggets here, but it's a nice place for a picnic."

"I'm all for it," he agreed.

Trey stashed their lunch in the deepest part of the shade, then carried their equipment over to the water's edge.

Following him, Nicole said, "I almost called Loretta yesterday to ask her for tips on how to do this panning thing. But I didn't want to make us sound dumb."

Laughing, Trey squatted on his heels and shoveled a small amount of gravel into one of the pans. "Why not? We are dumb about it. My guess is that, back in the old days, prospectors must have learned by trial and error. We'll pretend we're back in the 1860s and just starting out."

"Just starting out. I like the sound of that." Flashing him an impish grin, she reached for one of the pans and knelt down beside him. "Maybe we'll have beginners' luck."

* * *

For the next two hours they painstakingly sifted through pan after pan of rocks and gravel. Nicole tried to imitate what little she'd seen about panning on television shows and in movies, but she'd quickly discovered it was much more difficult than it looked to swish out the water and still leave the pieces of rock silt in the pan.

"I can understand why Loretta does this," Nicci spoke as she poked a finger through several colorful rocks. "It's addictive. I keep thinking, the next scoop, and the next pan will turn up a nugget."

"Guess I'm hooked, too," Trey told her. "I keep thinking the same thing."

She looked down the stream to where he was squatted over his pan. The sleeves of his shirt were rolled back on his tanned forearms while the hems of his jeans were wet from wading near the water's edge. For most of the morning, she'd tried to focus her attention on sifting through the endless rocks and pebbles, but even the idea of finding a gold flake or small nugget wasn't enough to keep her gaze from constantly straying over to him.

"Hey, here's something," he said suddenly. "But I think it's pyrite."

Leaving her pan, she walked over and looked down at the small rock he was holding between his thumb and forefinger.

"Oh, it looks like gold! Maybe it is! How can you tell?"

Rising to his full height, he dug a pocketknife from the front pocket of his jeans. "For one thing the color isn't yellow enough. This has a brassy tinge." He sliced the point of the small knife blade over the glittery streak running through the rock. "Not soft enough, either. If this was the real stuff, my knife would leave a mark. It didn't."

He handed the rock to her, and she held it up to the sunlight and angled it one way and then another. "Aw, that's a bummer. But it's pretty. Can I keep it? It might be the closest thing to gold that we find."

"It's all yours," he told her. "But let's not give up. I've heard if there's fool's gold around, there's usually a good chance the real stuff is nearby."

Slipping the rock into her shirt pocket, she turned wide eyes on him. "Wow! If that's true, then we might actually be in the right spot."

"Could be," he said. "But before we do more digging, I think it's time for lunch. What about you?"

"Eat? At a time like this? You've just made a discovery!"

Laughing, he placed his palm on her forehead. "Just what I was afraid of. You've caught gold fever. I should've never brought you out here."

Laughing along with him, she looped her arm around his. "Okay. We'll forget about gold for a while and eat lunch. Actually, now that I think about it, I'm hungry, too."

On a grassy knoll, beneath a shade tree, Trey placed his jacket on the ground to use for a make-shift table. Once they had the food laid out, they sat cross-legged on the ground and munched on fried chicken, potato salad and Western-style beans.

"Mmm. I can't remember anything tasting so delicious," she said. "I must have been hungrier than I thought."

"You've been working hard."

Glancing down at her yellow T-shirt, she hardly recognized it as the same one she'd started out with this morning. The front was blotched with mud and water stains, while her jeans were equally soiled. She could feel that parts of her hair had worked loose from her ponytail and were now glued in sweaty strands against the back of her neck. She didn't need a mirror to tell her she looked a mess. But she didn't care. She'd never felt this good.

"I'm having too much fun to call it work."

"You call digging through shovelfuls of gravel fun?" he joked. "My fingers are about to bleed."

"Really? Let me see." She put down her paper plate and grabbed up his hand. As soon as she turned his palm upward, she realized he was teasing. "What a faker! It would take more than a few rocks to make those calloused fingers bleed."

Their gazes met and locked, and then his hand

gently took control of hers. Nicole's heart began a wild pitter-patter as he drew her fingers toward his face.

"I think I'd better examine yours," he murmured. "Just to make sure they aren't bleeding."

"I—uh—I'm tougher than you think."

She didn't know if he noticed the breathless sound to her voice, but she figured he could probably see the rapid thump of her pulse on her inner wrist and know that he was causing an upheaval inside her.

"Let me see."

To her surprise, he brought the tips of her fingers to his lips and allowed them to linger there just long enough to cause her to lose her breath entirely.

"Wrong," he said gently. "Your fingers are as soft as the wing of a dove."

"Oh." She swallowed, then nervously cleared her throat. "How would you know—about the softness of a dove's wing?"

"I used to have a pair—for pets." His thumb moved slowly over the back of her hand. "Now that I think about it, your skin is softer than a dove's feather."

She was wilting inside, and if he didn't quit touching her hand as though it were a priceless jewel, she was going to fall right into his arms.

"What—er—happened to the—doves?"

"I decided to give them their freedom, and they flew away together. For a while they would show up and eat the feed that I threw out for them. But eventually, they left and never came back."

"Oh, do you think something killed them?"

A wan smile touched his lips. "No. I think they went south, made a nest and had a family. That's the way with nature. The birds didn't need me anymore."

Like a bolt out of the blue, tears suddenly blurred her eyes and forced her to look away from him.

His fingers tightened around hers. "Nicci? Is something wrong? Are you crying?"

He sounded concerned and a bit confused, which made Nicole feel like an idiot for the sentimental tears. He couldn't know that ever since she'd been a very young girl, she'd dreamed of having her own family.

"No! I'm fine." She quickly blinked away the moisture and forced a smile on her face before she brought her gaze back to his. "What you said about the doves and nature. I was just thinking how nice it would be if things were that simple for people."

He rubbed his palm over the back of her hand in a comforting way, and the sweetness of his touch brought an even bigger lump of emotion to her throat.

"To fly away? Or make a nest?" he asked.

Her smile turned wry. "Both, I suppose."

"Life isn't supposed to be that easy for people."

"Guess not." She shook her head and called up the cheeriest voice she could muster. "But that's enough philosophy. I'm ready to enjoy dessert."

He studied her for a moment longer, as though he wanted to make sure she wasn't about to burst into another spate of tears. To her relief, she must've convinced him, because he released her hand and reached for a plastic container holding a few slices of cake.

"Too bad we don't have coffee to go with this," he said.

He carefully maneuvered a piece of the cake onto a paper plate and handed it to her. Nicole quickly took a bite, but she hardly noticed the taste of the chocolate confection. Her mind was too busy trying to figure out why every little thing Trey did or said was affecting her in ways she didn't understand. She had to get a grip on her emotions. Otherwise, he was going to get the idea that she was either crazy, or prone to histrionics.

She said, "If we were real prospectors, we would've been smart enough to bring a pot and make the coffee over an open campfire."

"Hey, that would've been good," he said. "Along with some marshmallows and wieners to roast."

She laughed and was relieved the urge to throw her arms around him and rest her cheek against his chest wasn't quite as strong as it had been a few moments ago.

Once they'd packed away the lunch leftovers, the two of them returned to the spot at the stream where

Trey had found the pyrite. After sifting through several more shovelfuls of gravel, Nicole found another piece of pyrite, followed by an even larger chunk.

With each discovery, her excitement appeared to grow. Trey was relieved to see her mood had lifted, but he still couldn't dismiss the image of her eyes filled with tears.

After she'd told him about turning down the marriage proposal, he couldn't help but think she was living with regrets and those tears in her eyes were for a lost love.

And what if they were, Trey? You're not going to let yourself fall for her. You're smarter than that.

"We're on the right track, Trey. I'm feeling those vibes you were talking about."

The sound of her voice interrupted his nagging thoughts, and Trey glanced over to see her head bent over her pan as she pushed a finger through a clump of tiny pebbles. Even with her damp, dirty clothes and her disheveled hair, she looked vibrant and beautiful. And nothing like the woman he'd met that first day in Chandler's office.

"Not getting tired yet?" he asked.

"Gosh, no!" Her brows pulled together as she glanced at him. "Are you wanting to call it quits for the day?"

He said, "No, I'm fine. I just don't want you to get too tired. We've been at this a few hours now."

She shot him a bright smile. "Not a chance."

"Good girl," he told her, then leaned forward and scooped up another panful of gravel.

He was carefully allowing the water to slosh over the sides when something flashed in the sunlight. Quickly, he dug through the mud and pebbles until he found the bright yellow object. It was smooth with rounded edges, and it had only a single streak of black ore on one side of it.

Excitement rushing through him, he stood up and rolled the pebble between his thumb and forefinger. "Nicci, I think I've found it."

"It?" She echoed the one word in the form of a question before she glanced at him. The moment she saw he was standing, her jaw dropped. "You mean— a piece of real gold?"

"That's what it looks like to me."

She dropped her pan and rushed over to him. Trey held the piece in the middle of his palm for her to see. She drew closer and touched the nugget with the tip of her forefinger.

"Ooh, that's a yellow-gold color, all right! And it feels rather soft." Then she questioned in a half-whispered voice, "Do you think it's actually gold?"

He grinned. "I'd bet the money in my wallet that it is."

She let out a delightful squeal, then flung herself straight at him. "We found it, Trey. The real thing! This is wonderful!"

Laughing, their arms holding each other tightly,

they jumped up and down together with pure jubilation.

When the celebration finally ebbed and they stood catching their breath, Nicole tilted her head back and looked anxiously up at him.

"Oh my, you didn't lose the nugget in all of that, did you?" she asked.

Drawing his left arm from around her waist, he opened his fist to reveal the golden pebble. "No chance."

Smiling, she continued to gaze up at him. "I'm so happy for you, Trey."

"Don't be happy for me," he corrected. "Be happy for *us*. It's ours—together."

Still beaming, she shook her head. "No. That's to go in your savings. For the ranch you want."

Even though the nugget would probably bring no more than two or three hundred dollars, the fact that she wanted him to have it touched Trey deeply. "Now Nicci, that's not how this is going to work. We agreed before we started that we're in this prospecting together."

"Right! So I have a say on how I want to spend my share. I'm investing it in you and your ranch. You can repay me with your first calf crop."

He chuckled, and then, because he couldn't help himself, he pulled her even tighter against him. "Nicci—I—I've never known a woman like you," he murmured.

"I'm glad."

Her words were muffled by the front of his shirt, and he gently lifted her face up to his. "You are?"

"Very glad. That way you won't forget me."

"No chance of that happening, either." His gaze dropped to her lips and suddenly nothing mattered but kissing her, tasting all of that sweetness.

Trey lowered his head toward hers, but the second his lips landed on hers, his brain turned to a mass of swirling fog. With her soft body draped against his and her lips urging him to deepen the kiss, he was totally lost.

Eventually, as the embrace wore on, he began to register the hot sun baking his back and shoulders and a trickle of sweat rolling slowly down the middle of his chest. Behind them, he heard the wind swishing through the salt cedars and desert willows, the faint buzzing of the bees and the distant screech of a hawk. But none of those things were enough to overpower the taste of her lips and the incredible pleasure pouring through him.

At some point, he realized her arms were wrapped tightly around his neck and the front of her body was pressed so tightly to his that her breasts were flattened against his chest. One of his legs had found its way between her thighs, and his hands were gently cupping the fullness of her bottom.

By the time she opened her mouth and invited his tongue to delve deeper, he was only too happy to fulfil her wish. As he explored the ribbed roof and the sharp edges of her teeth, desire exploded in his loins and shot straight to his brain. He wanted her. So much so that he was practically paralyzed with the need to make love to her.

Did she want him as badly as he wanted her? The question was racing through his mind when a loud sound of falling dirt and overturning rocks forced him to pull away from her.

Stunned by the interruption, they both looked to a spot some fifty or sixty feet on down the arroyo to see a small herd of horses descending a steep bank and gathering to drink around one of the deeper pools of water.

"Wild mustangs," Trey said as he struggled to regain his senses.

Swiping strands of tumbled hair from her eyes, she focused her attention on the horses. "I don't think they know we're here," she whispered.

"They know. They're just too thirsty to be concerned about us," he murmured.

The shaggy winter coats of the animals were beginning to shed, exposing darker patches of hair along their necks and around their flanks. Most of them appeared thin from the lack of winter grazing, and their long manes and tails were ratted. Even so, they were a magnificent sight.

She said, "Something about them being wild and free makes them even more beautiful."

"I wish I could adopt the whole herd."

"Why don't you?" she asked.

He turned his gaze back to her face, and when it settled on her pink, swollen lips, desire clenched deep in his gut. If the horses' arrival hadn't interrupted them, how much longer would he have gone on kissing her? How much time would've passed before he carried her off to some grassy spot and made love to her?

"I don't have enough pastureland." He sounded like a robot, but that was only because he couldn't think straight. Not with his body still aching for hers. Not when he was having to fight like crazy to keep from reaching for her.

Turning back to him, she rested her palm against the side of his face. "When you get that ranch you want, you'll have pasture space for plenty of mustangs," she said, her voice full of gentle certainty. "And that's going to be sooner than you think."

Darn, but he wanted to believe her. Not only about the land, but also the passion he'd felt in her kiss. The tenderness in the way she touched him. Did she really want him that much? Believe in him that much? He was afraid to think about it. Afraid these moments with her were all too good to be real.

"You keep this up and I'm going to have a fat ego."

She laughed softly, and then her expression grew somber as her fingers played with the hair curling over his ear. "In case you haven't yet guessed, you're making me feel pretty good about myself, too."

"That's good. I—uh—" Pausing, he tried to assemble the right words to convey how he was feeling about her and the two of them together. But he quickly realized that was impossible. Not without making himself sound like a goofy sap. "Nicci, that kiss—I don't know about you, but it meant something to me."

Her gray eyes were solemn as she studied his face for long, long seconds, and then the corners of her lips tilted upward in an expression so soft it reminded him of a moonbeam, filling his heart with silvery light.

"It meant something to me, too," she whispered.

He wanted to reach for her, to kiss her again and let their desire for each other play out to the finish. He wasn't sure when, or if, there would be a right time for them to make love. But something told him that now definitely wasn't the time to put their relationship to the test.

Smiling down at her, he clasped a hand around her arm and turned her back to the stream. "Come on. We still have a few hours of sunlight left. It's time we got back to being prospectors."

Laughing, she squeezed his hand. "One nugget found and several more to follow."

Off to their left, the herd of mustangs finished drinking, then disappeared on down the arroyo. As

Trey watched them go, Nicole's prediction about him getting a ranch of his own circled through his thoughts once again.

The land, the cattle and the horses would mean nothing to him without her at his side. Even if she hadn't realized that fact yet, he had. And it was a damned scary feeling.

Chapter Seven

"Trey, take the end of this tape measure and start walking. Don't stop until I tell you to."

Trey turned a frown on Chandler. The two men were at the large barn that sat on a high knoll behind the animal clinic. Five minutes ago, they had finished doctoring a small herd of cattle suffering pink eye and were about to leave for a ranch call up in the northern part of Yavapai County. A job that, if they were lucky, would get them back here to the clinic by closing time.

"What are you doing? I thought we were driving up to the Bar 40 to take care of those bulls for Mr. Seeley."

"We are," Chandler told him. "This won't take

five minutes." He thrust the end of the metal tape at Trey. "Get going. Straight north from where we're standing."

Trey took off walking with the tape unfurling behind him. When Chandler finally called out for him to stop, Trey turned and looked back at his boss for further instructions.

"That's eighty feet. Think that will give us enough space?" Chandler asked.

Trey glanced around at his surroundings. Off to the left were several holding pens made of iron pipe, beyond was a loafing shed and next to it was a larger barn they used for examining cattle.

"Depends on what the space is for," Trey answered. "More parking area for trucks and trailers?"

Rolling in the metal tape, Chandler started walking toward the spot where Trey was standing. "Heck no! We already have plenty of room for parking. Where is your mind anyway? Don't you remember me talking about a new stalling barn for the horses?"

Trey could've told him that his mind was stuck on the clinic's receptionist. But he wasn't ready to admit to Chandler that he was already a cooked goose. Or that Nicole had him so mixed-up he hardly knew whether he was coming or going.

Biting back a sigh, he said, "I remember. But that's been months ago. I thought you'd scrapped the idea for a bigger and better horse facility."

"Why would I scrap it? The hospital needs improvements, and I've finally located a contractor to do the work."

"I hope he's better than the last one who put a new roof on the clinic."

Chandler groaned as he slipped the small tape measure into the pocket of his jeans. "Don't remind me of that disaster. No, this guy does excellent work, and he's dependable. All I need to do is make sure I have the blueprint designs exactly how I want everything."

Trey shot him a wry look. "You don't want a stalling barn. You want a horse hotel with all the amenities. Like air-conditioning, heating and a therapy pool."

"What's wrong with that? A sick or injured horse deserves the best of care. Extra comfort means faster recovery. Plus, the more available treatments I have, the better. I've talked Blake into building one just like it on the ranch. Holt has needed such a facility for a long time. And it will make things much easier for me in both places."

"You already have a damned nice foaling barn on Three Rivers. It has luxury stalls."

"That's for the brood mares and foals. Holt needs this for the whole remuda—'cause there's hardly a day goes by that a few of them don't require treatment for one thing or another."

Trey shook his head. "You're talking about lots

of money, Doc. You think it will actually pay off in the end?"

"I'm not worried about the profit," he said. "Not here at the clinic or on the ranch."

No, Trey thought, Chandler was all about the care of the animal. Not the cost.

The two men left the knoll and began walking toward the white work truck they intended to drive to the Bar 40.

"Speaking of money," Chandler said, "I heard you found a small fortune on your panning expedition this past Sunday. Why hadn't you mentioned it to me?"

Two days had passed since Trey and Nicole had panned the arroyo up near Congress, but the time they'd spent together was still just as vivid in Trey's mind as if it had just happened. Before the waning sunlight had finally forced them to leave the stream, he and Nicole ended up finding three more gold nuggets. But compared to the passionate kiss they'd shared, the gold was insignificant to Trey. Now the memory of having her in his arms was burning a hole right through his brain.

Not bothering to look in Chandler's direction, he said, "I guess you heard that from Ros."

"I hate to say it, but she's almost like a mother hen to Nicci. I've told Ros she needs to mind her own business, but they've been friends since they were little girls."

"No matter. It's no secret," Trey said, while wondering what Chandler really thought about Nicci spending time with his assistant.

"How much gold did you find?" Chandler asked.

"I'd say maybe five or six hundred dollars' worth. Give or take a little. When I get a chance, I'll take the stuff to an assay office and find out the actual value of it."

By now the two men had reached the truck. After they both climbed inside and buckled their seat belts, Chandler looked over at him.

"Didn't Nicci find any gold?"

Trey started the engine. "Two pieces. But she gave it to me. For my ranch savings." He reversed the truck, then turned it onto the highway. "Doc, would you call Nicci a wealthy woman?"

Chandler thoughtfully rubbed his chin. "I couldn't say for sure. I've heard Ros say that Nicci's parents have plenty of money, but whether they share their wealth with Nicci is another matter. Or whether Nicci would accept it, would be hard to say. She doesn't live like she has an abundance of money. And she does need to work to support herself. Why do you ask?"

Feeling a bit foolish, he shrugged. "I just wondered, that's all."

As the truck picked up speed, Chandler settled comfortably back in the seat. "I think what you're really wondering is how long she's going to continue to make her home around here. Right?"

Trey cast him a sheepish look. "Well, it's a reasonable question. She's different from us. And she still has strings attached to Fort Worth. Sometimes I get the feeling those strings are always tugging on her."

Chandler frowned. "She's trying to break them. Especially the strings her mother has thrown around her. Although, to Nicci, they probably feel more like chains than strings."

"What do you mean? What's the problem with her mother? She one of those smothering sorts?"

Chandler shook his head. "She needs to tell you all about that. Not me. Besides, I only know bits of the situation—and that's only because Ros has told me."

Other than mentioning the marriage proposal, Nicci had not shared all that much about her life back in Texas, and Trey was reluctant to push her for information. Especially when she wasn't pressing him for details about his own past.

"She's told me that before she moved out here, she worked for a travel agency, that she studied business in college and that she had a boyfriend who wanted to marry her but she turned him down."

He could feel Chandler eyeing him with curiosity. "What have you told her about yourself?"

Trey's chuckle was a mocking sound. "Now Doc, you know I'm an open book. Besides, me and Nicci are just friends. That's all a guy like me can be to a woman like her. I don't want to have a serious girlfriend. Dating a woman now and then is enough for me."

Rolling his eyes in Trey's direction, Chandler quipped, "Is that so?"

Trey glowered back at him. "Heck yes, it's so! And you know it. Don't try to act like you've forgotten the messes I got into ten years ago when I tried to be more than friends with a woman. First with Rhonda and then with Lacey." Pressing harder on the accelerator, he fixed his eyes on the broken white line separating the two lanes of traffic. "You would think I learned my lesson with Rhonda when I got the idea that she actually wanted to be my wife. But after she left for greener pastures, I licked my wounds and tried my luck with Lacey. When she walked away, that was enough for me."

Chandler's only response to that was a tired grunt.

Trey frowned at him. "I know what you're thinking. That I shouldn't blame either one of them. Well, you're right. Both of those women could see I was never going to be anything special. That I could never give a wife the things she needed or wanted."

Chandler let out a caustic laugh. "Oh sure. Even a one-eyed woman could see you couldn't give her a sixty-foot yacht, and a three-story house with a kidney-shaped swimming pool, or a four-car garage filled with a pair of Maseratis and a couple of Corvette convertibles. She'd probably be expecting you to have enough money in the bank to travel the world, too. No. I don't expect you could give a woman those things. So it's best that Rhonda and Lacey saw you for the loser you are and moved on."

Trey snorted. "All right, poke fun at me. I don't care. At least I know my limitations."

Chandler scowled at him. "Damn it, Trey, that's your problem, right there! You look at your limitations instead of the blessings you've been given and the assets you have. But you know what? I think for the first time in your life a woman has come along who sees the real Trey Lasseter and what he stands for."

"You mean Nicci? Well yes, I expect she does. That's why we're just friends. I make her smile and laugh. That's all."

"Take it from me, Trey. A woman prefers to laugh instead of cry. If I don't make Ros laugh at least a couple times during the day, then I start worrying. I know I'm not doing something right."

The idea of Chandler not keeping Roslyn happy was ridiculous. The woman was crazy in love with him and he with her. And they had the children to prove it.

"When it comes to your family, you know what you're doing. It's different for you than it is for me. You had a great dad. He worshipped his children and his wife. My dad—well, he tried. But being married and having a kid just wasn't his thing. He's better off single. And I'm a chip off the old block."

From the corner of his eye, Trey could see Chandler shaking his head. "You're wrong, Trey. You don't want to be like your father. That's why you didn't go with him to Montana all those years ago when your parents divorced. It's why you're still here and not up there with him. You view life differently than him."

Chandler had that much right. Trey loved his father, but he didn't want to live out his life in a bunkhouse with a crew of men who didn't care if they ever had a home or family of their own.

"Maybe so," Trey said, then hoping to direct their conversation elsewhere, he asked, "Has anything new been happening with solving your father's murder case? Sorry, I guess I shouldn't have said murder. But I don't know what else to call it."

"No need to be sorry. Naming it something else won't make it any less ugly." Heaving out a breath, Chandler turned his gaze toward the passenger window. "The situation is in a holding pattern right now. There's not much going on with the case. Joe and Connor are still waiting for Ginny Patterson to set up a meeting with them. Apparently, she has an abusive husband and doesn't want him to know about it."

Joseph Hollister was Chandler's younger brother and had worked more than a decade as a deputy sheriff for Yavapai County. Over the years, Connor Murphy, his friend and fellow deputy, had been helping Joseph dig into the cause of Joel Hollister's death. Together, the two deputies had recently discovered a major lead in the form of a woman named Ginny Patterson.

"You really believe this Ginny woman has important information about your dad's death?" Trey asked.

Lifting his hat a few inches off his head, Chandler raked a hand through his hair as though he wanted to plow the whole situation out of his brain.

"She has to be the key. From what we can gather from the personal notes of the late Sheriff Maddox, Dad was spotted with this woman several times at the Phoenix livestock auction. Mom even found an old day planner of Dad's where he'd penciled in a reminder to meet her, but the meeting didn't take place. He was killed the day before. Joe and Connor learned that shortly afterward she suddenly quit her job at the auction barn. And from what my brother says, she was a poor woman then and is still living in poverty."

"Could be coincidence about the meeting and quitting the job," Trey said.

"Could be. But it's too coincidental for me to swallow."

Trey thought about that for a moment before he asked, "Does your brother, Joe, and his partner, Connor, think this woman could've killed Joel? Or helped someone commit the crime? Frankly, Doc, what would be the motive? If the woman needed money, kidnapping for ransom would've been more logical."

"You're right. And that could've been the initial plan," Chandler said. "We all have our theories on the matter."

Trey shook his head. "Well, I don't know that I'd have the patience to wait around on this woman to decide when and where she wants to talk. What if she gets it in her head to run? Your link would go missing."

"She hasn't run in all these years since Dad died. Not likely she will now. Besides, we've waited this long for the truth. We can wait a little longer."

Trey glanced at him. "I'm not anything close to being a lawman or private investigator, but am I stupid to think she could use the phone? Maybe somewhere away from her husband? What's wrong with that form of communication?"

"There's too much that needs to be discussed. And Uncle Gil says you have to be face-to-face when you interrogate someone. To read the nuances in expressions—that sort of thing. Anyway, they need to see firsthand that they're actually speaking with Ginny Patterson."

"That's true. And your dad's brother was a detective for the Phoenix Police Department for, what, thirty years or more? He ought to know."

"Yes. Uncle Gil has been a godsend to the family

in more ways than one," Chandler admitted. "Especially for Mom. Before he moved back to Three Rivers, she'd really sunk into a dark place."

Trey said, "I never noticed Maureen acting like she was in a funk. But then, anytime I'm ever on the ranch, she's always working—helping the hands do something, or helping Holt with the yearlings. But now that I think about it, she has seemed a lot more chipper since Gil come home."

"Come home." Chandler thoughtfully repeated the words. "Funny how natural it seems to have Uncle Gil around now. I'll be honest, Trey, in the beginning I wasn't sure how I felt about Mom falling in love again—especially with Dad's brother. Actually, thinking of her with any man, other than Dad, seemed weird to me. But Dad is gone and life goes on. Mom deserves to have love in her life again."

The highway was cutting through a plateau of red rock and shell. Scrubby pines and twisted juniper clung to the steep cliffs, while ahead of them, a line of bald mountains rose above the desert floor. Even though Trey had seen this area thousands of times, he never grew tired of traveling this particular highway. Today, however, he wasn't noticing the beauty of the landscape. Chandler had given him too much to think about.

"Yeah," he said pensively. "Like Granny. She deserves to be loved, too. Here lately, I've had to remind myself of that."

Chandler looked at him. "Why? Does Virgie have a fella now?"

"I think it's more like he has her," Trey said wryly. "He's asked her to marry him and she hasn't turned him down. That tells me she's thinking hard about this guy."

"Hmm. Sounds serious. Do you know him?"

A few days ago, Chandler's question would've drawn a curse word from Trey. But something had happened to him since his visit with Virgie. And his changed attitude had everything to do with Nicole; he could admit that much. She was making him look at everything and everyone around him in a different way. Did that mean he might be falling in love with her? No! Not that. She'd just made him a bit more open-minded, that's all, he assured himself.

"I know him. You do, too. It's Harley Hutchison. The farmer who raises melons over by Aguila."

Trey expected Chandler to turn a shocked look on him. Instead, he merely nodded.

"Last time I saw Harley was when he brought that nanny with a ruptured teat to the clinic," Chandler recalled. "I kept her for a few days of treatment. Nice guy. You ought to be really happy for Virgie."

"I'm trying to warm up to the idea," Trey conceded, then asked, "You don't think he's too young or, uh, too much of a man for Granny?"

Chandler laughed. "If Virgie doesn't think he's too young and Harley doesn't think she's too old, then more power to them. That's what I say." Stretching his arm across the back of the seat, he turned so that he was looking at Trey head-on. "Your problem is that you've never been in love."

"Damn it, I don't—"

"No. Don't start reminding me of Rhonda or Lacey again. You weren't in love with either of those women. If you had really been in love, you would've gone through hell and high water to make it work. But you didn't."

"Hellfire! You think I deliberately chased those women away?"

Chandler groaned. "No. But you didn't make much effort to keep either of them around, did you? Let me tell you, Trey, when you do finally fall in love, you're going to know it. Because nothing else in the world will matter except having *her* in your life. And you'll do whatever you have to do to make sure that happens."

Trey could admit, at least to himself, that he wanted Nicole's company. But he couldn't imagine having her in his life on a permanent basis. What would it be like to wake up with her lying next to him? How would it feel to see her sleepy eyes open and rest lovingly on his face?

The questions caused a lump to form in his throat. When it finally eased enough for him to speak, he said, "Aw, Doc, you know me. I'm a confirmed bachelor. I need my space. I need to be able to go to the Fandango anytime I get ready."

"Fandango, hell," Chandler muttered. "That'll keep you warm in your old age."

Trey fixed his gaze on the highway and didn't say another word until they reached the Bar 40.

Hours later, the waiting room at Hollister Animal Clinic was finally empty, and Nicole was organizing the work on her desk as the clock wound down to closing time. With two minutes to go, the phone rang and she didn't hesitate to answer.

After the client gave her a brief explanation of what she needed, Nicole said, "Doctor Hollister reserves Thursday mornings for feline spaying and neutering, Mrs. Roberts. I have one vacancy left for this coming Thursday if you—" The woman interrupted with a frantic protest, forcing Nicole to pause. At the same time the woman's voice was rattling in her ear, she sensed a presence behind her and swiveled her chair just enough to see Loretta giving her a look that said she was thanking her lucky stars she was a bookkeeper instead of a receptionist.

Giving her coworker a grin, Nicole rolled her eyes helplessly before focusing her attention back on the caller. "Yes, on occasion Doctor Hollister will make exceptions. I can ask him and get back to you tomorrow," Nicole suggested. "Presently, he's out on a house call and won't be back before closing hours."

Thankfully, the woman agreed, and after Nicole had carefully jotted down her name and number, she hung up the phone, then turned her chair so that she was facing Loretta head-on.

The young woman had dark green eyes and vibrant red hair that curled upon her shoulders. Several inches taller than Nicole, she had a statuesque build that curved in all the right places. Nicole was still wondering why the woman didn't have a fiancé or even a steady boyfriend, but apparently from what Nicole could gather, Loretta preferred living a solitary life.

"Everyone thinks they should be an exception to the rule, right?" she asked.

Nicole chuckled. "Not everyone. But probably the majority. At least the woman was very nice about it. And she did have a legitimate reason for needing another day besides Thursday."

Loretta leaned her hip against the edge of Nicole's desk. "Nicci, you're too nice for your own good. No matter how hard you try, you can't make everyone happy. Although, I'll have to say you've made Trey one happy fellow," she added slyly.

The mention of Trey's name caused Nicole's heart to break into a tap dance against her rib cage. "What are you talking about? Trey is always a happy guy. Since I've started work here, I've never seen him unhappy."

"That's my point," Loretta said, then laughed at

the confused look on Nicole's face. "Oh, Nicci, I'm teasing. Well, kind of teasing," she admitted. "I ran into Trey yesterday in the break room. He was telling me you've turned into a regular little miner."

"Oh. He did? Well, he's exaggerating. I struggled trying to get the hang of swirling the water out of the pan without losing all the gravel," Nicole told her.

Loretta shook her head. "You must've done something right. You found gold. Do you have any idea how long I tried before I found a few flakes? Probably twenty trips."

Nicole hadn't said much to her coworkers about her and Trey's panning expedition last Sunday. For one thing, she figured the women wouldn't be thinking of the prospecting trip in terms of searching for gold. All of them, including Roslyn, would be thinking of romance.

Well, your friends would be right, wouldn't they, Nicci? Spending that time with Trey had been about being near him, savoring each touch and kiss he'd given her, rather than digging for a golden treasure.

"We had good luck. But actually, it was even nicer to be enjoying the outdoors. I didn't do much of that in Fort Worth," she said. "Honestly, I was mostly an indoor girl."

Loretta nodded. "Roslyn has told us before about her life back in Texas. She said you two made trips to the malls and theaters and concerts—things like

that. It sounds exciting. Especially when you com-
pare it to scooping up gravel out of a creek bed."

Nicole closed her appointment book and switched
off a lamp sitting on one corner of the desk. "Not really, Loretta. I've had more fun since I moved here
than I've had in a long, long time."

Loretta fixed her with a pointed look. "Is that because of Trey?"

She'd not expected the woman to ask her such a
blunt question, and for a moment she floundered as
she wondered how to answer. Finally, she decided
on the truth.

"Yes, I suppose it is." The soft note in her voice
revealed the emotions he evoked in her, and though
she tried to clear them away with a little cough, she
knew Loretta had already heard them.

"The last time I remember Trey dating anyone
steadily was several years ago. We all thought he was
going to get married. He never told us what happened
to end it, but I'm sure Doc knows the whole story."

Nicole often wondered if Trey had ever loved or
endured a broken heart. Now she knew, and the fact
tore at something deep within her. She didn't want
to think of Trey anguishing over a woman. Not any
more than she wanted to think of him making love
to one.

Rising to her feet, Nicole said, "Well, that's really
none of my business."

Loretta continued to scrutinize Nicole's face.

"Why, Nicci, you've really fallen for the guy. Haven't you?"

"You're jumping to ridiculous conclusions. I've not known Trey long enough for something like that."

"Really? Whatever happened to love at first sight?" the bookkeeper asked.

"That's totally not sensible."

Laughing, Loretta asked, "Who gave you the idea that there was anything sensible about love?"

Nicole was trying to come up with a logical reply to that when Cybil entered the waiting room. Seeing it was empty, she walked over to the counter that separated the customers from Nicole's work area.

"Looks like we're all finished," Cybil said. "Are you two girls ready to lock up and go home?"

"I'm more than ready. My washing machine is trying to lie down and die. I need to go by the appliance place and price a new one or ask Malcom if he can fix mine without it costing me a fortune," Loretta said, then gave Nicole a conspiring wink. "See you two tomorrow."

Loretta left the room, and Nicole gathered up her handbag and the thin jacket she'd worn over her sundress early this morning.

"I'll lock the front door and we'll go out the back," Cybil told her. "Doc and Trey came in a few minutes ago. They can finish locking up whenever they get ready to leave."

Just hearing that Trey was actually in the building

caused Nicole's heart to take an excited leap. She'd not had a chance to talk with him since they parted late Sunday evening, and she'd missed him terribly. Several times, she'd come close to picking up the phone and texting him, or even walking up to the treatment barns to say hello. But she'd told herself that chasing after the man wasn't the answer. If he'd already forgotten about those kisses they'd shared in the arroyo, then she needed to forget them, too.

"Yes, I'm ready," she told Cybil, and after switching off the overhead fluorescent light, she joined the woman out in the hallway.

The two women walked side by side past the treatment rooms and on toward the back of the building where a large recovery area held the caged animals that needed to remain at the hospital for extended care. Along the way, the loud sounds of barking dogs and meowing cats carried down the wide corridor.

"What a day," Cybil said with a weary sigh. "I'm so tired I barely know my own name."

"It's Cybil. Just in case you're wondering," Nicole joked.

Laughing, Cybil wrapped one arm around the back of Nicole's shoulders and squeezed. "Thanks for reminding me. And just think, we have the pleasure of doing this all over again tomorrow."

Nicole laughed along with her. "I wouldn't miss it for anything."

A few feet ahead, the door to Chandler's office stood partially open, and she could hear the two men's voices drifting out from the room. Even though she was longing to see Trey, she didn't pause to look in, or say good-night. No doubt the pair were discussing work, and she didn't want to be a nuisance by interrupting.

Outside the back door of the clinic, the two women said their good-nights and walked on to their cars, which were parked on opposite sides of the graveled lot.

Nicole had just opened the driver's door and tossed in her purse when she heard the sound of crunching footsteps behind her, and then Trey's voice called out.

"Nicci, wait up!"

Her heart beating fast, she glanced over her shoulder to see him trotting up to her.

"Hello, Trey."

He was smiling at her, and the smile she gave him in return was so wide she could feel it stretching her face. So much for being subtle, she thought.

"I saw you walk by the office and I, uh, wanted to catch you before you left," he explained.

"Was there something you wanted to tell me?"

He reached for her hand and smoothed it between the two of his. "Just that I've been so busy since we started back to work Monday that I haven't had time to go to the front of the clinic and talk with you.

I—uh—didn't want you to think I was deliberately avoiding you."

The sun had already dipped behind the western horizon and shadowed the parking area at the side of the building, but Nicci suddenly felt as though bright sunshine were pouring down on her.

"I didn't think you were trying to avoid me. Remember, I make the appointments. I know how busy you are." Her gaze met his, and she instinctively stepped a bit closer. "I have missed you, though."

The smile on his lips eased to a tender slant. "I've missed you, too. That's another thing I wanted to tell you."

Feeling an overwhelming urge to touch him, she placed her free hand on his forearm. "I've been thinking that we—uh—should have dinner together again. What are you doing tonight? Is it urgent that you go straight home?"

His brows lifted slightly as he glanced down at his soiled jeans and shirt. "No. It's not urgent. But I can't go out like this."

"I wasn't thinking about going out," she told him. "We can have dinner at my place. I'll go by the deli and pick up something. You've not seen my house yet. I'd like to show it to you."

His eyes lifted back to her face, and judging by his expression, it was obvious to Nicole that her invitation had surprised him. Actually, she'd surprised herself. She was continually telling herself that she needed to sit back and wait for Trey to do the asking. But she was quickly learning that he was far from the forward type—at least, with her he wasn't taking the lead. She didn't know if that was because he felt unsure about having a relationship with her, or whether he'd rather they remain friends.

When he didn't immediately respond, she quickly added, "It's okay if you'd rather not, Trey. I'm sure you're tired and you probably want to get home and rest."

He suddenly chuckled. "Rest. What's that? I don't need rest."

She let out a pent-up breath. "Does that mean you want to come?"

"Sure. I'd like it—a lot," he said softly. "I have a few things here to wrap up, but I can be there in thirty minutes. Is that okay?"

Impulsively, she rose on her toes and kissed his cheek. "It's perfect. I'll see you then." She started to climb into her car, then remembered he didn't know where she lived. "Oh, I'd better give you my address so you can find me."

Reaching into the car, she fished a pen and scrap of paper from her purse and jotted down the address.

"And just in case you have trouble finding it, the house is pale yellow with brown trim and the yard has a chain-link fence. You'll see my car parked beneath the carport," Nicole added.

"No worries. I'll put your address into my phone. It has a navigational app. I'll see you in a bit."

He jogged off in the direction of the treatment barn, and Nicole hopped into the car and practically threw gravel as she hurried out of the parking lot.

She had thirty minutes to stop by the deli and pick out something yummy for dinner and then get home and make herself look presentable. That was hardly enough time to take pains with her appearance, but she didn't care. She was going to be with Trey again and that was all it took to send her spirits soaring.

Chapter Eight

Trey usually kept a set of clean clothes in a locker at the clinic just in case he might need a change. But a few weeks ago, he'd used the clothes and hadn't bothered to replace them.

Now, as he walked onto Nicole's porch, he looked ruefully down at his chambray shirt and blue jeans. Both were covered with sweat, dust and dark patches where cow manure had splattered and dried. Maybe she wouldn't notice the stains too much, he thought, but the smell might knock her for a loop.

He was in the process of lifting the small brass knocker on the door when it swung open and the precious sight of Nicole's smiling face made him forget all about his disheveled appearance and the fact that he smelled like a bull pen.

"Hi, Trey!" She pushed the door wider and gestured for him to enter. "Welcome to my house."

Stepping past her, he found himself standing in a small foyer furnished with a brass hall tree and a potted cactus with a pair of red blooms in front of a single long window. But his attention was hardly on his surroundings. Not when she looked like a sweet dream in a blue checked sundress and her hair wound in a loose knot atop her head.

All he wanted to do was pull her into his arms and kiss her senseless. Instead, he stood patiently to one side while she dealt with the door. But when he heard the lock click, the reality that they were entirely alone sent a spurt of panic through him. How was he going to keep his hands to himself and his mind on something other than making love to her?

She didn't give him time to come up with a strategy as she quickly looped her arm through his and urged him out of the foyer.

"Other than Roslyn, you're the first guest I've had since I moved in," she said as they strolled into a rectangular-shaped living room. "Actually, one of my neighbors came as far as the porch to say hello. I guess I could count him."

"Him?"

She smiled coyly up at him. "Mr. Bains. He's eighty and a widower. He retired here in Wickenburg so he could play golf year-round. Sometimes I see him leaving with his clubs as I'm leaving for work."

Trey chuckled. "Now he's the kind of man Granny needs. Elderly and safe."

She gave his arm a playful pinch. "You leave your grandmother alone. She wants passion—not snoring."

Yeah, Harley was probably capable of giving Virgie plenty of that, Trey thought crossly.

You need to wake up, Trey. You have a problem with Harley because you don't have the backbone to be like him. Because you don't have the guts to go after the woman you want. Because you turn into a trembling coward when you think about marriage.

Fighting the taunting voice inside his head, he asked, "How do you know what Granny wants? You've never met her."

Her laugh was a little wicked. "From what you've said about her, she's a woman who enjoys life. That tells me plenty. As for Mr. Bains snoring, he has a hefty paunch. I'm guessing he raises the rafters every night."

Slanting her a wry look, he patted a hand against his abdomen. "I'd better start watching what I eat. I don't want to start raising the rafters."

Chuckling, she gestured toward the furniture grouped into a cozy U in the middle of the room. The couch and love seat were upholstered in dark red fabric, while the chairs were a deep moss green.

Brown leather hassocks were positioned in front of both chairs, while colorful throw pillows dotted all the plush furniture.

"Go ahead and be honest," she said. "All I need to add is a decorated tree and it would look like Christmas."

"Nothing wrong with that. I like it," he said truthfully.

"Thanks. Comfort was my main objective." She gestured toward the walls, which were painted a light gray color. "I don't have many pictures or wall hangings put up yet, and I still need a few scatter rugs, but its slowly coming together."

The room looked like a real home, he thought. Was that because it had a woman's touch? Or because he was standing next to Nicole, imagining himself as a permanent fixture in her life?

He cleared his throat. "If the rest of the house looks like this, then you've been busy."

She reached for his hand. "Come on," she said. "I'm sure you're tired and hungry. Let's go eat and I'll show you the other rooms later."

She led him through an arched doorway and into an angular space that intersected with two separate hallways shooting off to the left and right. Straight ahead was a pair of slatted swinging doors.

He followed her through the doors and into a kitchen with a long row of windows facing a backyard, plenty of white cabinets and a round pine table with matching chairs. A shaded lamp swung over the table, while a light over a gas range illuminated the work area.

Releasing his hand, she crossed over to the cabinet counter. "I got enchiladas and sides to go with them. I hope you like Mexican food. Otherwise, you might have to settle for a peanut butter sandwich."

"Don't worry," he assured her. "I love Mexican food."

She opened a microwave and pulled out a glass dish. "Go ahead and have a seat," she told him. "I'll bring everything over."

"I can help," he offered.

Shaking her head, she glanced in his direction. "Thanks, but you're my guest."

Is that how she considered him? Just a guest dropping by for supper and a bit of conversation? Trey wanted to be more than that. He wanted to be her everything. He wanted the right to hold and kiss her, make love to her. He wanted her to belong to him and him to belong to her.

He wasn't sure when or how he'd reached that conclusion. Or what he intended to do about it. He only knew that when she'd opened the door and invited him into her home, he'd felt happier than he'd ever been in his life.

"Okay, if you're so intent on spoiling me, I'll sit." He started toward the table, then paused midstride.

"I wasn't thinking, Nicci. I washed my hands before I left the clinic, but I think I ought to wash again."

"Oh, sorry, I'm not a very good hostess. I should've shown you to the bathroom." She placed the dish of enchiladas on the table, then motioned for him to follow her out of the kitchen. "It's right down the hallway."

Outside the swinging doors, she turned left and they immediately walked past an open doorway on the right.

"The dining room is in there," she explained, gesturing toward the doorway. "But I didn't think we needed to use it tonight."

He chuckled. "The way I look, I'm surprised you let me in the house. Much less into the dining room."

"Nonsense. You look like a man who's been working outside with his hands. That's very sexy."

Trey came close to stumbling. "I—uh—I'll take your word for it," he said sheepishly.

She laughed softly. "Trey, you have to be the most modest, guileless man I've ever met."

"Is that supposed to be a compliment?" he asked.

By now they'd reached a doorway on the left and she stopped and turned to him. The gnawing hunger in his stomach was instantly forgotten as her hands flattened against his chest and pushed their way upward.

"It's very much a compliment," she whispered.

His gaze collided with hers and then, all at once,

he was struggling to breathe. There was something in her gray eyes conveying far more than her words, even more than the pressure of her fingers wrapping urgently over the ridge of his shoulders.

"Then I should be thanking you," he murmured.

She rose up on her tiptoes and angled her mouth to his. "My very same thoughts."

Trey didn't waste time wondering why she was offering her lips to him, or even why the look in her eyes told him she wanted him in the most basic way a woman could want a man. The why of it no longer mattered to Trey. He was tired of trying to figure out her motives and even more tired of trying to resist the fire she built in him.

When his lips came down on hers, she let out a welcoming groan and curled both arms around his neck. Trey responded by wrapping his arms around her waist and tugging her body tightly against his.

The thought to keep the kiss gentle and contained lasted for about two seconds. After that, the contact of their lips turned to a reckless hunger that shot a hot blaze straight to his loins.

Along the way, Trey fought to hold on to his senses, but the taste of her lips was like sipping from a fountain of wine. By the time she opened her mouth to invite his tongue inside, he was desperate to be inside her and feel her warm body yielding to his.

The need for air finally forced their heads to part, and as they both sucked in several long breaths, Trey could feel his heart pounding like a sledgehammer against his rib cage. Beneath his hands, he could feel her shoulders trembling, and the fact that he'd had that much effect on her stunned him.

"Nicci, I—"

She suddenly looked up at him, and Trey forgot the words he was about to speak. Instead, he was taking note of how her eyes had darkened to a stormy gray and her puffy lips had turned to a deep shade of rose. The dimly lit hallway created shadows across her cheeks and chin, and before he realized what he was doing, his fingertips were tracing the flickering shapes upon her soft skin.

"I wondered how long I was going to have to wait for you to do that," she whispered in a raw voice. "I was beginning to think you didn't want me."

He groaned. "Want you? Nicci, if I wanted you any more than I do right now, it would kill me."

His throat was so tight it sounded like he was choking. She must've recognized the agony in his voice, because her palm was suddenly resting against his cheek and her soft gaze was delving into his.

"You're worried. Why?"

He groaned a second time. "This might be a huge mistake. I don't want to hurt you. I don't want you to hurt me. Maybe we need to forget—"

"Forget what?" she interrupted in a hoarse, shaky voice. "How we make each other feel? Forget what it's like when we touch each other, kiss each other? Maybe you can forget, but I'm past that point."

The urgency in her words was all the persuasion he needed to crush his mouth back onto hers, and as he gathered her into his arms, he realized he was also past the point of forgetting. All he wanted now was to let himself touch and feel and savor these moments of making love to her.

When the kiss finally ended, she grabbed his hand and tugged him on down the hallway and through a partially open door on the right.

Beyond the slightly opened blinds at the window, he could see the last bit of daylight rapidly disappearing. Shadows slanted across a queen-size four-poster bed and a nearby dresser, the top of which was scattered with perfume bottles and other feminine items. As she led him toward the bed, he noticed a dressing screen stretched across one corner of the room. A few garments were tossed over the top, while on the bed, a blue-and-white comforter was rumpled from where she'd sat on the edge of the mattress. Above it all, the scent of her perfume lingered faintly in the air and pushed his swirling senses to an even drunker state.

By the time they reached a spot near the bedside, she began to unsnap his shirt. Trey could only wonder if she'd pulled him into some sort of exotic dream where he didn't belong.

Shaking his head with confusion, he said, "This is too nice. I'm not fit for this room—or for you."

"That's crazy thinking," she murmured.

Each snap she pulled apart sent more muddling fog into Trey's brain. "I, uh, don't belong here." The front pieces of his shirt parted, and as her fingertips brushed his skin, his breath lodged somewhere deep in his throat. "Maybe I—should go get in the shower. And give you—time to think."

Seeming to ignore his words, she pushed the garment off his shoulders and down his arms.

"I don't need time to analyze you or this. And you're not about to go anywhere." Leaning forward, she pressed her lips to his bare chest, then proceeded to scatter a row of kisses down his breastbone. Once she reached the bottom of it, she made a sharp turn and directed her attention to his left nipple. Using the tip of her tongue to circle the flat brown flesh, she whispered, "I want you just as you are. Salty and sexy and oh—so—good."

While she continued to slide her parted lips over his skin, Trey thrust fingers into her hair and held the tips against her scalp. She had to stop, he thought desperately. If she didn't, he was going to break into a thousand useless pieces.

"Sweet Nicci," he said thickly. "Let me look at you—touch you—every inch of you."

His mouth dropped to her bare shoulder, and as he gently sunk his teeth into her soft skin, his fingers pulled down the zipper at the back of her dress. When the tiny straps slid off her shoulders, the rest of the garment followed, until the fabric pooled around her feet.

Trey stepped back, and as his gaze took in the pink lace bra and tiny matching panties, she said, "I'm not much of a curvy girl. I hope you're not disappointed."

Disappointed? Didn't she realize that having her standing here like this, offering herself to him, was nearly as incredible as him reaching into the sky and touching a star?

With a shake of his head, he wrapped his hands around the sides of her waist and marveled that his fingers very nearly spanned the distance.

"Don't you know how beautiful you are? How desirable?" His hands slipped up her back until they reached her hair. After fishing out the pins, the knot fell and the thick strawberry-blond curtain swung down around her face and onto her shoulders. He sniffed its lovely scent before sliding a thumb beneath her chin and lifting her mouth to his.

This time he held the kiss to a slow, seductive search, but instead of tempering the fire that was growing between them, it grew to mammoth portions. Soon her tongue was thrusting boldly between his teeth, demanding he give her more.

A tidal wave of desire washed over him, nearly drowning him with swirling heat. He felt his erection pushing at the fly of his jeans and heard a loud rush of blood in his ears. At the same time, he realized she was groaning and fumbling with his belt.

Stepping back, he gently took hold of her hands and placed them at her sides. "It's a tricky buckle," he said thickly. "I'll do it."

She sat down on the edge of the bed and waited while he rapidly dealt with his boots and jeans. When he was finally stripped down to nothing but a pair of black boxers, he joined her on the bed and, with his hands on her shoulders, gently eased her down onto the mattress.

Lying face-to-face, he rested his forehead against hers. "I didn't know this was going to happen," he said, then groaned as he realized how inane that sounded. "I mean—I thought it could—but I didn't know. I was hoping—not planning. Hell, I'm not making sense!"

She wrapped her arm around his waist and snugged the front of her body next to his. "You're making perfect sense to me. I hadn't planned on this happening tonight, either. But when we kissed—" Her sigh brushed against his cheek. "I'm glad it's happening. You'd probably have a red face if I told you how long I've wanted this."

"I think I'm blushing all over," he admitted. "And I'm going to quit asking myself why you want me. I'm just very, very glad that you do."

He didn't wait for her to reply. Instead, he closed

his lips over hers, and immediately her mouth opened beneath his. Her arm moved from around his waist to slip a tight circle around his neck.

In a matter of seconds, the kiss turned into another fiery exchange, and the need to be inside her caused his loins to ache, his jaw to clench with what little restraint he had left.

Eventually, the need to have her totally naked forced his head back from hers, and he turned his attention to removing the lacy lingerie. Once the bra was unhooked and tossed aside, he curved his forefingers over the waistband of the bikini panties and slid the scrap of lace down her silky legs until the fabric dangled off her toes and fell to the floor.

With a hand cupping the weight of each little breast, he studied the pale pink nipples. "Perfect," he whispered. "Everything about you is perfect."

Her eyelids fluttered open and she smiled up at him. "The room is full of shadows. You're seeing a blurred version of me."

Odd that she should say that, Trey thought. For the first time in his life, he felt as though he was seeing her and his surroundings with absolute clarity. He didn't belong here. He could see that, even if she couldn't. But for now, it didn't matter. Tomorrow and reality would arrive soon enough.

"Wrong, sweet Nicci, I'm seeing all of you," he murmured. "And I want everything I'm seeing."

"Then please don't close your eyes, Trey. Because all of me is what I want to give you."

A hot lump suddenly filled his throat, and to hide the sudden onslaught of emotions, he dropped his head and buried his face between her breasts. Beneath his lips, her skin was like velvety smooth cream, tempting him to lick and

taste. When he gently closed his teeth around one nipple, he felt her hand push its way past the waistband of his boxers, then on downward to his throbbing manhood.

The delicate touch of her fingers very nearly sent him over the edge, and with a great groan of resistance, he brushed away her exploring hand and practically leaped off the bed.

A confused frown on her face, she sat up. "What's wrong?"

The concern in her voice made him wonder if the last man she'd made love to had been some sort of superman with a will of iron. Or was she so innocent she didn't realize she'd been about to end everything before it ever got started.

Turning his back to her, he found his wallet and fished out a condom. "No! I just can't handle wanting you *this* much! That's all."

"Oh."

His fingers fumbled as he urgently attempted to roll on the protective sheath. When he finally managed to finish the task, he turned back to see she was watching him through half-closed eyes. The come-hither expression on her face was like nothing he'd ever seen on a woman before, and the fire that was already burning inside him launched into a raging blaze.

Holding out her arms to him, she murmured softly, "Come here."

He rejoined her on the bed and quickly positioned himself over her. As his knee slid between her thighs, she looked up at him and Trey thought he would drown in her gray eyes. Along with desire swimming in the luminous depths, he saw so much tenderness and caring that his boggled brain couldn't take it all in.

"Nicci—sweetheart. You're incredible."

The words barely made it past his tight throat, but they weren't so garbled that she didn't hear him. One hand snared a hold on the back of his neck and drew his head down to hers. Then with his forehead resting against hers, he lowered his hips and entered her with one smooth thrust.

Before Trey connected their bodies, Nicole believed she was ready for him. She thought she knew exactly what to expect from him and herself. But she couldn't have been more wrong.

The moment he entered her, she felt the hair practically lift from her scalp. Her fingers curled into her palms and the air in her lungs whooshed past her lips with such a force it sounded like a balloon let loose to fly across the room.

As he began to slowly and carefully move inside her, she wondered if he'd carried her off to an unworldly place where there was only soft, heated space and the sounds of their breathing.

His skin felt as hot as a sunbaked rock and tasted as salty as the sea against her tongue. While her hands made a roaming search of his muscled body, her mouth nibbled its way across his wide chest, down the corded arms and back to the strong column of his neck. And all the while, their hips moved in unison, faster and deeper, until the bond between them was so complete she wasn't sure where her body stopped and his began. She only knew that he was all she would ever want. Ever need.

Time continued to tick on as the two of them made love in the darkening room, but Nicole didn't have any idea of where the hands were on the bedside clock. She was aware only of Trey and the wild desire he was creating with each caress, each kiss, each plunge of his hips. If the night lasted forever, it wouldn't be long enough.

But nothing this good could last that long. The thought raced desperately through her mind and made her even more frantic to hold him close, to feel the rapid thump of his heart banging against her breast and have his hard-driving thrusts lift her higher and higher.

Somewhere deep inside her, coiled pressure began to build until she was certain it was going to spring open and shatter her body into a million pieces. She fought to remain in control, but Trey wouldn't allow it. His lips swallowed hers up, his hands clamped around the inner part of her thighs and lifted her lower body to an angle that left no space between them.

His strained grunts drifted to her ears, and then she heard nothing but the sound of her own heart as it hammered out a euphoric crescendo.

Suddenly she was crying his name and clutching his shoulders as she felt herself whirling, falling end over end into a vortex from which she never wanted to escape. At the same time, he buried his face in the curve of her neck while shudders of relief racked his body.

What was he doing here? How had this happened? Even before he rolled onto his side and opened his eyes to see Nicole's face lying next to his, the questions were revolving around in Trey's head. Now as he studied her soft features dampened with sweat, he was even more confused.

From the moment he'd walked into Chandler's office and laid eyes on her, he'd thought the most he could ever be to her was a co-worker. At best, a friend. The idea that they would wind up as lovers was like a page out of a fantasy book. This proved that dreams did come true. But did they last? That was the question that truly haunted him.

He was trying to shut out what it all meant, trying not to think about tomorrow, when her eyes fluttered open and the corners of her mouth tilted upward.

"My darling, Trey."

The whispered words were followed by the trace of her fingertips against his cheek. And because his heart was so full, he closed his eyes and brought the palm of her hand to his lips.

"Nicci."

Her name was all he could manage to say, but she didn't appear to expect more. Still smiling, she scooted closer and pillowed her head upon his shoulder.

"Forgive me for being a terrible hostess. I've kept you from dinner when you must be starving."

Laughing, he said in a teasing voice, "Well, bringing me into your bed instead of giving me a plate of enchiladas was kind of rude. Am I supposed to exist on you and air alone?"

"That is the idea." She made a purring noise. "But I won't let you starve. I'll heat everything again."

Trey reached for the corner of the comforter and pulled the cover over both of them. "There's no hurry." He slipped a hand down her arm, then on to the curve of her hip. "And lying here next to you feels too good to move."

"Mmm. I'm not sure I *can* move."

He rested his cheek against the top of her head. "I don't think you understand how you've made me feel."

She pressed a kiss on his chin. "Happy, I hope."

Happy wasn't the word for it, Trey thought. *Euphoric* was a closer description, but even that seemed tame considering the wild trip his emotions had taken as he'd made love to her.

Made love. He'd quit making love to a woman ever since Lacey had moved out of his life. No, that was hardly the truth, he thought. Because at some point during the past half hour he'd discovered that, before tonight, he'd never made love. For all these years, he'd only been performing the sex act. This thing with Nicole was entirely different. She'd caused an upheaval in his very heart and soul.

Even so, he was too cowardly to admit the truth. The most he could do was nuzzle his nose against her hair and murmur, "Yes. Very happy."

She nestled her cheek in the middle of his chest and wrapped her arm across his waist. The tender reaction had Trey wondering if this was how a king felt with all his treasures laid out before him.

"I guess by now you're thinking you've been chased and cornered."

He grunted with amusement. "No woman has ever chased me, Nicci."

"Until me," she said impishly. "I don't care to admit it. I mean, maybe it wasn't all-out chasing, but

I wanted to make sure you understood that I liked you—a lot."

"That's the mystery. What you've ever seen in me," he said.

"I've wondered the same thing about you. I'm not exactly a prize. But here you are with me anyway. And I'm so glad you are."

The hand at his side moved to his rib cage, and as she hugged him tightly, a weird pressure began to build in his chest and spread to his throat. He tried to swallow the feeling away before he took her chin between his thumb and forefinger and tilted her face up to his.

"Do you understand how special you are? How beautiful?"

Smiling wanly, she touched her fingertips to his cheek, and Trey couldn't help but think this was how it must feel to have an angel in his arms.

"There are plenty of beautiful women in the world," she said pointedly.

He stroked his fingers through the long hair lying against her back. "I haven't seen that many around here."

She chuckled. "I don't believe that. Fort Worth was full of them."

"Is that why you left? You didn't want to be a little fish in a big ocean?"

She playfully pinched a bit of flesh at the side of

his waist. "Is that what you think? That I need to be the center of attention?"

A chuckle rumbled out of him. "No. I was only teasing." He rubbed his cheek against her temple as his thoughts quickly sobered. "But I would like to know the real reason why you left Texas. You must've had a nice life there."

She let out a weighty sigh. "I did have a nice life there. I think I told you that Dad has always made plenty of money. And when it came to me and my brother, he and Mom never held back. We always had a nice home and most everything we wanted."

"Were you living with them when you moved here?"

"Yes. But that's a whole other story."

Her voice was full of regret and sadness, and Trey was suddenly remembering back to that first day he'd met her at the clinic and he'd walked into the break room to find her sniffing back tears. Had her distress been over her parents or letting go of the man who'd wanted to marry her?

"Would it bother you to share it with me?" he asked, even though better judgment told him that the less he knew about her, the easier it would be for him whenever she dumped him. And she would dump him, he thought ruefully. There was no doubt in his mind about that.

"It wouldn't bother me. Maybe with someone else it would, but not with you. Because I think—" She reached up and traced a fingertip down the side of his neck. "Because you're not judgmental like most folks are."

Trey suddenly felt like a snake, forked tongue and all. He'd already judged her as a woman who'd spend a bit of pleasurable time with him and then move on.

"You have me confused with someone else," he told her, then urged, "but tell me about your parents anyway."

Propping her head up with her hand, she studied his face. "They were married for twenty-six years when Dad went a little crazy and had an affair with a much younger woman. He thought he wanted a divorce so he'd be free to marry again. And even though it very nearly killed her, Mom gave him what he wanted and he moved away from Fort Worth."

He frowned. "Your parents divorced?"

Nodding, she said, "That's when everything went to hell. I wasn't living with my parents at that time. I had moved out several years prior and was living in an apartment close to my job, and I had spent lots of hours and money furnishing it just the way I wanted. But my parents' marital crisis forced me to give up my home and move in with Mom. You see, losing Dad caused her to have a mental breakdown. Angela—that's my mom—was in such bad shape she couldn't even take care of herself. I had to do most everything for her. And if I tried to leave for any length of time, she would fling hateful accusations at me like I didn't care—that I was no more of a faithful daughter than Big Mike had been as a husband. For a while, I even had to take a hiatus from my job because her doctor feared she would harm herself."

"Big Mike—is that your father?"

"Yes. His name is Michael, but since he was a young boy, everyone has called him Big Mike."

"I see. I guess you must have been pretty angry with Big Mike when all of this happened," he said, while trying to imagine the hell that must have been going on in Nicole's life.

"Well, I was somewhat angry," she agreed. "But I've always loved Dad and I tried to look at things with an open mind. He had reason to be unhappy. His job kept him away from Fort Worth most of the time, and Mom had become very uninterested in anything going on with him, even when Big Mike was home. They grew apart and his eye wandered— I think it was that simple."

"If your mother was so dependent on you, how did you manage to move out here? You mentioned having a brother—did he take over caring for her?"

She groaned and closed her eyes. "No. Trace lives in Louisiana and works on offshore drilling rigs. I told him to stay there because there was hardly any point to both of us disrupting our lives. And anyway, Mom had plenty of money to hire private nursing care or even a companion to make her feel not so alone. But she refused. She wanted to cling to me instead."

"That must have been damned rough on you."

"Yes, especially when she would beg me not to leave her," Nicole agreed. "But you haven't heard the half of it yet. Less than a year after my parents divorced, Big Mike came back to Fort Worth and begged Angela to forgive him. And, of course, she did. Now they're remarried and happier than I've ever seen them. In fact, they're like two different people. Like newlyweds who can't keep their eyes or their hands off each other."

"Aw hell, you're kidding."

Her eyes opened to settle on his face. "I realize it sounds like some cheesy movie plot, but that's actually what happened. And once Mom was off the anxiety and depression meds, I decided it was time for me to break free. So here I am in Arizona living an entirely different life. Except that—"

"Except what? Surely you're thrilled that your parents got everything worked out."

"I am," she said. "And my father has told me more than once how grateful he was that I'd stuck through the rough times with Mom. But I—well, I should be ashamed of myself, Trey. Because I—still can't rid myself of the resentment I feel toward Mom, especially. That makes me sound awful and look even worse, doesn't it?"

He shook his head. "No. It seems pretty understandable to me. You didn't tell your father to go have an affair or divorce your mother. It wasn't your fault that when trouble hit, she was too emotionally weak to hold up."

She studied him for a moment before she sat up straight and covered her face with both hands. As Trey watched her, he feared she was going to cry, and he wasn't sure he'd know exactly how to console her. But then her hands fell away and she looked at him with a mixture of gratitude and misgiving.

"Thank you, for being so understanding. And I agree with you. It wasn't my fault that my parents' marriage crumbled. Nor was it my place to try to put it back to together. But, as children, we're supposed to take care of our parents when they're in need. After all, they took care of us until we became grown-ups, right?"

"Uh, mine tried. I'll put it that way," Trey admitted, while thinking of the years of struggling he and his mother had gone through because his father had moved on without them.

"I guess—it's just hard for me to forget all that I sacrificed to keep her from—well, for a long time I feared she might take her own life. She seemed that low in spirit. Then when Big Mike returned, Mom flipped a switch and was suddenly a different woman. That was hard to take. And now I feel like I've earned the right to live my own life the way I want to live it."

He reached for her hand and pressed it between his palms. "Are you saying your parents want something different for you?"

Her lips twisted to a wry slant. "Mom calls me every day, urging me to come back to Texas. There are some days I get three or four calls from her, along with a half-dozen text messages. Dad wants to buy me a new house, a car—whatever my heart desires just to get me to live near them. Sometimes, Trey, it gets to be almost more than I can bear."

Whatever her heart desires. Exactly what did Nicole's heart desire, he wondered. And where did he rate among the things she wanted in life? Did he want to be a part of her wishes?

Even as he attempted to answer the self-imposed question, that unexplained pressure returned to his chest. In an effort to ease the discomfort, he sat up and wrapped an arm around her shoulder.

"Sometimes it takes more than a thousand miles to fix a problem, Nicci. If you don't want to go back there, then it's up to you to make your feelings clear to your parents. No matter how much they might protest."

She let out a long sigh and then twisted her head just enough to give him a smile. "Roslyn is always telling me I need to get more of a spine. Sounds like you're giving me the same advice."

Deciding it was well past time to lighten the moment, Trey chuckled and, starting at her waist, climbed two fingers up the middle of her back. "Your backbone feels sturdy enough to me. All you need to do is use it."

He began easing her down on the bed and she let out a provocative chuckle. "What are you doing? Testing its flexibility?"

"I've decided it bends perfectly." Once she was settled on the mattress, his hands left her shoulders to cup around the backs of her thighs. "Now I think I need to examine your hamstrings. It would be awful if you pulled one. Everyone at the clinic would want to know why you're hobbling."

Chuckling under her breath, she pushed at his chest until he was lying flat on his back and her warm little body was draped over his.

"Maybe you should be the one worried about hobbling into work tomorrow."

She teased the words against the corner of his lips, and Trey wasn't surprised to feel a fresh surge of heat rush through his body.

His mouth curved into a taunting grin. "You're quite a woman," he said slyly. "First you starve me, now you threaten to cripple me. What next?"

Her gray eyes glittered as she gazed down at his face. "How about me making love to you?" she whispered.

Slipping his arms around her back, he pressed her tight against him and forgot everything except the warm, tender joy filling his heart.

"I'm all yours, sweet Nicci."

Chapter Nine

"Here you are!" Roslyn sang out as she practically skipped her way into the break room. "I went to the front desk and found Loretta sitting in for you."

Nicole pulled out the folding chair next to her and motioned for Roslyn to join her at the utility table.

"I kept waiting for a lull in the action, but it never came. Luckily, Loretta offered to take over so that I could eat my lunch."

Roslyn glanced at her watch. "Lunch! Nicci, it's two thirty in the afternoon. Why didn't you yell for help before now?"

Nicole shrugged. "No big deal. I wasn't that hungry anyway."

And why would she be? she thought wryly. The

enchilada meal that she and Trey had finally gotten around to eating at one thirty this morning had stuck with her until recently.

Roslyn sank into the adjoining chair and looked at her with kind concern. "I know you want to prove to Chandler and me and everyone else here at the clinic that you're a dedicated worker. But there's no need for you to go overboard. You're always here early and leaving late. You rarely take a short coffee break and—"

Nicole held up her hand to interrupt her friend's assessment. "Listen, I'm not trying to prove anything. I'm just doing my job. That's all."

Roslyn rolled her eyes, and as Nicole studied her pretty face, she realized the young woman who'd been her friend all those years back in Fort Worth was basically gone. Since Roslyn had moved here to Arizona, married Chandler and created a family, she'd morphed into a different person. Instead of being little more than Martin DuBose's sad, dutiful daughter, she was now a happy, confident wife and the mother of two children. She never stressed over the heavy workload at the clinic. Nor did she chew her fingernails if everything wasn't perfect at home; she took it all in stride.

"Well, I'm only trying to point out that you don't have to do your job quite so much."

"Don't worry. I'll pace myself." She returned the last section of her sandwich to its wrapper before she turned a thoughtful look at her friend. "Ros, when did you realize you were in love with Chandler?"

Roslyn's features twisted with comical confusion. "What is this? Are you doing some sort of survey on the subject of love?"

Hating the idea that she probably looked like a blushing teenager, Nicole grabbed her coffee cup and took a couple of sips. "I've been wondering, that's all."

Daring a peek at her friend, she watched Roslyn's brows form a straight line. No doubt she was worried about her, Nicole thought. She was acting out of the norm. But wasn't that typical behavior for a woman who'd fallen in love? To go around with her head in a foggy dream?

"Oh honey, don't tell me you're still agonizing over giving up Randy?" she said in a frustrated voice. "I remember how crushed you were when your dreams of marrying him ended. But face, it, when you told him you were staying in Texas with your mother instead of going with him to California, he didn't care enough to even put up a fight to win you over. A woman wants her man to love her passionately. To do everything humanly possible to keep her at his side. Randy was a sap. He wasn't the man for you."

"He went into the Marines, Ros. You can't say he lacked ambition or gumption." Even as Nicole said the words, she realized that Roslyn's assessment of the situation was right on target. Randy hadn't cared enough to fight for Nicole's love. In fact, he'd simply said he was disappointed with her decision not to marry him and walked away without a backward glance.

Roslyn snorted. "A guy with brawn and muscle can be a wimp in the ways that really count. And in my opinion Randy was a big one."

Nicole laughed with relief. "Thank God I didn't waste any more time on him."

Roslyn arched a brow at her. "I do believe you've seen the light."

Nicole smiled as the image of Trey's handsome face flickered into her mind's eye. "Seeing the truth changes everything. Now, back to my earlier question. How did you know it was love with Chandler?"

She tilted her blond head one way and then the other. "If you're looking for a simple answer, then I guess I realized I was in love with Chandler when I considered moving on to California. The idea of life without him was like staring into a black hole. It was incomprehensible."

Nicole sighed as her thoughts drifted back to last night and the intimacy she'd shared with Trey. Making love to him had changed everything for her. Now all her hopes and dreams and priorities led straight to him.

Roslyn's hand was suddenly waving in front of Nicole's line of vision.

"Yoo-hoo, Nicci? You're off in outer space!"

"Sorry. I was thinking about what you said," Nicole explained.

Leaning closer, Roslyn peered at her. "Why, Nicole Nelson, I believe there's a dreamy fog in your eyes! Have you—" Pausing, she left the table and went over to the open doorway. After a quick glance down the hallway, she shut the door, then returned to her chair and grabbed hold of Nicole's hands. "Have you fallen in love? With Trey?"

A hot blush stormed over Nicole's cheeks. "Go ahead and tell me I'm an idiot. For the past year or more, I've been avoiding men at every turn. I haven't wanted to think about marriage or love or anything remotely connected. My plan was to wait until—well, until I'd gathered some common sense together. I believed I needed to take the time to decide whether that's really what I wanted."

Roslyn laughed. "That's ridiculous! You don't have to ask yourself what you want! From the time we were young girls, all you ever talked about was being a wife and mother—having your own family. It's been your dream."

Nicole groaned ruefully. "Sure, I remember that dream. But it turned into a nightmare after going through my parents' divorce and remarriage fiasco. When I left Fort Worth, I had just about closed the door on wanting anything to do with love. But then I came out here and what do I do? Swoon over a man that I've only known for a few weeks! I must be out of my mind."

Roslyn shook her head. "Do you remember when I first started working here at the clinic? You thought I'd lost my mind. Me, city-girl Roslyn, helping nurse a bunch of sick animals. You thought I was mixed-up and probably making a mistake about leaving Fort Worth and my pampered life behind. I believe you even thought I was crazy for jumping into marriage with Chandler after I'd just given birth to another man's baby."

Deciding she had no option but to take the honest route, Nicole nodded. "Okay, I'll admit it, I'm guilty on all those counts. I can also see quite clearly that I was wrong about everything. You made all the right choices."

Roslyn's gave her an encouraging smile. "You'll make the right choices, too, dear Nicci. All you have to do is follow what your heart is telling you."

"I can do that. Trouble is, I don't really know what Trey is thinking or feeling about me. He, uh, likes me enough, I guess. But he's not one to talk much about his feelings or his wants for the future. The only plans he's mentioned is wanting land, cattle and horses. Nothing about a wife or children. And then he keeps giving me these impressions that he thinks I'm too good for him, or he's not good enough for me."

"Nicci, Trey needs time to adjust. You're a different type of woman than he's accustomed to dating."

Dating? Was that the word for it? The times she and Trey had spent together seemed like so much more. But maybe she was reading too much into his smiles and kisses, the tender way he touched and held her.

"What do you mean?" she asked. "Has Trey dated a lot? Loretta mentioned that he had a serious girlfriend once. But that's all."

Roslyn shook her head. "From what I know about Trey, his idea of dating is going to the Fandango to drink beer and dance with the local girls."

"I see," Nicole mumbled thoughtfully. "So it's not his nature to get serious over a woman?"

"I've never seen that side of him. But from what Chandler has told me, Trey had a couple of serious girlfriends in the past. Although, that was several years ago and long before I moved here and married Chandler. But as for you—I'm thinking Trey probably sees you as a princess sitting high up on a pedestal and he's a lowly court jester."

Nicole frowned at the thought. "That's plain silly. Just because my parents have money or that I've graduated from college doesn't make me a princess!"

"I understand that and so do you, but Trey needs time to figure it out for himself. That's what I think." Roslyn's gaze swept up to the clock on the wall, and she suddenly jumped to her feet. "Oh my gosh, I need to get back to the recovery room!"

Nicole began to gather the leftovers of her lunch. "Uh, Ros, I think I must've sidetracked you. Did you come in here hunting me for a reason?"

Roslyn snapped her fingers. "Right! I wanted to invite you to Chandler's birthday party Friday night at Three Rivers Ranch. Maureen's shindigs are always fun, so I think you'll enjoy it. And Trey will be there, too, so you shouldn't get lonely."

She winked at Nicole, then hurried out of the breakroom.

A half hour past the clinic's regular closing time, Trey and Chandler had left the treatment barn and were on their way to the clinic building when Nicole met them halfway on the beaten path.

Since Trey had left her house in the wee hours of this morning, he'd been so busy he'd not had the opportunity to see her or even send a text. Now as his gaze took in her wrapped red dress sprinkled with yellow flowers and the long hair draped upon her shoulders, Trey felt his heart jump into a happy jig. Has this woman really held him close and rained passionate kisses, not only on his lips, but on every other part of his body? Had she really made love to him as though he was the most desirable, precious thing she'd ever touched? He was still having trouble believing the night had been real instead of a fantastic dream.

Chandler was the first to speak. "Hey, Nicci, you should be headed home, shouldn't you?"

She shook her head. "Not yet," she answered. "I needed to let you know there's an emergency call on the phone. A horse has been injured at a roping arena south of town. I've put the person on hold—in case you need to speak with her."

"Thanks. I'll take the call in my office," he said to Nicole. To Trey he added, "I'll need to get some meds from the supply room. You might make sure the truck has all our equipment."

"Right. I'll wait for you there," Trey told him.

As Chandler hurried away, Trey turned his attention to Nicci. The soft smile on her face had him wishing he could gather her up and kiss her right here in the open, no matter who might be watching.

"Hi," she said gently.

"Hi, yourself. I've tried all day to find a moment to text you, but it never came. We've been swamped."

She moved closer and placed her hand on his forearm. "I know. And it looks like you're far from finished. I guess this means you won't make it by the house tonight."

There was a shade of disappointment in her voice, but not the petulant kind. The idea that she could be so understanding made him want her even more.

"Wrong. I'll be there. Even if it's midnight and I have to wake you."

Her chuckle was incredibly sexy, and Trey couldn't stop himself from bending and placing a quick kiss on her forehead.

"You won't have to wake me," she promised, then gave him a little push toward Chandler's work truck parked beneath a mesquite tree. "Now you'd better go before Doc finds you dawdling with the receptionist."

Close to three hours later, Chandler and Trey were standing outside one of the clinic's horse stalls watching a palomino gelding limp over to a water trough.

Once the two men had arrived on the scene and Chandler had carefully examined the horse, they'd managed to load the animal into a trailer and transport it here to the clinic. Since then, they'd made several X-rays of the horse's foot and cannon bone and determined there were no life-ending breaks, only a strained tendon.

After treating the horse with injections and a leg soaking, the worried owner had finally decided it was safe for her to go home and leave her beloved animal in Chandler's care for the next few days.

"At least he's going to get well," Trey said.

"Yes. Luck was with him. Anytime a horse collides with a steer and both animals are running full blast, the result usually isn't pretty." He slapped a hand on Trey's shoulder. "Let's go home. What do you say?"

Trey wasn't going home. Not in the technical sense. But he was beginning to think of home as anywhere he was with Nicole, and that was a scary thought. One he'd been trying to ward off ever since he'd climbed out of her bed and drove to his place.

"Will Ranger be all right, you think?" Trey asked, as the two men turned away from the penned horse and started toward the parking area. "I can drive back over in a few hours and check on him."

"No need for that. The pain meds will last until tomorrow evening and hopefully the steroids will keep the swelling down. All he needs now is rest. And speaking of rest, you look like you could use some yourself. Did you eat lunch?"

"Don't worry about me, Doc. I'm fine." The mere idea of being with Nicole again was enough to make him feel like he could jump a dozen fences, forward and backward.

"I don't have to tell you we've been as busy as hell around here. But we've been this swamped with work before and it never made you look like this. Have you been sleeping?"

Damn, did he look that wrung out? "Uh—yeah. I've been catching a few winks here and there. Only last night Nicci had me over for dinner and I stayed kinda late," he said, while thinking that was the most he was going to admit to Chandler.

"Uh-huh. I'm beginning to understand now," Chandler said slyly. "Are you two getting close?"

If they'd gotten any closer, it might've killed him, Trey thought. "Guess you could call it that. We— enjoy each other's company. For now, that is."

Chandler paused his long stride to peer at Trey through the falling twilight. "For now? What the hell does that mean?"

Trey wished Chandler wouldn't push him for an explanation. He was already having enough trouble trying not to think too far ahead. It was easier on his mind and his heart to stay in the present and not dwell on the time when this thing with Nicole came to end. And it would. Because sooner or later she'd wake up from her dreamworld and see that he didn't fit into her future plans.

Shrugging, Trey tried to sound casual, but his troubled thoughts brought a tinge of bitterness to his voice. "We've had this discussion before. You know nothing lasts with me."

Chandler's brows slowly arched upward as he studied Trey's face. "Have you stopped to think that Nicci might be expecting more from you? Maybe you ought to make it clear to her that you're not a serious kind of guy. You'd be doing her, and yourself, a favor."

It took lots of pushing and prodding to stir Trey's

temper. Especially from Chandler. The man was his best friend in the world. But at this moment, curse words were boiling on the tip of Trey's tongue.

"Nicci is a grown woman. She understands where I'm coming from," he said sharply. "And I know where I stand with her. So there's no need for you to worry about either of us!"

If Chandler was surprised by Trey's retort, he didn't show it. Instead, he laughed. A fact that irked Trey even more.

"Me worry about my best buddy? Why would I do that? Apparently, you have everything under control and exactly the way you want it." He lifted a hand in farewell. "See you tomorrow, Trey."

By the time Chandler opened the truck door to climb behind the wheel, a feeling of remorse washed over Trey and he hurried over to him.

"Doc, wait a minute."

With one boot resting on the running board, Chandler paused to look over his shoulder. "You wanted to say something else?"

Trey cleared his throat, then wiped a hand over his face. "I'm being a jackass. Go ahead and tell me so. I deserve it."

Chandler laughed again. "If you ask me, you're putting yourself in a mighty high animal bracket," he joked.

Grinning sheepishly, he said, "You're right. Don-

keys aren't dumb, just stubborn. Sort of like me—
sometimes."

"Sometimes?"

Trey chuckled. "Yeah. Sorry, I guess I'm tired
and a little on edge."

Stepping back to the ground, Chandler asked,
"Why? You worried about this thing you've started
with Nicci?"

Trey let out a heavy breath. "I don't understand
it. I've never been happier in my life. Nicci is—she's
just wonderful. But deep down I know that sooner
rather than later I'm going to disappoint her."

Chandler shook his head. "All you have to do is
be yourself and be honest with her. I promise you
won't disappoint her."

Sighing, Trey looked down at the ground. "That's
not exactly what I mean."

"Hell!"

The curse word jerked Trey's gaze up to Chandler's face. "What's the—"

"Trey, sometimes you're slower than molasses!
And sometimes, like right at this moment, I'd like
to set the seat of your jeans on fire!"

Trey lifted his arms and let them flop against his
sides in a helpless gesture. "See? If I make you so
frustrated, just think—"

"Close your trap and listen!" Chandler interrupted. "Nicci doesn't want a rich man. Nor does
she want a perfect man."

"How do you know that?"

Chandler groaned with frustration. "I'm a genius. That's how! Now get the hell out of here before I kick your rear!"

"Mom, I really think you and Dad should take a vacation. A long one. Some place that's new and interesting to both of you," Nicole suggested as she stood at the kitchen counter, attempting to make cold-cut sandwiches with one hand while the other held the cell phone to her ear.

"That sounds great, Nicci dear, but Big Mike has to fly to New Mexico and oversee a job out there for the next month," Angela said. "That means I'll have to find something here to keep myself occupied."

The whiny sound to her mother's voice sent an uneasy thought darting through Nicole's mind. Was her parents' relationship already headed on a downward spiral again?

"Why don't you go to New Mexico with Dad," Nicole suggested. "I'm sure he'd love your company. And you wouldn't have to be home alone and wondering what to do with all the time on your hands."

"I wouldn't be alone if you were living back in the city," she pointed out. "Oh, Nicci, we used to have such fun going shopping together, having lunch and gossiping about all our friends. It could be that way again, honey."

Nicole closed her eyes and pinched the bridge of

her nose as she recalled the time when she and her mother had been very close. Those happy years were something Nicole would always cherish. But neither of them could go back to those days. They were over. Just like Nicole's life in Fort Worth was over.

You have to quit worrying about your parents and think about your own future. You've taken the first step by moving out here and away from them. Now get a backbone and make the most of it.

With Roslyn's advice suddenly echoing through her thoughts, Nicole straightened her shoulders and spoke firmly, "Not on a permanent basis, Mom. I'll come back for short visits. But that's all. You have to accept my decision. You're fine now. Both mentally and physically, you don't need me to lean on. You have to accept the fact that I can't be around to fill in for Dad's absence."

She could hear Angela's soft gasp and knew her mother had been shocked by her daughter's frankness. But back when Angela had been under a doctor's supervision, he'd told Nicole that the best thing she could do for her mother was to force her to stand on her on two feet. For everyone's sake, Nicole had to hold fast to the doctor's advice.

"I don't want you to fill in for him. I—"

"Yes, you do!" Nicole interrupted before her mother could continue to lie to herself. "And you have to stop it, Mom. Dad needs you."

"Big Mike has his job. He's always had his job,"

Angela argued, then added in a placating tone, "But don't worry about your parents, darling. We're better than ever—the happiest we've been in years."

"And I want you two to stay happy. You need to focus on Dad instead of trying to lure me back to Texas. If you really care about his feelings, then you won't mind bearing up to a little desert dust and making yourself comfortable in portable housing. He would love having your company and I know it would be good for you to be there with him."

"Are you serious? What would I do?"

Nicole refrained from rolling her eyes. After all, it wasn't totally her mother's fault that she'd become so spoiled over the years. Big Mike had done a good job of pampering her. So much so that Angela considered her own needs rather than those of the people she supposedly loved.

"You could start by taking care of Dad's needs and showing him how much you appreciate all the hard work he's put in over the years to give you anything and everything you've ever wanted. Including two children."

A long stretch of silence told Nicole that, for once, she'd managed to grab her mother's attention.

Finally, Angela said, "Why, Nicci, what have they done to you out there? I've never heard you talk like this. And anyway, I thought you were still angry with your father for his—well, bad behavior."

The last thread of Nicole's patience very nearly

snapped. "I'm still angry with the both of you," she said bluntly. "And I need time and space to get over it. So please give me that much."

"Space?" Angela croaked. "You've already put a thousand miles between us. Isn't that enough space?"

Nicole realized she'd be wasting her time trying to explain the context of space to her mother. Angela was focused on one thing. Getting her life back as it used to be before her marriage dissolved, before Nicole decided she deserved to have her own life.

"Sorry, Mom. I've got to get off the phone. I have a date and he'll be arriving any minute."

Angela gasped. "A date! But what about Randy?"

Biting back the urge to scream, she gave her mother a curt goodbye and ended the call.

Fifteen minutes later, Nicole had pushed her mother's annoying call out of her head and had just finished making a pitcher of ice tea to go with the sandwiches when she heard Trey's knock.

Her heart humming with joy, she hurried to the foyer and opened the door to find him standing hat in hand, smiling back at her. Nicole didn't waste time with words. She reached for his hand and tugged him over the threshold and into her arms.

Hugging her tight, he said, "Mmm! If I'd known I was going to get this kind of reception, I would've driven faster."

The scent she'd come to know as uniquely his wrapped around her senses as she buried her face in the middle of his chest. "I've been thinking about you all day and wanting to do this."

He said, "I hope you've been thinking about this, too."

He tilted her face up to his, and the long, searching kiss he planted on her lips left her sighing for more. "You almost make me want to forget about eating," she admitted.

A sexy lopsided grin carved out dimples in both his cheeks. "Almost?"

Chuckling under her breath, she stepped around him and dealt with closing and locking the door. "We're not going to get sidetracked tonight. Not when I've gone to the trouble of making a stack of sandwiches with my own two little hands."

"Just for me? I feel honored," he teased.

She laughed again, and as she clasped her hand around his, she realized that Trey was the only man who'd ever made her feel truly deep-down happy inside. It was like he'd unlocked a secret part of her that was filled with nothing but joy.

"One of these days I might actually learn how to cook something edible. And then I'll fix you a real dinner," she promised.

"What's more real than a sandwich?"

Laughing, she led him out of the living room and into the intersecting hallway. "You know where the bathroom is. This time I'll wait for you in the kitchen."

As he headed down the hallway, he taunted playfully over his shoulder, "Fraidy cat."

Inside the kitchen, Nicole put the platter of sandwiches, along with a basket of chips, onto the table and was filling two iced glasses with tea when Trey emerged through the swinging doors.

As he drew closer, she could see he'd washed the dust from his face and combed damp fingers through his blond hair. The sleeves of his white cotton shirt were rolled back upon his tanned forearms, while the tail was tucked neatly into the waistband of his jeans. He looked incredibly rugged and sexy, and as her gaze drank in his tempting image, she wondered if she'd gone crazy. Eating a sandwich was hardly the first thing on her wish list tonight.

He said, "You look like you're about to laugh. Do I look funny or something?"

Her cheeks warm, she walked over to the table where he was standing behind one of the wooden chairs.

"Actually, I was thinking I didn't want you to get the idea that I only wanted you for sex."

His brows shot straight up. "No wonder you were about to laugh. That idea is hilarious. Where did you come up with it, anyway?"

He pulled out a chair and helped her into it. After she was settled comfortably in the seat, she said in a teasing voice, "Well, I haven't exactly behaved in a

shy manner around you. You're going to start thinking I'm a brazen hussy."

Chuckling, he joined her in the chair sitting kitty-
corner to her left elbow. "I'd rather think I'm so irresistible that you can't control yourself," he teased.

And he'd be right, Nicole thought. She was drawn
to him in so many ways that she couldn't resist.

"I am glad you didn't have to work very late tonight." She pushed the platter of sandwiches toward
his plate. "How did things go with the injured horse?"

"Good. We brought him back to the clinic and
Doc will be treating him for the next few days. It's
going to take a long recuperation, but eventually he'll
be fine."

"I'm happy to hear that," she said, then casting
him a curious glance, she abruptly changed the subject. "Did Roslyn talk to you about Chandler's birthday party? They're having it at Three Rivers. I forgot
to ask if the party is supposed to be a surprise, so
I wasn't sure if Chandler might have already mentioned it to you."

Nodding, he speared a pair of sandwich halves
onto his plate. "Maureen always puts on such big
shindigs that it would be impossible to make it a surprise. Doc has already invited me. I promised him
I'd be there. What about you?"

"I assured Ros I'd be there," she said, then slanted
him a hopeful glance. "I thought the two of us might
go together. It's a long drive out there."

"Sure. I'd like that," he said.

She lifted a sandwich to her lips but lowered it back to her plate before she could take a bite. "Sorry, Trey," she said sheepishly. "I'm being forward—again—putting the two of us together without considering the thought that you might want to go alone. Just tell me if you'd rather go stag. I won't mind."

He shook his head. "I'm here because I want to spend time with you. As much time as I can before—"

He broke off so suddenly that her expression turned quizzical. "Before what?"

Clearing his throat, he said, "Nothing. Er—I only started to say before Doc and I get even busier. That's all."

Skeptical now, she frowned at him. "I can't imagine you two being busier. You're always running all over Yavapai County and parts of Maricopa County, too. If you got any busier, you'd be working twenty hours of the day."

"That's actually happened before."

Her lips twisted to a wry slant. "Somehow that doesn't surprise me."

She picked up her sandwich and managed to take one bite before a cell phone lying on the cabinet counter dinged to announce an incoming message.

Trey glanced in the direction of the sound. "I hear your phone. Were you expecting anything important?"

"No. I'm certain it's my mother. We had a conversation not long before you arrived. Now she thinks I'm angry with her."

"Are you?"

"Not exactly angry. More like frustrated. And a bit worried."

The weary sound in her voice sent a ripple of unease through Trey. What would he do if she suddenly announced she had to move back to Fort Worth to deal with her mother?

You've been left behind before, Trey. Your ego was squashed for a while, but you got over it.

Yeah, but things were different this time, Trey argued with the daunting voice in his head. The feelings he had for Nicole were already rooted deep inside him. Tearing them out would leave him full of empty holes.

Trying not to think about that possibility, he asked, "Is something wrong with her?"

"Nothing new. Dad has to leave soon on a work trip to New Mexico. Instead of going with him, Mom thinks I should be there to fill the void." Shaking her head, she said, "It's so wrong, Trey."

"I thought you told me their marriage was going great now. Are you worried that might be changing?"

Nodding, she said, "The way I see it, marriages take work, and I'm not sure Mom has that much work ethic."

She'd barely gotten the words out when the phone dinged twice in rapid succession. Nicole put down her sandwich. "Excuse me. I'm going to take care of this."

Trey watched her walk over to the cabinet, and after a quick glance at the screen, she punched a button on the side of the cell phone, then dropped it into a drawer and pushed it shut.

Out of earshot and out of sight, Trey thought. But was that enough to push the problem out of her mind, at least for tonight? She'd explained what had happened to her parents and how she'd felt the need to get away and move here to Arizona. But with her mother continuing to tug at her, how much longer could she stand being torn between her life here in Wickenburg and her family back in Texas?

"Sorry for the interruption," she said as she rejoined him at the table.

He made himself smile at her. "Don't worry about it."

She reached over and placed a hand on his forearm. Her gentle touch reminded him how much he needed her, how much it meant to him to be a part of her life. But he was very afraid to let himself love again or dream of having a family. He'd tried in the past and failed and it had taken him years to get over the hurt and humiliation of being rejected, not once, but twice. He couldn't bear to think of falling short in Nicole's eyes—of losing her.

"Trey," she said softly, "this is our time—for me and you only."

He gave her a pointed glance. "If an emergency happened right now, Doc would call and I'd have to go help him. That would be a huge interruption."

"A call from Chandler would be different. That would be a medical crisis. Mom isn't in crisis. She's in denial."

"You sound certain of that."

"I am. And I'm very certain that I want you here with me."

As Trey's gaze scanned the gentle expression on her face, he realized Chandler had given him sound advice when he'd suggested he be himself and be honest. Being himself would be easy enough, he decided. But how could he be honest and admit that he didn't want to live without her?

Even if he had all kinds of courage, he couldn't admit such a thing to her. She'd think he'd gone and fallen in love with her. And that wouldn't be true. Trey had quit falling in love a long, long time ago.

"Trey, are you okay?"

Her voice jerked him out of his reverie and he saw that she was leaning toward him, a look of real concern on her face.

Thinking he probably looked like a fish lying on a creek bank, he snapped his mouth shut and swallowed hard. "I, uh, was just thinking."

"Must have been some deep thinking," she remarked.

He laughed in an effort to cover up his embarrassment. "No. Just thinking about the birthday party and—other things. And there's something I've been thinking about asking you."

Her face lit up with a smile. "If I'm ready to go panning again? I've been thinking we need to go again—and soon. It would be nice to put a few more nuggets into your ranch kitty."

"That would be nice. But there's somewhere I thought—" He reached for her soft little hand and squeezed it. "Uh—how would you like to drive over to Aguila and meet Granny?"

Her jaw dropped as she stared wide-eyed at him. "Seriously? You really want me to meet your grandmother?"

She made it sound like meeting his grandmother was the next thing to a marriage proposal. Trey was wondering if he'd made a mistake by offering the invitation when she suddenly hopped out of her chair and wrapped her arms around his neck. But as soon as she began to rain kisses all over his face, he realized that anything that made her happy made him happy, too.

Laughing between the smacks she was placing on his cheeks and chin, he said, "Sure, I want you to meet her, or I wouldn't have asked."

"Oh, I can't wait! When can we go? Tomorrow night?"

Her eagerness amazed him. It also made him feel about ten feet tall. Was that what a woman's love did for a man? he wondered. Made him believe he could lift the whole world and balance it in one hand?

Hey, Trey, you're getting way ahead of yourself. You might have Nicole's attention, but she's never talked about loving you. She's never hinted at the word.

Refusing to listen to the doubting voice going through his head, Trey said, "Granny works late at the café on Thursday and Friday nights. And we'll be at Doc's party on Saturday. I'll see if she's going to be home Sunday. Can you go then?"

Pulling her head back, she touched the tip of her nose to his. "I'll be ready and waiting!"

With a hand at the back of her head, he pulled her face near enough to fasten his lips over hers. She moaned softly, and without breaking the kiss, she slowly sank into his lap.

When she wrapped her arms around his neck, Trey gathered her closer and deepened the kiss until their tongues were mating and his hand was sliding over her hip and onto her buttocks. Along the way, desire began to lick at the edges of his brain and send red-hot signals to the rest of his body.

He kissed her until he could no longer breathe and was forced to pull his mouth away from the intoxicating sweetness of her lips.

"We haven't finished eating," he murmured huskily.

Her gray eyes were like silver smoke as her lips tilted into a sexy smile. "Who cares about eating?"

He chuckled under his breath. "You said we weren't going to get sidetracked. Remember?"

"I have a very short memory." Smiling impishly, she tugged him up from the chair.

Trey willingly allowed her to lead him out of the kitchen, and as they walked hand in hand down the hallway to her bedroom, he realized he'd been all wrong when he'd called himself a stubborn jackass. No, this thing he had with Nicole had turned him into a helpless little lamb, too lost in her charms to stop her from shepherding him straight off a cliff.

Chapter Ten

Saturday turned out to be a blazing hot day, but as darkness fell over Three Rivers Ranch house, the temperature dropped dramatically. To make it more comfortable for the birthday party guests, a fire had been built in a large stone firepit located at one end of the covered patio. Festive colored lights hung from the rafters, while a portable bar had been set up to provide before-dinner cocktails.

With her back to the warmth of the flames, Nicole's gaze vacillated from the family and friends milling about on the patio to the ranch yard in the far distance. A half hour ago, Chandler and his younger brother Holt had insisted Trey join them on a trip to the horse barn to check on a very pregnant mare. So far none of the three men had returned to the party.

Nicole was wondering if a medical emergency had detained them when she spotted Holt's wife, Isabelle, walking toward her. Dressed in a floral skirt and blouse, the lovely blonde was carrying a long-stemmed glass filled with orange-colored liquid and slices of citrus fruit.

Having met her several weeks ago, Nicole already regarded the woman as a friend. Besides being warm and down-to-earth, she'd also learned Isabelle was an excellent horse woman, and along with being a wife and mother, she worked her own horse ranch, the Blue Stallion.

"Nicci, where's your drink? You need to get in the partying mood," she scolded playfully.

Nicole smiled. "I just finished a margarita. If I had another, I'd have to be helped to the dinner table."

Laughing lightly, Isabelle turned her back to the heat radiating from the fire. "Same here. This will be my one and only cocktail. And speaking of the dinner table, Maureen has decided to have dinner inside tonight. Even with the fire, our food would be cold by the time we filled our plates."

"It is a bit chilly." She glanced over at Isabelle. The woman didn't appear a bit fidgety about Holt's absence. No doubt she was probably accustomed to her husband disappearing in the middle of a dinner party. "Did you bring your baby with you tonight? I've not had a chance to see him yet."

Smiling fondly, Isabelle nodded. "Carter is upstairs with the rest of his little cousins. Probably trying to hoard up all the little horses he can find in the toy box. For some reason, he's obsessed with the animals," she added with an impish wink.

"I don't suppose both his parents being horse trainers has anything to do with that," Nicole joked.

"Not a thing," Isabelle said with a chuckle. And in case you're wondering, Roslyn is still upstairs trying to get Billy to sleep. If you'd like, we'll go up later on and you can see the whole brood of kids."

"I'd like that," Nicole told her. "I've been trying to remember all the children's names. I know Evelyn and Billy belong to Roslyn and Chandler but I'm not sure about the rest. There're so many I get them mixed up."

Isabelle smiled. "Maureen calls her grandchildren the little herd. By the way, what do you think of my mother-in-law?"

The first time Nicole had visited Three Rivers to meet Roslyn's family, Maureen had walked into the room wearing jeans and boots and a crumpled cowboy hat with a stampede string drawn tight beneath her chin. Nicole had been amazed by the woman.

"Oh my, she's everything and more than I expected. She's so beautiful and warm. She seems ageless."

Isabelle nodded. "Not to mention strong, hardworking and loving. There's no way any of her daughters-in-law could ever fill her shoes. Blake, Chandler's older brother, manages this ranch and does a fine job of it, but underneath, their mother, Maureen, keeps the wheels turning."

"Speaking of beautiful women, your mother is no slouch," Nicole said of Gabby Leman, a lovely blonde, who'd been hanging on to her husband's arm ever since the couple strolled out here to the patio. "And her husband, Sam, is just delightful. It's amazing that he's in his seventies and able to work as foreman of the Bar X."

Loving pride shone on Isabelle's face, and Nicole had to wonder how it would feel to have a mother she could count on to be strong and understanding. Back in Texas those who knew Angela would say that wealth had spoiled her. But after being around the Hollisters, Nicole wasn't so sure. Maureen had been blessed with incredible wealth, yet she appeared to be a pillar for her family. Gabby was a successful artist, but she was happy to live a down-to-earth life with her cowboy.

Isabelle replied, "Lots of people predicted their marriage would never work. And not just because Sam is more than twenty years older than Mother. The fact that she's an artist and originally from San Diego and he's a rawhide-tough cowboy makes it look like such a mismatch. But none of that matters to them. They adore each other."

Nicole felt the same way about herself and Trey. They were different, too, and yet when they were together, it was like everything fit perfectly.

"They're lucky," Nicole said, "to have found each other and to be so happy and in love."

"So true. I was divorced when I met Holt. Back then I wasn't necessarily looking for love. Funny how it seems to find a person even when you're trying to avoid it." She sipped her drink, then turned a clever smile on Nicole. "Roslyn tells me you and Trey came to the party together tonight."

Nicole's cheeks grew warm. "We did. He's gone with Chandler and Holt to the horse barn right now."

Isabelle laughed. "And that was a half hour ago. Holt loses track of time when he's with his horses. And a mare that's foaling is a real party for those guys."

"Taking care of animals makes Trey happy," Nicole told her. "And that's good, because I want him to be happy."

Isabelle regarded her closely. "You sound like a woman who really cares about her guy."

Her guy. Nicole wanted to think of Trey as being her man. That the feelings between them were growing into an unbreakable bond. But so far, she was still waiting for him to give her a sign that their relationship meant more to him than physical pleasure.

"We've not known each other all that long," Nicole replied.

"Time is irrelevant," she said with a clever grin. "The first minute I saw Holt, I felt like an earthquake had hit me. And back then he was such a womanizer that I tried to convince myself that I despised him. Obviously, my strategy failed."

Nicole was thinking how loopy she'd felt when she'd first laid eyes on Trey when Isabelle suddenly gestured to the far end of the patio.

"Speaking of men, here they come," Isabelle said. "And if we're lucky, the mare will hold off until we eat dinner."

Through the years, Trey had attended many Hollister parties. Some had been huge affairs, others low-key. But he'd never had a date at his side. Especially one like Nicole. Now as the group headed into the house for dinner, he gave her a rueful smile.

"Sorry we were gone so long to the barn, Nicci."

"No problem," she replied. "Isabelle has been keeping me company. How was the mare?"

"Doc thinks she'll deliver in the next few hours. Two of Holt's assistants are keeping an eye on her right now."

She looked incredibly lovely tonight in a green-and-white strapless dress with a white lace shawl draped around her creamy shoulders. Her hair swung like a bright flame against her back and reminded Trey of the times he'd tangled his fingers in the silky strands and fastened his mouth over hers.

He was quickly becoming obsessed with her, he decided, and the fact was starting to worry him. But how did a man go about turning off the feelings in his heart?

"Chandler is probably hoping she'll hold off until tomorrow."

Her remark interrupted his thoughts, and he managed to chuckle. "Are you kidding? Doc thinks it's fun when a mare foals on his birthday. Just like there hasn't already been thirty or forty foals here on Three Rivers born on this day. Some are even named after him. Like Doc Do Too Much, CH Star and Chandler's Charge. He loves his job."

"Yes, and I think you love your job, too," she said with a knowing smile.

He slanted her a guilty look. "Just a little."

Inside the house, Trey and Nicole followed the crowd into a long dining room where three separate tables were set up to accommodate the large number of guests.

Nicole was seated to Trey's right side, while Taggart O'Brien was to his left. Beyond the Three Rivers Ranch foreman was his wife, Emily-Ann, who'd recently given birth to a boy they'd named Brody. Across the table, Holt and Isabelle were gazing at each other as though they were the only two people in the room.

Each of the Hollisters had a loving mate, he thought. Even Maureen had moved past the tragedy of losing her husband, Joel, and now seemed to be head over heels in love with his brother, Gil Hollister.

As Trey looked around at all the happy couples in the room, he couldn't help but feel like a little lost doggy. Everybody had somebody, he thought. Not just for tonight, but forever.

Why the hell are you feeling sorry for yourself, Trey? You have a beautiful woman sitting next to you, and she looks at you with stars in her eyes. If you really wanted a lasting family like the Hollisters, you'd be telling Nicci how much you loved her. How much you wanted the two of you to spend the rest of your lives together. Instead, you get scared if you even think she's going to mention the word love. You're a coward. Nothing but a sniveling coward.

"Trey, are you coming down with something?" Holt asked. "You look like you've eaten too many green apples. Is Nicci making you sick?"

A spate of chuckles penetrated Trey's wandering thoughts, and he glanced blankly around the table before his gaze settled on Holt's teasing face. "Did you say something to me?"

"I said you look miserable. I realize this isn't like going to the Fandango, but Mom does throw a decent party."

Hoping his face wasn't red, Trey said, "Oh—it's a great party." He glanced over at Nicole's curious expression, then back to Holt. "I was doing some thinking. And Doc always did say it made me sick to use my brain," he attempted to joke.

"Want to share those deep thoughts of yours?" Nicole asked.

The impish little smile on her face made him want to grab her and kiss her and forget all about the doubts rattling around in his head.

Snatching at the first thing that came to his mind, he said, "I—uh—was just noticing how especially happy Maureen looks tonight."

The thought was partly true, Trey decided. Earlier, when they'd first entered the dining room, he'd noticed the Hollister matriarch standing next to Gil, holding his hand and smiling up at him in the same endearing way that Nicole smiled at him.

"Maureen is happy," Isabelle spoke up. "Gil has changed her life for the better."

"Mom's hopes are high right now," Holt said, then added in a lower voice, "Joe and the Phoenix police are planning a meeting with Ginny Patterson. Sometime in the next few days. Mom believes the woman can fill in the blank spots about Dad's death."

"And that's the only thing that's holding Maureen back from actually planning a wedding with Gil," Isabelle added.

Next to Trey, Taggart quickly added, "I can tell you that Blake has his hopes up, too. We all do."

"Yes," Holt agreed with the ranch foreman. "For years we've had a cloud hanging over us, and we're praying that Ginny Patterson is finally going to help shine some light."

Trey started to question Holt about what this so-called meeting with the woman was going to involve, but the food suddenly arrived and everyone turned their attention to eating.

For the remainder of the party, the subject of Joel's death and the hope to solve it wasn't mentioned again, until much later when Trey and Nicole were driving back to Wickenburg.

"The whole thing is so—well, just thinking about it makes me shiver," Nicole said. "Who knows if this Ginny woman can be trusted? She might lead Joe and Connor into a trap?"

"We don't know if Joe and Connor will actually be in on the meeting or if the Phoenix police will handle the whole thing. Either way, they're professionals. They'll know how to deal with the situation."

She pondered his words for a moment before she finally said, "Yes, I suppose so. I wonder if Chandler and Roslyn know about this plan. Has he mentioned anything to you about it?"

"Yes, they know. The whole family has been waiting anxiously for Ginny Patterson to finally agree to a definite date for the meeting. Now it looks like that's finally in the process of getting done. I only hope it gives them answers." He looked over to see her head resting against the back of the seat, her eyelids lowered to sleepy slits. Just looking at her made his heart ache with feelings so strange and strong that he could never begin to understand them. "Have I told you how gorgeous you look tonight?"

A faint smile touched her lips. "Maybe two or three times. And you're changing the subject."

"You *are* my subject."

"Is that why you've been so distracted tonight?" she asked. "Even when we were dancing, I had the feeling you were somewhere else."

To add to the festivities, Maureen had hired a small three-piece band and pushed aside the living room furniture to make space for dancing. Trey had hoped having Nicole in his arms and moving to the music would help soothe the uneasiness that had come over him during the evening. Instead, it had made him even more impatient to get her alone.

"I was somewhere else," he admitted. "I was in bed making love to you."

She leaned across the console and reached for his hand. "We're almost home, darling."

Home. Yes, something about tonight had changed Trey's definition of that word. To have a real home, it took two people loving each other, working together, laughing at the good times and crying through the bad. It meant making roots together. And that meant he had to believe Nicole would never want to go back to Texas. He had to put his trust in her and truly believe she was different than the women who'd hurt him in the past.

Hours later, Nicole lay curled against Trey's warm body, her head pillowed on his arm as she gazed past the open curtain of the bedroom window. A moment ago, she'd heard the distant sound of a rooster crowing, and even though she couldn't see the clock on the nightstand, she knew that daylight would soon be pushing away the moonlight.

The party at Three Rivers had lasted for hours, and Nicole had enjoyed it immensely. Still, she'd been relieved when Trey had finally suggested they leave. He'd not been himself tonight. Even while they'd made love, she'd felt a part of him was far away.

She'd hoped that sleep would blot out her nagging thoughts. But instead of sleeping, she'd lain wide-awake, listening to Trey's even breathing and wondering what was in his heart. Why couldn't he share his feelings with her?

Maybe because his feelings for you aren't worth sharing, Nicole. Did you ever think of that? Just because he's in your bed doesn't mean he loves you, or anything close to it. You're dreaming. Hoping for something that is never going to be.

The mocking voice going on in her head caused tears to fill her eyes, and she prayed the salty moisture wouldn't roll down her cheek and onto his arm. Not for anything did she want him to wake and find her crying.

"You should be asleep."

The unexpected sound of his voice caused her to rapidly blink her watery eyes and attempt to swallow away the lump in her throat.

"You should be, too," she murmured. "We're going to be red-eyed when we go to see your grandmother later today. Do you still want to go?"

His cheek rubbed against the top of her head. "Sure. Why wouldn't I?"

"I thought—you might be out of the mood."

His hand slid gently down her arm to rest on the curve of her hip. "I want us to go. I don't know why you're thinking my mood is off."

With her back still to him, she drew in a deep breath and closed her eyes. "I'm sorry, Trey. I guess I'm just being a woman and getting the feeling that—" Turning to face him, she rested a hand in the middle of his chest. "Maybe you're getting tired of me."

"Tired?" His laugh was incredulous. "That's not going to happen."

The moonlight slanting through the windows illuminated his face. She carefully studied each rugged feature before she finally asked, "Do you remember after we went to the Wagon Wheel and I asked you what you would do if a woman got serious about you? You said you'd probably run. You've never explained why. Did a woman hurt you?"

He was silent for so long that Nicole had given

up on an answer, but then he sighed and turned his gaze toward the ceiling.

"I really don't want to talk about it, Nicci."

Rejection washed over her, and she quickly sat up and swung her legs over the edge of the mattress. "Oh. Okay."

His hand was suddenly wrapping around the side of her waist. "Where are you going?"

"To the kitchen. To make coffee." Anything would be better than lying next to him and thinking about things that made her want to burst into tears.

"You're angry with me," he stated.

"No. Just disappointed. That's all."

Suddenly he was sitting behind her and his hands were on her shoulders, drawing her back against his warn chest. "Doc told me that if I was honest with you, then you'd never be disappointed in me. I guess maybe I'd better be honest with you now."

Frowning, she twisted her head around to look at him. "I don't want you to do or say anything just because you feel I'm pressuring you. That's not good. So let's forget this. Okay?"

She started to rise, but he held her fast.

"It's not okay. I should've told you in the beginning that I—well, let's just say I tried the serious thing a couple of times before. Both of them ended in a bad way. For me, that is. Not for the women."

After Loretta and Roslyn had hinted about his past romances, she'd been thinking it would help her to understand him better if she knew what had happened. But now, the deepest part of her was revolting against the image of him loving another woman.

Trying to brace herself, she asked, "Serious? Like considering marriage?"

He nodded. "I was only twenty-one back then. Rhonda worked as a farrier's assistant. I thought we'd make a perfect match and so did she. Until she got the chance for a high-paying job on a ranch near Reno. She lit out and never looked back. I heard later that she'd found herself a sugar daddy."

"I'd say you made a great escape."

"That's true enough," he said ruefully. "But I doubt you've ever been deserted like that—it bruises the ego, Nicci."

She couldn't imagine any woman walking away from Trey. Not if she'd really loved him. "Your ego must have healed over time."

"It was a couple of years or more before I met Lacey. She was my age and the single mother of a little two-year-old girl. She worked hard as a waitress, while trying to take college classes on the side. I thought we matched up just fine. And I grew darned attached to the little girl."

"What happened? The baby's father showed up to make trouble?"

He shook his head. "No. He was out of the picture. It was Lacey's family that caused the problems. They were a dysfunctional group, including her parents. Always begging for money or help of some kind. Their interference finally got to be too much."

He was practically describing what Nicole had been going through with her own parents. Had Trey noticed the parallel? Was that why he'd not wanted to take their relationship a step closer to love and marriage?

Trying to quell her runaway thoughts, she asked, "Did you break up with Lacey?"

"No. She packed up and moved her and the baby to California. Ironically, after Lacey left, her family moved away, too. But whether they followed her, I never heard."

"You could've gone after her."

He shrugged. "She obviously didn't care enough to stay with me and try to make it all work, so I didn't see any point of putting up a fight to keep her."

It didn't sound like he'd put up a battle for either woman. In some ways Nicole was glad he hadn't. It could only mean that deep down he hadn't loved enough or cared enough to fight for what he wanted. Only, somewhere along the way, those bad experiences had pushed him into believing he never wanted to be a family man. If that was the case, she might never change his mind.

"I see," she murmured thoughtfully.

A look of disbelief crossed his face. "That's a surprise. I didn't expect you to understand why I'd basically given up on women—until you came along."

She practically stopped breathing as she waited for him to say more. Like how much he would always need her. How much he would fight to keep her in his life. But the silence in the room began to stretch as far as the lingering shadows. And after a while Nicole decided the best and only thing to do for the moment was to show him that she honestly did understand.

Nestling her cheek against the curve of his shoulder, she said, "Before I ever moved here to Arizona, I had promised myself that I wasn't going to look at another man. At least, not anytime soon. Then you walked into Chandler's office and made me break that vow."

His chest shook with a chuckle, and the sound brought a smile to her face. "What's funny about that?" she asked.

"Be honest. I caught your attention because you'd never smelled a man who was covered with cow manure."

She hugged him tighter. "Better than any designer cologne."

His fingertips drew lazy lines upon her cheek as he bent his head and touched the tip of his nose to hers. "And you're better than an armful of paradise," he whispered.

"Mmm," she purred. "Then we'd better not waste the rest of the morning."

"I thought you wanted coffee."

She angled her lips against his. "We'll have plenty of time for that—later."

The waning afternoon was spreading long shadows over Virginia Lasseter's vegetable garden as Nicole followed the woman through rows of snap beans, tomatoes and corn.

Pausing, the tall, slender woman with long dark hair pointed to a portion of the garden to their right. "I normally have cantaloupe and watermelon growing there, but with Harley raising acres and acres of melons, he told me not to bother with those—he'll keep me supplied. So I planted more onions, carrots and radishes instead of melons. Trey hates radishes, but he's rarely around to eat."

Virginia looked at her and smiled, and not for the first time this afternoon, Nicole thought how much Trey's grandmother reminded her of Maureen Hollister. Not that the women's appearances or lives were similar in any way. Maureen was an incredibly wealthy woman and the owner of one of the largest ranches in Arizona. The family's holdings raked in more money in a single year than Nicole could imagine. As for Virginia, she lived in a very modest old house on a small acreage. She worked as a waitress to support herself, and yet she had that same regal quality that Maureen possessed, that same youthful beauty that was timeless. Both women's eyes shone with strength and wisdom. The two important qualities that Nicole often prayed her mother would find.

"I love radishes," Nicole said. "Actually, there's not a vegetable in your garden that I don't like."

"Good. When everything is ready to pick, I'll call you. I'll have plenty to share with you."

"I'd like that."

Virginia's gaze moved from Nicole to where Trey was sitting on the steps of the back porch, playing with one of the woman's several cats.

"I think my grandson disapproves of my decision to marry Harley," she said. "When I showed him my engagement ring, he looked like he'd swallowed a few fence steeples."

Not long after Nicole and Trey had arrived at his grandmother's house, she'd sprung the news of her engagement on them and showed off the hefty sparkler that Harley had slipped onto her finger.

Nicole felt incredibly happy for the woman and had given her a sincere hug and well wishes. As for Trey, he'd mostly remained quiet about the news.

"I wouldn't say he's unhappy, Virgie. I think the word *marriage* just makes him feel a bit squeamish."

The older woman sighed as she tucked a strand of black hair threaded with silver behind one ear. "That's understandable. His parents were always at each other's throats. Our son Amos was, still is, a good man in his own way. But he's the sort that never should've gotten married or been a father. Not that he ever was much of one," she admitted. "When he and Emma divorced, it was a blessing all around. After that, James and I hoped our marriage would be an example for our grandson. But then Trey had some bad tries at romance."

"Yes. He told me a little about them. But I believe he's over that now."

Virginia batted a hand through the air. "Over those women? Pooh. He didn't love either one of those gals in the first place."

Nicole wondered how Virginia could be so certain of her grandson's emotional state. "What makes you think so?"

Smiling, she patted Nicole's shoulder. "I never saw hide nor hair of either one of them. But I've seen you."

Was this woman implying that Trey might possibly love Nicole? Just because he'd brought her here today? No. She'd be foolish to let her hopes go that far.

Nicole was trying to think of some sort of appropriate response when Virginia nudged her shoulder toward the house.

"Let's go in," she said. "I have something to give you."

They strolled back to the porch where Trey still sat with the black cat.

"What are you two doing?" he asked. "I thought you were going to gather the eggs."

"We have plenty of time to do that before dark," Virginia told him. "You just stay put. We have some girl business in the house to take care of."

Trey arched a skeptical brow at his grandmother. "Are you filling Nicci's head with stories about me?"

"I don't want to scare her off," she answered sassily, while gesturing for Nicole to follow her onto the porch.

Trey winked at Nicole. "Okay. You two just go on and leave me all alone. At least, Cleo likes me."

"Cleo likes anybody who'll rub her belly. And by the way, all the cats need their vaccines. Think you can take care of them the next time you come? That's much easier than me hauling seven cats into the clinic."

"I'll bring all the vaccines next time," he promised.

The two women entered the house, and after walking through the small kitchen, Virginia guided her to a small bedroom at the back.

"This used to be Trey's room while he was living with us. That was years ago, before he went to work on the Johnson Ranch. Now I mostly use it to store things," she explained.

The small room had a linoleum floor printed to look like river rock. A single long window covered with sheer priscillas was located next to the side of a full-sized bed made with a wooden bookshelf for a headboard. A matching chest stood across from the bed, and on top of it was a framed photo of Trey that appeared to be taken at his high school graduation. Everything was simple and neat and spotless.

"Trey has confessed he's not much of a housekeeper," Nicole said. "Was his room messy back then?"

Virginia chuckled. "It was usually a disaster. But I didn't clean it up for him. I made him do it."

She moved to the head of the bed where a cedar chest was pushed up against the wall. After removing a small lamp from the top and setting it aside, she pushed up the lid.

Nicole was wondering what the woman could possibly be wanting to give her when Virginia pulled out a handmade quilt.

"I made this many years ago. It's done in a double wedding ring pattern," she said, her hand smoothing over the calico. "For a gift for Trey whenever he got married. I'm giving it to you now."

Nicole's mouth fell open as she handed the quilt over to her. "But Virgie, I can't take this!"

"Why not? I'm giving it to you."

"But Trey is—"

"Trey nothing. He'll come around. Just like I did with Harley," she added with a coy grin.

Nicole was virtually speechless. The mere fact that Virginia Lasseter had accepted her as Trey's girlfriend so quickly and without question was amazing in itself. But to give her such a keepsake was more than she could grasp.

"I don't know what to say, Virgie," she murmured, and then before she could stop them, tears sprang to her eyes. "This is—the most beautiful gift anyone has ever given me."

"Oh, I doubt that. Trey said you were a city girl and wore fancy high heels. I figure you've had lots of nice gifts before."

Was that the way he'd described her? Thought of her? Maybe when they'd first met, she'd seemed materialistic, but surely he'd learned differently now.

Shaking her head, Nicole said, "Virgie, a gift from a store isn't like this one. My home back in Fort Worth—my parents have always had money. But I wish—" She paused and blinked back the moisture burning her eyes. "I wish that home could've been more like yours."

Virginia's understanding smile made it even harder for Nicole to keep from bursting into tears.

"You'll get to do it your way now," she said, curving her arm around Nicole's shoulders and giving them a squeeze.

"But you and Harley will be getting married soon," Nicole reasoned. "You should keep this quilt for the two of you."

"Nonsense. Harley wouldn't care if he was sleeping under a piece of canvas. And you know something, neither would I. We're just going to enjoy each other. In the end that's all that matters."

Blinking back her tears, Nicole planted a kiss on Virginia's smooth cheek. "Thank you. For the quilt. For everything."

"You're welcome. Now come on. Let's go see if Trey's ready for some fried pies and coffee."

The two women started out of the bedroom, only to meet Trey at the open doorway.

"What's the matter?" Virginia asked. "Did Cleo get moody and claw you?"

He glanced at Nicole and then his grandmother. "No. I—uh—was coming after Nicci. I've got to get back to town—to the clinic to meet Doc. As soon as I can get there."

Nicole said, "Chandler never works on Sunday. Has there been an emergency?"

"Not exactly," Trey answered. "Doc needs me for something."

"Well, darn. I wasn't nearly finished visiting with Nicci yet." With a tolerant smile, Virginia patted the middle of her grandson's chest. "You'll just have to bring her back, Trey."

"I will, Granny."

"Soon."

"Yes, soon."

He sounded impatient, which was totally out of character for him, Nicole thought. Even when an emergency arose at work, he always reacted in a cool, efficient manner. But here in front of Virginia was hardly the time to question him. Instead, she said, "I'll go fetch my handbag."

Chapter Eleven

Trey had barely driven away from his grandmother's house when Nicole asked for an explanation.

"I thought you said this wasn't an emergency. Why are you in such a hurry?"

He glanced over to see a confused frown on her face, and for a split second, Trey considered stopping the truck on the side of the road and pulling her into his arms.

From the time he'd made love to her early this morning until now, something had happened to him. Whether it was the way she'd clung to him, or how she'd seemed to understand when he'd talked about his past mistakes, he wasn't sure, but it had felt like some sort of dam had broken inside him. And then when he'd watched the way she and his grandmother had interacted, it was like a foggy lens had been peeled from his eyes.

Before he received Chandler's call, he'd decided that as soon as he and Nicole returned to her place, he was going to have a long talk with her. He was going to put his heart, everything, on the line and find out exactly where he stood with her. She needed to know that he didn't want just an affair with her. He wanted more. Much more. If she wasn't willing to give him those things, he had to be prepared to tell her goodbye.

"It's nothing about rushing to treat a wounded or sick animal," he said. "Doc wants me to go to Phoenix with him—right now. As soon as I get there."

She squared her knees around so that she was looking directly at him. "Phoenix? On a Sunday?"

He grimaced. "I didn't want to say anything in front of Granny. Not that she would've repeated anything to anyone, but it might have worried her. I'll explain everything to her later."

She arched a brow at him. "How about explaining to me now?"

Fixing his gaze on the highway, he said, "The police have set up a meeting with Ginny Patterson. Doc wants me to be there with him."

"Why does Chandler want you with him? He has three brothers who can go."

Her question felt like an ice pick driving right through him. "I guess it's hard for you to understand, but Doc considers me a brother, too."

There was a pause of silence and then she said, "I'm sorry, Trey. I didn't mean it that way. I know that you two are practically tied at the hip. I just thought—well, to be honest, it makes me uneasy to think of you going anywhere near someone who might be a murderer."

"Don't worry. We'll only be listening in on some conversation," he said in an effort to assure her. "And later I think you and me need to talk."

From the corner of his eye, he could see a guarded expression come over her face.

"Talk? About what?"

"Oh, about whether we're going to go panning anytime soon. There's treasure to be found out there, you know."

She reached for his hand, and his heart winced with longing as her fingers tightened around his.

"I do know. And we're going to find it—together."

Trey could only wonder if they were talking about the same kind of treasure.

After dropping off Nicole at her house, Trey drove on to the clinic and found Chandler waiting for him.

"What about your brothers and Gil?" Trey asked as he climbed into Chandler's truck and fastened his seat belt.

"Joe and Connor are already in Phoenix with police detectives. Blake, Holt and Uncle Gil are traveling just ahead of us in another vehicle," Chandler explained. "Normally, we wouldn't be allowed to listen in on something like this, but Gil pulled some strings with the department."

"What about Maureen? Did she go with the others?"

"No. Mom is at home. Being on the ranch gives her comfort."

That was understandable, Trey thought. Three Rivers Ranch had been Maureen's home for more than forty years. "Holt mentioned at the party that this meeting might be happening soon. I wasn't expecting it to be today."

"Joe got a call late last night that things were quickly falling into place." He blew out a long breath and slanted an uneasy glance at Trey. "Guess this is it, buddy. The last chance to find the truth about Dad. If this falls apart, there's nothing else left. It kills me to think of Mom living the rest of her life wondering what really happened to Dad."

"This isn't just about Maureen. It's about you and your brothers, too. You've all suffered over the unknown." Trey glanced at Chandler's stern profile. "Just how much does this Ginny seem to know about your dad's death, anyway? Has she told anyone?"

"She has her suspicions, and that's all that Joe knows. Other than the basic facts that she had some sort of connection to Dad via the Phoenix Livestock Sales and she's scared to death of her husband. Supposedly that's why she's not come forward with information before now. Has to be conscience, or the opportunity to get the husband out of her life, that finally made her agree to help. Take your pick."

"Doesn't matter as long as you find the truth," Trey told him.

Once they arrived at the police department in Phoenix, Trey and Chandler were directed to a section of the building designated for the homicide division. When they entered a small sparsely furnished room used for interrogations, they found Blake sitting at a table, while Gil and Holt were standing together at the back of the room. To one side, three men wearing street clothes were gathered around some sort of technical equipment.

Spotting Chandler and Trey, Gil immediately strode forward and began to explain what was happening.

"Where are Joe and Connor?" Chandler asked, his gaze circling the room. "I thought they'd be here with the detectives. Has the meeting already started somewhere else?"

Gil said, "There's not going to be a meeting. Not in the sense you're thinking. Ginny agreed to having a hidden camera with sound placed in her kitchen. That's the issue that was holding up this whole thing.

To get the bug installed without her husband suspecting or finding out."

Chandler and Trey exchanged looks of surprise.

"You mean this is sort of like a sting?" Trey asked the retired detective.

"Exactly," Gil said. "And frankly in this case, we're at Ginny Patterson's mercy. If she doesn't get her husband to talking, or if she tips him off in any way, this could all be over before it begins."

Chandler groaned. "This is a hell of a situation. She wants us to believe her husband was involved in Dad's death? And not her? How can we trust her on this?"

"We don't have any other choice," Gil said, then motioned for the two men to follow him. "Come on. I'll introduce you to the guys who'll be operating things on this end."

A few minutes later, Holt walked up to Trey and Chandler. A cup of coffee was clutched in one hand, while a frown marred his face.

"This stuff tastes like ground-up parsnips," he muttered as he glanced down at the black liquid. "I wish Jazelle was here to pour me a bourbon and Coke. This waiting around is hell."

"Yeah, it's hell all right," Chandler agreed. "But if you're worried about Maudie foaling tonight, don't be. I checked her before I left. The baby is lying just as he should be."

A half-hearted smile on his face, Holt slapped

a grateful hand on Chandler's shoulder. "Thanks, brother. I'm not worried about Maudie. I just want all of this stuff about Dad to be over and done with. It's been eight, close to nine years since Dad died. It's time for our lives, and Mom's, to move on."

Trey felt the same way. He wanted his relationship with Nicole to move on from what it was now. He wanted to know that she would be with him forever. Not just until she grew bored with him, or decided her family needed her back in Texas. Maybe she wasn't expecting or wanting to hear that he loved her, that his whole outlook about marriage had changed. But one way or the other, she had to understand where his thoughts were headed, and he needed to know whether any of it really mattered to her.

Trey was still deep in thought when one of the technicians suddenly spoke loud enough for everyone to hear. "If you men want to gather round, we're picking up image and sound now."

Trey followed Chandler and his brothers and uncle over to a computer screen on a metal desk.

"I hope to hell the picture gets better than this," Gil said as everyone stared at the grainy images.

The eldest of technicians quickly turned a dial on the machine, and the screen immediately cleared to show an area of kitchen cabinets and one end of a farm table covered with checked oil cloth. The white wooden chairs had lost most of their paint from years

of use, but the shabbiness of them or the nearby cabinets was hardly important.

It was the large man sitting at one end that caught
Trey's attention. He was a seedy-looking character,
somewhere in his late fifties, with thin balding hair
combed straight back from a low forehead. His rough
features looked puffy, as though he either drank or
had some sort of health issue. The dark-colored shirt
covering his slumped shoulders looked to be splattered with something like paint or wet concrete. He
was forking food into his mouth as fast as he could
chew and swallow.

"What is this slop anyway?" the man asked. "I
might as well be chewing one of those bones you
throw out for the dogs!"

"It's pot roast. I cooked it for you special," a feminine voice spoke from somewhere beyond the table.
"You always liked it before."

"Not with these damned rotten teeth!" he bel-
lowed. "I need something soft!"

"I'll fix you some scrambled eggs," she said.

"No, you won't fix me any scrambled eggs,"
he mimicked, every word dripping with sarcasm.
"You'll sit your ass down and quit hovering over
me!"

A woman with drooping features and short blond
hair pinned out of her eyes came into view as she
walked over to a nearby chair and rested her hands
on the top of the backrest. She was wearing a cotton

housecoat that gaped at her bosom, while the edges of the sleeves were frayed. She hardly looked nervous, Trey thought. Instead, she looked like a person who was merely going through the motions of living.

"You know, Ike, you could get those teeth fixed if I went back to work," she suggested. "I've been thinking I might get my old job at the sale barn again. I hear Walt needs help in the concession now."

The man she called Ike suddenly jerked his head up and stared menacingly at his wife. "You're gettin' damned sassy tonight. You askin' for a beatin'?"

Trey was wondering why the woman was living with this animal of a man when Chandler looked at him and silently mouthed the word *sick*.

On the screen, Ginny moved away from the chair and was out of sight for only a second before she returned with a pitcher filled with tea or some sort of dark liquid. As she refilled Ike's glass, she said, "I'm trying to help. We could use a little more money around here. Especially with you getting fired from that concrete job."

He slapped his fork down so hard that the table actually shook. "That was no fault of mine! And don't you ever mention that sale barn again! You think I'm gonna let you go work there and get yourself another man? You ain't nothin' to look at, but I'll be damned before anybody else gets you!"

To the right of Trey, Holt whispered, "God help her."

On the other side of Chandler, Blake muttered, "I'd like to get my hands around his throat."

Back in the Patterson kitchen, Ginny seemed to gather some energy or courage, or both, as she straightened her shoulders and stared down at her husband. "What are you talking about? Another man? I've never had another man. Why would I want one when I have you?"

Forgetting the food on his plate, Ike glared at her. "Don't stand there and lie to me in that catty voice! I'll knock your head off your shoulders!"

"If you're talking about Joel Hollister, I have a bit of news for you, Ike. I read in the newspaper that the Yavapai sheriff's department has come up with some new evidence that says the rancher wasn't drug to death by a horse—he was murdered. You know anything about that?"

Ike looked like a man who'd just seen the devil and didn't know whether to get ready to fight, or run. But after a moment he quickly gathered himself and sneered at her. "You're worse than stupid. Why would I know anything about that rancher? He was a rich bastard. Somebody killed him for his money."

Seemingly unfazed by his retort, she said, "The law doesn't think so. And I don't think it, either. I believe that you killed Joel Hollister! Just because he was my friend!"

The damning accusations came out of Ginny so suddenly and unexpectedly that everyone in the room stared in stunned fascination at what was unfolding before them.

His voice low and threatening, he said, "I'll give you one thing, Ginny, you got more guts than I ever thought."

Ginny put down the pitcher and moved a few inches on down the table. "Yeah, I finally got enough guts to face the fact that I'm living with a murderer."

An evil grin twisted his face. "Hell yeah, I killed that son of a bitch Joel Hollister. Just what do you think you're going to do about it?" he goaded. "I'll tell you what. Not one damned thing. Or I'll smash your head the same way I did his!"

"That's it," Blake said in a hushed, incredulous voice. "We got him!"

While Holt was making a fist pump, Trey was expecting the woman to run out of the house and to safety. Instead, she continued to stare at him as though she wanted to go after him with a carving knife.

"Why, Ike? You never knew the man. He didn't do anything to you."

"Nothin'? He was going to help you leave me. Yeah, I knew about the plans you two made. You think I'm as dumb as you are, but I'm not. Back then, you were actin' awful happy for some reason. I couldn't figure out why until I heard you on the phone talkin' to Wanda, that loopy old friend of yours. Hollister was gonna help you get you and your things to the bus station without me knowin'."

Ginny blinked, and Trey prayed she wouldn't break down now.

"No one else around here ever had the guts to help me—except for Joel," she said. "I'll never forgive myself for asking him—for causing his death."

"Aw now, ain't that sweet," he drawled sarcastically. "You think the man died a hero."

Trey noticed Ginny's hand wrap around the handle of the heavy glass. Was she going to use it as a weapon? Why didn't she just get the heck out of there?

Trey was about to whisper the question to Chandler when he saw Ike pick up his fork and point it at Ginny in a bullying manner.

"In case you'd like to know, I didn't find out the man was a rich, well-to-do rancher until the next day. That's when I called Hollister and told him I wanted to meet him. I made up this cock-'n-bull sob story about how much I loved you and wanted him to help me win you back. Just like I figured, he didn't want his family knowin' he was mixed up with a woman like you, so he agreed to meet me on the backside of the ranch."

"That's where you killed him," she stated in a stricken voice.

"It was so easy it was pitiful. He turned around to tend to his horse and never knew what hit him. At first, I didn't plan on making it look like an accident. That came to me after the fact. Worked, too, didn't it? Joel Hollister was drug to death by his own trusty steed. That's what the newspapers all printed." His laughter was a satanical sound. "You know, Ginny, the only thing I regret is that I didn't get some money out of him before I killed him. That was stupid of me, but a man can't think of everything."

"No. You never thought of the most important thing," Ginny dared to say.

"What's that?"

"Good lawmen don't give up on righting an evil wrong. And you're evil, Ike. Right down to the core."

"Somebody needs to get her out of there! The monster will kill her!" Blake moved desperately toward the screen as if he could pluck Ginny out of danger.

"Hang on, Mr. Hollister," one of the detectives assured him. "Officers will be moving in any second."

Trey was about to echo Blake's fears when Ginny suddenly threw the glass pitcher directly at Ike's face.

Roaring and sputtering, he jumped to his feet, but by then three detectives burst into the kitchen and quickly shackled his hands behind his back.

When the video feed went dark, Ike was cursing a blue streak and Ginny was weeping.

The room full of men went quiet until Gil finally turned to face his nephews. His usual swarthy complexion had gone pale and his features were taut. No doubt he'd been struck hard by what they'd all just witnessed.

After clearing his throat and wiping a hand over his face, he said, "I don't know about you guys, but that was damned hard to watch—to hear why my brother died."

Blake stepped forward and placed a hand on his uncle's shoulder. "Hard, but necessary. Everything is going to be good now, Gil. Especially for Mom. And that's what matters the most."

Gil gave his eldest nephew a grateful nod. "Yes, she does matter the most. And if any of you are wondering about the legal end of this, I'm fairly certain the DA of Yavapai County will prosecute Ike Patterson. A lawyer will probably advise him to retract his confession, and there might be a fight about entrapment, but one way or the other, he'll pay for his crime."

Beside him, Trey could hear Chandler let out a long breath of relief. A reaction, not only to the end result of tonight, but to years of unanswered questions.

Holt said, "I don't know how the rest of you feel, but I think Ginny Patterson deserves a medal for bravery."

"I damned well second that," Chandler added. "He would've killed her. Maybe not tonight, but at some point in the coming days, he would've silenced her."

"Poor, poor woman," Trey said. "All these years

with no one to help. Except for your dad. And he died trying."

Chandler looked at him, and Trey didn't miss the mist of tears in his friend's eyes.

His voice raw, Chandler said, "Dad died because he loved helping people. He wanted everyone to be as happy as he was."

Gil said, "You're right, Chandler. And that's the way we're going to honor Joel. Let's go home and be happy."

As Trey followed the Hollister men out of the interrogation room, he couldn't think of anything he wanted more.

Monday mornings were always chaotic at the clinic, but that didn't stop the staff from celebrating the happy news that Joel's murderer had been arrested and would likely remain behind bars.

Knowing the Hollisters had suffered for years over the ordeal, Nicole was thrilled for all of them. The family could finally put the how and why of that awful incident to rest. But at the moment, Nicole wasn't celebrating; she was doing her best to stop a flow of tears from streaming down her face.

Why, oh why, had she answered her cell phone? One glance at the ID had told her the call was from Texas. She should've ignored it. But the waiting room had momentarily cleared and the business phone was quiet. And since her father often updated his cell phone, she'd feared it might have been him calling to tell her that Angela had relapsed with another mental breakdown. Instead, she'd been totally shocked to hear Randy Dryer's voice in her ear.

The Hollisters weren't the only ones who could put the lid on an unpleasant memory, she thought, as she dabbed a tissue to the corners of her eyes. And now that she had a moment to think, she realized she was thankful for the call. For so many reasons, it had been cathartic.

"Wow! No one in the waiting room and the phone is quiet! Ready for some lunch?"

The sound of Trey's voice entering the room had Nicci sniffing back her tears and swiveling her chair to face him.

"Hi, Trey! Uh—yes—I'm ready for lunch." Another pesky tear slipped from the corner of her eye, but she managed to give him a bright smile. "I'm—"

As soon as he spotted the tears on her cheeks, his smile turned into a frown. "Are you crying? What's wrong? This is a happy day! You're supposed to be celebrating."

Gripping the tissue, just in case she might need it again, she rose from the chair. "I know I'm supposed to be happy. And I am, really. I just need a moment to compose myself."

He frowned as he eyed the cell phone lying on the desk. "Why? Has your mother been giving you a bad time? Is that it?"

"No. I—" She paused as she tried to think of the right way to explain her emotional state without sounding crazy. "Mother hasn't called yet today, thank God. But I did get a call from Texas—from my old boyfriend—Randy Dryer."

One of his brows cocked to a skeptical arch. "The man who asked you to marry him?"

Nicole's stomach roiled at the very thought. There would never be any other man in the world for her except Trey.

She took a step toward him, and in a hurried voice answered, "Yes. The one I turned down. He—uh—he's a marine now and back in Fort Worth for two weeks and wants me to fly back and join him. He's dropped his current girlfriend because he says he still wants to marry me."

One of the things she'd always adored about Trey was that he had such an expressive face. His eyes and mouth, even the dimples in his cheeks, were constantly revealing his thoughts and feelings. But now as she looked at him, all she could see was a stone-faced stranger.

"Oh, I see."

The odd expression on his face and the three-worded response were hardly what she'd expected from him.

Frowning with frustration, she said in a wary tone, "I'm not sure that you do."

"Don't worry, Nicci. I get the whole picture—

now. Those are happy tears. Congratulations. I can't say that I blame you for changing your mind. I hear that's a woman's privilege, and God knows I've learned that the hard way. How soon will you be going back to Fort Worth? Does Doc know yet that he's going to have to find a new receptionist?"

She was so stunned by his questions that her whole body began to quiver. But the reaction was only momentary as, right behind the shock, anger poured through her, causing her cheeks to redden and her hands to clench into fists. How dare he assume something so ridiculous! The man had shared her bed. Did he not know her at all?

She forced her gritted teeth to relax enough to push a retort past her lips. "I haven't decided yet! It might be sooner than you think!"

Before he could make a reply, a buzzer announced the door of the main entrance being opened, and Nicole looked across the waiting area to see a beagle trotting into the room followed by a young woman holding the dog's leash.

Oh great, this was a fine time for an interruption. She turned back to Trey to tell him she'd talk with him later, but there was nothing but empty air in front of her.

He'd walked off without a word. He was accepting without a fight what he thought was her decision to marry Randy. Apparently, he was going to let her go just as he'd let the other women in his past walk away. So much for hoping he might actually love her, she thought sadly.

Drawing in a deep, bracing breath, she blinked her eyes and walked over to the woman standing at the check-in counter.

Any other time, Trey would've been thrilled that he and Chandler were headed to the Johnson Ranch. Trey would always be a close friend to Mr. Johnson, the man who'd single-handedly persuaded Trey to enter the profession of animal welfare. Along with seeing Mr. Johnson again, Chandler was in an especially jovial mood. From the moment he'd arrived at the clinic this morning, the veterinarian had been laughing and joking. Trey wanted to join in on the man's merriment, but how could he feel any sort of happiness when his heart felt like two hands had torn it right down the middle?

He was deep in the misery of his thoughts when Chandler's hand suddenly landed with a loud pop on the console between their seats.

With a visible jerk, Trey whipped his head around. "What the hell was that for?"

"I'm trying to wake you up! I've been talking to you for the last five minutes and getting no response. Haven't you heard anything I've said?"

Trey's shoulders slunk as he fell back against the truck seat. "No. Sorry. I've been thinking."

"Is that what you call it? I'd call it sulking."

Frowning, Trey cut his eyes toward Chandler. "Okay, I'm sulking. Who gives a damn anyway? I hope we get this job over early. I'm going to the Fandango tonight and getting drunk! I don't care how long it takes me. Or if Joe hauls me off to jail for public intoxication."

Chandler shot him an indulgent look. "I don't have to remind you that intoxication is a fool's remedy. What's brought on this sour mood? You were fine until lunch."

"Something left a bad taste in my mouth. Mainly a strawberry blonde who has a horrible penchant for talking on the phone."

Chandler's laugh was loud and long. "Hell, Trey. She's a receptionist. It's her job to talk on the phone."

"This has nothing to do with her job," he argued. "Did you know that she's constantly getting calls from her mother? That sometimes she even turns off the phone so she won't hear it?"

Chandler shrugged. "I'm aware that her mother is problematic. But I'm sure all of that is going to get better. Once Mrs. Nelson accepts the fact that Nicci isn't going back to Texas."

Trey's teeth snapped together. "That's where you're wrong," he muttered, then shook his head. "I shouldn't be the one to tell you this, Doc, but Nicci *is* going back to Texas. She's going to marry that marine she used to date."

Chandler laughed again. "You're messed up, Trey.

I think you need to take off tomorrow and get some rest."

"Right. I'll need it to nurse my hangover," he agreed in a petulant voice. "Guess this will teach you not to be hiring city girls. I tried to tell you she wouldn't last. The only thing that surprises me is that she hung around for this long!"

Losing his patience now, Chandler pulled the truck to the side of the highway and braked the vehicle to a jarring halt. "Gabe is waiting on us right now! But I'll be damned if we go to the Johnson Ranch before you explain all of this to me. And not in those damned innuendos!"

Lifting his hat from his head, Trey raked both hands through his hair as he related the whole encounter he'd had with Nicole and then ended it with a self-directed curse word. "I was a fool, Chandler. That's all. I should've never let myself get to thinking that she could seriously care for me."

"She does seriously care for you. Are you an idiot?"

Trey leaned his head toward the passenger window and stared at himself in the side mirror. "Yep. That's me."

Chandler muttered a curse. "Tell me this, Trey. What did Nicci say when you left her desk?"

"Nothing. She went to wait on Mary Ferguson and her beagle. I didn't hang around to hear more. And what else could I say?"

"Damned plenty!" Chandler blasted at him. "Why didn't you grab her up and tell her you loved her? Why didn't you say there was no way in hell you'd ever let another man have her? That he'd have to go over your dead body to get her!"

Trey's mouth fell open as the gist of Chandler's words slowly sank in on him. "I've messed up."

Chandler made an impatient sound. "Did she say that she loved this guy? Did she come right out and say she wanted to marry him?"

"No. Not that I can remember, but as soon as she said the word *boyfriend*, my brain turned to scrambled eggs. Besides, she was crying. And she said she was happy. And that's the way I want her to be."

"Yeah, you've messed up." He put the truck in gear and gunned the vehicle back onto the highway. "But I wouldn't worry. Nicci will forgive you for being a lamebrain."

She might forgive him for being stupid, Trey thought miserably. But what about the rest? Like loving him. Marrying him.

"I'll talk to her tonight."

"If I was you, ole buddy, I'd be doing more than talking. You might think about stopping by the flower shop before you see her."

Chandler reached for the knob on the radio and tuned it to Trey's favorite station. As soon as the Frank Sinatra tune floated out of the speaker, Trey turned a grateful look on him.

"Thanks, Doc."

"Brothers have to help each other out at times. That's the way I see it."

That's the way Trey saw it, too.

"Nicci, what were you thinking?!" Roslyn exclaimed as she scrubbed a wire dog crate with disinfectant. "Why didn't you run after Trey and explain exactly what was going on with you? Now the poor guy thinks you're going back to Texas to marry Randy!"

At thirty minutes past closing time, the front door of the clinic was locked and Nicole had gone back to the recovery room to help Roslyn with the last of the cleaning chores.

"I was about to explain everything to him when Mary Ferguson walked in with her beagle." Nicole sprayed cleanser on a countertop and methodically wiped the hard surface, while wishing she could wipe that whole scene with Trey out of her mind. Yes, she'd handled the whole thing badly, but he hadn't exactly been a model of common sense.

"Oh pooh! Mary wouldn't have cared if you'd made her wait!" Roslyn straightened up from the cage and leveled a pointed look at Nicole. "I think you were too afraid to tell Trey that you love him. That's what this is all about."

Clutching the disposable cloth in one hand, she walked over to where Roslyn was standing. "That's not so!" she exclaimed, then followed it with a miserable groan. "I—well, it was hardly the perfect time or place."

Roslyn rolled her eyes toward the ceiling, while across the room a dog barked in protest.

"Perfection doesn't fix things. Honesty does," Roslyn said. "Does Trey know you've fallen in love with him?"

"I'm not sure if he's guessed how I feel about him," Nicole said. "But I've showed him in plenty of ways that I love him."

Roslyn shook her head. "But have you said the words to him? Have you made it clear that you're totally besotted with him?"

Clasping her hands behind her back, Nicole walked over to the rows of stacked crates where a few dogs were recuperating until they were well enough to go home. As soon as the dachshund noticed that Nicole was headed in his direction, the bark turned into a happy whine and his tail started wagging.

"Not exactly. I've thought about it, but—I felt like it was a bit soon to spring that on him. And—well, to be honest, I have been afraid. Trey hasn't said anything to me about his feelings or the future." She poked a finger between the wires and stroked the dog's nose. His tail thumped harder. "He told me about those women who left him and how it felt to be deserted. Now I guess he thinks I'm deserting him, too. Oh, Ros, I don't know what to do."

Roslyn turned the crate upside down to drain before she walked over to Nicole. "He and Chandler should be home from the Johnson by dark. You need to be at Trey's place—waiting for him. That way he can't run. He'll have to hear you out."

Nicole frowned. "Why couldn't he run off? If he drives up and sees my car, what's to stop him from turning around and leaving?"

"You think he's that angry with you?"

Angry? The more Nicole pondered it, the more she'd decided the look on his face had been bottom-of-the-pit disappointment. That was even worse than anger.

"No. But he—"

"No buts!" Roslyn interrupted. "This isn't a time to pussyfoot around. You need to be lying for an ambush."

Nicole laughed in spite of her misery. "You've been watching too many Westerns."

"I don't need to watch a Western to know how to deal with a man. But it helps," Roslyn said with a chuckle.

Nicole's mind had already moved on to planning mode when Cybil stuck her head around the door.

"Hey, you two, I'm going home. Are you going to lock up?"

"I'll take care of it," Roslyn answered her. "See you tomorrow."

After the blonde disappeared from the doorway, Roslyn turned back to Nicole and smiled.

"Go home and change, then get over to Trey's house. And don't worry. When he gets home, you'll know what to do."

Trey wasn't coming home. Not anytime soon, Nicole decided. Roslyn had predicted the two men would be home by dark, but twilight had come and gone and now the only light that remained was coming from the yard lamp.

From her seat in one of the wooden rockers, she gazed down the dirt lane that led to Trey's house and desperately wished his headlights would appear. Was she crazy for sitting here in the dark, waiting for a man who probably wouldn't want to see her, much less talk to her?

She loved him more than anything. She'd sit here all night if it would help right things between them. No, she'd camp here on his porch for days, even weeks, if that's what it took to convince Trey that the life she'd led in Texas was truly behind her.

The sound of her ringing phone jerked her from her swirling thoughts, and she hurriedly fished it from the handbag sitting next to her feet.

"Nicci, where are you?"

Nicole frowned at Roslyn's abrupt question. "Silly, where do you think I am? I'm sitting on Trey's front porch—waiting. He's still not here! I'm beginning to think he's probably gone to the Fandango or somewhere to have a few beers."

There was a short silence and then Roslyn said, "He's not doing anything like that. I just got a call from Chandler. There was some sort of accident on the Johnson Ranch. Something about Trey having a run-in with a bull. The men are on their way to the hospital in Wickenburg."

Her heart was suddenly pounding. "Hospital! What's wrong? Is it serious?"

"Sorry, I don't know. Chandler didn't explain. He promised to call me later—after Trey is examined."

Nicole shouldered her handbag as she hurried off the porch. "I'm on my way!"

"Go ahead and kick my rear, Doc," Trey said. "If I'd had my mind on my business, none of this would've happened."

"Forget it. We'd already finished the job," Chandler told him as he walked alongside the wheelchair being pushed by a male nurse. "And you'll mend all right. You just remember what I told you earlier."

Trey looked ruefully down at the cast on his left forearm. He was going to be hampered by the cracked bone for a month, but he could deal with the nuisance. All that mattered to him now was convincing Nicole that the only man she belonged with was him.

"About Nicci, you mean?"

"Exactly," Chandler answered. "It's only nine thirty. You still have time to go by her house."

"Can't. I penned the horses for work tomorrow," Trey told him. "They'll need to be fed and watered."

"Forget about the horses. I'll go by your place and take care of them. Besides, you've been administered pain meds. You don't need to be stumbling around in the dark, trying to carry a heavy feed bucket."

"You shouldn't be trying to feed livestock tonight," the nurse said. "You need to go straight to bed."

Trey couldn't argue with that advice. The only thing that could cure him was to go to bed with a strawberry blonde with a pair of soft lips and more love in her heart than he had a right to. But would she be willing to look past the blockheaded way he'd behaved this morning?

The three men passed through a glass door and onto a concrete area covered by a large overhang.

"I'll go get the truck and pick you up here at the curb," Chandler told him. "No need for you to walk."

"Heck! I'm getting out of this thing!" Before the nurse could stop him, Trey jumped out of the wheelchair.

Seeing it would be useless to argue, the nurse handed him several sheets of paper stapled together. "Here are the instructions to follow. And don't forget to make an appointment with your regular caregiver."

"Don't worry, he will," Chandler said. "And I see her coming right now."

Her? Dear God, he'd finally gone and done it, Trey thought. He'd driven Chandler crazy.

Glancing around, he saw Chandler grinning at the woman trotting toward them.

Nicole!

Stunned, Trey watched her rapid approach. Roslyn must have told her about the accident, he decided. But why had she bothered to come?

Standing next to him, Chandler said, "You don't need me any more tonight, buddy. You're going to be in good hands."

Chandler walked off in the direction of his truck at the same time Nicole rushed up to Trey. Her face was white, and for a split second he thought she was going to burst into tears. Had she actually been that concerned about him?

"Will this young woman be taking you home?"

Compared to the doubts swirling in Trey's mind, the nurse's question was trivial.

"Yes. I'll be taking him home," Nicole answered. She leveled a pointed look at Trey. "And I'll be taking care of him."

"Then you're all set to go, Mr. Lasseter." After winking at Nicole, the nurse said to Trey, "And don't be running into any more bulls. We don't want to see you back here at the hospital."

Trey thanked the nurse, and once the man departed with the wheelchair, he turned to Nicole and said, "You really don't have to do this, you know."

"Do what?" she asked.

In spite of the medication they'd given Trey to dull the pain in his arm, Trey's heart jumped into a runaway rhythm.

"Give me a ride—or anything." He grimaced as he realized he didn't make any more sense now than he had this morning. "I mean, uh, not unless you want to."

Her lips pressed together. "Do you feel like walking out to my car? If your legs are wobbly, I can pull up here to the curb."

"I can walk. Let's go."

Both of them remained silent as they made their way to her vehicle, but as soon as they were seated inside, she turned to him.

"What's wrong with your arm? What happened?"

"It's just a crack. I'll be fine in a few weeks," he said. "I wasn't paying attention, and about the time I stuck my arm through the slats of a loading chute, a bull shot forward and tried to wrap it around an iron pipe."

"Oh." She released a long breath with the one word. "I'm glad you weren't hurt worse."

He gestured toward the keys dangling from her hand. "Aren't you going to start the engine?"

"Not yet. There's something I want to say first. About this morning and the—"

"Just tell me one thing, Nicci," he swiftly interrupted. "Are you going back to Texas and marrying that marine?"

She looked thoroughly disgusted. "You still have to ask those questions? I feel like cracking your skull to match your arm! I'd never marry Randy. Not in a million years. Nor will I be moving back to Texas for any reason. If you hadn't been so quick to assume the worst this morning, I could've explained. But you made me angry. And then you made me even angrier when you left without—" She paused and shook her head. "As though you didn't care at all!"

Groaning, Trey used his good arm to reach for her shoulder and drag her toward him. Once her face was nestled against his neck, he said against the top of her head, "I realize I was wrong. I should've howled in protest. I should've told you that you're my woman— the woman I love—and that I'll never let you go."

She tilted her head back far enough to look at him, and as Trey studied the doubtful shadows in her eyes, he realized she'd been just as uncertain about his feelings as he'd been about hers.

"You love me?" she asked. "Honestly?"

"Honestly. I should've told you that days ago," he admitted. "But I thought it was impossible for a woman like you to love a man like me. I was afraid to risk my heart. Afraid you'd end up leaving me."

"I love everything about you, Trey. Everything! And you might as well get ready to put up with me for the rest of your life, because I'm not going to let you go. Not for any reason!"

His hand cradling the back of her head, he eased his mouth down on hers and kissed her with all the love and tenderness his heart had to give.

When the kiss finally ended, he whispered against her lips, "Let's go home. Like the nurse said, I need to be in bed."

She let out a sexy chuckle. "What about your arm?"

He rested his cheek against hers and wondered if he could possibly be any happier than he was at this very moment. "I'm feeling no pain."

Her fingers pushed through the hair above his ear. "That's because the medication has numbed it."

"No. The hurt is gone, my darlin', because I know you love me and you're going to be my wife."

Easing out of his arms, she settled herself behind the steering wheel, and after starting the engine, she cast him a coy smile. "Is that a proposal?"

"Uh, now that you ask, it is," he admitted. "But don't worry, I'll give you a better one tomorrow. With flowers and a ring and—all my love."

"I only need that one thing from you, Trey. And that's your love."

She drove out of the parking lot, and as Trey settled back in his seat, he realized that, like the Hollister men, he was well and truly going home.

Epilogue

Six weeks later, on a hot May night, a large group of friends and family crowded the roofed patio and spilled over into the yard behind Three Rivers Ranch house. Champagne was flowing and spates of laughter drowned out the distant sound of bawling calves being weaned from their mothers. Spring roundup was being planned for next week, but for tonight no one was thinking about riding and branding.

"I've seen some big shindigs here at the ranch," Trey said. "But I believe this is the biggest."

Standing with his arm around the back of Nicole's waist, Trey gazed across the milling throng of people. He'd never seen the Hollisters so jubilant, but he doubted they could be feeling any more joy than he'd been experiencing these past three weeks since he and Nicole had eloped to Reno and spent several days honeymooning in the cool mountains.

Since they'd returned, Nicole had moved all her things into Trey's house and put her property in town on the real estate market. She insisted that the money from the sale of it would eventually be added to their savings for the big ranch Trey had always dreamed about. At first he'd protested about her plans for the money, but she'd managed to convince him that she wanted what he wanted—a perfect place to raise a big family.

Nicole inclined her head to a spot across the patio, where Roslyn and Chandler were speaking with Maureen and Gil.

"That's a whopper of a diamond Gil slipped on Maureen's finger," she remarked. "I can see it flashing all the way over here."

Trey lifted Nicole's left hand and kissed the knuckle just above her wedding ring. "Yours is a fraction of that size, but it means just the same," he told her.

She turned her beautiful smile up at him. "I love my ring. And I love you, too, Mr. Lasseter."

He hugged her closer to his side. "Are you sorry now that you eloped? Instead of staying here and having a fancy ceremony?"

She shot him a quizzical smile. "Are you kidding? And miss all that planning and stress? And my mother smothering me with well-meaning advice? No, thank you. Eloping was the best thing for you and me. It was very romantic with just the two of us."

Neither Trey nor Nicole had known what to expect from her parents when they'd gotten the news that their daughter was married. Fortunately, Big Mike had been full of congratulations, while Angela had seemed to have experienced a wake-up call. Not only had she quit pestering Nicole with whines and demands, but she'd also happily gone with her husband to New Mexico.

"Hopefully your parents are having a second honeymoon right now," Trey voiced his thoughts.

Nicole smiled up at him. "Yes. I think we've been an inspiration for them. And Mom seems like a different person now. I'm actually looking forward to them coming for a visit. Which might be in time for them to attend Maureen and Gil's wedding."

"Doc tells me the ceremony will be held at the church in town," Trey said. "I was surprised. The ranch is such a huge part of their lives. I thought it would take place here."

"I've been told that she and Joel were married here on the ranch, so I'm thinking she probably wants something different with Gil."

From their shady spot in the yard, Trey urged Nicole toward the patio. "Let's go to the bar. I feel a beer coming on."

She laughed. "Beer when there's expensive champagne to be had?"

"I'm a simple guy," he reasoned.

"Okay, simple guy. What else has Doc told you about the wedding?"

"You'll have to ask Ros for more wedding details. That's all I know. But Doc did give me some very surprising news."

"Oh, what's that?"

"The ranch has hired a new man to work with Holt as his assistant trainer. He's supposed to be arriving soon. You know, the family has tried for years to convince Holt that he needed help, but he wouldn't give in. Because he's so damned particular with his horses, Blake says. But now that he's married and helping Isabelle with the Blue Stallion, he's realized he can't keep stretching himself so thin."

"Apparently, Holt must have found a guy he can trust to do the job the way he wants it. The way Chandler trust you," she added proudly. "The longer I work at the clinic, the more I realize why he wants you to study for a veterinary degree. He needs you in that capacity. But of course, that's a choice you'll have to make."

Trey had been giving the idea more and more thought. But now that he and Nicole were married, there were other things to consider. Not for anything did he want to put a hardship on her, and yet he knew that if he did decide to enter veterinary school, she would give him her total support and never complain. The idea that she loved him that much made him realize just what a blessing he'd been given.

"Hey, you two! Over here!"

They both paused, then seeing Chandler standing at the far end of the portable bar sipping from a fluted glass, they grabbed their drinks and walked over to join him.

"Quite a party, isn't it? Mom is walking on a cloud."

"She looks like a dream, too," Nicole added. "You must be so happy for her."

"And there's something else we're happy about, too. A few years back, Mom put up a several-thousand-dollar reward for the apprehension of the person or persons who might've had a hand in Dad's death. Joe delivered that reward in person to Ginny Patterson today. She was overwhelmed. The money will help her move to a nicer place. And Joe's halfway convinced the woman to make her home in Wickenburg. He's assured her that no one will ostracize her because of Ike."

"That's great," Trey replied. "All she needed was a little help to turn her life around."

"Speaking of Joe," Nicole said. "Why are he and Connor climbing up on the edge of the fire ring?"

Before Trey or Chandler could speculate, Joseph cupped a hand around his mouth and spoke loud enough for the crowd to hear.

"Attention everyone! As law officials of Yavapai County, Connor and I have the duty of seeing that no one overindulges in spirits tonight. So we're ordering all of you to set your glasses down! No one is allowed another drink for two hours."

Gasps and groans rippled through the crowd.

From somewhere in the crowd, Joseph's father-in-law, Sam, yelled out. "What the hell is this, Joe? Jazelle just poured my bourbon. I'm not going to waste it!"

Joseph and Connor exchanged amused glances before they both burst out laughing.

"Just a little joke, Sam. Connor and I actually want to make an announcement. Everyone is here to celebrate Mom and Gil's engagement. Well, we have something more to add to the merriment. I just learned that Tessa is expecting our third child. And Connor got the news this morning that Jazelle is expecting their second. So drink up everyone. It's a happy night."

As everyone rushed forward to congratulate the two men, Trey felt Nicole's hand wrap around his, and he looked down at the coy smile on her face.

"If we ever expect to have a family as big as the Hollisters', we're going to have to get busy," she told him.

Bending his head, Trey pressed a kiss on his wife's cheek. "I promise we'll get started on that tonight, darlin', as soon as we get home."

* * * * *

MILLS & BOON

Coming next month

FROM BRIDAL DESIGNER TO BRIDE
Kandy Shepherd

"I'm thinking of the questions people might ask us at the wedding."

"Where did we meet?"

"Perhaps we met in LA. At a party."

"To which, sadly, I was not invited," he said with a mock mournful expression.

"Shame. There was a party at a waterfront venue in Santa Monica. I went outside for a breath of fresh air. You were outside—"

"Taking a break from a particularly boring business dinner." He paused. "And I saw this dark haired girl leaning against a palm tree. I was struck by her beauty."

Eloise giggled. "I like that. So what happened?

"I opened a conversation with a witty remark."

"I responded with something equally witty."

"We struck up a conversation. You hung onto my every word."

"Huh! How about I made you laugh?"

"You do that in real life, so that could work. Then you said you had to get back to the party."

"No! I'm sure I would have wanted to stay with you."

"Would you?" he said.

"Yes." Her gaze connected again with his in that surprisingly intimate way.

"I got your number. And I called you straight away to check I got it right."

"So when did you call me?"

"I asked you to call me when the party was finished. You did. Then I took you back to your hotel room."

"And…?"

"We talked all night until the sun came up," he said a smile dancing around the corners of his sexy mouth. "I was a gentleman."

"And I was wishing you weren't." She slapped her hand over her mouth. "Scratch that!"

He laughed. "So I wasn't such a gentleman the next night."

"Really," she said trying to sound prim instead of turned on.

It took a real effort not to focus on imagining the exciting details of his fictional ungentlemanly behaviour and her fictional response. Since that first kiss she had spent too much time fantasying over the prospect of making love with Josh. Now he sat so near to her in the privacy of her home, it was impossible not to acknowledge that intense physical pull. "And we spent as much time as we could together before you had to go back to Boston."

"We did. In fact, we hardly left your hotel bedroom." His tone was so exaggerated in its lasciviousness it made her laugh.

"If you say so," she said.

"I wished so," he said with a grin.

She was glad she had decided not to sit next to him on the sofa. It would be only too easy to let this game get out of hand and practice for real.

Continue reading
FROM BRIDAL DESIGNER TO BRIDE
Kandy Shepherd

Available next month
www.millsandboon.co.uk

COMING SOON!

MILLS & BOON

THE HEART OF ROMANCE

A ROMANCE FOR EVERY KIND OF READER

MODERN

Prepare to be swept off your feet by sophisticated, sexy and seductive heroes, in some of the world's most glamourous and romantic locations, where power and passion collide.
8 stories per month.

HISTORICAL

Escape with historical heroes from time gone by. Whether your passion is for wicked Regency Rakes, muscled Vikings or rugged Highlanders, awaken the romance of the past.
6 stories per month.

MEDICAL

Set your pulse racing with dedicated, delectable doctors in the high-pressure world of medicine, where emotions run high and passion, comfort and love are the best medicine.
6 stories per month.

True Love

Celebrate true love with tender stories of heartfelt romance, from the rush of falling in love to the joy a new baby can bring, and a focus on the emotional heart of a relationship.
8 stories per month.

Desire

Indulge in secrets and scandal, intense drama and plenty of sizzling hot action with powerful and passionate heroes who have it all: wealth, status, good looks…everything but the right woman.
6 stories per month.

HEROES

Experience all the excitement of a gripping thriller, with an intense romance at its heart. Resourceful, true-to-life women and strong, fearless men face danger and desire - a killer combination!
8 stories per month.

DARE

Sensual love stories featuring smart, sassy heroines you'd want as a best friend, and compelling intense heroes who are worthy of them.
4 stories per month.

To see which titles are coming soon, please visit

millsandboon.co.uk/nextmonth

MILLS & BOON

HISTORICAL

Awaken the romance of the past

Escape with historical heroes from time gone by. Whether your passion is for wicked Regency Rakes, muscled Viking warriors or rugged Highlanders, indulge your fantasies and awaken the romance of the past.

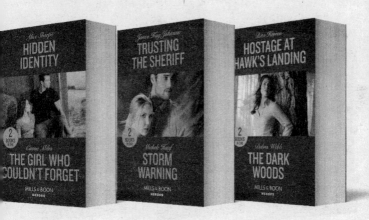

MILLS & BOON
MEDICAL
Pulse-Racing Passion

Set your pulse racing with dedicated, delectable doctors in the high-pressure world of medicine, where emotions run high and passion, comfort and love are the best medicine.